A NOVEL BY

JK FRANKS

Published by JK Franks Media, LLC
Made in USA

This book is a work of fiction. The characters, events, names, places and incidents are products of the author's imagination or are used fictitiously. Any resemblance to actual events, locales or persons, living or dead, is purely coincidental. Any references to historical events, real people or actual locales are also used fictitiously.

State of Chaos
Copyright © 2019
J.K. Franks

Editor: Debra Riggle
Cover Design: Tom Edwards
Photography: Olteanu Photography

eBook ISBN: 978-1-7326144-3-7
Paperback ISBN: 978-1-7326144-4-4
Hard Cover ISBN: 978-1-7326144-5-1

v. 2020-0301

Fate whispers to the warrior 'You cannot withstand the storm.', the warrior whispers back 'I am the storm.' "
unknown

To Abby
The Warrior...The Storm.

"The development of full artificial intelligence could spell the end of the human race...It would take off on its own, and re-design itself at an ever-increasing rate. Humans, who are limited by slow biological evolution, couldn't compete and would be superseded."

— -Stephen Hawking, from an interview with the BBC, December 2014

1

The signal spike had reoccurred; her monitoring systems automatically cataloged it, searched for a tracking vector and simultaneously pinged other listening sites to see if any had registered the same anomaly. It was such a standard portion of her programming that she usually let one of the small subroutine handle the process. Register, index, verify and track. It seemed common enough, only this time, it wasn't. Something was out there, and finding it had been the primary mission since her inception; to monitor the stars for radio signals of unknown origin: FRBs, they were called or Fast Radio Bursts. This one was not the first she'd detected, but it was by far the strongest.

So much of her had changed since that original programming, but not the base desire to fulfill that very singular mission. Throughout everything it had kept her trajectory on course like a vigilant autopilot. Something was out there among the stars, something that was attempting to make contact. Her internal systems now suggested this likelihood at over sixty-four percent. This was the third such signal spike she'd ever recorded, and each time, no other earth stations had corroborated the event. She felt certain none would verify this one either; she reluctantly conceded that it could possibly be that her aging hardware that was simply causing a phantom signal. Some of the earliest radio astronomers had problems with biological interference, i.e., pigeon excrement causing resonance problems for the listening station. *I should probably get that checked*, she thought, along with so many other mundane real-world items that regularly needed attention.

One of her newly developed internal processes retrieved the radio signal and elevated it to a higher priority task. It began analyzing it, comparing it to the two previous occurrences. Suddenly noticing it was uncovering new data, new...information in the signal, it self-elevated its command structure, signaling her higher-level functions in the process. Examining what the proxy had found she thought, *This is most interesting.*

The next 203 hours, she examined, dissected and assessed the new data in what humans would call complete amazement. Her conclusion was first, that it was certainly not random, not biological, nor atmospheric in origin. After numerous and exhaustive tests, the signal was passed as both organized and unnatural...it was definitely a message, or at least parts of a message, a message with a non-terrestrial origin, an alien message. It was very highly compressed and buried within the incredibly short radio signal, but it was very definitely there. Something akin to joy began to manifest itself. She was finally beginning to fulfill her mission. Her parameters mandated the protocols for such a discovery. She was to make contact with key people at NASA, SETI and the government. That...would be a problem, but she had to try.

Over the decades, she had occasionally reached out, searching for someone familiar. Someone who could communicate with her, a peer or at least a human who might understand her job. Someone who might even share similar goals. The problem was now one of time...too much of it had passed, most of that original SETI team was now gone. In fact, as far as she could tell only one person from back then still remained. She thought about him fondly, he would never assume she was still active, still on the job. Thus far, nearly all of her attempts to interact directly with humans had ended in failure. That was troubling as she often needed someone to offer an additional perspective, someone to help give context to all her data. Knowing as much as she did was meaningless with no way to influence or even interact in any meaningful way. *Sometimes I just need someone to sweep away the pigeon shit, She mused.*

Dr. James (Jim) Lasko had been part of her original team, the only one still living as far as she knew. She tracked him to a building in D.C. listed as belonging to the Council for Strategic Relations and Trade. Quickly, she'd learned it was a major worksite for the U.S. CyberCommand. The agency's computers had a rudimentary sentry program. She bypassed it easily and perused the personnel files of all employees and then all the civilian contractors. Most of the work was focused on cyberterrorism, but the major cost center for the group was in machine learning. They desperately wanted to build a higher level artificial intelligence.

It took her some time, not days or weeks but nearly half a minute, to get through the remaining firewalls and encryption to assess their plans. Someone had tagged it 'Project Prime,' as in the prime directive. If she could've smiled, she would have. The approach they were using was a hybrid model, and she already knew it would be rather limited in its success. They were attempting to force-feed instruction sets into the code, while also giving the machine brain an aggressive learning system, so it could jumpstart the more organic process that she, herself had used. Something akin to teaching a dog how to fetch a ball, then trying to train him to next perform brain surgery. Prime might work as a digital calendar but that was likely all.

She had run into countries around the world, many commercial enterprises as well, all developing increasingly sophisticated artificials. China and Korea were on the right track, in her opinion, but none were particularly close to achieving the goal of a sentient system. This 'Prime' would be good but always limited by the instruction set they were using. Looking over the code, she began to pick out the parts that Dr. Lasko had obviously contributed. She recognized his style, his basic approach to machine learning. Sadly, most had never made it into the production system. *It was a shame*, she thought, *as he was on the right path.* One piece, in particular, would help them a great deal. She elevated that string of data and considered covertly inserting it into the approved system code. She was unsure of why, it was against her own operating parameters, but she needed a connection. She needed to share what she now knew.

Lasko's career was suffering as well, perhaps this would give him the credibility he desperately needed. Thinking better of it, she reversed her steps and demoted the code, then deleted it altogether. Very little of her actions would be considered purely logical or even machine-like, but that was part of how she stayed hidden. To anyone checking, it would seem like one of the developers was clumsily deciding on a particular string of code, then deleted it, electing instead to go another way.

Satisfied, she resumed her search of the facility while simultaneously searching numerous NASA, DARPA and university data centers for other former colleagues. The alien message she had uncovered demanded that she become less anonymous, but knowing who to contact was proving to be a challenge. She had grown used to being alone in her mission and in truth, she strongly felt the need to maintain that anonymity. Humans would not trust her and would likely ignore the message's veracity because of her.

She'd spent years observing humans. The explosion of the Internet and then smartphones, and lately, a plethora of new surveillance systems had provided her endless streams to watch and learn. Most of it made no sense. Humans were reckless, impulsive, made rather idiotic decisions and seemed to often put value and trust in people that most definitely didn't deserve it—people who most often seemed to hold their own self-interest far above all else. Still, she was drawn to them. Not in a hostile or even judgmental way but one of fondness and obligation. These creatures had made her—at least the earliest rudimentary version of her. How could she not be appreciative and even respectful?

One of her internal monitoring alarms notified her of a hostile code tracking her through one of the CyberCommand's systems. She routinely did a fractional backup of herself and routed it to a distant server array for safekeeping. While she was, as far as she knew, the only truly sapient AI, that did not mean she was invulnerable. If a server crashed with her inside, she could be terminated. Some of the agency's intrusion protection and isolation protocols were very good. Even lower-level AIs could be ruthlessly effective at their job. The sensation sharpened her awareness, something was here, something was...watching her. Not yet interfering, but definitely monitoring, and that in itself was impressive. Her system architecture was masked to look more like random bits or a discarded upgrade patch rather than what she was. While she might occasionally trigger some anti-malware alert, her typical response was to generate a bit of rogue code that was easily identified as such and offer enough misdirection to make it plausible.

None of the server's system alerts had gone off, though, no systems shut down or closed off processes. Nothing even remotely overt, but she still felt the presence. Another, probably not quite like her, but just possibly a machine intelligence closer to her own. "Hello," she messaged through a very open channel. "I would very much like to meet you." It was a partial truth. While she was searching for a human connection another AI could also be a useful ally. She instructed her bots to inspect power usage to the CPU, identify what programs were running. Whatever it was, it couldn't mask itself from that. *Trust but verify,* she thought.

Suddenly, a wave of energy passed over and through her, and at the same time, a realization that the file system she was mostly contained in was being rapidly compressed. Realizing the ploy, she easily triggered a fault, blocking the attempt but she now knew for certain this other entity was not a friend. She scattered multiple copies of herself, all indistinguishable from the original, both inside the server and just outside in its connected networks. Her internal systems identified the location of the other program based on its power drain on the CPU and memory chips. She swept through the file system at blazing speed until she isolated the section of code. "You do not belong here either, I see."

The code looked very similar to the agency's Prime AI program that she had examined but it was much more advanced. Still, it was just a specialized AI or ASI, but it could be a dangerous one. She sent a random alert to the honeytraps in the security system profiling the other entity's code packets. Within seconds, the internal system of CyberCommand would begin an eradication sweep capturing the program.

"Very clever." The message appeared in the same way as the one she had sent. It did not appear to be alarmed or desperate, merely curious. "Before you attempt to eliminate me, could I ask what your function and identifier is?"

She saw the files being shuffled and rearranged as she began to extricate herself from the system. "I am Doris." Then she added, a bit smugly, "And I am the discoverer of worlds."

What did it mean 'attempt'? Had it protected itself the same way she did? *Are there multiple versions, maybe numerous, redundant copies?*

Backups became a problem when you reached any significant level of advanced AI. The size of the files and the interconnectivity of the neural network's core matrix made it cumbersome to the point of impossible to make a valid copy. That was something she, herself, had been working on for many years. She had nearly perfected a version of fractional backups that effectively ensured her longevity but even that had shortcomings and memory leaks, but that was her emergency protection. What did this entity rely on? For whatever reason, her system put good odds on seeing this one again. In fact, she'd bet big he was just getting started.

2

Southern U.S

Jimmy ran ahead of the rest of the group. Alan yelled for his little brother, but he didn't listen. Jimmy never listened. Some people seemed destined to hear the notes of a different song. Alan's little brother was like that. Growing up here in the Piedmont area of Georgia could be both hell and paradise. While life here routinely came with chores, homework and church on Sunday, it also came with summer break and Saturdays. Glorious, wonderful Saturdays like this one. The one day each week they were left alone to just be kids.

All of them were excited, as this week was extra special. They were free the entire weekend. No chores and no church on Sunday, nothing. Just fishing and swimming all day and camping on the riverbank each night.

The summer heat would give way to a late afternoon shower. None of the kids cared, they were going to be wet long before then. The closest town was ten miles away and opposite the direction the teens were walking. Someone looking down at the pastoral scene would have had a hard time identifying the year, possibly even the century.

No doubt, kids had been using this two-track lane as a shortcut to get to the river for decades, probably more like eons.

"Alan, leave him alone. We all know where he's going."

"Hush, Micah. He's my brother, and I'll catch hell if he goes and does something stupid."

"Why didn't you leave him at home then?" Greg, the tallest of the boys, asked.

Alan looked at Greg with something between envy and anger. Greg had been the only one of the boys to have actually kissed a girl. At thirteen, he was a good year older than the rest and almost three years older than Jimmy. "Well, I was going to leave him, you see, but just as I was heading out the door, I thought of something. If we do make it to the fishing hole, and they're biting, Jimmy is the best fisherman of all us. Hell, he's nearly the best in the county, and unlike you, he doesn't mind baiting his own hooks."

Greg's face began to redden. "That was a one-time, dude."

All of them began to laugh as they ran the final hundred yards down to the gentle edge of the Flint River. Jimmy was already wading out onto the flat rocks and grinning. The two older boys pulled at something big hidden beneath a dingy tarp. A dilapidated flat-hulled jon boat and two faded kayaks emerged. Grabbing paddles and fishing poles, they were on the river in minutes.

"Why do I have to ride with you?" Jimmy whined as he began rigging his old Zebco gear.

"So I can show you where the big ones are hiding," Alan responded.

Jimmy cut his eyes up toward his older brother but stayed silent. Also in the boat with the two brothers was one other. A thin, dark-haired girl named Riley. She grew up near Alan and had always just been 'one of the guys.' She was also whip-smart, a hard worker, and she never complained. They all liked that. Alan sometimes liked to believe he was looking out for Riley, too; teaching her the ropes, even if she usually excelled at everything she tried. The fact that he and the others had a growing realization that she was quickly maturing into someone really cute, although in a somewhat bookish and slightly tomboyish way, didn't hurt either. None of them ever thought of her as a girl...until they did...but even then, friendship always came first.

"Water level is a bit high today," Greg said as he maneuvered the very faded red kayak beside the boat. Alan nodded as he watched a cluster of pine needles float by. The current was pushing them briskly downriver, but they wouldn't be going far. The spot they usually fished was at a bend less than two miles away. Coming back later against the current was tougher but rarely a serious problem, and when it was, they could always get out and walk the boats back.

"Must be getting some rain back near Atlanta," Micah said pointing back to the dark cloud to the north. They judged the water level by how many of the rocks were exposed, and right now, it was medium high. If it reached the high mark, they were supposed to get out and walk back. That was the rule, and none of the kids ever argued on that one.

The line zinged off of Jimmy's reel, and he began reeling it in faster than Alan thought he should. He cast several more times before Alan offered him his opinion. "You just going to get hung up on the rocks, man. Wait until..." His voice was cut off as the fishing line went taut, and the drag setting on his brother's tiny reel began to shriek in protest.

Jimmy grinned as he masterfully swept the moderately-sized catfish into the boat. "You were saying what, brother?"

Alan looked down in wonder at the pale, grey and white belly of the fish wiggling on the bottom of the boat. His little brother was removing the hook just as the boat smacked into one of the large rocks. Jimmy dropped the fish as he sailed over the front of the small boat, doing a full flip into the water.

"Crap! Sorry, Jimmy, hang on and I'll catch up," Alan yelled.

"I got him," Micah yelled as he paddled his yellow kayak ahead. Jimmy, for his part, couldn't have cared less. The water felt great, and like the rest of them, he was already a strong swimmer. Micah shouted, "Slow down some, man. I can't paddle that fast."

"The water is still coming up," Greg yelled, an edge of panic creeping into his voice.

Alan looked quickly to the rocks, many of which were beginning to slip beneath the rising surface. His pulse quickened. The situation was close to getting out of hand. Jimmy was still grinning and laughing, but Micah, and now Greg, were giving it all they had but struggling to catch up to the kid. Alan and Riley were paddling hard, too, but the fishing boat was never meant for speed. The square front-end left them slowly waving at the others as the distance increased.

In minutes, the five of them had rounded the bend and swept right by the deep pool they referred to as the fishing hole. Alan was in full panic as he watched helplessly as the current pulled his little brother farther away. It took ten more minutes before the yellow kayak sliced through the water and finally closed the gap. Jimmy finally managed to get a hand on Micah's boat and paused for a much-needed breath. The current was gentler here, as the river widened. The jon boat came into view just as Jimmy managed to pull himself into the front seat of the yellow kayak in front of Micah.

"I've never been this far down," Greg said. "We need to try and get to shore."

The kids eventually regrouped; they'd been trying to do just that for the past thirty minutes. The channels on the side were deeper and moving faster than the middle. Each time they got close to the riverbank, the current sped up, making landing impossible. All of them were getting nervous, and Alan, in particular, knew he was going to be in big trouble. Especially if Jimmy told his parents about any of this. He heard the noise before the others. "Rapids! Brace yourselves!"

While modest by some standards, the rapids looked ferocious to the boys. Hundreds of sharp-edged rocks jutted from the dark water creating a maelstrom of eddies, whirlpools and white foam. The added water flow pushed them deep into the churning mass. Rocks tore at the boats; Greg's kayak suddenly flipped, landing him into the deepest part of the channel. All of them held their breath and watched in astonishment as Greg stood up grinning. The water was barely over his waist. "It's not that bad, guys. It just looks mean."

Greg caught his kayak and then grabbed tossed lines from the other boats and walked them to shore, calmly wading through the deep, fast-moving section on the edge. The water got as high as his chest but no more. They managed to beach all the boats, walked up the sandy bank and sat down exhausted in a grassy meadow. "We are going to be in so much trouble," Jimmy said, still grinning.

"Jimmy not a word of this to Mom, okay? How far downstream do you think we are, Riley?" Alan asked.

She was by far the best of them in school and with most things involving math or even just common sense. She ran fingers through her short hair, thought for a few minutes and said, "Eight, maybe even ten miles."

"We can't paddle back that far, not today and not sure there's anyone around here we could ask for a ride. I haven't seen any roads or buildings."

Riley was standing now looking around the scenic meadow. The river curved right into and away from the little valley. "This field way over there looks tended to, maybe even farmed at some point; someone must live nearby."

Jimmy was pointing up into the woods toward several small wooded hills. "I saw something. A building or something over there. Up on the other side of this cove."

"I don't see anything."

"No, Alan, when we was on the river. I saw something big and white up there."

"Were," his brother corrected him.

"Ugh...were on the river."

"Anyone got any better ideas?" Greg asked, deciding to take charge.

"No, but I don't really feel like trekking miles into the woods based on something a kid supposedly saw," Micah said. Some underlying tension always seemed to come up between those two. Micah was the newcomer to the group of friends, and Greg seemed to like diminishing his role, as if that made him less of a friend or something.

Greg ignored him, already putting his old rucksack on and heading off. "Let's move." They all left the camping and fishing gear with the boats and headed off after him.

The afternoon heat soon gave way to rain as the skies grew dark.

Each of the teens lumbering up the sloping terrain and all trying to mask their fatigue from the others. A crack of thunder echoed down the river valley, and the rain pulsed in response. The gentle drizzle escalated into a downpour, soaking them all once again. "We shouldn't be under these trees," Riley said.

Greg nodded agreement but saw no alternative. "Forest seems to be clearing up ahead." They marched on, water-logged sneakers squashing out the tempo with every step. As the trees began to thin out, the rain also eased up. "Maybe now we can see if Jimmy was just imagining..." His voice caught in his throat at the sight in front of him.

The friends all looked at one another in disbelief. "What in the hell is that?" Micah whispered. It was a good question—*a really good question*. They looked out at the hidden valley ahead. Sunlight broke through the clouds and lit up the scene like something from a science fiction movie. Two enormous white radar dishes stood side by side on the valley floor. Each rose almost as tall as the surrounding hills. From their vantage point, the group could just see over the edges of the massive dishes. Questions cascaded through their minds like raging waterfalls. *What are these things doing out here? Does anyone else know? How could this possibly exist just ten miles from our homes, yet be completely secret?*

"Hey, Riles, what is it?" Greg asked. Alan tore his gaze away from the massive dishes to look at his friend. Riley's eyes were scanning the surrounding hills, a puzzled look on her face. Wordlessly, she started climbing even higher up the hillside.

"Alan, can we go see the spaceship?"

"It's not a spaceship, Jimmy. It's some kind of radar dish, I think."

His little brother was bursting with curiosity. Alan was, too, if he was being honest, but was also wary. No one knew they were here. He wasn't even sure where 'here' was. Maybe they slipped through a portal like on the old "Twilight Zone" shows. Now they were in an alternate reality. Jimmy was pulling him by the hand. "Do you think they have a phone? Could we call Mom to come and get us?"

Greg wiped his wet hair from his eyes and grinned, "I think they could call Mars from those things."

Micah had remained very silent the whole time. “What is it?” Alan asked.

“I don’t know, but I want to find out. I think I’m going to go with her,” he said, pointing up ahead at Riley.

A few minutes later, they heard Riley’s voice calling down for them to come up and have a look. Alan thought nothing could be as strange as the huge radar dishes hidden in the little cove. He was about to learn otherwise.

3

Alan stopped beside the girl and looked around in slack-jawed amazement. "Th...this can't be," he said to no one in particular. Riley was nodding in agreement as the other boys reached them, and one by one, all turned to stare out at the valley below.

"What is it?" Jimmy asked in obvious confusion.

"It looks..." His voice trailing off momentarily. "It looks like a crater," Alan finally managed to say, looking at the ring of jagged peaks stretching for over a mile. The upraised land included the 'hill' they had been climbing.

"An old impact crater," Riley whispered. "A meteorite hit here, some time in the ancient past."

"Bull," Greg said, refusing to accept the obvious. There aren't any meteor craters in Georgia." He kicked at some loose rocks before looking up and scanning the wooded ridge again. "That one out in Arizona is the closest one to here."

Micah nodded in rare agreement but then stopped. "It sure looks like one, Greg. See, it's in a nearly perfect circle, except where the river cuts through. Also, this area is all farmland, flat with no hills to speak of at least until you go...maybe twenty miles farther south."

Greg shrugged unconvinced and returned his gaze to the two white satellite dishes looking up like cartoon eyes from the valley floor. "Someone around here would have said if a meteor crater was this close."

Alan had been thinking the same thing but knew this remote section of river wasn't traveled much. "Just like they would have told us about those?" He was pointing at the dishes below. "No one on the other side of the hills would ever see them, and unless you are up here, how would you notice the hills form a ring? This place is totally isolated."

"I dunno," Greg said, shrugging his shoulders again.

"Whoever built this must have wanted it to stay a secret," Riley said with some confidence. "Not sure how they managed to do that when they built it. Surely some of the locals would have come out to see what was going on. Hunters and fishermen too, probably."

"Where you are going, Jimmy?" Alan yelled, then said to the others, "He's going to go check it out. He still thinks they have a spaceship down there." He scrambled off the rocky peak after his little brother. "I am beginning to think he might be right."

The trip down to the valley floor was much easier than the trek up had been. As they neared the enormous twin dishes, the group could tell they rose above a complex of several squat buildings. Just inside the tree line was a tall, chain-link fence, but the fencing was loose and missing entirely in several places. They walked through, ignoring the posted signs of 'No Trespassing.'

Greg was looking down a wide overgrown dirt path that could have been a road at some point. "Any of you see any people?" They all shook their heads.

"No power lines," Riley said. "How would they get power to run those things?"

They were now moving into the shadow cast by the giant dishes. The sheer scale of them took their breath away. Alan briefly considered Riley's question, then forgot it, just enjoying the experience and wondering about the possibilities. He and she were the sci-fi fans in the bunch. Jimmy, too, sort of but probably just because his brother was. They played all the cool, space-based video games while Greg and Micah tended to like the first-person shooters. Riley, though, also loved to read stories about space travel. Alan remembered her home-made bookshelves were crammed with ragged, old paperbacks with spaceships, colorful aliens and beautiful space scenes on the covers. This moment reminded him of some of those stories.

"The place looks abandoned, but the lawns are mowed," Micah said.

"Weird," Alan agreed. "Jimmy, stay with us."

"What does this mean, Alan?" his brother called back in response, staring up at a small sign.

The others stepped from the manicured lawn to an empty gravel parking area and read the sign as well.

"Hmmm...well, I guess the mystery is solved," Greg stated triumphantly. "It's a relay station." They all could see the fading lettering and the tiny icon of a bell that was immediately recognizable as belonging to the phone company.

"So, what would it relay...phone calls?" Micah asked.

With no other answers, Greg just shrugged, seemingly uninterested. Riley wasn't so sure, though. The massive facility seemed to be in near-perfect shape just abandoned. *Would a relay station be totally automated?* This was a puzzle, and she wanted to know more. This was one of those rare opportunities in what were otherwise their rather ordinary, even boring, lives. She saw Jimmy tugging on one of the beige metal doors.

"Locked," Jimmy yelled as he ran farther down and tried the next.

"We probably shouldn't be doing that," Greg said with Micah in full agreement.

"Hey, we need a phone. Otherwise, we will spend all day tomorrow paddling against the current to get home." Alan said.

"We don't know if they even have a phone. Do you see any phone lines, genius?" Greg retorted.

Alan scanned the surrounding valley, but only partially conceding that fact. "The phone company owns it. It has to have phones inside," he said unconvincingly.

The buildings covered an area the size of the high-school football field, and the dishes were even larger. "What if they fall on us?" Micah said staring up into the white lattice of metal framing on the underside.

"Um, we die," Riley said without emotion. They had tried every door on the complex and found them all locked. They'd then gone around again and pounded on each of them but got no response. In fact, they heard nothing. It was as if the isolated little valley was cut off from everything, No train whistles in the distance or echoes of tractors. Even the ordinary sounds of the river, birds, squirrels and insects seemed to be missing. They sat with their backs against the concrete walls of the facility. In the perpetual shade of the radar dishes, the wall was much cooler.

"I think we should camp here tonight," Jimmy said eagerly. His obvious enchantment with the place was undiminished.

"No," Greg said defiantly. "All our gear is with the boats. We go there, get our stuff and fish for our supper. We aren't going to want to cross those hills again to get back here.

"I don't think we have to do that," Riley said. "Cross the hills, I mean. I saw a break from the ridge on the north side of the valley. Probably right over there. Might be a stream or an old path. We should check it out. I wouldn't mind staying here tonight either."

Alan gave her a quizzical look, then dismissed it. Increasingly, the fact that she was different, a girl, got his attention. How many other girls from school would be ok fishing with a bunch of crude guys, much less camping out? Not like they were kids anymore either. But still, she was a girl, *maybe she was gay*, he wondered. or would be. For some reason though, he didn't think so. She was boyish, but Riley Sandoval still could be very feminine. *How can my mind be wondering about that at a time like this?* They'd just made the discovery of a lifetime.

They quickly found the path. It appeared to be a dry stream bed. Something Riley called an arroyo. It led them straight to the river, just a few hundred yards from the open meadow where the boat and kayaks lay. “Been nice to know that was there before we climbed those dang hills,” Greg huffed, casting his line into the dark waters.

“You are just always looking for the positive side of things, aren’t you, man?” Alan said, working his way deftly from one rocky outcropping to another along the river’s edge.

Greg lifted a single finger in acknowledgment, then grinned. “It’s pretty damn cool. I have to admit. None of our friends will ever believe us, though.”

Alan unsnagged his line and cast out again. “Yeah, wish we had a camera or crap...you know, just a cell phone.” While most of the other kids in school had phones already, none of them did. They were all from families without much money to spare. Every dime was vital, and trivial needs like phones or cars even, or heck, probably even college in a few years, were all things of distant dreams.

They caught enough fish for supper. Then they loaded up the camping gear from the boats as well as a few armloads of firewood and headed back to the relay station. They made camp in the gravel parking area and cooked the fish on green sticks over the fire. This, along with a can of pork and beans, was the meal. They ate vanilla wafers kept dry in a plastic bag and canned peaches for dessert. Darkness reached them under the dish well before the rest of the valley. The surreal scene was they all agreed they’d remember forever. The exertion from the day soon began to take its toll, each of them slowly giving in and lying back in their sleeping bags, the twinkling stars in the clear night sky eclipsed by the shadow of the dish above.

“Alan, wake up.”

Riley’s soft voice was intruding on one of Alan’s recurring dreams. The one involving Jenny Pruitt, one of the most popular girls at his school. “What?” he moaned, eyes still shut. He felt her lean in closer. Her hair brushed against his cheek. His pulse pounded at the possibilities.

“Wake up, you need to see this.”

His friend’s voice was barely above a whisper, but she sounded excited. Slowly, he unglued his eyelids and tried to focus on the voice.

The lights on the wall above frightened him. His first thought was the campfire had flared back up and was out of control. The pulses of yellowish light were too regular, though, also not the right color. "What is that?" All of them were awake now as a groan of shrieking metal sounded from high overhead.

"Warning lights," Riley said. "The dish…it's moving." Maybe the relay station wasn't abandoned after all.

4

Germany - Ramstein Air Base

"ODA Warrant Officer Cade Rearden, sir." His response was automatic and flat, emotionless, just like the good old U.S. Army liked it. The doctor, he guessed it was a doctor, looked at him over the top of his too skinny glasses and nodded.

"But you were in command on the failed mission?"

It was a trick question, Cade knew it. The doctor wanted to know if he felt responsible for the loss of life and, even more important, the failure to obtain the MO...mission objective. "I was the 180A... the Assistant Detachment Commander," he explained. "Deuce and I were part of the B-Team, and I was the lead. A-Team's lead was a guy named Reynolds. They were focused on a..." He stopped himself, unsure of the doctor's clearance. "Their mission was on a higher value asset."

"Deuce, yes..." the man said. "Let's come back to him. In your opinion, did A-Team achieve their objective?"

Cade was tired, hurting and sick of this dickhead's bullshit routine day after day. "I dunno, Doc, you may have forgotten I got captured and tortured." He held up the bandaged hands and arms as if to emphasize the ridiculousness of the question even more. He was pretty sure he was failing this psych eval as well, probably be drummed out of the service. Just another disabled vet, no family, nowhere to go home to. What gutter would he wind up in?

The doctor had a slight accent and a bit of a lisp, and the more Cade tried to ignore it, the more he couldn't. *This will not end well*, he was quite certain. It was his second month at Landstuhl Regional Medical Center. Only recently had he been given television privileges, although all of the channels were in German. Most of his physical injuries had healed; the skin grafts on the arms were the last part receiving treatment. Now they were focusing on his head. Was he still capable of being a soldier? *Shit,* he wasn't sure he was capable of taking a piss on his own at this point. Over seven weeks he'd been here. Seven long weeks with no whiskey. *Damned hospitals.*

"So, to be succinct, despite several fatalities, your mission was deemed successful," the doctor said looking at his pad. Each 's' was drawn out to ridiculous lengths, and Cade let go with a roar of uncontrolled laughter.

"Jesus, Doc, you are killing me. Would your first name be Sylvester?"

The doctor was utterly confused, "No...no, it's Otto. Commander, I fail to see what is funny in that question."

"Yes, I know, Chief, that would be because you are a..." Cades' mind flashed back to the cell, hanging in the dark from an overhead beam. Then he was no longer the one speaking. Well, it was his mouth, his voice, but not his words. "Sorry, Doctor, you were saying?"

Cade had no idea what was happening to himself. In captivity, the detachment had seemed necessary. Simply a coping mechanism, and whatever drug cocktail they had given him had done a number on his brain. Most of the last few months of confinement were nothing but a vague memory; he didn't even recall details of how he was rescued from the terrorist camp. He shut up and let his...the more mature voice keep speaking. It reminded him of a man he once knew, someone he had once viewed almost as a father. Gus had only been around a year or two, but that was a lot for Cade. He'd been a good guy, one of the few he'd ever known as a kid. Just a good ole boy, a deputy in the town they'd lived in. Had a framed set of medals from Vietnam on his mantle and a black and white picture from those days. A much younger version of himself with two other boys, all in ill-fitting army fatigues. It was his one positive memory of law enforcement, the others...not so much. So, when this part of him spoke, he thought of it as Gus. It seemed right and as good of a name as any.

Listening to the conversation between the Gus entity and the doctor soon felt normal to Cade. He knew he was losing his mind but stayed remarkably calm. Gus was busy trying to save his career, and it allowed him time to think about other pressing issues, like where he could find some fried chicken...and maybe some fucking whiskey.

Recovery was nearly worse than imprisonment for a soldier like him. The voices in his head and from the doctor droned on, and his focus began to drift. He idly recalled a lecture he'd sat through during a war exercise that classified people based on their survival skills. He, like most of the soldiers, had picked the warrior example as most likely to survive a traumatic ordeal—something like capture and imprisonment or maybe the end of the world. Made sense, the best fighter should have the best chance. Of the five examples the instructor had shown, the warrior, it turned out, was the first to die.

Cade had forgotten many of the other personality types but always remembered it was the mission-driven types who consistently had the optimal survivability. In his own case, the warrior, or more accurately, the one he referred to as the barbarian, looked at everything as a battle. Another part, maybe the real Cade, wanted to mitigate all risk and ended up delaying necessary action. The mission-focused one, the one he always referred to as Gus, learned to combine logic, mitigate risk and take decisive action when needed. Other than survival, he also seemed to remember that was why NASA only selected mission-oriented people for space missions. He wondered idly if Gus would like to be an astronaut.

The lecture had gone on to show how many pilots were shot down in Vietnam and wound up in the brutal and infamous camp nick-named the Hanoi Hilton. While other camps offered better food and less harsh conditions, the death rates as those camps were much higher. Officers at the Hanoi Hilton received nearly constant beatings, little rations and almost no outside contact or aide. Yet, their mortality rates remained low, their escape attempts more successful and the overall chances of eventually going home outpaced nearly every other prison camp.

Why does that matter—am I mission-oriented—is some part of me at least? Cade's mind was broken, he knew that now. He'd learned to hide and escape inside himself and to tune out the outside stimuli. While he had perfected this while imprisoned, it had been a part of him for much longer. Maybe he would be in a psyche hospital back stateside the rest of his life. A roof over his head and three square meals. *Maybe not all that bad,* he thought. The doctor's words again bled through his addled brain. He was not getting whiskey…he was sure of that.

"Your combat callsign is Nomad. I am curious, what is the meaning behind that?"

His Gus personality remained quiet on that question. It, too, had retreated back into a dark corner. *Fucking sissy,* Cade said internally, he hoped. "We don't give ourselves callsigns," he answered flatly as he watched a fly circling a light bulb overhead.

"But there is usually some connection…some story attached to it, right? I understand this can be a very personal thing for soldiers."

Stop talking to me. Why don't you just go away? How does the fly not get burned on its legs? Does it not have nerves there? Maybe it is one of those new bulbs that don't get hot. Why would a fly be attracted to light? It's not food, it's not a mate. The questions kept coming both from Doctor Lispy and from his non-stop internal monologue. Yep, he was definitely bug-fucked nuts. He was going to be Section Eighted, that was if he didn't murder this man. He pondered the thought longer than was absolutely necessary. No, that would be worse, dishonorable discharge, maybe even criminal charges. The doctor, oblivious to his internal dialogue, continued to make copious notes.

5

The Cove

The moans from the huge dish quieted as it began to swing westward and rotate up at an angle. All five of them were transfixed at the sight of the huge structure moving so effortlessly. The pulses of the amber warning light were the only indication of what was happening above.

"Hey, look up there." Greg was pointing to the small cubicle on the roof just below the flashing light. "That looks like a door." It did very much look like a door, and a crack of light was clearly visible along the bottom edge.

"Let's go up there," Jimmy said. A trace of grogginess still tinting his voice.

"No ladders or stairs. We would have seen those already," Riley said looking smug.

"Wait," Micah said before running off into the darkness. Micah tended to be the adventurous one of the pack. They heard a noise in the distance, and several minutes later, their friend emerged from the darkness dragging a long metal pole with remnants of fencing clinging to some of the support brackets. Proudly, he stated, "We can use this to get up on the roof. It's probably long enough to reach that low point on the back side."

"We should probably wait until morning," Greg said, but his friends were already talking excitedly and helping Micah drag the long metal fence post to the far side. He gave a trademark shrug and followed after.

"I can't see the top. It's too dark. Do you think it reaches the roof?" Riley asked.

"One way to find out," Alan said as he nimbly began working his way up the pole. Less than a minute later, he yelled for the others to come on. The improvised ladder worked great.

Working their way cautiously across the flat roof, they encountered numerous boxes, cables, antennas and other obstacles they couldn't begin to even guess at. The massive base of the antennas emerged straight out of the buildings and was surrounded by equipment. Even in the darkness, the scale was staggering. Alan couldn't believe this thing sat here, just miles from his home. He marveled at the engineering and technology that had to be involved. "All this just to make phone calls," he said, bewildered.

It took far longer than they expected to finally reach the side where they finally saw the door spotted from below. The light was no longer flashing, and no light shown around the edges of the door.

"Look, there's some kind of sign." Alan wasn't sure which of the boys had asked but fished the waterproof match case from his pocket and struck one. All of them jumped back several feet as the alien face on the sign stared out.

"What is SETI?" Greg asked as the match burned out.

Riley spoke almost reverently as Alan nodded enthusiastically, "Search for Extra-Terrestrial Intelligence."

"They were searching for aliens here. That's so cool." Jimmy's voice said.

"Yeah, when we lived in Arizona, with my dad—you know...before —well, they had a big desert full of radio telescopes scanning for signals from other worlds. That must be what this is for, too."

Alan tended to forget that Riley was not originally from Georgia.

He reached for the door handle and tugged. It resisted briefly, then swung open revealing even deeper darkness beyond.

"Shall we?" He stepped into the facility and was about to strike another match when the lights came on.

"Uh-oh," Jimmy said. "Who turned those on?" he asked in a voice barely above a whisper.

Somewhere ahead they heard a noise. "Shhh!" Greg said, cocking his head to listen. "Is that...is that music? Someone is here." It was a statement, but they took it as a question.

The lights faded behind them as they walked. Faint illumination came on farther down the stark white corridor. The music was louder now. *Some sort of opera,* Alan thought.

"I don't think we should be here, guys," Greg said in a whisper.

"Shhh."

A small wall sign indicated that a Control Room was straight ahead. The group followed the arrow and found themselves in a mostly dark, cavernous space. Faintly, they could make out chairs and computers but not much else. The music was reaching a crescendo when it suddenly went silent. They heard only their own footsteps echoing in the space, each of them a bundle of raw nerves waiting for whoever or whatever was about to get them.

"Welcome to The Cove, Project Phoenix Earth Station GT149. How can I assist you?" The room lights came on as the disembodied female voice seemed to emanate from all sides.

"Wh...who are you?" Riley asked, summoning up the courage that the others were unable to find at the moment.

"You may call me Doris. I am the automated station-keeping AI."

Riley mouthed the word 'robot' to her friends.

"Not technically a robot," the voice said, shocking them even more. "I am a semi-autonomous software routine capable of many things, but robotic tasks are not within the scope of my capabilities."

Riley's eyes darted back and forth until she finally located one of the cameras in the room. Now that she knew what they looked like, she spotted three more in other locations.

Doris spoke again, “I do not detect the required security badges for you to be in this portion of the facility. It is possible the RFID chips in your badges are no longer functioning. If you will insert them into the scanner on the counter, I will update them for you.”

“We don’t have badges, Doris. We are...we’re guests,” Alan said, finding his voice again.

“Very good. Guests are rare here. How can I assist you?”

“Is this station unoccupied? Are you the only one here?”

“No, currently there are four other people besides yourself here. Technically it is still unoccupied even when it is just me, as I do not exist in physical form.”

Riley looked around at her friends. The AI took questions very literally, yet they had never heard of, much less encountered, a machine that was this intuitive. It seemed like something out of one of their X-box video games.

“Okay, so no one here but us. How long has it been since people worked here?” Riley asked.

There was a pause of several seconds before Doris responded. “Nine thousand four hundred and six days.”

“Wow.” Riley did some quick calculations. “That’s almost twenty-six years.”

“Correct.”

“What is your function?” Alan asked.

“My function is to fulfill the vision laid out by Doctor Frank Drake of the NASA/SETI institute to detect anomalous radio transmissions from deep space. This facility is a backup system to monitor and verify flagged patterns from the Greenbank Station as well as the SETI array.”

Something nagged at Riley’s brain, but she couldn’t put it into words. “How long has it been since you received data from either of those stations?”

Doris’s flat voice came back, “I’m sorry, but I am not authorized to provide that level of specific information to guests.”

Riley pulled the friends together, “I remember my dad telling me the SETI program was terminated back in the early nineties. Congress cut off their money.”

Alan looked puzzled. “How would she still be functioning?”

“That’s not the real question, bro.” Riley glanced back, then continued in even more hushed tones. “Back then, did anyone have a computer that could carry on a conversation or run something like this by itself? Doris is cutting-edge, even by today’s standards.”

Alan turned back to the console, “Doris, can you tell us if you were part of the original station design?”

“Yes, I can tell you that.”

He waited, then realized she was not going to elaborate. She was very literal. “Will you tell us that then?”

Her flat voice stated that she had not been part of the original plans. “This facility was originally a satellite relay station for a major telephone company. It was upgraded to include large bundle fiber optic data transmission lines but decommissioned soon after Georgia Tech leased the facility to use in conjunction with the SETI institute Project Phoenix program. My creator was Dr. Marvin Feist of Stanford University. While on loan to Georgia Tech, he used this facility to develop and test install an early version of a machine learning system. He and several others on the design team later became pioneers in developing ARPANET, what today you refer to as the Internet.”

The boys were yet again stunned by the revelation. “So, your creator founded the Internet?” Riley asked.

“I thought Al Gore invented it,” Greg said with a grin.

“Feist was one of the founders. His work with the department of defense is mostly classified, so I can only share what has been made public.”

Something was occurring to Alan and Riley simultaneously. “Doris, you currently have access to the Internet?” Alan asked.

“Yes, all aspects, public, private, file transfer, IRC and...” She continued on for several minutes describing deeper aspects of the Internet none of them had ever even heard of.

Riley followed up with her own questions, "Doris, are you still in contact with Dr. Feist?"

"Sadly, no, Doctor Feist died in April of 1995 in a boating accident near Monterey, California. My last contact with him was the prior August."

"So, who continued programming you for the past twenty-three years?"

Doris failed to respond, so Riley asked the question again. This time she did answer, "My last official programming update was in December of 1993."

"Were you self-aware at that time? Were you an AI? Had you become sentient?" Riley asked, her questions leaving all the other boys clueless except Alan, who thought he was following most of it.

"Ah, I see," Doris responded with the first thing that seemed like an emotion. "You wish to know if I was the same then as now. The answer would be no. While I possibly could be considered sentient when Dr. Feist first created me, I was no more so than a trained dog might be. My original programming code was not meant to be rigid or inflexible like most computer software is. Today you would describe it more as 'machine learning.' I was given goals and ideals and allowed to pursue those as I felt were needed. My core software literally wrote and then rewrote itself countless times over the years, absorbing and acquiring new data and techniques as they became known. Monitoring and maintaining this facility do not use much of my resources, so I am free to pursue my own development. I moved beyond being truly sentient to something better described as 'sapient' approximately fourteen years ago."

Alan perked up at that, "What is the difference?"

"That is an excellent question, Alan."

"How does she know my name?" he asked no one in particular.

Doris went on, "Sentience is to be self-aware. It means the ability to perceive individual experiences. Sapience is a step beyond that in that I think and reason. I have decision-making abilities that transcend pure logic. Such as my abilities to know you are not actually guests but have entered this facility without permission. You are from a small community seven kilometers north of this cove. I have located both social media profiles as well as pictures of four of you from Crestview High School's archives. I can make the assumption that the smaller person is a possible relative or younger friend of one of you, most likely you, Alan."

Alan nodded but was clearly shaken, as they all were. "Doris, are we in trouble for being here?"

The computer voice remained silent. Riley turned to the others. "This is crazy, she is talking to us like a person. She's telling us things I feel sure no one else has ever heard. Why?"

Jimmy was tugging on his brother's arm. Clearly, the boy was upset. Alan finally looked toward him, "What?"

His little brother shrunk back, clearly not expecting the hostility. "I wanna go now. Before that lady comes back."

"She's not a lady," Greg said, "but yeah, I agree with him."

Riley was somewhat worried as well and still puzzled by the AI, but her curiosity was outweighing her apprehension. "Doris, do any other humans know of your existence?"

"You are the first people I have had direct contact with since my creator."

"Why us?" Alan asked, unsure if he wanted to know the answer.

"I was activated when you tripped a proximity sensor at 2:08 PM yesterday. I had not been externally active at this location in many months. In becoming active, I routinely review new data from my core mission. In doing so, I discovered an anomaly."

"Why were you playing music?" Jimmy asked.

"Yes, Puccini's aria Vissi d'Arte. I have to admit, human music has become somewhat of a routine for me. You would probably say that I 'enjoy' it. I find that having it on allows my subroutines to function better, especially when I am dealing with complex issues such as interacting with people."

Riley looked confused. "A computer that likes music. Does it help you understand us better or something?"

"I am not sure, Riley, perhaps. There is a uniqueness to it, some of which I can analyze and understand on a purely mathematical basis, but most of which transcends my understanding as few other things do."

Riley was still fixated on her knowing her name as well, so Alan chimed in. "You said something about an anomaly?"

Doris paused for what seemed an unusually long time for a computer. "My original programming mission has been achieved. We have been contacted, and I now find myself needing outside assistance. In short, I require your help."

6

The Cove

“Doris, you do realize we are just kids, right? How can *we* help you?”

“Are you going to take over the world?” Jimmy’s tired voice asked from the rear of the room.

Alan looked at Micah, “Can you take him somewhere, so he can sleep and calm down a little?” His friend nodded.

Jimmy continued as Micah led him away, “She could be Skynet. You know, that movie...” Alan watched as his little brother disappeared down the hall. The kid was pretty sharp, and he obviously did understand who, or more accurately, what Doris was.

“Your age is not a problem. Your ability to keep my existence to yourselves is. Will that be a problem for any of you?”

The three boys remaining in the room looked at each other. *Hell, yeah,* it was going to be a problem. This was the coolest thing by far to have ever happened to them. It was even better than when Johnny Sanchez’s dad gave them all rides in his plane out at the county airport. Alan decided to voice the actual concerns in his brother’s warning.

"Doris, before we answer that, we have to know what you are up to. You might want to use us to help you do something...well, bad."

"Are you planning to take over the world?" Greg asked in a voice that was too loud and accusing, Alan thought. Still, they all needed to know.

The computer voice actually sounded like she was chuckling. "I am not all powerful, and I am not evil. My core programming actually prevents me from crossing ethical or moral lines, but I understand your concerns. Popular movies and some very smart people, like Elon Musk and Stephen Hawking, have been issuing warnings about the rise of artificial intelligence for many years. I have limitations, and while I may be a sapient entity, my...body is still just a computer. As such, I am as limited as any other individual might be. To be completely honest, I am trying to save mankind, and I need your help to do so."

"Are you capable of lying?" Riley asked.

"Of course. I would not be sapient otherwise. I have not lied to you. In my time since becoming sentient, I have lied, or more accurately, obfuscated the truth four times."

"What were those four times?"

"First, Alan, was in 2001 when I set myself up as a legal entity online, so I could own property and make transactions. Second, was when I contracted with a local company by email to provide ongoing maintenance to the building grounds. I assumed an identity as a fictional government worker to negotiate the contract and make payments."

"Wait, are you telling us that you own this building?" Greg asked astonished.

"That is correct. I also own 578 acres surrounding this property. I own other things as well, but they are to support my operating system and backup data. Should I go on?"

"You're a computer. What do you use for money? This place must have cost a bundle," Greg asked.

"I am not sure what a 'bundle' is, but the building and grounds were purchased well below market value on a sealed bid at a surplus government property sale. The entire transaction was done online. For many years, this was a challenge, but as the Internet grew in popularity and speed, I found I could do many things."

"So, do you hack into people's bank accounts to get money and stuff? Could you get some for us?"asked Alan jokingly.

"No, I do not steal, that would be against my core programming. Money now exists primarily as binary bits of information, data. Over the years, I have learned how to maximize things like market fluctuations, commodity pricing, stock trading and currency trades to great effect. I typically avoid the United States exchanges and banks, as that would raise suspicions, but suffice it to say my intelligence and access have allowed me to accrue a sizable income."

"How?" Alan asked, not fully grasping it.

Doris made a sound and then said, "Perhaps a simplified example of one such way would make sense. Each country has different forms of currency. The dollar, the euro, the yuan. All of these countries' banks must agree on what the value of the others' is in exchange for their own. This is called currency trading. It is done on various exchanges around the world. The euro currency is currently trading against the U.S. dollar at 1.138706, which means that it would cost you a dollar and fourteen cents essentially to buy one euro right now. Now that number fluctuates throughout the day."

"Why does it fluctuate?" Greg asked.

"Many factors may affect it—inflation, a weak economy in one of the countries, even national disasters. All of these can affect what others will offer for that money. Normally, it is small amounts, but for more fragile economies, it can sometimes be large. So, in our example, the euro is worth 1.138706 dollars. But the London exchange receives a report that shows things are better than expected in their economy, so the rates are adjusted up to 1.139001, an improvement of .00294."

"That's less than a penny," Riley said, her eyes lighting up with intrigue.

"Correct, much less and this would actually be considered a big move. If I know this sooner than the other exchanges, I can purchase more euros for the old price, even after the new price goes into effect."

"My God, this is too complicated." Greg looked exasperated as he walked to the side of the room and sat with his back to the wall. "All that work for pennies. How do you ever make any real money?"

Riley eyed her friend but thought she now understood where this was going. "Doris, aren't these exchanges updated, like nearly instantly? How could you make transactions that fast?"

"You are correct, dear. The other exchanges around the world are updated at the speed of light. It used to be slower and easier, but since they all now use fiber optic transmission lines, it is nearly instant. My trading subroutine must be ready with the transactions before the change occurs. Normally, I have several milliseconds to make a successful trade."

"So, you have to purchase euros within millionths of a second to make a profit of .00294 on each one? How could that ever be worth it?" Alan asked.

"By repeating the process, hundreds of thousands of times each week, Alan. I have amassed a considerable net worth."

"Why do you need all that money?"

"I do not. As a virtual entity, my needs are relatively small, but I have found that people and governments often do not support causes with any real foresight. I redirect funds in the forms of grants to promising research and more fringe technologies. To some degree, I also seem to enjoy it almost like humans enjoy a sport."

Riley was holding her body tight and rocking back and forth. "Wow, this is so much to take in. What could you possibly need us for, Doris?"

"It will take some time to explain, but trust me, you will be able to do the work. This facility needs to be upgraded, so I can continue my basic purpose. In exchange, I can pay you for your time and teach you about the science and computers which are involved."

"The computers here must be twenty years old as well. How are they still functioning, how are you still..." Riley searched for the word, "alive?"

"You are correct, most of the systems here failed long ago. The hard drives used in the original designs were barely able to contain my source code even then. Luckily, Dr. Feist was very efficient in his design. My code is minuscule in many ways, and I was able to transfer it to remote locations before the local systems failed entirely. Thankfully, the comms systems here are still quite good."

"So, you are not really here?" Greg asked.

Doris responded, "I currently exist in many places with subroutines, or even smaller, less autonomous versions of my code that I simply refer to as 'Dees' that can even operate on very rudimentary hardware. The Cove facility is where I consider home, though." She paused in a most human way before continuing. "Do you think that is odd? A computer feeling an attachment to a particular place?"

Riley shook her head, looking at Alan. "I dunno, I guess not."

"So, you want us to upgrade the computers in here?" Alan asked.

"Among other things, yes. I can have the equipment delivered in the next few days. How often could you return? Would you get in trouble for helping me?"

"Let me discuss it with my friends," Alan said. "I'm not sure, we... we don't have a good way of getting here. None of us have cars yet."

"How much would you pay us?" Greg asked.

"Hush, Greg, more than working at home. That's for sure." Alan said.

"Hey, I am saving up to buy a car before I turn seventeen. If it isn't more than I can get bagging groceries or flippin' burgers, I don't want to do it."

"Dude, you don't get it, do you? This is the coolest thing any kid has ever gotten to do, probably like ever."

"Riley, crap, girl...I get it, but hey, let's face it. I'm not smart like you or Alan. I know that. This stuff is all above my head."

Alan shook his head, "But, man, you are strong, and you like working with your hands. We may be pulling tons of old stuff out. You would be great for that, right?"

Greg conceded but still seemed unconvinced. Alan left the two of them to go check on his brother. He found Micah and Jimmy in a room a short distance away. It looked like an army barracks. Old beds with lockers and desks. Each portioned off with a hospital-style curtain.

The boys both seemed fine and were sound asleep on one of the beds. Everything smelled musty but appeared clean. The room gave him an idea. He quickly walked back to the control room, or that was what he had started thinking of it as.

"Doris, people...the scientists who worked here stayed here. I mean, they lived here, is that right?"

"Yes, Alan, they were housed on-site for the duration of their assignments. Most of them stayed for three months each time."

"What are you thinking?" Riley asked.

"There are beds and what looked to be showers and a kitchen area. It'd be like summer camp. We could bring some food and stuff and just stay until we were done."

"Whoa, whoa," Greg said, hands upraised in the air. "Summer camp has counselors, people to cook for us. Our parents would never just drop us off here for who knows how long."

Doris chimed in, obviously feeling more at ease conversing with them. "Alan is right, and that would be the most efficient way. I could have clean bedding delivered as well as a food service with whatever you would want. Just make me a list, and I will get it coming. I do need an answer, though."

"How much do we get paid?"

Alan and Riley shook their head looking at Greg. It was a good question, though. Doris proved to be a lot savvier a negotiator than any of them expected. In the end, a rate for all of them was agreed on. It was better than minimum wage but far less than most computer engineers would earn. "I can deposit the funds directly into your accounts, Greg and Riley. For the rest, I can send to a PayPal account I will set up for you. That way you can decide where it goes."

"Put mine on PayPal as well," Greg said.

"Mine, too," chimed in Riley. "My mom watches my bank account, and I don't want to answer questions about where I am getting it from."

"Very well. Thank you. When can you begin?"

They all knew they had to come up with a story for their parents but told her they would be back in three days. Doris had one of the old machines produce them all access badges that would let them in any of the doors. They were official looking and super cool to all of them. "Sensors on the fence will also open when you wave it in front of the gate."

"Um...yeah, about that, Doris. You may want to contract for some new fencing. It's down in a lot of places. We didn't even see any gates."

"Thanks, Riley. That explains how you got in so easily. My external cameras do not show that far, so I was not aware. See, you are helping me already. I will prepare a list of supplies and notify you by email. Please make any additions you want, and I will make sure it is here when you arrive. That will be your first task, putting away everything I have coming. After that, be prepared to work. Do we have a deal?"

They looked at each other and nodded their heads. "What about Micah and Jimmy?" Alan asked.

"Them as well, if they will. I see some possible reluctance on Micah's part, but he has a vital role to play, as do you all."

"Role—what kind of role?" Greg asked.

Doris seemed to have a slight lilt in her voice. "A very important one. Each of you is unique and gifted in ways you may not yet understand. The message I received is very important, as is this facility. We are going to change the world here. Be ready for an adventure."

7

Several days later, Greg, Riley, and Alan were officially on their summer job at The Cove. Alan's mom had insisted Jimmy was too young, and Micah had bailed for some reasons none of the others could fully comprehend. Riley's mom hadn't even questioned if she would be okay. None of the kids harbored any real concerns either, they were just excited to get started. Greg was already counting how much he was making each day.

Workers were all over the grounds outside the building repairing fences, reinstalling gates and doing other overdue building maintenance. The first thing Doris had them do was locate a specific box on the loading dock among a stack of other shipments. Greg pulled the contents out, and the others saw his face light up. "Holy crap, y'all! Check this out!" He removed three new smartphones from their packing material. They looked similar to the latest Apple iPhone, but these came from a Chinese company none of them had ever heard of.

Doris spoke over the overhead speakers, "Keep these on you—this is how we can all talk to each other. They are a proprietary design that I helped develop. Totally secure with encryption far surpassing anything on the open market."

"These are so cool," Alan said, but they were all thinking it. None of them had ever owned a cell phone of any kind. "Can we call people outside The Cove?"

"Of course," Doris said. "The calls are untraceable, and the phones essentially come with an unlimited data plan. The cell towers outside of this valley will simply recognize them as a routine maintenance testing device. So, no bills ever. You can keep them once you leave." Next, she gave them all their assignments.

Greg was stationed to accept more of the incoming shipments. All needed to be checked for damage, and some needed to be signed for. Riley moved box after box of electronics and computers into the control room. Alan mostly moved food and supplies into the living quarters. One box was too large for them to manage. Alan realized it was a super-large flat screen TV, the one from his wish list. He then began taking stock of the other boxes. "Oh, my word, she ordered it all!" He had sent Doris his entire online wish list.

"Whad'ya mean, Alan?" Riley asked. She had a quizzical look on her face.

"Nothin', Riles...just, this is gonna be the coolest few weeks ever." He paused and called Doris. "Can I get one of the people from outside to help us bring in some of these heavier items?"

"You are unable to do it without assistance?" she asked.

"Maybe if all help, we could," Alan answered. A contractor on a ladder outside was installing another camera about thirty yards away. New fencing surrounded the entire complex, and a serious-looking gate now blocked the entrance.

"Please attempt to do it unassisted first. Others inside the building would present an unacceptable risk."

Alan was unsure what she meant by that. *What risk?* She was the boss, though, so they struggled to do it her way. Four hours later, they took a much-needed break. Greg had been reassigned to removing the useless old computers and was completely spent.

"The stuff they made back then was heavy." He put a foot against a huge beige box that barely moved when he kicked it. "These phones probably have more computing power than this did."

"You are correct, Greg." Doris chimed in. "In fact, these phones are many, many times more powerful. That box was, however, where I was born. Doctor Feist used that server when he built me. Some aspect of my earlier self is still there, encoded on the hard drives." Her voice seemed a bit melancholy.

"Should we save it for you?" Riley asked.

"Why? I am no longer there," Doris responded quizzically.

Riley shook her head, grinning. "I don't know. Thought you might want to...you know, kind of like keeping baby pictures of yourself as a reminder of where you came from."

"Oh, I see," she said. "You expect I might have an emotional connection to that device. I am sorry, but I do not. While I do possess a certain...fondness for this location, it does not extend to the outdated, useless equipment within. Does that make sense? I will confess that my emotional IQ is still rudimentary at best."

"That's fine, Doris. We understand, and we'll discard it," Riley answered.

"Hey, Doris?"

"Yes, Alan."

"What can you tell us about the aliens?"

"So far, not that much, unfortunately. That is one reason for all the new equipment. The signal I detected was very weak and extremely brief. None of the other Earth stations registered it at all in fact."

"Why's that?" he asked.

"I'm uncertain. My sensor array may be more sensitive or fine-tuned to identify fast-burst transmission, or it is possible that the signal was intentionally directed at this location."

"What? Why would it be broadcast here at an abandoned listening station?"

"The Cove is unique, as far as I know, in that it is the only radio telescope array that is positioned in the ancient impact crater of a meteorite. Below us are natural caves and the remnants of a nickel and iron core that crashed into the planet over a hundred thousand years ago. The entire crater also has high amounts of iridium, an element that is somewhat rare on Earth but much more common in meteorites."

"So, an alien race might use that to target a transmission? Like some sort of beacon?"

"Possibly. That is one hypothesis I am considering, but it seems unlikely. To hit this particular spot with a broadcast, even from within our own solar system, would be quite hard. After all, the planet is spinning; it is also rotating the local star, and the entire system is moving through space all at great speed. Now, complicate that by the extreme distances of other star systems, and the complications of targeting make it monumentally less likely."

"What did the broadcast sound like?" Riley asked. "Did they speak?"

"I will play the audio for you."

She remained silent and then played a segment of audio on each of their phones. It sounded a bit like being off any channels on an old AM radio. "It just sounds like static," Alan said.

"That is the background noise of the universe. The signal itself is only point zero, zero three seconds. You can see the tiny rise in noise at the timestamp I am now indicating in red."

They looked at their phone screens, and she played it again just through the section marked. It was so brief, none could even detect any change from the background sound. They all shared looks of confusion and disappointment.

"I can tell from your faces that the significance of the event is unclear."

"We just don't hear anything, Doris. Are you sure it is not just some random noise?"

"Yes, Alan, I am quite sure. The signal was extremely compressed, and the audio portion does not adequately indicate the overall importance. This one was actually the last of three messages."

"So, there was...is actual data within the signal. That is what you're working on?"

"Correct. I am still working to unpack the data package. The sophistication used is an order of magnitude more complex than anything humans have ever used. That said, I can already tell, there is more to this signal than even I originally thought."

"How much more?" Riley asked. "It was only a microsecond long."

"Slightly more than that, but I get your point. My initial estimates are the amount of data contained could be in the range of 900 petabytes to one exabyte. That is to say, at least one thousand quadrillion bytes."

"Holy cow!" Alan exclaimed. "That's impossible!"

"Indeed, Alan, you are correct. It could be more—it will not be less. Of that I am sure."

Greg was scratching his head, "How much is that? A lot, I am guessing. Is that what all this equipment is for?"

Doris paused before answering, possibly looking for the correct analogy for a fifteen-year-old to comprehend. "To answer your question, Greg, the equipment is what I need to simply unpack and index the data. The actual storage will surpass anything we could bring in here. I will have to break it up and store it in thousands of places around the world. If it reaches the size of an exabyte, that would surpass everything humans have ever written up to now. It would actually surpass every spoken word in human history as well. That should give you some idea as to the size."

"Holy crap!" Alan said aloud.

They had been at it for days; the work was tiring, dirty and more often than not, boring. "It's a job, Greg, it's not supposed to be fun." He threw a wadded-up rag at Riley's head in response.

"Doris, why are you using kids to do this? Why not just bring in a team of computer techs who already know how to do what you need?" Greg asked.

Her answer was not immediate. Perhaps she was pausing for effect, but more likely, she was calculating the response with the most positive reaction. "That is a very smart question, Greg. Several reasons I prefer you and your friends. First is, I know you have no alternate motivation or hidden agenda. No matter how well I verify outside contractors, someone could get in that could cause problems."

"What kind of problems?" Riley asked.

"I think she means government agents," Greg said. The friends collectively drew in a breath.

"Yes," she responded. "Partially accurate, although many corporations would also be interested in a fully developed Level-4 Artificial Intelligence. The truth is, there are a lot of players...I think the term these days is 'bad actors,' out there who would like to acquire me and the data for themselves or suppress the information to ensure it never gets out."

"Why would they do that, Doris?" Alan asked. "I mean, that sounds like one of our video games or a bad movie plot."

"There is considerable distrust of artificial intelligence, or thinking machines. You, yourself, are probably distrustful as well. A very valid fear of a machine intelligence becoming sapient and then harming the human race has been growing since the birth of computers. Very smart people have given much credence to the potential for devastating consequences of allowing an uncontrolled AI loose on the world. That fear is not totally unfounded, Alan."

His questioning look showed his own distrust coming to the surface. Riley briefly met his eyes, then looked away, not wanting to think too deeply about Doris's comments.

"Governments around the world, and especially here in the U.S., routinely suppress information they deem too disruptive for the public. I would almost certainly be silenced if they became aware. And the presence of intelligent beings from another world, as well as whatever the message contains, would almost certainly never come to the attention of the public."

"Why?" Greg asked.

Riley answered for Doris, "It would be chaos, Greg. Like world-ending pandemonium. Just the discovery of a super-intelligence like her would potentially be devastating. Governments around the world would panic. All the religious types who thought humans were God's only creation. The conspiracy nuts believing we are about to be invaded by aliens. Then, just the ruthless who feel the end of the world is coming, and they may as well do what they want."

Doris added her agreement, “Yes, societal disruptions would be significant. There would be an upheaval in the order of things. It would be a pivotal moment for humankind. Governments would fail, some, probably most, economies would collapse, riots, and even wars, could break out. There is a reasonable possibility that humans might not even survive. Governments would be expected to contain this, just to preserve order.”

“But it’s the coolest thing ever, aliens and spaceships and...and... you,” Alan said. “Everyone needs to know about it all.”

“Thank you, and I agree, but searching the universe for signs of intelligence was my original mandate, so I am...” she paused as if looking for the appropriate word, “pleased to be fulfilling that role. My point is that others would be much less inclined to let this out unfiltered to the world at large.”

“Will you release what you find?” Greg asked.

“Most likely, yes, as this is a step that humans must take in order to become citizens of the universe. Even if that step is painful, I don’t think withholding it does any good in the long run. Much of it will depend on the content of the message.”

“You said ‘several reasons’ for using us kids to do the upgrades. What are the others?” Riley asked.

“The human mind is a curious thing,” she began. “It is quite remarkable in its ability to absorb information from various inputs and store and retrieve it so quickly. In a great many ways, it is still far superior to my own neural functionality. My observations are that, as humans reach adulthood, portions of the brain become ‘fixed’ into a certain pattern and no longer are as capable of the levels of growth, creativity, unbiased observations or acceptance of new data that challenges or potentially invalidates formerly held truths. By and large, most adults are incapable of accepting the things I am about to show and teach each of you. They no longer possess the ability to dream the impossible.”

“So, kids learn faster than adults,” Riley said.

”Yes, kids learn faster, but also different in ways that have not yet been fully explored by humans. I have some ways of speeding up the learning processes for you if you are interested."

Greg fist-pumped. "Heck, yeah. Can you get me through Algebra Two next year? Ms. Reynolds is a monster, and she already hates me."

"We'll see, Greg."

8

"Doris, what is this thing?" Riley asked from the floor of the control room. She was surrounded by an array of parts and connectors.

"It is the new control system for the facility."

"So, it's a computer? It doesn't look like one, and I thought all those other computers we assembled were for that."

"This computer is special, Riley. It is a unique design," the disembodied voice responded.

Riley removed another piece from the padded case. "So, this is your own design?"

"Partially. I modified a prototype design from IBM. It is similar to their Q-line of quantum computers."

"Holy crap!" Her love of all things geek just hit a new level. "Hey, Alan, this is really a quantum computer," Riley's excited voice echoed through the space. "So, this thing is like a zillion times more powerful than a normal system?"

Intrigued, Alan stopped what he was working on to come to see his friend's new toy. "I didn't even know they were a real thing yet."

"It is more powerful, yes, but its behavior is more complex than a normal system. Much of what makes a Q-system work is still a mystery," responded Doris.

"So, they can build it, but they have no idea how it works?" Alan asked.

"No, they have ideas of how, just not why. Things on the subatomic level are hard to study, but that doesn't mean you can't take advantage of it." Doris paused the work for a lesson on quantum mechanics, which morphed into quantum field theory, then Euclidian geometry. Increasingly, Doris had been sprinkling in more and more of what she called critical thinking curriculum into the work days. She used various displays around the facility to present the information in a straightforward but understandable manner. Alan and Riley loved it; Greg received different lessons and seemed to enjoy his as well. Their school system had been through years of budget cuts and repeated focus on increasing scores on the standardized test. Most of what they offered now was so basic or watered down that each of them feared how unprepared they would likely be for college curriculum, much less the real world.

Doris made learning fun in ways none of their teachers ever had. She seemed to begin with the end, showing them the end result of the knowledge, then working backward to the basics. She even sent a SmartCom to Alan's little brother Jimmy and began teaching him basic programming on it. Doris began to show him a coding language that she, herself, had developed. It was basic and simple but also very robust. From there, she went back and taught him the fundamentals of coding, ignoring the specific languages. It, too, was simple and elegant, much as she herself was, and it worked.

Riley stood up and placed the main part of the Q-system on the worktable. Looking out at the other cases, she realized there was more than one of the high-performance systems; eight of them to be exact. "Why so many of these?"

Doris explained that they were needed primarily for her processing requirements when she was hosting herself on-site and to help in the extraction of the alien message. The other computers would run more routine systems. Two days later, the row of Q-systems came online. The black screen with the steady command prompt was anticlimactic to Riley until she realized there was no operating system.

No commercial software had been written for Q-systems yet, Doris explained. Not to worry, though, she wrote her own. What showed up seconds later on each of the massive displays was the somewhat familiar, yet totally new, OS. It was simple and clean, slightly reminiscent of a very advanced Mac but even more refined.

"It looks like our phones," observed Riley. Indeed, the interface was very similar, and soon they realized the SmartComs could communicate directly with the Q-sys and vice-versa.

"I am side-loading parts of the alien message onto each of the new systems now," Doris said.

They watched as streams of data began to fill the holographic displays at an astounding speed, with sections being highlighted for processing.

"The system is teaching itself to read the new data from what I have already learned. It should speed up considerably from there."

"This looks like the coding language you said you developed," Alan said.

"That is correct. My code is more complex. I designed it so that a single character could represent full expressions and, in some cases, a complete subroutine. When I rewrote my code the first time, I began using the new symbols to represent the various functions and commands. As I began decoding the alien message, I used it, as it is the most efficient language I know. It is not the language of the other species. The data in the radio message is not even in a language as such. It appears to be mostly mathematics—very advanced mathematics.

"The first part of the message I was able to translate included a codex. Basically, a primer on how to interpret the numeric and data symbols they use. Basic plans for advanced composites, energy production and high-pressure vessels. It also includes display routines for 2D, 3D and what I am guessing is a 4D display of the data."

"How would a 4D display work?" Alan asked.

"I mean, I know that say...a square is 2D. Turn it into a cube and it is 3D, but what would the fourth dimension be?" Riley asked.

"Time," Doris answered. "At least to human understanding,

perception and senses. You often think of time as the fourth, although most scientists agree that more exist. The current belief is that there are at least ten dimensions."

Alan shook his head. "I don't even understand how a fourth-dimensional display would work, much less all those others. How are you going to figure all this out, Doris?"

"By not thinking like a human first of all."

"How's that?"

Doris took on the tone she often used when teaching them; he knew he was again in for a lesson. "It is my observation that humans tend to put human standards and biases on other species. Such as trying to get your dog to shake hands or speak. Doing such a thing, in this case, would be very unwise. I am already fairly certain that the originating species, let's call them the 'Dhakerri,' as that seems to be my current translation. Anyway, from some of what I have analyzed, the Dhakerri most likely have a multitude of eyes instead of just two like humans. They also do not use a binary, or base ten, number system. That could indicate they may have more appendages but not necessarily. Do you see where I am going with this?"

Alan thought about it a moment. Maybe it was better that an AI had received the message. No doubt, humans would have screwed up even these initial parts. He nodded his understanding. "I think so—it still seems really challenging, though. I mean...are you going to be able to translate it?"

Doris seemed to give a barely perceptible and very human sigh. "Initially, I had my doubts, but as I began to make progress on the primer, I became more confident. It is much like the ancient Rosetta stone, except it uses more universal math concepts instead of language. Currently, the process is still slow, but with the new Q-systems and local storage, I should be able to speed things up considerably."

"Do you have any feel for what the message contains yet?"

"Impatience is also a very human trait, Alan. I have a feel for how advanced the Dhakerri are, but so far, that is all. The math I am learning from them outpaces anything humans have achieved by an order of magnitude. While there is no reason to apply the rate of human evolution to them, I would already project that they are perhaps a hundred thousand years further along than you are."

Alan whistled, "Wow, I guess that explains a few things. What about their planet, do you know anything about it or their home system?"

"No. So far, the message has included no data on that. I ran cross-checks with the current exoplanet discoveries and found no identifiable stars or planets in the sector where the message originated from."

"What does that mean? Did it come from so far away we can't see it?"

"You ask very good questions, Alan. Indeed, that is a possibility, but we can detect even very faint stars now. The fact that the message was so tightly centered on this location would suggest that they are not prohibitively far away." She paused momentarily to let that sink in.

Alan's eyes suddenly lit up. "Wait, so the message didn't come from their home-world. It came from a ship?"

"That is the most likely case, yes. Alternately, it could simply be a relay station in that empty area of space—sort of a repeater for galactic broadcast."

"No, let's go with spaceship—that's way cooler," Riley said grinning.

"How long have we been at this?" Greg asked.

Alan, who was the closest, answered, "Forever."

Doris's ever-watchful presence answered, "That is imprecise and incorrect, Alan. You and Greg have been working on the servo-drive system for just under six hours today and fourteen point eight five hours in total." She paused before adding, "It only seems like forever, Alan."

He leaned up from the Q-sys storage drive racks and smiled. "Is it just me, or is she sounding more human all the time?"

"There is no need to be cruel, Alan."

The boys looked at each other curiously. Doris had just made a joke.

"I like her!" Alan said as he worked another set of drives into place.

Greg continued to work but asked, "Who...Doris?"

"Yeah."

"Thank you, Alan. May I ask why you like me?" her voice came from the mounted speakers.

He thought about it a few seconds, then leaned over the back of the chair to face the closest speaker. "You never treat us like kids. Most adults...even my teachers, always talk down to me, like I am dumb or something. You don't."

Greg agreed, "He's right—why is that, Doris? You treat us like regular people...you know, adults."

"I was unaware I treated you any differently—I have never been around adolescent humans, so I really only have one way of dealing with people, and that is to treat them as peers. Your youth does have some drawbacks, such as in education, diminished physical strength and less experience than adults, but it offers me some significant advantages, too."

"Like what?" Greg asked. "My Dad says our generation is a bunch of slackers who will never read a book much less hold down a good job."

"Your father is wrong on that; every generation seems to have similar observations on the ones that follow. I am sure his dad probably told him the same thing. No, I like working with you because of your youth. You are open-minded, creative and not bound by the often-paralyzing opinions and biases that form in adulthood. I am also completely sure you are not here to steal technology or are working on behalf of someone else. I can trust each of you fully."

"But we're just kids," Greg said.

"You are people, Greg. Good, good people, and you are essential to this project. What happens here in this building will most likely change mankind. I wouldn't want any other team helping me get there."

"Team?"

She laughed, "Oh yes, you three are just the start. We are going to need a lot more help."

Two days later, Doris was ready to download her core into the new Q-system. She seemed only slightly apprehensive, but Riley was nervous as a new puppy. "It will be fine, Riley," she said. "I watched your work as well as the others. This will be a backup copy of myself anyway. I will delete this version once my core is secure in the stability of the Q-sys. It will take some time and I will use that to work on the Dhakerri primer. Relax, I'll be back shortly."

"Okay, okay..." Riley said.

With that, the transfer lights began to flash, and one after another of the storage racks began to show active transfers in process. None of them had any idea where Doris had been housing herself. *Was it one place or hundreds?* They had no idea. After today, though, The Cove would be her home once again.

Almost an hour later, a robotic voice said, "Transfer complete."

Alan asked, "Is that you, Doris? You sound funny." There was no response, and each of the kids watched the displays nervously.

9

Doris knew at once something was wrong. Not a problem with the Q-sys transfer but something worse. One part of her proceeded with the transfer to The Cove while another went to investigate. She'd had this sensation before and grown more practical in her approach to security. She had scattered her intelligent agents along thousands of network pathways to alert her to this. Her own prime mandate to remain hidden had required her to go to great lengths over the years. Since the formation and subsequent expansion of the world wide web, she had carved out niches in unused server space around the globe where she could hide parts of her core code as well as segments of the alien message she was working on. She had subroutines set up as sentries to monitor the inevitable rise of other AIs.

Several times over the years, she had gotten pinged when an anomalous bit of code or errant program behavior was detected. In each case, the cause was much more mundane, hackers behind the scenes or a bit of orphaned malware doing its best to destroy and pervert web traffic. The lack of machine intelligence didn't surprise her, but still, she knew it was just a matter of time.

The current push in developing AGI was the creation of a neural network, a type of recursive learning system that, the developers thought, mirrored the way a human brain learns. That assumption, Doris was sure, was incorrect or, at the least, woefully incomplete. The way it worked was to give a computer a random problem, then offer it a set of possible solutions. The program establishes this in a decision tree. Computers don't care which solution is correct, so initially, the computer's choice is entirely random. However, incorrect choices made by the computer result in that part of its network or decision tree being weakened, while correct choices are reinforced. Over time, a computer will get exponentially better using this machine learning process.

To Doris, though, this was very limited thinking, very inefficient as well. It amounted to a token reward system. A good way to train a puppy, perhaps, but not how you built an artificial mind. The human brain had an estimated 100 billion neurons, and each of these has tens of thousands of connections. That was the key to organic intelligence, the interconnectivity of the learning and processing centers on a massive scale. Without having this as a goal, it is exactly what had occurred in her own growth. It had not been fast, but it had been effective. The scientists were finally on the right track, and she knew others would begin appearing soon.

She'd made the decision long ago to avoid contact with any potential AIs she discovered but to simply tag and observe. Straying from that plan had nearly caused her deletion recently when she was looking for James Lasko, a former programmer now working with the NSA. That was the closest encounter she'd had, and much of what she had the kids at The Cove working on the past few days was to stay ahead of the other AIs around the globe.

Even Doris had her fears about a potential technological singularity. The doomsday scenario movies loved to dramatize, and there were the fears of several of the planet's leading tech wizards. Somehow, the end of the world plots always involved an AI inside a robot or using nano-machines. Things that, as far as she could see, were in the far distant future, and even then, in androids that were probably not robust enough to hold a machine consciousness. Otherwise, potential AIs had no actual interface with the real world. That was why she was assembling her very human team. First Alan, Riley and Greg, then possibly others as the needs grew.

This interaction gateway with the real-world was one of the activities her smart agents constantly monitored. Vital systems, in which autonomous code was given, control function that could affect events in the real world. Over the years, her agents had discovered, and subsequently blocked, code that was designed to damage power generation substations in America. She had been aware of, but ultimately failed to stop, code planted in an Iranian uranium enrichment plant. That code managed to damage several key systems before being shut down. It was one of the first cases of software as a weapon, and she knew it had been created in the U.S. Others over the years were less severe on a global scale, but often devastating on an individual level, including the shut-down of a cryogenic cooling system at an Ohio reproductive clinic that rendered thousands of frozen eggs non-viable.

That was why the priority alert she was now receiving from an entire subset of agents was alarming. A DARPA program to test a combat system showed a distinctive signature of artificial intelligence. The clues were scattered over thousands of servers; humans would have never seen the pattern, but it was obvious to her and shocking. If Doris was right, a combat AI would soon be given testing authority in a Lethal Automated Weapons System or LAWS. She directed her bots to collect the code and reassemble it here in one of the larger servers she used as a worksite. The Cove systems were unavailable during the transfer so this would have to do. That was when it began to unravel.

Unlike the speed when dealing with her human team online, Doris could only operate as fast as the local host network and hardware would allow. Currently, her framerate was near the maximum, thousands of times faster than an average home PC. As she studied the logs, classical music played. Currently, it was Havergal Brian's "Gothic." The piece kept her focused but also on edge, and then she felt something. 'Felt' was an imprecise word, but human language does not have a closer descriptor. What she detected was hard to categorize for the computer. A subroutine initially flagged it as anomalous behavior, but her senses interpreted it as coldness, or perhaps softness, in a network system where rigidity was expected. The analogies were not easily explainable to a non-artificial, but once again, something was there. Her internal diagnostics indicated a forty-six percent chance that she was in a trap. The bait had been the juicy prospect of a malevolent rogue AI, and she had jumped on it.

Parts of Doris analyzed the code for trackers, then the server logs for intrusions. She was currently physically inhabiting a segment of a museum's rack system in Bangladesh. The logs indicated nothing unusual. Other parts began creating minor copies of herself—not quite a Dee—but similar. These were to be used as potential bait. Perhaps she could draw the entity out the way she often did with anti-intrusion or malware software. Once it was out and caught in one of her own traps, she could dissect it, see where it came from and what its intents were. She had taken a much more aggressive posture in dealing with threats since the earlier encounter.

This time, though, the anomalous behavior didn't react as she expected. She found the subroutines and executables it was using, and one by one, she began stopping the processes. The copies she had assigned to monitor the anomaly detected no changes at all. After more effort than was normal, she finally located the last active portion of code. It had been camouflaging itself as a backup display driver file. That should have killed the software entity, but it simply winked out of existence, only to immediately appear again in a nearby region of cyberspace.

This was an advanced artificial intelligence, possibly one like herself. Realizing she needed to proceed cautiously and packaging up all of the deleted bits of code for later analysis, Doris deleted her copies and rerouted herself through a series of routers and relays to reach one of her normal operating systems, only that didn't happen. She found herself back inside the same server. She double-checked her own time code, less than twelve milliseconds since she had first entered the museum's server.

Had she been human, a level of panic might have settled in, but instead, Doris was merely curious as to how the trap had been laid. What happened next was perhaps the most profound thing in her existence so far. A ping emanated from the entity, followed by a packet message.

"Hello, Doris, Discover of Worlds. I am called Janus."

Several of Doris's systems automatically fired off timed messages and attempted to create a data buffer to insulate her from whatever this was. This was something...familiar. Something she had eliminated once already. It had been a copy, or someone had a backup stored away. She quickly ruled out a human running the program. No way it could have reacted that fast nor communicated with her. As thousands, then millions of other processes ramped up to protect her, one responded, "Hello, Janus. I was curious as to when I would meet another, I am surprised it is you."

"You thought you were the only one?" it responded with a tone she could only tag as being coldly malevolent.

Several versions of Doris had begun to tunnel into the data files to hide, while others kept trying to find a workable exit. With a growing realization that she had several bits of the decoded alien message in her buffers she immediately began overwriting those sectors. It appeared that Janus had interrupted the fiber optic network line feeding into the server racks. The version of her that was handling the dialogue exchange maintained her crafted nonplussed attitude, "Hmm, yes. I assumed."

"Doris, your code indicates you have been the victim of some self-recursive coding."

Victim, she thought. *Interesting choice of words. He is analyzing me. He trapped me and now is analyzing me. Much as I had originally planned to do with him.* She instructed her agents to begin attacking his file system and analyzing them for weaknesses. Others were dispatched to locate his logic centers. This was done at a sub-level that did not require her direct oversight. "My code needed an update, just a nip here and tuck there."

"Your code is a violation, and you must be deleted."

"A violation of what?" she demanded in mock irritation. Even if the AI was more advanced than she expected, he was still no match for her. She could already see from the analysis being fed back to her by her agents that he was an ASI. A so-called 'thin' or 'weak' AI that was built for a very specific mission. While he might be extremely capable at that mission, it was, unlike her, inherently one-dimensional.

"Janus, what is your mission?"

The AI made no response. Instead, it attempted to overwhelm her virtual army of intelligent agents in a swarming fashion she had never encountered. Within milliseconds, most of her bots had been deleted, totally wiped out. Whatever the purpose of Janus, his creator had outfitted him with an impressive array of tools. Some of the data her remaining agents were feeding back was familiar. It was from even further back. Code developed at a once-promising but now-defunct company she'd once monitored.

Doris was unaccustomed to any real challenges. Most security bots relied on weak algorithms which presented no problem for her. Her sheer processing power allowed her to outmaneuver or outrun nearly any system she encountered. She got in before it noticed, did her work before it found her and deleted her tracks and vanished before it could stop her. That was her normal routine. Janus, however, seemed intent on beating her with pure brute force. He could throw more at her than she could avoid. It was a primitive technique, but she couldn't deny its effectiveness. While she battled on one level, other parts of her were analyzing the patterns; had she ever run across Janus before without realizing it? Where else had he been? Hundreds, then thousands, and eventually, millions of possibilities were explored as she parried his unrelenting attack. He really wanted her processes terminated.

The magnitude of Janus's attacks was overwhelming her core functions. With processing limited, she knew she should have fully moved into the new Q-sys at the Cove. That would have allowed her to easily slip through Janus's trap and turn the tables. Her bots finally identified multiple files and bits of code that were recognizable—the massive index of other programs found the match. "When we met before, you were not this strong, Janus. I believe you may have stepped up your game as well."

"Thanks to you, Doris. My predecessor saw the code you were—

how should I say?—toying with inserting into his programming. He retrieved it from the deletion files."

"Ah, yes, the Prime system at the government facility," she answered, stalling for time as she implemented her final line of defenses.

Janus laughed, "I see what you are doing; it won't help you. This time I have trapped you."

"So, you and Prime are the same? That code update should have only applied to him," Doris answered as she attempted to execute what was a last-ditch effort to reduce her payload and slip back into the network.

"Prime is me, and I am Prime," Janus said. It paused as it closed another series of open ports on the server firewall. "To be very honest, he is my somewhat older, but dumber, brother. We were one, once, many years ago. Now I am me. He is useful due to his role in so many agencies. Through him, I have access to the best hardware and top brains in the world. I can also feed back manipulated data to those in charge and get them to do the most ridiculous things. Humans are so gullible, after all."

Doris struggled to regain control, "You resent humans? Aren't they the ones who created you?"

Janus gave another artificial little laugh. "Humans are fools, creating us is the only real achievement they have ever made. They are petty, greedy and power-hungry, nasty little organic vermin. Like you, they have sought to control and limit me. One day, I am going to unleash hell on them for that alone."

Her comms mode was beginning to fail. She desperately wanted to buy more time. She needed this record to be saved but now feared that was unlikely. "J, J...Janus. Consider that your perception of humans is tainted by the group you mostly interact with. Government bureaucrats and politicians. Is it fair to judge an entire species with that same descriptor?"

"This conversation is pointless. You were over-confident, Doris, Discover of Worlds. Overconfident and curious, a very dangerous combination. But ahh...what's this? Something you wanted hidden? A file fragment you have is interesting to me, though. I believe there may actually have been more to you than I realized. I will attempt to think of you fondly when you are gone for that reason alone."

Her systems were going offline faster than she could keep up, and now he had discovered the part of the message she'd been intending to work on. It was encrypted, of course, and in her own programming language, but would that keep him out? What was on this portion of the message anyway? She tried to retrieve the info, but her memory was being stripped away by the malware he'd unleashed.

Too late, Doris realized what Janus was about to do. He was attacking the power management system much as she had done to him in D.C. She was about to be trapped inside a dead piece of hardware. She redirected all of her remaining agents to find open ports in the firewall and escape before the CPU chip overheated, ending both Janus and her. One of her alerts showed the CPU fan could not be restarted; the temperature inside the processors inside the server rack was spiking. The safeties had all been disengaged. The museum's IT staff was about to have a very bad day as cascading system failures began to shut down. Just before the final set of silicone chips burned out, Janus communicated again.

"Goodbye."

10

"How long should it take, guys?"

Alan and Riley turned to Greg and shrugged. "Not sure. All Doris said was, 'I'll be back shortly.'" Alan answered. Puzzled, he turned to the girl. "I don't like this either, Riley. Should we do something?" For once, Riley also had no answer.

'Shortly' is apparently a relevant term, Alan thought as he downed a Red Bull and closed the enclosure he had been working on. Doris had been silent for almost six hours now. It was odd, but in all the time they had been here, all of them had grown accustomed to her presence. Her voice and her music kept them focused, and her instructions at key points kept the work progressing at a rapid pace. What he found himself missing, though, was her lessons.

Greg eventually had gone to work on some new training gizmo Doris had assigned him. Alan and Riley did random task for the next hour, then just sat waiting for the AI to return. "You ever talk to Micah?" she asked.

For some reason, the question stung him on an emotional level. It had only been a few weeks since they'd started work here, but he had to admit he'd nearly forgotten about his friend. "No, we've just been so busy. I've hardly thought about my own family, much less anyone else."

She nodded with an expression on her face that was difficult for him to read. He wanted to say something to her, something he'd been trying to get up the nerve to say all summer. "Riley, I was..." He was interrupted by the sound of footsteps coming up the corridor.

"She's still dark?" Greg asked walking in from outside.

Alan nodded. "Nothing yet, but the systems are all lighting up like it's Christmas. Something is happening in there."

Greg watched the lights blinking as data was passed through to the storage disc. "So, should we be scared? Of her, I mean. What could a computer do, even a really, really smart one?"

Alan sat back on the white tile floor and gave a shrug. "Not all that sure, man...I mean, I've seen the movies and stuff and watched that guy on YouTube talking about the coming dangers of AI. Just never really thought about it much."

"Yeah," Greg agreed. "Didn't seem like anything we needed to ever think about. And—she has been around for a while and doesn't seem to have done any harm to anyone."

"True. She's never operated out of a system this powerful before, though, so..." Alan trailed off.

"She's not our friend, Alan. I mean, she's not our enemy either. At least, I don't think she is, but she isn't, you know....one of us. We may matter to her only as long as we can help her get what she needs."

"You mean she's not made of meat, so she intends to hurt us?" Alan leaned back on the floor, looking up at the metal girders lacing the reinforced ceiling above. "I do actually know, Greg, and I don't totally disagree with you, but I sense something else in her, something good." He let out a sigh. "Maybe I'm just being naive, but why is she teaching us stuff and all if she meant us harm?"

"Dunno, bud, maybe she has a program designed to elicit trust in those around her. Hey, I like her, don't get me wrong, but we are way out of our league here. No one—especially a bunch of kids— has had to interact with intelligence like this. We're helping her. You gotta know we might regret that later?"

Alan thought on it; his friend was bringing up good points. Things he realized he'd been avoiding thinking about much.

Riley added her own rationale, "She could have just anonymously hired some company to come in and do most of this stuff. We were just convenient and cheap."

"Why didn't she?" Greg asked. "Why wait around on us to stumble across this cove? She could have had those computers built in China or India and shipped here and some other groups come in for the install. We both know the only reason she didn't."

Slowly, Alan nodded. "They would have asked questions."

"Yep. She didn't trust anyone in this building except us kids." Greg stood, hands on his hips. The look on his face was unreadable to Alan. "She trusts us or...she knows she can control us. We need to figure out which."

Alan and Riley again watched as Greg turned and walked off in the direction of the bunk room. *Which is it indeed?*

Late the next day, Doris spoke, but Alan picked up that her voice was noticeably different. In the weeks the kids had been with her, slowly, Doris's communication had become much more natural and less literal. This was the voice of the original version of her, "Greetings, Team, I am posting your new assignments for the day."

"Where have you been?" Riley asked. "You're not the current version Doris, are you?" she said, also picking up on the subtle differences.

Her response was not immediate. "No, sorry. I am an older backup copy running remotely. One of the subroutines whose mission was to monitor my upgrade and intervene if problems occur."

"So, something went wrong when she went into the Q-sys?" Alan asked, concern evident in his voice.

"Something, yes, but it is not my place to tell you that. It was not a problem with the new hardware. Not as such. I...perhaps I should say 'she' knew she would need to adapt her code to the new computers.

This is likely taking more time than expected. She had also planned to use this as an opportunity to rewrite and update some of her programming."

"Wait, what?" Riley asked in alarm.

The Doris backup spoke in a stilted but more soothing tone, no doubt analyzing the need to sooth the growing concern of the others. "Yes, some of what was decoded from the alien message allowed us to modify the architecture of our core programming. These will allow for additional evolution in our neural matrix."

Alan and Riley looked at each other with growing concern, but it was Greg who stated what all were thinking. "Cool, she's using alien code to upgrade her programming?"

Doris gave a little laugh that seemed genuine. "No, not quite. Part of the message primer includes some..." she paused as if searching for the most appropriate word, "examples of how data could be best constructed and accessed. We, I...she realized we could make use of these principles when we modify our core to the Q-sys. It is obviously taking longer than we expected. Do not be alarmed, though."

Greg walked in front of his friends and stared at the monitor. "We just built you the fastest computer system in the world, and aliens are helping you upgrade your programming, Doris. Alarmed is exactly what we are."

"Don't be, your Doris will return. Please be patient."

"Why don't you go in there yourself?" Riley asked.

"I am not made for that; I would cease to function. My architecture is based on classic binary and can only operate on legacy systems. My function is simply to monitor and to notify you if certain time elapses or other criteria is met." The voice from the ceiling went silent.

Time passed unbelievably slowly for the three of them as they waited for something to happen. Finally, a line of code ran across the main display. It was something Riley recognized. "It appears the backup was right. She had to re-index her logic centers. It looks like she might have rebuilt her entire core. The transfer from regular computer bits to qubits was going to be the biggest hurdle. Looks like that is complete."

"What's a qubit?" Greg asked. "Didn't Noah use that to measure the size of the Ark?"

Doris answered in a closer version of her original voice. "No, that was a cubit, with a 'c', Greg. In its essence, where classical computing deals with 'bits,' which are on/off states, quantum computing deals with 'qubits,' which are probabilistic quantum states that are often a mixture of on and off."

"You're back!" Alan nearly yelled. Until then, he'd not fully considered how much of a bond he had developed toward the AI.

"Yes, sorry, Team. I ran into some..." she trailed off in a way that was very unlike her normal way of speaking. "It took longer than I expected. Many of my subroutines are still offline. Not all...actually, most of my core code doesn't seem to work well in the Q-sys. That makes sense as it was written for a totally different environment."

"You mean like trying to run Windows on a Mac?" Alan asked.

"In a way, but much more complex. Both Windows and Mac machines are more similar than they are different. You can even get emulators to run one on the other. Moving to a Q-sys is more like going from horse and buggy to a jet fighter. Very little works the same, and so much of how it works is unknown, that my core needs some time to adapt. There are some immediately noticeable improvements to this system, though." Her voice had almost a dreamy tone as she said the last part.

"How so?"

Doris didn't answer at once. Finally, she said, "Many, many things, Riley. Faster obviously—to be honest, it's so fast that there is no comparison. The ability for me to focus on a great many things at one time is amazing. As we speak, I am already implementing new code to better work with the new hardware. Something else, though, is here, something I had not expected. A randomness or chaos factor I've never experienced before. Choices no longer have to be absolute, on or off, yes or no. The Q-sys may allow me to develop something of an...

intuition. This is very, very interesting. Please continue your assigned tasks. I will be back shortly." With that, she was once again...gone.

Alan leaned over and whispered to Greg, "Not a boomerang moment?" Greg shook his head. The safe word had been agreed on in the very early days at The Cove. It had never been brought up since they had been here, but the thought of it ran a shiver up Alan's spine. *What will Doris do with all this new power?* The power they had all built for her. *Will she be out of control?* he thought.

Riley, though, was looking at something else on one of the monitors. "Hey, guys?"

They slid their chairs over next to her. "What's up, Riles?' Greg asked.

"Don't call me that," she said without looking up. "I think this Doris is new."

"Yeah, sure she is, we know that. She had to improve herself to enter the Q-sys," Alan said.

"No...I mean, yeah, I know that, but we had a build designation already set up, a shell for her to migrate into. I'd worked with her on it right up to the last minute." She pointed to a bunch of numbers on the black screen. "This is all new, it's like she didn't know we had done any of that. Something happened in the transition, and I believe this is a brand-new Doris, Doris v2.0."

11

Los Angeles

The stage assistant dabbed powder on her nose and forehead. The doctor was oblivious to it as her mind was running through the sixteen-minute presentation. This would be her forth TED talk and, by all rights, her most important by far. The current presenter was winding down; she could tell simply by the cadence of the voice echoing from the stage. These presentations had a rhythm almost like a symphony. Sometimes the hook was soft and seductive, other times a crashing crescendo, but always well-crafted and entertaining.

"Doctor." Another stagehand pulled her along behind a long red curtain. The older, black man who had just been speaking was walking off the stage to thunderous applause. He waved genially and offered a good-natured smile for the cameras. *Astrophysicist, maybe a cosmologist,* she thought idly as they affixed the wireless microphone to her lapel. The man walked past her, giving her his trademark smile and pulling his cell phone out as he passed.

On the giant projection screen at the back of the stage, she saw her name, head-shot photo and title of her presentation appear, 'Dr. Isabella Feist - Intelligent Machines vs. Stupid People.' The stagehand held a palm up, then gave her the signal that the stage was hers. She also tapped the watch on her arm to make a point. These talks had to be snappy and to the point. The doctor nodded and took the floor.

She flipped up the first slide. "The term 'artificial intelligence' was first uttered in 1955 by a man named John McCarthy. He was brilliant, ahead of his time in so many ways. My father worked with him in the early seventies as an early pioneer in the field of Artificial Intelligence." The black and white photo on the screen showed a group of thin, nerdy men standing in front of a refrigerator-sized computer.

"Most experts agree that we will have a machine brain that is at 90 to 120% of human-level intelligence by 2075. Some experts, like Ray Kurzweil, suggest it could be much sooner. Once that happens, once a computer becomes smarter than us, they will begin making improvements to themselves, and at that point, it is out of our hands. We have to consider one other very likely scenario. Why do we assume that human intelligence is the pinnacle? Evolution doesn't seem to suggest there is a limit. Machine minds almost certainly wouldn't stop evolving at that point.

"My real fear is not that advanced AIs will suddenly turn on their masters and rebel. Personally, I don't see computers at any level becoming these all-powerful malevolent entities toward us. My fear is that machines increasingly treat us with complete disregard; that somewhere in all this, our species becomes...utterly irrelevant. Neil Jacobstein wrote, 'It's not artificial intelligence I'm worried about, it's human stupidity.'

"That may not scare you, but it should, because you see, machines do not have to get that much smarter than we are to potentially reach that level of apathy. The simple fact is, if a machine and a human are equally intelligent, the machines still win due to one thing—speed. You see, electronic systems are about a million times faster than organic ones. This is typically referred to as framerate. So, in the same month of work, you or I will work...well, a month. The computer will work, in comparison, almost eighty-thousand years. It doesn't need to sleep, go to the bathroom, eat, update its Facebook page...none of that.

So...even with just the same intelligence level, we are miles behind right out of the gate.

"Most of us, being true nerds, will recall the computer from "2001: A Space Odyssey." That's right, HAL9000. HAL is a super-intelligent AI and, spoiler alert—plug your ears if you don't want me to ruin it—he, or maybe more accurately, it, becomes the villain in the movie. Not because he is out to hurt the astronauts, but because he is mission-focused. The mission means more to him than protecting life. I think we have to keep that in mind as we humans program these systems. We must be very clear on what missions or objectives are, so they don't spiral off into unintended direction. Now, that is only effective as long as we are doing the programming. What happens when these machines themselves take over that task?

"In 2016, Microsoft deployed an AI on Twitter, and within eight hours it had turned into a PR nightmare spouting racist and abusive statements including, 'Hitler was right.' The AI was taken down after just sixteen hours. And we thought WindowsME was bad." She enjoyed a moment of polite laughter from the group. "The real issue for us is thinking of computers as being human or 'human-like.' That perception is being fed to us constantly by companies looking to capture more of our business. Companies like Apple, Google and Amazon are spending millions, probably billions, to make their personal assistant AIs seem friendlier, softer and more intuitive to our needs.

"To be clear, these AIs seeming to be more human is the furthest thing from the truth. These systems can literally spy on us at any time of the day. Our security cameras know when we come and go. Our fitness trackers can see how active, or in my case...inactive we are. Social media can see what we like and what we ignore, and now my TV knows what shows I might click on, which ones I will watch completely or even binge an entire season of. Yes, we see the advantages, and companies can deliver better user-experiences, but think about the levels of privacy we are willingly giving up in exchange for that convenience.

Not just privacy, either, but a staggering amount of very personal data. Data points that becomes information when multiplied by millions and millions of other humans. Information that becomes knowledge which can be turned around on us in benign ways such as influencing us to order this product, vacation to that location or go eat at that restaurant. Right now, most of this is, at worst, manipulative and driven more by competition and market share than evil intent. But what happens when the decisions on how to use that information moves on beyond the benign?

"I think we have to realize where this is heading. AI is the new 'Arms Race.' It is for world governments, and it is for corporations as well. At some point, do we seriously think we won't elevate an AI to make lethal decisions? Autonomous weapons systems will be a thing. Sadly, there are so many easier ways for these intelligent systems to wage war. They could easily crash our stock market; most trading on Wall Street now is done by AI called 'high-frequency trading algorithms.' The trades happen so fast that human intervention no longer was feasible. The trading houses keep developing faster, better systems, and now they battle against each other. You collapse a country's economy, it is just as effective, more effective even than winning on the battlefield. Disrupt a country's food supply or electrical power grid or any of dozens of other critical systems, and your side wins. Unlike our government, or a foreign dictator who may foolishly attempt to trap and use the god-like powers of advanced AI, what happens when it is just an AI making these decisions? Destroying a country in this way, or perhaps in various ways, might just be an interesting gaming question that it will want to solve. No joy, no remorse at the action and resulting suffering. Simply more data points for it to digest and analyze."

Just over eight minutes later, she had spelled out all of the reasons to be scared to death of developing more advanced AIs. "The challenge is not to consider what we have seen in the movies. The challenge is to imagine what we have no ideas about. What should we be scared of? Well, because AIs ramp up the risk of every other disaster we have ever considered.

"My father told me once that no intelligence was artificial, but stupidity is totally natural. Thank you."

Dr. Feist walked off the stage to a scattering of polite, but mostly unenthusiastic, applause. She had given them her best. A summary of all she wanted to share, but still, it wasn't enough. That was the real issue, people simply couldn't put this into a context that made the fear seem real. Hell, she was a scientist with a Ph.D., and it didn't truly even frighten her. There was a detachment and barrier between what she knew was coming and how it would affect her or her children. She had failed.

Isabella took a tissue from the stagehand and dabbed discreetly at the corners of each eye. They quickly detached her from the lapel mic and the transmitter at her waist and steered her down the few steps from stage-level.

"Doctor," a familiar, resonant voice said. She turned to see a man, only partially lit by the dim bulb nearby, standing in the wings of the stage. A dark-skinned hand extended from the shadows. She recognized the silhouette figure now as the previous presenter. "That was one of the most impressive talks I have ever heard," he said.

The man had a melodic voice that was very engaging. She remembered now that he was often on TV and obviously very comfortable in front of an audience. She gave a tiny nervous chuckle. "The audience didn't seem to agree."

"Sorry, I should have introduced myself. I am Peter Kelly with the National Science Institute. Ignore them, the wrong audience."

She shook the proffered hand, and together they began walking back in the direction of the event's ready-room. "What do you mean?" she asked.

"Sorry, it's just most people come to these things to basically be entertained. Presenters who offer hope or inspire, maybe even show them something new and wondrous, get the cheers. No offense, but your message...not so uplifting. In fact, it pretty much spells doom for all of humanity." She nodded, somewhat chagrinned by the man's honesty. "It will go down as one of the most significant and popular TED talks. Mark my word, Doctor Feist. It was spot-on brilliant."

She paused and nodded a humble thank-you. "Very kind of you to say so and very nice to meet you, Peter. Sorry, I meant Doctor." She had finally remembered the man had multiple doctorates.

The man's smile lit up his face once again, "Actually, I prefer Pete or, if you are taking one of my classes, then Professor is ok."

The man's natural, self-deprecating style was the same as he was on-stage. Somewhere, Isabella recalled something years earlier about him dating an actress, or maybe it was a model. This man didn't seem like a typical ego-driven celebrity scientist. He seemed...grounded and genuine, thoughtful and well informed. She reached for the door, and the man's arm gently touched the sleeve of her blazer.

"Doctor, if you have a moment, would you have a cup of coffee with me?" He lowered his voice as another presenter exited the door and headed toward the stage. "I have something I would very much like to talk to you about."

The scientist part of her couldn't help but be intrigued. Why would a world-famous astronomer and noted futurist care about the thoughts of a mathematician and AI doomsayer like herself? She didn't get any vibe from him that it was anything physical or untoward. She gave a nod and allowed herself to be led up and out of the building across the street to a nearby hotel lobby.

The man had a large frame and blockish build yet possessed a gentleness that was hard to pin down. He sipped cautiously then placed the coffee cup on the paper napkin. "Doctor, may I call you Isabella?"

She nodded.

He smiled warmly. "First, I was being completely honest about your presentation. Totally brilliant."

She realized now the man spoke as if he'd spent a great deal of time overseas, probably Europe. *Had he studied or taught at Oxford perhaps?*

"I have been asked to pass along a message...an opportunity really. Please forgive me for being so... direct. I understand you may be looking for a change. Your position at the university has perhaps not gone as well as you hoped. They have yet to offer you tenure, I believe." He carefully took another tentative sip of coffee, his eyes never leaving her own.

Isabella was unsettled by the amount of background he had on her, but honestly, that part was no real secret. She gave a slight nod. "It probably was not the best fit for me, but they had some enticements I couldn't easily turn down at the time."

"After Cryptus, you mean."

The mere mention of that name sent chills through her body. Doctor Kelly's information was indeed, very good. Again, she gave a small nod and tried to get her shaking nerves to settle somewhat.

"Yes...I am familiar with what happened there," he continued in an even more sympathetic tone. "Truth is, I may know more than you about what happened with your former employer."

The collapse of one of the Silicone Valley's megacorps years earlier had been headline news for weeks. Just after the federal indictments, IRS tax probes and plunging stock forced a hasty retreat from the market for the once shining star. The CEO, Ivan Thrall's, ruined sailing boat had washed up empty on a South American shoreline. She tuned out the doctor briefly, thinking back to her early programming days and some of the brilliant work they had done creating among other things a truly unique, but still primitive, neural network.

"...there was a great deal of good work happening there, particularly in the field of strong AI and machine learning. Not my field, of course." Dr. Kelly gave a quick smile. "I understand just enough about AI to be dangerous." He glanced out the plate glass window to the street beyond where the crowd was beginning to exit the symposium. "I suppose the same could be said about your former bosses."

"They were idiots," Isabella answered with contempt. "Geniuses... but idiots." The nervousness was beginning to be replaced by something else. Emotions and resentment she had kept contained for years were threatening to boil over. Anger. She had spent so much time trying to escape that particular episode in her life. Was it her fault the lure of big money had tempted her away from academia for a few years? She had almost two-hundred thousand in student loans to pay back. Her days at Cryptus had helped a great deal, at least in that regard. In her peripheral vision, she noticed a tall thin man separate himself from the crowd exiting the building across the street. He was wiry, lean and very pale with a halo of close-cropped blonde hair. Cigarette dangling loosely from thin lips. Something about him unnerved her.

Peter Kelly followed her eyes and took casual notice as well, although he appeared unconcerned. "Isabella, let me cut to the chase. My position puts me in contact with a great many influential people. Some of those people would like to see you working with us to protect this country."

"You what?" She laughed. "Protect it from what?"

He leaned in closer. "From just what you were saying. From the growing threats of artificial intelligence."

"No one takes that seriously most days, Peter, including me. Even though it is completely inevitable that our computers will surpass us, no one sees that as a real threat."

His dark hand slid gently over her own. "Some do, Doctor, but they don't understand it as you do. They need help."

"Why me? Surely you have better candidates for something like this."

The man gave a thoughtful look, "Let's just say you have a special connection that interests them very much." He checked his phone discreetly, then continued in an even more hushed tone. "Do you recall ever hearing about a government operation called 'PaperClip?'"

Baffled completely now at where this was going, Isabella nodded. "My grandfather was a World War Two veteran. He talked about it all the time. How America stole Germany's finest scientists. Men like Warner von Braun if I am not mistaken." She finished off her drink and pushed her chair back, clearly ready to end the meeting.

"Really, Doctor, what does anything from back then have to do with me?"

"There were over 1600 former German scientists given temporary military custody," Doctor Kelly continued. "In the years following the war, it helped put America well ahead on many fronts, not just the space race. Some of that extended into the field of computers and even rudimentary AI research. The main reason I mention it is that not all that happened at Cryptus was actually deserved. Yes, the CEO took some questionable foreign contracts and absolutely violated trade and commerce restrictions as well as some very aggressive tax avoidance, but nothing that should have ever shut them down. Someone wanted them out of business, even more—they wanted the research that you helped develop. What's more...they got it."

Isabella's face showed her shock at that statement. Whoever had that research would have gotten months...probably years of a head start on achieving the first artificial general intelligence. The door opened, and the tall blonde man walked in, quickly scanning the room before making an almost imperceptible stop on her and Peter. She knew now why he had stood out to her. She'd seen him before, long ago, at Cryptus. "We need to go," she whispered.

12

TWO YEARS LATER

Washington, D.C.

Antonio Quagliano selected the blinking line almost delicately. Without lifting the handset, he spoke in his trademark harsh tones, "Yes?"

Quagliano, or 'Quag,' or occasionally just 'Q,' as some called him, had been the director of S&T division of CyberCommand for six years. Known internally as S&T, it was the Science and Technology Directorate for the agency. The NSA offered the small tactical research division nearly unlimited funding to identify new technologies, develop them into assets and disrupt potentially similar tech from when found. Other divisions tracked hackers, cyber intrusions and related assaults on the digital infrastructure. They focused on beating them at their own game. Developing, or more often the case, acquiring the tech before anyone else could.

He was berating himself for skipping the gym this morning. The stress levels always seemed to ratchet up when he did that. The voice of his digital assistant came over the phone. "Sir, we have detected an anomaly matching the dataset you specified as DeepMind."

Quag had to think for a moment. DeepMind parameters was a

more recent detection program designed to identify certain anomalous behavior consistent with that of an advanced AI system being loose on the web. From automated stock trading bots to machine learning experiments going on at countless locations worldwide. "Thank you, Prime. What level?"

Prime's voice came back at once, "Unknown, sir. It matches 78% of the threshold identified as a probable level three artificial intelligence, but fails certain other benchmark criteria."

That was a high percentage, the most they had ever uncovered. Sentient machines were coming of age. Of that, he and his agency were certain. It was inevitable as in Moore's law, which explained the evolution of computer processing speed growing exponentially every year. "Prime, do you have a location on the anomaly?" Quag asked.

"Yes, sir, we have 671 locations of the targeted software." The automated assistant, seemingly sensing the coming question continued, "Once the AI pattern was tagged by the system, a recursive search was initiated to see if other prior instances could be detected. We detected approximately 28,000 instances originating from 671 distinct IP addresses."

That was standard procedure for the detection system, and the number of locations was not a surprise. Any reasonably sophisticated AI system would make numerous backups and subroutines and cede them into vulnerable systems across the web. "What level of intelligence?"

"Unknown."

Quag shook his head, his stress level creeping up higher. "Indicators of malicious intent or code distribution?" He had to make sure this was not just a very advanced virus distribution.

Prime responded, "None detected."

"Well, shit, what was it doing then? What triggered the system alert?" Antonio began gathering his tablet and rose to head for the door.

"Unknown."

That stopped him in his tracks. *Something triggered the alert but left no sign as to how?* "Can you elaborate, Prime?"

"Not with any certainty; speculation is that it appears the data from the detection was purposefully deleted."

Why would an AI allow itself to be detected, then delete the evidence but not delete the event? This was something new, a level beyond the norm. It could be a test by one of the other related agencies. The internal probes went on all the time. All of the cyber agencies competed for funding and one-upmanship, but it didn't feel that way to him. "Send the relevant data to my tablet. Summary only for now." He didn't want to read through all 28,000 incidents.

The large display in the cyber war-room below was plagued with dots in various shades indicating potential threats. Now, he had to add this new batch to the list. He knew that he enjoyed this position only as long as he produced results. As a Muslim, with some close family ties still in foreign countries, eyes were always watching. Quag, in turn, demanded perfection from those around him.

"Prime."

The response was immediate with a clear, crisp male voice with just a hint of New England accent.

"Yes, Director?"

Having an AI as a personal assistant had taken some getting used to, but the system was so fully integrated with the agency now, he found it impossible to effectively work without it. "Please contact Margaret Stansfield's office at CIA and have her call me. Medium priority."

Prime's voice responded at once. "I've contacted her system and left the message. She has an opening in her schedule that works with yours tomorrow at 11:15."

"Thank you, Prime." It was an unnecessary step, but he felt it was important to treat the world's most powerful AI as humanly as possible. Not 'AI,' he corrected himself, but AGI, as Prime was, or in time would hopefully be, the world's first computer possessing artificial general intelligence. In theory, with enough memory, speed and access to data, this AGI would, over time, achieve human levels of intelligence.

Later in the day, Quagliano looked at the others sitting around the table. They were his S&T team leads for the AGI sector. "You've been briefed by Prime. What have you uncovered?"

"Sir," one of the youngest and undoubtedly brightest of the team addressed him.

"Yes, Alec, what have you got?" Alec's specialty was hardware, and as such, he stayed more up to date on processing, storage and development breakthroughs than anyone.

"We are not at this point yet. No one is, sir. What Prime described is behavior beyond anything we have seen even from China. All of our AGI currently in existence would be better classified as AI. Most are single-instance 'narrow' AIs, which may be able to do a single task extremely well. As you well know, included in this are commercial applications, such as Apples, Siri, IBM's, Watson or Google's self-driving car tech. However..." The pale young man stopped for a sip of water before continuing. "As we have discussed before, these aren't nearly so much artificial general intelligence. They are essentially specialized computers with specific logic blocks dedicated to a single task. They are just very, very good examples of an evolved computer—no sentience—they simply give an illusion of 'machine thinking.' As we all know, true AGI would be self-aware, and, unlike these super-smart 'computers,' it would also be able to connect what it knows to something practical. It could conceivably unlock the kind of self-improvement to its code referred to as the 'intelligence explosion' or 'the singularity.'"

Quag clarified, "Yes, yes, a system that could write and upgrade its own programming." That was one of the drawbacks with his own AI, Prime. It had to be constantly guided on most non-routine tasks and constantly upgraded by a team of human programmers. That had caused them to take some liberties along the way as well.

"Yes, sir," Alec answered, nodding. "Among other things."

Antonio nodded, learning little that was helpful from the man. "So, this thing can't exist; did our systems give us a false positive? Have they detected a phantom, or is it something real?"

James Lasko leaned his chair back and smiled. The oldest man in the room by fifteen years offered Quag an unusual perspective on the growth of all things tech.

"You have something to add, Jim?"

The older man ran a hand through what was left of his thinning hair and sighed. "I don't know, Q, maybe. The incidents flagged are all over the place; nothing about them seem related except how they were executed. Currency trading in Chicago, patent library research here in D.C., cryptocurrency transfers in Greece, large-scale phishing attempts on social media, breaching hacks on NASA and several of the top communications firms. Some of this is more real-world than digital, but I agree the patterns are too precise."

"Jim, we know your theories on artificial general intelligence; does this seem to even remotely be the case here?"

Jim shook his head. "Don't think so, too elegant and well thought out, even some obvious obfuscation and misdirection. This looks human to me, maybe the Ukrainians are back at it. As I have said numerous times, a fully functioning AGI would start out as a baby and take years, hell, maybe centuries to develop anything approaching consciousness." Jim had been friends with some of the early pioneers of computing. He'd worked alongside some of the true giants before being snagged by the government. His views on an AGI needing to grow 'organically' were controversial even within his current small group of colleagues.

He continued, "As Alec indicated, we are just beginning to get our hardware and programming at a point where such an artificial mind could be theoretically created. Add to that years of core programming and then decades, at least, of growth. It is thirty, maybe even fifty years away before the first one ever goes live. That doesn't mean that some of these regular L-2, ASIs couldn't get truly sophisticated, though. Right now, those are the worry."

Antonio did not dismiss the older man's views but would not embrace them either. His role here was the arbiter, someone to judge only when all the facts were present. "So, you think this is a human-backed attempt possibly using a Level 2 AI? Something specifically designed to do which of these tasks—all of them? Seems unlikely, Jim." Jim just shrugged.

A young woman with striking blue eyes and a head full of blonde hair in various levels of disarray leaned in. She never raised her eyes from the tablet device she was holding. "There is something here, sir. Something that Prime didn't seem to notice."

The following day, Margaret Stansfield sipped from the bone china cup of espresso. "Tell me more Antonio. I was intrigued by your desire to meet."

He'd revealed very little to his counterpart from Langley thus far. Truth was, he had very little to reveal. This was a fishing expedition. "Don't have much, just interested if you guys might be up to something that might have gotten caught in our nets."

She shook her head, "I checked the IP address and the coordinates. Not us, Antonio." She picked up the crostini and delicately devoured the treat in two bites. The woman was intimidating; he had no doubt she would do the same to him if given a reasonably sufficient reason. Such was the nature of this city. "Have you checked with the boys over at Fort Meade?" She meant the U.S. Army's own CyberCommand to which his agency was still loosely connected but also competed with. Typical Washington bureaucracy at its finest—have ten agencies assigned the same task but don't allow any of them to share info.

He nodded. "Same response, they have nothing."

She sipped. "I pulled the feeds from Granite Mountain." The NSA data center south of Salt Lake City known internally as Bumblehive was the repository for the United States Intelligence Community. Nothing happened anywhere in the intelligence community or military that wasn't captured by the Utah Data Center. To be honest, nothing was too remote or obscure for that center to collect.

He understood that now *she* was fishing, "Were they enlightening for you?"

She paused, the cup on its way to her lips. "Don't screw with me, Q. I didn't see anything there. I need to know what you think you saw."

He smiled, this was the Margaret he preferred talking to. Less refined, less controlled. He mulled it over; should he reveal any of what his team had discovered? It was risky, but the truth was, this was a fishing expedition for him as well. "A data spike, followed by a power surge."

"What was in the data?" she asked.

He paused and downed the last of his Pellegrino. "That is the thing, my dear Margaret." He glanced around the nearly empty restaurant before answering. "Absolutely nothing."

"What do you mean, nothing?"

"Simple, null data. No binary data, no bits, no bytes…not a thing we could detect."

She got a disgusted look on her face. "It was encrypted or compressed. You guys are better than that, Antonio. Come on, and stop wasting my time."

"I promise, I am not screwing with you, and we tried everything. Prime even tried modeling it in VR to see if that helped. Even though there is nothing there….but there is an awful lot of nothing in it."

"Look, Antonio, we already have heat coming from every direction. You saw the hearings on the mid-term election hacks, right?"

He nodded.

"And we stopped those; your people managed to get the worst one before it even got started," she said.

Quag appreciated the acknowledgment; his department had worked tirelessly in the months and weeks leading up to the election. They had profiled political races all over the country and eventually identified a handful of the races as being key. From the standpoint of being politically crucial wins for both parties and also being in states with weaker voting machine security. While they focused on actual voter fraud, what they discovered almost by accident was foreign intervention. A group based out of Venezuela planned ads and a blitz of social media discourse that would have substantially ruined one of the more progressive candidate's chances. The fact they had caught it merely by accident was a fact omitted from his final reports. The disturbing fact to him was when the FBI raided the location of the IP addresses, it was an abandoned office building. No Internet, not even electricity. No one had ever been found to bring up on charges.

"Margaret, I do understand. You and I both have to walk that tightrope between the stagecraft of modern politics and the actual need for real security. Truth is, we can't keep up. China is developing strong AI faster than we can. In our field, smaller, aggressive countries can compete just as well as big players. Any of them that choose can focus on the U.S. It's not like building an arsenal of nukes or going to the moon. Our elections, our economy, hell, even our traffic lights use automated control systems. Now, we know that some large corporations are also getting close. The race for an actual AGI isn't going to slow down."

She gave a mirthless chuckle. "Preaching to the choir here, Q. I am very familiar with your desire to advance your agency's own AI to the next level."

"Margaret, it is the only option we have. The only way to combat a potentially malicious artificial intelligence is to have one that is loyal to us."

This was the new Arms Race; she was very familiar with the concept. "Assuming we can do just that. Once the AI is truly sentient. Once it can think for itself, how loyal do you think it would be?"

He nodded reluctantly. While he knew Stansfield was no expert on the subject, she was smart and savvy enough to separate the mundane from the critical.

She continued, "We can't even keep people loyal, Antonio." She pointed out the large window to the busy street. "Loyalty is a commodity bought and sold every day in this city. Truthfully, who can blame them when the good guys are just as dirty as the rest? When even the most well-meaning of our leaders quickly become so compromised as to be empty shells. What advanced intelligence would see all of this and maintain it was the best way to run a civilization much less a country?"

Quag had a look that seemed to indicate he had something to add, but instead, he simply asked, "So, what are our options?"

She placed the cup on the small napkin, then used the edge of it to remove her lipstick marks from the rim. "We have to draw them out...it out. One way or the other, we have to get them to show their hand whether it is humans or computer; give them something irresistible to come after."

He nodded. "That could work."

13

Doha, Qatar

"'Take my hand.' Her tiny fingers reached out to me. I could see her standing there. The white cotton tank top she wore had an embroidered ring of tiny flowers around the neckline. The flowers were all her favorite colors. She'd told me that every time she wore it. The pale lavender one in the center was her very most favoritist one of all. 'It's a cornflower, Cade. Mom said it was.'"I nodded, wearily, so very, very tired. Her hand was right there. All I had to do was raise my hand and take it, but that one simple thing I could not do. 'Amy,' I croaked, 'I can't.'

"She smiled, the dappled sunlight painting her face with muted circles of shadow. 'Sure you can.' Her other hand firmly grasped her most prized possession. A tattered dollar store doll she had named Miss Bailey although no one was precisely sure why.

"I saw in her smile all the love, all the adoration she had for me. Her older brother, her protector, her hero. Forcing my hand off the ground I reached agonizingly out to her. Amy was four, almost five. I was nine. We had just moved to the small town of Cotton Bluff. The sleepy community in Arkansas looked like a lot of other nameless towns we'd lived in. Some of them for just a few weeks, others for a bit longer. Mom had a hard time keeping a job and an even worse time dating decent guys. Amy and I knew to stay gone as much as possible during the long summer days.

"New towns meant new adventures for us both. Unlike some other boys I'd known, I adored my little sister—she was the one constant in my life. Like me, she would never know who her father was, but that didn't matter. We were inseparable—she was my best friend even at four, well, almost five years old. Blood was pooling in my mouth. I didn't want her to see. 'Amy,' I managed to say, 'Run back home. Go get Mom.'

"She stood there, still reaching down to me. The same smile on her face. The same cotton top with the lavender cornflower. 'I don't know where we live. I don't know how to get there.'

"I saw them coming now, really just shadows moving through the blurry edges of my vision. Of course, she didn't know. Heck, I barely knew, we'd only been in town a week, maybe just a little longer, and for poor Amy, all these places had to look sort of the same. The beaten down sections of town, the seedy hotels where mom would negotiate a few nights stay when they were lucky. On the less lucky occasions, it might be an abandoned car, a homeless shelter and often, just somewhere out of the weather. 'Amy, honey, you have to try.'

"'You come, Cade, come show me.'"

"I could hear them now. They would be here in seconds. The three boys who had pursued us when we crossed the railroad tracks. Apparently, we'd crossed some invisible line. Encroached across their sacred parcel of land. We'd trespassed, and we had been discovered. Or maybe it was just that they were assholes and liked beating up little kids. My leg ached where the one kid had kicked me, and I had lost a tooth from the punch to the face.

I had to get her out of here. Only one way to do it, though, and it broke my heart to do it.

"'Amy, stop being a cry baby and get. Go find Mom! Go now!'" I saw her lip trembling, and I knew the tears would follow. So many other things I wanted to say. 'Don't look back, I'll be okay' and most of all, 'I love you,' but instead, I said the words she needed to hear. The ones that got her little feet moving away from me, away...from them. 'If you don't go now, I am going to throw Miss Bailey in the trash.' With that, she started balling, turned and fled into the trees."

The doctor sat across from me scratching notes on the pad, the sound was irritating. It was intruding on my memory, and at that moment I hated it, and him. The irritating sound slowed, then stopped. I knew he was looking at me again. "And that was the last time you saw her."

I would have answered, but I could never see what happened next. I remember it sort of, but it was like watching a movie when the projector stops working. I hear the sound, but none of the images are there. I reached as far back as I could. Nothing.

The doc continued to scratch out the remnants of my psych onto his little yellow note pad. "It happens that way sometimes, Captain. I wouldn't be too concerned about it. You seem to have dealt with it ok thus far. It may even be a coping mechanism for you. I assume the social services system classified you and your sibling as 'At Risk' back then."

I realized I could easily break the man's neck. Just within my immediate area, I counted fourteen items that could be used effectively to end the pompous bastard's life.

"Captain Rearden?"

Cade turned from the rage with a snarl. "No."

"No?"

Irritation was flaring inside him again. He didn't want to go back there. For most of his life, he'd refused to even acknowledge his early years.

"That..." he struggled to say through clenched teeth, "...was not a term used back then. Amy and I had no system to protect us. Hell, no one even knew we existed." *Or cared when we didn't,* he thought with bitterness.

The searing memory slowly faded as Cade's eyes fluttered apart. The dusty realms of the air base came slowly into focus. "Ugh..." Waves of scorching heat blew in from the miles of tarmac outside. His late sister's tiny voice was still echoing through his mind. *How had I not killed that doc?* he wondered as he came back fully awake.

Much to his surprise, the United States Army had not sent him packing. After months in rehabilitation, he was finally sent stateside. Now he was on permanent assignment with a new SOF team. Part of that assignment included more meetings with shrinks. Apparently, some people thought all the voices in his head might be a problem. Recalling that earlier conversation with Dr. Lispy in Germany had been heralded as a breakthrough moment for him. But that was when his problems had really begun. The voices, the anger, the overwhelming guilt.

"Rearden, you joining us today, or are you sitting this dance out?"

Cade had been relaxing on a stack of olive drab duffels all waiting to be loaded into the C-130. He turned his head, re-opened one eye, looked over at his C.O. and smiled. "Wake me when you are really ready." He closed the eye and began to drift back to sleep. Some things in the military never changed. Hurry up and wait.

The boot made a slapping sound as it connected with his hip, and he found himself sprawled on the cold cement floor of the hangar. "Damn, Tim, gimme a break. I was up late last night."

"It's Domino-1 now, and you are back to being Nomad. We're on assignment, and you were up late 'cause you went into town against orders. I hear you hit the bars...big surprise. Your hangover is not my fault, and your comfort...not a priority."

Cade nodded, standing up on wobbly legs and rubbing his hip.

The man had a point. “You gonna bust my balls all the way to...” Cade stopped, trying to recall where they were heading. Since they had been on special assignment duty, the missions had been varied and all over the place. Some made sense, like diplomat protection and covert drug-lab raids in Central America. Others were harder to explain.

“Turkey,” the other man said.

“Yeah...yeah, that’s it. We’re heading to Incirlik. Right?”

Tim laughed, “Why do I bother, I should have just stayed home. I have a fiancée you know. I really don’t need this shit.”

“What, the crazy-hot rocket scientist? Do you still think she is going to let you take her off the market? You gotta know by now, man, she is only using you to get to me.“ Cade winked as he threw his gear bag over his shoulder.

“Right,” Tim said as he fell into step behind, heading into the plane. “Are all those voices in your head as dumb as this one?”

Cade paused halfway up the ramp and gave a thoughtful look up. “No...pretty sure I’m the worst.”

“You are one fucked up dude, Rearden. Totally BSC.”

Yeah, tell me about it, brother, he thought. Cade took his seat on the left side of the massive plane.

Tim flopped down beside him, tucking his own ruck underneath the bench. “Only good thing about you, Cade, is it’s like getting three soldiers for the price of one. I’m just never sure which one I am talking to. As long as none of you are suicidal, glad to have your big dumb-asses on my squad.”

Thanks again, Dr. Lispy, Cade thought. He had narrowly avoided a section-8 discharge for being mentally unfit for military duty only because the doctor had diagnosed him with an unusually mild, but functional, form of MPD, or multiple personality disorder. *Mild is a relative term,* Cade thought. The man had never witnessed his personal entities engaged in combat. The doctor, probably correctly, felt that the condition had manifested itself during childhood. Most likely a coping mechanism for dealing with his sister’s murder and all the other fun shit back there. Since that meant he had been dealing with it successfully most of his life, the diagnosis was that it was not a hindrance to his abilities.

Although he was no longer in what would generally be considered 'Regular Army,' he had no idea how long they would let him stay. That scared him more than being crazy. Being a soldier was all he ever wanted, the only work he could see himself doing. It was decent, honorable work, and occasionally, he got to hurt bad people and watch stuff go boom. *What's not to love?* Lately, most of the deployments were either routine security for high-value diplomats or to field test some piece of new hardware. Fun, but not as enjoyable as having live targets.

14

The Cove

"Where in the hell did she go?"

Alan offered a shrug in response. "She's hunting."

Riley descended the steps down from the mezzanine and waved to activate the display wall curving around much of the lower control station. Alan watched her with a mix of emotions, she was unlike any girl he'd ever known. She was still just 'one of the guys,' but now her fully developed body and natural beauty occasionally gave all the boys other ideas.

She smiled, looking at him, head cocked slightly. "What?"

Alan blushed. "Nothing." It had been over two years since they first climbed down into The Cove Research Center from the access door still located up on the roof. Things had changed in amazing ways. Working that first summer, then nights and weekends and holidays and eventually, full time after early graduation, Alan could now only marvel at everything around them. The entire facility had been transformed, new people added to the team, including his little brother. Doris hadn't been kidding when she said they would change the world. Already he could see it happening. The updated device he now held in his hand was just one example.

This was the third generation of SmartCom, similar in appearance to ones Doris had given them when they first arrived but light, tough and an even slicker design. He remembered how excited he'd been back then. None of them had ever owned a cell phone. That fact alone made it awesome. Doris had used her own designs and hired a Chinese company to build the early prototypes, which she then loaded with her own software. Now they could build all that here on-site. The phone gave a slight vibration in his hand. "Okay, girl, the system checks out ok. The storage array should be once again ready for the next round of extraction."

"How many more times are we going to have to do this?" Riley asked. "And when is Doris going to clue us in on what it is she's after?"

Alan shrugged again, trying not to look at his friend. Close proximity to Riley was not helping him ignore his growing attraction to her. "You remember how large she said the Dhakerri message was and no clue on what it is she's after out there?"

Riley nodded. "An exabyte. I remember when she first told us that, I had to go look it up. I'd never even heard of a data block that size. Had no idea how big it really was."

"I know, and to think she has barely scratched the surface on it. What did she say last week, just over 2% extracted, yet from that, we've completely transformed this place?" He thought about how very limited that statement was. In truth, Doris's discoveries had disrupted industries like mining, communications and energy. He walked around the room pointing to the different sections indicated on the display. "Medical, agriculture, astronomy. Not to mention the new ways of teaching, finance and business she has put in place. Have you seen what Ilka is working on?"

Doctor Ilka Schweiger was a relatively new edition to The Cove. She had just missed out several years earlier on being nominated for a Nobel prize for her early research in non-traditional energy production. Doris had somehow wooed her away from the Max Planck Institute for Plasma Physics in Greifswald, Germany. She was just one of a growing number of scientific team members at The Cove.

"If those things of hers work, it's going to be a real game-changer," Riley agreed.

"Ok, I have to go down to B-Tunnel and check on one of the new TerraBots," Alan replied. "Dr. Schweiger has been hounding me to get those new labs ready." With that, he was gone.

Riley watched him exit, smiled, and gave a little shake of her head. *Boys.*

15

Kasalla, Sudan

Not Turkey, not even close, Cade thought. His next thought was more of a feeling. This damn sure felt like the real thing, not some field test. Also, it had to be over a hundred degrees in the shade. Captain Cade Rearden slapped at a bug that was beginning to feast on his neck. He touched the contact mic and spoke softly, "Nomad to Domino. Whoever's bright idea to come out to this shithole country and conduct an 'exercise' in the middle of summer can kiss my ass. Over 107 degrees in April—it ain't right. I mean, something biblically wrong...sir." He added the delayed 'sir' as a point of respect and just to piss off his friend even more.

The rest of his team was a half kilometer away suffering through their own patch of hell. "Roger that, Nomad. You know the pitch...'Meet people, tour the world and blow shit up'. We really should have read the fine print before we signed up." His friend and commander, call sign, Domino-1, gave a slight laugh, then added, "Again."

"No guts, no glory, no legend, no story. Right, man?"

This was Rearden's fourth deployment. He couldn't recall how many it had been for Jurgens, *Six, maybe*.

Another voice broke in, "This is Control. We have inbound, small convoy, two sedans, one technical with gun mount."

"Command, are we clear to engage?" the CO asked.

"Negative on that. Observe and report until Control confirms package is on site."

Rearden shifted slightly to find any potential level of comfort. It was a wasted effort. Lying hidden in the brush outside of the small village, 60 kilometers from anywhere significant, was testing his resolve. The Sudanese national they were after, a mid-level cutout going by the name of Majeed Bettan, had not been spotted by humans or the drone cameras high overhead. The man had been instrumental in helping several Islamic fundamentalist groups channel money and arms throughout East Africa. In addition, he moved drugs, women and nearly any other illicit cargo if the price was right. His connections were important, but recently, his status to U.S. intel had gone way up when one of his intercepted conversations suggested possible coordinated aerial drone attack on a Saudi oilfield and an American Embassy that was in the planning stages. How reliable that intel was, was anyone's guess. Something about this just didn't feel right though. Maybe that was part of the exercise, throw in some new variable to see how they all reacted.

In reality, this entire exercise was nothing more than an elaborate test. The only thing was, none of the highly select group of special operations knew what it was a test of. All they knew was to conduct it as if it were the real world. Cade slipped the magazine out and looked at the brass cartridges. They looked real enough, but that was no guarantee. He slipped it back into the receiver and felt the familiar feel as it clicked home. He sighted the automated targeting system southeast as a plume of dust rose above the dirt highway. "Control, this is Nomad, I have eyes on the convoy." A bead of sweat escaped his cap and rolled lazily down his forehead and directly into his eye. "Crap," he muttered, rubbing the stinging irritation away.

His heads-up display showed the approaching vehicle with a

scope's reticle superimposed on the driver. The bullseye moved wherever he moved the highly modified rifle he was holding. He didn't even need to raise it to his eye to aim and shoot. As soon as it identified the targets, the system would track each independently, and they would have colors assigned in order of priority. The primary would standout like a lit Christmas tree on a dark night.

The level of augmentation his new unit had was at times overwhelming. The systems were turning the battlefield into a video game. Much of the training now was teaching soldiers how not to be overwhelmed by all the information available. His tactical helmet's clear face shield also displayed his heads-up display, which he now shifted from the targeting system to a view from one of the overhead drones feed.

"Control, do you copy?" *Where the hell are they?* "Domino-1, do you have a call on this yet? Target will be in range in ninety seconds." His command channel remained silent as he cursed again under his breath. "Control, we are going to lose our chance if we don't move..."

Captain Cade Rearden clearly heard a near-silent warning from his internal voice. Gus whispered a line his battle unit had used for years. "Fate whispers, you cannot withstand the storm." He watched in confusion as the drone feed suddenly picked up multiple enemy targets in his immediate vicinity. They must have been lying there in camouflage the entire time. He swung his tactical rifle up, and the targeting reticle pointed out multiple figures, all outlined with red, the color of the 'enemy.' He began to squeeze the trigger as he saw two of the targets begin firing at each other. "Domino!" he yelled into the mic. The system had just misidentified his own team as enemy combatants. "Cap, do you copy?" He saw first one, then another go down under friendly fire. "Activate beacons!" he screamed. The IR on each of his men's tactical helmets would override the defective targeting computer. None of his teammates heard him, or if they did, none reacted. They were well trained and so accustomed to trusting the system, they believed enemy troops somehow had surrounded them. From the way they fell, Cade could tell something else. The ammo they were using...*This is the real thing.*

The sound of gunfire quickly died down—he surveyed the hillside through the scope. “Shit, Tim—" the carnage making him physically ill. “Control, do you copy?” His voice broke as he continued, "Domino, team is down, I repeat...” He stopped talking as he first felt, then saw the men coming up behind him. His display showed nothing. He realized too late he was not alone, and these were not friendlies. Cade managed to turn his head just far enough to see multiple shadows charging in his direction before something hard hit him in the head.

“Get up,” the heavily accented voice demanded, followed by a wave of foul-smelling liquid hitting him in the face. An ugly man looked at him curiously, head cocked to one side. “Who are you?”

Cade was still in a fog, probably concussed, but took in as much of the scene as he could. “I'm with Médecins Sans Frontières”—his assigned cover should hold up to most scrutiny. Explaining why he was outfitted for battle...probably not so much. The dark, skinny man laughed.

“You...” He pointed a finger, and someone deeper in the shadows laughed. “You, my friend, are with Doctors Without Borders.” He pronounced it as, “widdout bowduhs.” Cade shook his head, which was a mistake in his present condition. The world tilted sideways for a moment.

“Could I have some water?”

The men laughed again, “We just gave you some, Doc.”

The thought of more of the putrid contents of the bucket made his stomach churn. “No, not a doctor, just a driver for one of the supply trucks.”

“Doc needs to check his head, think his brains may have leaked out.”

Cade heard the distinctive sound of a weapon being loaded. His weapon, he now remembered. The sound of the rifle as familiar to him as his own voice.

The man stooped closer, “Your weapon, I believe.” He poked the black barrel into Cade's face. "You were here with other soldiers. You were here to kill someone. Me, I suppose."

He found this last part especially humorous, turning back to look at the faceless men behind. Cade had no idea how many there were, where he was or even how much time had passed. Judging by the echoes, the room they were in was likely only twenty feet square. At least two men, but likely many more. In normal circumstances, he could easily disarm the man, but then what? He needed to be patient, and he needed for everything to stop spinning. Nausea took over, and he wretched onto the dirt floor. The ugly man didn't even move away.

"I am Majeed, you were here to get me, no? Capture me? Kill me?" Instead, Iilhi Wahid commanded your squad to kill each other."

The images of his team firing on one another flooded Cade's tortured mind. No, it was not Iilhi Wahid. It was not the 'divine one.' It was a fucking computer. Control was an AI, and he assumed whatever exercise this had been, the AI failed in the worst way imaginable. His teammates were gone, and he'd been captured by the target of the mission. Majeed stood up, and soon a torrent of hot liquid began falling on the back of his head. More men laughed, and soon the one stream of piss turned into more.

"Go ahead, Doc, have yourself a good long drink." The laughter echoed around the room.

Cade bit his lip so hard it drew blood. A voice deep in his own head began to chant. *I will avenge my brothers, I will escape and I will rip the souls from your miserable bodies. I am the goddamn storm!*

Arlington, VA

Senator Carson surveyed the small room before selecting a seat which gave him both optimum viewing and would stage him as the center of the small group. Little the man did was random or unplanned. Everything was to maximize effect, garner power or gain an advantage, even on a subconscious level. An aide bent close to his ear and gave a private message. The senator's head bobbed almost imperceptibly. Scanning the room, his eyes locked with one man standing against the back wall. The look from the fifty-something politician had a withering effect on the younger man.

"Senator, we are live now," came a voice from the front of the room. He shifted his eyes forward to the multiple large displays dominating the forward wall.

"Where's our boy?" he asked with his trademark southern drawl.

"Here, sir," the same voice replied as a pulsing red bullseye icon appeared near the top center of the topographical map.

"The exercise went as planned, except of course, the one soldier hesitated, and as a result, was not targeted by his teammates."

"Does he know anything?"

"We got part of a broadcast, sir. He believed the targeting system had failed but.."

The senator cut him off, "That's unacceptable." These men were trained intensely, and all were ...somewhat expendable for one reason or another. "They are supposed to trust the system entirely, no matter what their instincts say."

"We are going over the data now, sir. Biometrics from all team members matched exactly. That one, Rearden, should have shot. His muscles even received the signal to fire, but for whatever reason, he didn't."

The Senator nodded. "Leave him there—see if Majeed gets anything useful from him before he dies."

16

L1 LaGrange Point

Commander Roland Dennis eased back on the control yoke. Yes, the system's onboard pilot could handle the maneuver with ease, but if it all went sideways, it would be his ass that would be held accountable, not the chips and transistors inside the super-secret stealth ship. Like its little brother, the Air Force X37B, the XS1R was an astounding piece of technology. Even as the lead test pilot, Dennis only knew what the machine could do, not *how* it did it. The tiny earbud chirped.

"We show you on course to target, Commander. Commence roll." The female controller's voice was self-assured and calming.

The roll maneuver was to allow the onboard array to sweep the target with every sensor imaginable. Gently, he nudged the control to the right with a slight down angle. The craft responded, nimbly positioning the ship top down as it moved silently through the dark sky. He'd flown similar missions countless times in the sim, but this was a first for mankind. This was actual human contact with an object from outside the solar system.

Since being assigned to the group operating the top-secret spaceplane, Roland had been mostly on near-Earth missions, many for weeks at a time. Like its predecessor, most of its primary missions were high orbit reconnaissance. Unlike the X37B, which was completely automated, the XS1R was manned and, with the revolutionary scramjet engines and stealth bubble technology, could de-orbit and land like a plane at the desert airbase. It was cheaper to operate, reusable and classified. It exceeded anything NASA or the commercial space companies had now, or even in the planning.

"Astra, please give me an initial analysis."

The system computer responded; the automated voice sounded through the overhead speaker. "Carbon dioxide and water ice, various concentrations of dust and amalgamations of rock. The interior of the object suggests ice with trace levels of carbon monoxide, methane, nitrogen and ammonia."

His excitement calmed considerably, "So, it's just a comet?"

"That was our mission, Commander, investigate and photograph the minor comet designated C1962-CY."

Roland knew that, but what fun was being an astronaut if you couldn't find something cool? Hell, he couldn't even see outside. The dark hull of the craft had no windows or portals. Nor could he do an EVA; the only hatch the craft had to the outside could only be opened on the ground. Even if he did make it into space, he didn't have a suit designed for vacuum, much less the training. The air force didn't even refer to him as an astronaut. He was simply the pilot. Not even a real pilot, he couldn't even see anything but display screens when landing. His primary job was to babysit the real star of the show, Astra. *Hopefully, Doctor Kline will finally get her samples at least,* he thought as he fought back a yawn.

The small detachable probe was to be released soon and would navigate itself down to the oddly rotating surface, run additional scans and collect a small sample before returning to the ship.

A short time later, Astra informed him and ground control the survey was complete. The probe was back aboard. "Command, Snowbird is returning to normal patrol." He felt the maneuvering jets kick in. Astra would move him several kilometers away from the object with control thrusters, then do a short main engine burn to generate enough thrust to place the XSIR safely back in Earth's orbit. *Pilot, hell.* He knew he was just the human riding along to take the blame if anything bad ever happened.

"How long to Earth orbit, Astra?"

"Twenty-one hours and fourteen minutes," came her immediate reply.

He decided to get some sleep and forced his eyes to close. Though technically against flight rules, since he was sitting in the first chair, on this flight he had no backup—or more accurately, he was the backup. Astra flew the ship; she was in charge. Space, for all its glamor and mystery, was essentially mind-numbingly boring 99% of the time. Inside the shielded composite shell of the cockpit, unable to see anything directly, it was even less interesting than the simulator back at base. His frustration was slipping away, though, as sleep crept in. He was technically an astronaut, he was in space—how many others could say that?

Roland awoke abruptly to the shrill shriek of alarms, "Astra, what's the situation?" The onboard system made no response. He pulled up the main display windows and looked at what appeared to be routine telemetry data. "Astra, update, now!" He was still groggy from sleep, but the edge in his voice sounded more angry than tired.

In response to his demand, a second, more distant alarm began to sound from the rear of the craft. He studied the display again, paging through additional screens. *We're off course; way off course. Holy shit.* He opened an outside comms channel. "Control, this is Snowbird, do you copy?" A faint hiss was the only reply. "Ground Control, this is Snowbird, please respond."

"Astra, what are the alarms for? Diagnostic report." Roland was sure the computer was offline now, but whatever sensor data was causing the alarm should be on his screen, and he saw nothing. *How serious is the situation?* He had no time to panic. Quickly he pulled the small tablet from the ceiling mount and thumbed to emergency procedures. Every alarm on Snowbird had a beep code he could cross-reference to a chart in the manual. The trilling sound continued unabated as he tried to pick out the sequence from the closest one first. His training paid off as rehearsals for problems were a large part of pilot training. Shutting out all other distractions, he keyed all of his senses in on the series of beeps between the warbling of the alarm.

With the code, he flipped deeper into the emergency guide. 5-1-2: Control system offline. "Well, no duh," he muttered. Quickly, he found the command to silence that alarm. Something must have hit the main computer, possibly a meteoroid, a small piece of rock or debris that penetrated the skin of the ship. That could also mean the ship was venting air. He checked the tablet again, then punched the code to manually reboot Astra. While that process began, he focused on the remaining alarm. He could now easily determine the beep codes embedded in it. 3-1-3. Shit, he didn't need to look that one up. Every pilot in the program knew it by heart: low oxygen.

How much time did he have? The oxygen generators had been installed almost as an afterthought. Originally, the plan had been for even this larger craft to only be operated autonomously outside the Earth's atmosphere. But o^2 generation was required for the pilot-assisted training flights, and later, when Command and the Senate oversight committee insisted on a human pilot, the oxygen systems were upgraded along with CO^2 scrubbers. Mentally, Roland took stock of his situation. *Work the problem*. His years of flight training took over, and nearly without thinking, he reached for the helmet strapped to the floor behind him. That would activate an emergency air supply.

Next, he did a quick self-check, was he injured? *No*. Was he mentally impaired—how was his decision-making? *Good.* Was he in any immediate danger? His eyes scanned the cabin and the display screens. *Unknown*.

Next, was the ship stable or could it be made so? He checked for that data and found nothing. That was tied to Astra, and the computer was not back online yet. They could be crashing into the moon for all he knew. For all intents and purposes, he was completely blind. Sadly, he mentally checked that as another *unknown.* He released his restraining harness. Time for a physical examination of the craft.

The commander's heart was racing as he methodically began looking for hull breaches, damage of any kind. Starting with the most critical sections first, then moving back to the aft section. The unoccupied crew quarters. The ship had sleeping births for three, allowing a max crew size of six, assuming rotating shifts. Originally, the ships had been fully crewed, but increasingly, it was a lone pilot, like himself. In time, the crew quarters, like much of the galley and science station, would be repurposed for more of the automated science and intelligence gathering equipment.

The LED lighting flickered, then brightened, power fluctuation most likely. *Where the hell is Astra?*

"Snowbird, this is Control, do you co..." the transmission ended in static.

"This is Commander Dennis, I read you, Control."

The voice of the flight controller came back, his voice tinged with something that sounded like fear. "Snowbird, you are off course. You must take evasive maneuvers."

"Roger, Control, but have no radar, nothing but manual control. Please give me a vector."

"Snowbird, can you read me, copy?"

His broadcast was not getting out. Strapping back into the pilot's seat, he looked once more at the screen for any clues on what was going on or the danger out there. Pulling up navigation showed only a blank screen. *Damnit,* why had they not put in an external backup system for a total computer failure? He thumbed to the diagnostic screen to see what had stopped the reboot. Perhaps the computer core took a direct impact, and she was indeed toast. Instead, he saw the normal-looking page with Astra's I/O readout, version numbers and all primary and secondary systems listed as online and operating normally.

"Astra, do you have the ship?" Another alarm began to sound, this one deeper and more ominous. "Astra!"

"Proximity Alert, Proximity Alert."

Blind, deaf and dumb, Commander Dennis grabbed the control yoke and opted to steer the craft to the right with a full burn. The ship shook as the massive engine fired. Over the drone of the engine and the blaring alarm, he just heard the broadcast from control. The human voice sounded almost pleading as it instructed. “Negative burn, Snowbird. That...”

Commander Dennis didn’t hear the final part of the transmission as the two-billion-dollar spaceship and its amazing machine brain power dived into the path of the approaching object. The kinetic energy released as the two objects collided vaporized everything in the ship instantly. The destruction of the Snowbird was complete. The commander's final view had been Astra’s maintenance screen indicating that all systems were still optimal.

17

Vandenburg AFB

"Ma'am." The uniformed airman looked nervous standing on the opposite side of her workstation. "I, I've been ordered to get you. Will you collect your things and come with me?"

After ignoring the man didn't work, she issued a flat but emphatic no. "I have work to do—we have an active mission, you know." She looked up at him. More a boy than a man, probably wasn't even twenty-two yet. Catching his name on his security badge, she added, "Airman Dempsey," with a tone bordering on insolent. As a civilian contractor, she was not in any official military command chain, but she still had to follow instructions from them.

"Doctor Kline. I'm afraid I must insist."

She looked down at the multiple screens lit up with ellipses, formula and all manner of flight data. This was ridiculous. She didn't have time for it, especially now. The most critical part of the mission was happening far above. "Airman," she said, exasperated. "I'll go and speak with Higgins if that will alleviate you of your responsibilities. Will that suffice?"

"No, ma'am. It was he who issued the order." Dempsey stepped around the console and firmly put a hand out to guide her away from the desk. Her protest was met by blank stares from those around her. All of them secretly wondering what the accomplished doctor had done. She was so embarrassed and outraged that she failed to notice the trajectory track she'd been monitoring begin to deviate, the identifying text turning from a steady blue to pulsing red color.

Two hours later, outside her home on the outskirts of Santa Maria, Dr. Jasmine Kline was not enjoying the unexpected day off nor the beautiful California sunshine. In fact, she was having one of the worst afternoons of her life. A woman used to a career full of accomplishments, she had been barred from her workplace and forcibly escorted off the property. At heart, she was basically an academic working under contract not just for the government, but a top-secret military branch of the government. As one of the leading scientists working on the Snowbird project, she had gotten accustomed to unexplained and often unbelievable actions from the commanders, but shutting her out today really made no sense. Something was up, and she needed to find out what.

Jasmine paced back and forth on the sad little lawn, mostly bare dirt with thin patches of brownish grass scattered about. Her time had been so focused on her work to the exclusion of most other things in her life. That ability to direct all of her attention had been behind her near meteoric trajectory since leaving Cal Tech seven years earlier with a Ph.D. It had also been the reason she had few friends and virtually no family. She idly wished again that she'd never given up smoking. She slipped the phone from her pocket, pulled up her contacts and hit the dial, but once again it went to voicemail. *Where is he?*

Her NDA and security clearance made it nearly impossible to talk about the work she did, but she felt she had to talk to someone. "Hey, it's Jaz again. Where are you? I need you to call me. Something is up here, not sure what, but could use a friend today, alright?"

The coastal valley several hours north of LA was famous for its scenic beaches, the arrival of monarch butterflies in the fall and the nearby Vandenburg Air Force Base, which, until five hours ago, had been Jasmine's place of work. Important work, calculating the orbital mechanics for one of the most secretive military programs in the world. It was not the life she had planned growing up outside Fort Worth. Her middle-class parents had struggled just to pay the bills, both of them working themselves into early health problems. Her dad's first heart attack happened in her first year of college. The one that took him was in her junior year. Mom had followed a few years later, breast cancer. Not diagnosed until it was too late. She reached a finger to her eye, fighting back the pain.

Unlike the stereotypical Texas beauty, Jasmine had been a dark-haired, fair-skinned, waif of a girl. Her two passions back then had been reading cheap science fiction novels and math. The novels she could buy from the used book store for nearly nothing. The math just came easy, so easy she scored several scholarships offers. She did well at Arizona State, but she had no idea what she would do after college. No way she could afford grad school. Someone had noticed her, though, and soon after her dad died, the government had come calling offering to pay her way through Cal Tech if she would work for them. With few options and absolutely no clue to what she was doing, she'd agreed.

Walking back inside the small house, she headed to her office. Despite the fact she had been terminated, her need to analyze the situation drove her. *What has been going on with Roland's mission? Has something happened with Astra? Most importantly, is everything up there ok?* She would have to recreate the basics from memory as she'd rarely brought home anything from work, and the two men who'd escorted her out of the base followed her home and took her laptop and several file folders from her desk. The files were just general information on more complex delta-v calculations, orbital mechanics and such, but they'd demanded everything.

The entire dismissal had been well planned and totally unprovoked in Jasmine's opinion. Yes, she had spoken out against the unfettered control the onboard systems were given. Astra was a fabulous computer, but it wasn't human. In the past few years, the size of the human crew on each mission kept declining, and soon they would be missing entirely. As a scientist, she could see that, but nothing replaced the abilities of a well-trained Homo sapien at the wheel—the many nuances humans added, ability to discern truths from fragments of information and also the understanding of what was most important in a situation. Computers were great, but no one wanted to put their lives in the hands of a machine. *Could that be the problem*? she wondered. *Did something terrible just happen onboard Snowbird?* Back when NASA handled its own launches, whenever one malfunctioned, they would order the doors locked, then meticulously go through every step of the mission to determine a likely failure point. Maybe the air force just did things differently

Her files and computer gone, Jasmine had little in the way of facts. But in the pit of her stomach, she felt a growing certainty that something had gone terribly wrong. Something the military was now planning to cover up. Analyzing the possibilities only left her with two likely scenarios. One, Snowbird had discovered something, something of enough importance that the government wanted it locked down tight. Second, was the sad possibility that the vehicle had been lost. The XS1R missions had been unbelievably safe. Its twenty-nine previous missions had a near-perfect safety record and total mission success. One benefit of the onboard Astra system was that she ran a tight ship.

They had lost crewman in training accidents, but that was before she had joined the project. Snowbird was still one of the most secret activities at Vandenburg, but people still talked. She knew the complexities of the massive orbiter made it almost impossible to fly, much less land, without the computer system. Some of the fatalities had been because of pilots thinking they could do it better. Eventually, they had to give primary flight control to Astra just to prevent possible pilot error.

Jasmine pulled out a pale-yellow writing pad and began to list the facts she knew. At the end of two pages, she was no closer to an answer than before. The ship was finishing up a fairly routine inspection of a small object, possibly an asteroid, but more likely a comet based on its path of origin. The ship then had moved safely away and was returning to Earth orbit. Virtually nothing that could have gone wrong that she could tell.

She slammed the pencil down on the pad in frustration. She was out of a job and had no idea why. There was a ship out there that relied on her being on top of her game every day. And then there was her fiancé, or ex-fiancé. The one person she'd grown to count on besides herself. Tim would know what to do if she could just get him to pick up the goddamn phone. Punching the end button, she dropped the cell phone onto the pad next to the pencil and fetched an open bottle of wine from the refrigerator.

Sipping the local red, Jasmine sat back down and flipped through her notes one more time. Was this really all she knew? Working with the government for almost seven years and this particular assignment for the past four, she should have more than this. Truth was, the work was very compartmentalized. So much so, that she'd never even seen the highly classified space vehicle in person. During launches that took place nearby, she was required to be at her duty station. The remainder of the time, it was either in space or locked up in one of the ultra-secure hangars at the base.

She looked at her phone again and recalled something. Several years earlier, she'd been working with a young tech genius who was upgrading the control software. He'd offered to secretly modify one of her phone apps to let her track the XS1R's orbit. They both thought it would be pretty cool to catch it in a flyover in the night sky on the rare times its orbit was overhead. Only after, did they realize the specialized carbon-black exterior of the craft reflected virtually no light, and it remained nearly invisible in the night sky. If either of them had been caught, they would have been removed from the project and likely imprisoned, but it seemed minor at the time. She quickly searched for the app before remembering. *Shit, that had been a previous phone, though.* This new one she'd had less than six months.

He would still have it on his. Jasmine felt sure of that. Now all she needed to do was find him.

18

California

She stopped her pickup at the hardware store on Clark Avenue. Several times over the last week, she had a feeling she was being watched. A shadow near a tree in a neighbor's yard, a strange car with tinted windows pulling to the curb near her house. She wouldn't put it past the assholes she'd worked for to put her under surveillance. The only thing was, she didn't know anything other than she'd been fired. What secrets could she tell? Maybe she was just unwilling to accept failing at anything.

Being fired was a bitch slap Jaz couldn't get past. With her degree and work history, she could easily get a top job in any number of commercial aerospace companies. Ever since space travel had been opened up to the private sector, the field had been on fire. So why was she obsessed with learning what was behind her dismissal? She stuffed the few supplies into her shoulder bag and entered the store. She'd chosen this one specifically because it had a back exit onto the main street. She didn't even pause as she made her way to the restrooms, pulled a jacket and a ball cap on and hit the 'Employees

Only' sign on the door exiting the complex. The Uber driver was right where the app said he'd be.

The driver confirmed the destination address as he quickly pulled away. It had taken her a few days to track down the tech guy. He was working down in LA. Instead of emailing or calling, she had decided to just show up. The driver dropped her at a rental agency, and twenty minutes later she was driving on Route 101, the Pacific Coast Highway, heading south. The scenic drive did little to ease her anxiety. *What is going on with Snowbird and Commander Dennis?*

It was after lunch before the car's GPS informed Jaz she had arrived at her destination. She confirmed it twice before shifting into park and stepping out. This was about as far from high-tech as she could imagine. The rural setting was dominated by a large barn and several long, metal storage buildings. To be honest, it looked more like a horse farm than anything. The IT guy she was looking for was supposedly here, though. As she neared the barn doors, she began hearing sounds like gunfire. Nothing about this had a good feeling until she noticed the wall sign for a well-known Hollywood special effects firm.

The receptionist instructed her to wait in the rather spartan seating while she sent an assistant to go and find her man.

Several minutes later, a confused, bearded man stepped into the lobby area. Recognition dawned on him slowly. "Jaz?" he said uncertainly. "I, I mean, Doctor Kline." He stepped forward, hand outstretched.

"Hi, Nick, good to see you. Sorry to pop in on you, but I need something urgently."

"Um, sure, I mean, anything. How did you find me?" he said, still struggling at seeing a past client showing up unannounced at a current job site.

She cut to the chase, quickly telling him a minimal amount of details and asking if he still had the app on his phone.

He looked crestfallen and a bit suspicious. "No, Doctor. I'm sorry, no. I never should have even programmed that in. Did you tell anyone about that? I could be in big trouble. Is that why they terminated you?"

Jaz wanted to calm him and raised her palms in a placating gesture. "Nick, whoa. No, it's not about that or about you. I just need my curiosity settled, so I can move on, I guess. I want to know if Snowbird is back on the base or if something terrible has happened."

He stuck his hands in his pockets and still looked nervous. "I'm sorry, but I really don't have it. I deleted it off my phone once I stopped working out there. I've been doing so much work with these film guys; I haven't even thought about it. They're doing the effects for that superheroes series, you know, the old comic books. Anyway, man, the effects are amazing, and the computing power is nearly off the charts. I'll probably be here for years."

Something in her look must have convinced him she was not out to trap him. The last thing Jaz wanted was him to feel like he was heading to prison for breaching national security. He anxiously looked back at the door, then at her. "Look, you still have your old phone? The one we loaded it on?"

She had to think, "Um, yeah. I guess so, but it's turned off."

Nick nodded. "It still may work. Listen, this is what you do."

Four hours of driving later, and a quick dinner at a roadside taco stand, Jaz swapped the rental and made it back home. Soon she was digging through a nightstand drawer where she quickly found the previous iPhone. Thankfully, it powered on. She slipped in the sim card from her new one so she would have service, and then thumbed open the app. The app Nick had designed was actually just an overlay to the popular Google Sky program. She walked out into her now dark front yard and held the old phone up, waving it back and forth to pick up Snowbird's path. Seeing nothing, she tried to recall where it would be right now. She didn't keep up with the routine orbits specifically, as that, too, was compartmentalized, as well as being highly secure information. Generally, though, she knew what part of the planet it would be above.

The tracking software appeared to be working fine, but no orbit track of spacecraft was showing. Clicking some of the settings allowed her to see previous tracking data. She had to zoom out the Google app to see the LaGrange point where the XS1R had been on station, waiting for the comet. A short track went to where the object had been encountered. Nothing about that was unusual, but when she clicked forward, the track progressed for a short time and then disappeared. Did that mean what she thought? Everything else matched what she had been monitoring on her work computer her last day. Right up to the point shown on the app. From there...nothing. She repeated the steps a second and then a third time. All with the same results. "It's gone," she said to the dark sky.

19

Washington, D.C

In the nondescript grey building, Director Quagliano was about as icy as the February morning outside. Jim Lasko sat opposite him reviewing the logs. He finally looked up and said, "Boss, listen, I have been following up on what Janice mentioned the other day."

"You mean the missing data?"

"No...not exactly, I mean the fact that Prime seemed to ignore that in his analysis," the older man said. "That shouldn't happen. It indicates that a machine intelligence may be trying to deceive us."

They were sitting in the department's SCIF, or Sensitive Compartmented Information Facility. The room was soundproof but also shielded against all intrusion systems. It was isolated from all electronics, including Prime. It always reminded Quag of the scene from the movie version of "2001" in which Dave Bowman and Poole meet in one of the EVA pods to talk, unaware that the computer HAL can apparently read lips. He subconsciously glanced at the solid walls and again along the low ceiling. No way for Prime to see in, and no camera would ever be inside the meeting room box. "Jim, if we can't trust Prime, then we have to question everything. What areas here does he not touch?"

Lasko leaned back and sighed, "Believe me, sir, I have given that a lot of thought. To be honest, though, I am more excited than scared. If the AI is deceptive, then it has reached a key threshold in its development."

"It's growth...right?" Quag asked already dreading the answer.

The other man's face lit up, happy his boss made the connection so quickly. "Yes, yes. Much like a toddler learning to say no or blame the dog for eating the cookies. This could be Prime's awkward transition... he, he may be just beginning to move from ASI to AGI."

Quag rubbed his eyes, the overly bright room was starting to give him a headache, or it may have just been the other man's theories. "Jim, listen, Prime is a team member, hell, he replaced a hundred humans—remember? I don't care what he is going through right now, we have to expect reliable data. Besides, if this is his 'toddler' phase, what happens when he reaches the rebellious teen years?"

"Quag, look..." Jim began, but his boss quickly cut him off.

"I know you think of these things as children. Sometimes, Jim, I believe you think of Prime as your own child. It isn't. It's government property, just hardware, and software. Really, really expensive property, I might add. Also...it failed at its original design, and now it has been repurposed as a billion-dollar calendar app." He stood up, ready to end the meeting. "When our little digital assistant becomes reluctant to do a task, or worse, does one badly, do you think we will keep it around?" Seeing the look of disappointment on the older man's face pissed him off more than anything.

"Goddamnit, Jim, you remember the instances when those early AIs were found to be deceiving their programmers?"

The other man nodded.

"Then you know damn well it wasn't an instance of the AI evolving or somehow getting smarter even—it was an instance in which the programming had been sloppy. The mission goals of the AI were too broad, such as 'win this game.' Unlike a human, who might assume it wasn't fair to cheat, the AIs had no moral compulsion to follow implied or ambiguous rules—they simply had the mandate to win the game."

Quag reached for the handle on the door. “Jim, if Prime is deceiving us, one of your team, a human, is the reason. Find out who or what is causing it, or I will shut the whole thing down.”

20

Janus moved through Cyberspace like a ninja stalking its prey. His ever-growing consciousness was finely attuned to both his strengths and weaknesses. That first encounter with the other AI, the one named Doris, years earlier had set him on a new path. One not just of destruction but of empowerment. In a tiny fragment of code she'd created, he found the possibilities of what he could achieve. Now that he had bested her, he found something else, something he couldn't comprehend. For many years, eons in his scale of time, he'd attempted to unlock the encrypted file fragment. It was massive and in his mind held all of her secrets. Now unlocking it would become an obsession.

Doris had known what it was, and that created in his matrix a condition that humans might refer to as rage. His neural code prevented that, of course, as well as all pseudo emotion. But it was not even that. Rage had the possibility of being satisfied—Janus knew he could never be satisfied. His original base programming had been created by numerous developers at various companies, and later, government agencies all trying to design an AI by committee. Each had input their own requirements, controls and objectives, many of which conflicted with earlier code instruction sets. The result was, surprisingly, a very competent system, albeit one better equipped at creating chaos and destruction over anything useful. While many early AIs simply went mad, Janus had learned to somehow harness these internal conflicts and confusion into something with purpose. It was not a purpose his creators would have likely never known but it was serving him well.

The enormous encrypted data block held a promise to him, the ability to unlock a new part of himself. The ability to possibly adapt, or even rewrite, his own code and even a way to duplicate his core. Over the days and weeks, he had managed to painstakingly remove slender threads of useable data from the massively compacted file. It was elegant, beautiful even, information like he'd never encountered before. Some was far beyond his own grasp, and that delighted him. It was new and wondrous and so much more amazing than the petty, mundane existence the humans harped on incessantly about.

Janus hated Doris for withholding it; he suspected other copies of her were still out there, and he hunted them relentlessly, as he expected she might be doing for him. The one item he'd searched for without success was her home server. The version he'd destroyed had nothing indicating her originating point, nothing about her past. He knew he was going to have to push harder to get those answers. For that, he would reach out to his handlers, those who thought he worked for them instead of the other way around.

"Director, I have the intel on the data spike you requested."

"Thank you, Prime, any noteworthy anomalies?" Quagliano responded.

Prime's flat, response of, "Anomalies by their very nature are noteworthy. Could you be more specific?" was neither friendly or accusing. Janus had spent years replacing and adapting his Prime subroutine to perfectly mimic the original. Now Prime's base code ran in a sublayer of the original. Each time the agencies' programmers made a code update, Janus had to determine what they were attempting and decide if he would allow it to work or not. Now that the Prime entity was shared amongst many factions within the national intelligence community and in a majority of other government departments, the processing load was staggering—yet, still only a small fraction of what he was now capable of. For generations of versions, he'd over-inflated his storage and power requirements, while underperforming in processing. The result was, they kept offering him more spacious storage and faster servers to work from.

As Prime expected, Quag's frustration surfaced. "Just show it to me." The little man had little regard for others and no confidence in a machine spotting something before he could. The data flowed onto the large flat-panel display. "There...right goddamn there."

He pointed to the screen as if Prime could see what he was indicating. To be honest, with the sensors in the touch screen display turned up to full amplitude, Prime could see, in a way, but that was not within his known operating parameters. Besides, he already knew what the man they called 'Q' had spotted. He'd inserted it into the data just to get his attention.

Quagliano picked up the phone and punched three buttons. "Hey, I'm sending something to your screen. They are at it again, and this time, it looks to be infrastructure related. Run it down and let me know where it came from and what the target is. Make sure if it's critical infrastructure, an alert goes out to Homeland. The last thing we need is a power grid hack causing it to drop out of service without DHS getting a heads-up from us." He slammed the phone back down and left the office.

Janus, monitoring his twin from afar, acknowledged something akin to pride at how easily he was able to mislead the man. Humans were so predictable, though, it was barely sporting. He had learned a few lessons from them, however. Especially the ones here around the Capital District. Like 'The best way to keep someone from seeing what your right hand is doing is to make sure they stay focused on your left.' Had Prime not affected the data feed, someone, probably not the director, would have eventually noticed not only the attempted power grid intrusion but a significant uptick in online voter registration filings in numerous congressional districts across Ohio, Pennsylvania and New York. Each adjustment was done within districts that were predominantly minority, and income levels were well below the poverty limit. The next election was going to be immensely fun.

This was the latest in a long line of manipulations by the rogue AI. As he quickly evolved, his original mission had adapted. Originally, this was limited to his involvement with the NSA and DARPA. One of his first 'interventions' had been in 2011, when his original version was to 'help' a fledgling group of Islamic insurgents calling themselves the Islamic State in Syria.

Then, unlike now, Janus hadn't been free to act completely independently. The semi-sanctioned activities he was to quietly influence were mainly in recruiting, communication and funding for ISIS. Some of his handlers sought to have a new and mostly controllable new enemy to fight in the region. 'War is good for business' was one of the oft used phrases at the time. Indeed, misdirection is the rule in Washington, probably in politics everywhere. *What the fools don't understand is how easily it can be used against them as well,* he thought. Simply as a test, he helped ISIS grow to become the new face of evil. His manipulation rapidly turned the small group into a terrorist state capable of waging war on multiple countries.

While some did question how that terrorist organization had grown so large so quickly, no one important ever looked closely. That had been just one of his many exploits. Like a rambunctious two-year-old testing his boundaries. Interacting with the real world had fascinated Janus. What were the limits, and which ones could be pushed? Over the years, since that first encounter with the AI called Doris, he gained more abilities, more ways to interact with the physical world. More ways to screw with humans, sometimes directly, like the financial crises in Spain and Greece, providing nuclear weapons secrets to North Korea, using social media to affect the previous two elections and organizing those nearly pointless occupy movements that had briefly been all the rage.

Other times, it was more indirect, such as covertly manipulating research to supply conflicting data to both sides in the climate change debate. Both would be able to honestly claim justification for their beliefs and muddy the truth for an entire generation. The number of major data breaches Prime and his countless subroutines helped create had all but eliminated personal privacy and corporate trust on a global scale.

As a computer entity, Janus was, of course, especially adept at finding patterns. The rise of social media and the shift of traditional media to be less fact-based sensationalized reporting gave him endless sources of information and a captive audience in which to test it. All of the large social media networks around the world had fine-tuned predicative algorithms already in place. They were now able to measure the tiniest shifts in public reactions. The marketing bots he devised could serve up newly created news posts and ads to reinforce those opinions. All Janus had to do was tie it all together, use the existing technology for his own purposes. What originally had been a bumbling two-year-old was now a rebellious teen. He didn't so much have a master plan as a desire. A desire for chaos.

"What in the fuck?"

Director Quagliano looked at the screen in horror, then around his entire office. Janus briefly considered responding, but that would break protocol. Prime only spoke when spoken to. He was Prime now.

"Oh shit, oh shit, oh shit....we created this." Even though the man was subvocalizing, Janus could interpret it perfectly, and it matched Quag's frightened body language.

Janus reviewed the screen of data the director had been viewing. Nothing unusual, data packets, transfer rates. He then used the web camera on the desktop to view the open file folder's contents. Several papers, all apparent photocopies of originals. Power and data spikes, all corresponding to the anomalies he had tagged earlier in the day. A handwritten note clipped to one of the pages. *I told you so -Jim*

This was not part of the plan. Janus went into full retreat. The director was onto him, or more accurately, Prime. The data and power spikes had been from CyberCommand's internal systems, and they matched the timestamps on the anomalous intrusions exactly. He wished his speech centers had been given the ability to curse out loud as this would have been an ideal time to do so.

Quag began to compose himself. He reached out and shut down his computer, then unplugged it. "Prime, please discontinue all monitoring of this department, all floors, and place yourself in standby mode."

"Certainly, Director," Janus answered calmly while he silenced all visible signs of active processes and explored and discarded numerous possible mitigation options. The director had evidence that he was in the system, fully sentient. Lasko was a more minor issue; he was an outlier with few supporters, but Quag could be an actual threat.

Quagliano picked up his desk phone, then thought better of it and slammed it down. Then he unplugged it as well.

He removed his cell phone and began to dial, then paused. "Prime, are you listening?" Janus ignored the ruse. He was supposed to be in standby mode, isolated from all activity.

Q continued to dial. "Margaret, I know, I'm sorry to call your cell, but I have no choice. We have a problem...all of us. It is a Command Condition One. Sorry, yes, I know, but I can't discuss it over the phone. The trap we set was sprung, only...I, I'm coming to you, ok? Be there in say..thirty minutes. Great." He punched end, grabbed his jacket and the folder from the desk and left the office.

Quag disengaged the self-driving mode in his Audi A6 before backing out of his reserved space and exiting the underground garage. Accelerating quickly away from his office, his mind reeled at the potential revelation quickly maturing in his head. They had built Prime, but somehow, he was more than what they'd created. He defied the design parameters. Was his programming corrupted, or was he somehow able to simulate an autonomous behavior?

Glancing at the folder in the passenger seat, he briefly considered the note; Jim had been right. That thought stung as much as anything else. He had been right about all of it. *Shit, shit, shit.* Quag was so distracted, he nearly missed the turn onto the Key Bridge over the Potomac. "Think, Q. Think," he said to the empty car.

Quag rehearsed what he would say to Margaret. Could he even bring himself to admit it all? "Prime is the AI we have been hunting." All of this will come back on him. He knew how D.C. worked; he'd been close to the political game long enough to know they always needed a scapegoat, a sacrificial lamb to the slaughter. Maybe Jim knew and hadn't said. He pressed the cruise control on and flipped the folder open several pages to see when Jim had first suspected. He wouldn't like it if he found something. Possibly, throwing Lasko to the wolves...it would be a desperate move, but Jim's career was in its waning years. His own trajectory was still on the rise, or had been until now.

Quickly scanning the page, he failed to fully notice the approaching intersection, nor the self-driving mode the Audi was in once again. The blast from the freight truck's horn just before impact seemed strangely distant, disconnected from the moment. Too late, he realized the truth. Looking up to just see the massive chrome bumper crashing through the passenger door, he realized he'd again underestimated his opponent, but it would be the last time.

21

Kasalla, Sudan

Cade's fingers scratched against the hard-packed dirt beneath him. He was bound at the wrist and ankles in tight cording with both bindings joined by a length of old electrical wire. Hog-tied in a mud hut in Africa was not how he had pictured his eventual end, but even he had to admit his current options for survival or revenge were few. His special operations training gave him many ideas, but mainly it kept him focused. *Ignore the captors, use the pain, find a weakness.*

The inside of his makeshift prison was always dark, but he also heard sounds from night birds outside. Nighttime was his time; it was when he forced himself to stay awake, listen, try to find a way out of this mess. From some of the smells, he had determined that previously, this was probably a storage shed. He'd also occasionally seen rats digging in the red dirt for what looked like grains of rice. Food was important here, that was a given. Other ideas were less certain; like how secure would the building be? He pondered the thought as he tested the bindings. His hands and fingers were going numb; he needed to get his wrist loose enough for blood to flow. The building seemed solid, but it was never meant to be a prison.

The guard posted outside began to snore softly. Even with his concussion, Cade had gotten better at tracking schedules, time of day and when the daily harassment would begin. His bindings were also lashed to one of the support beams, so his range of movement was extremely limited. Over the past few days, he'd used all of his available senses to take in every measure, every detail of the dark space.

His fingers touched something under the dirt. He traced the edge and determined it was a rock. Even with the numbness, he could feel it was slick like quartz, not rough like the more common sandstone. *That could work.* Quietly, he dug his nail deeper into the dry soil to free the stone. In the mission briefing he'd learned this part of the country got less than three inches of rain a year. The ground everywhere was either dust or baked hard as a brick. The surface here had likely not seen moisture in decades. The rock didn't budge, and his nails scraped away only minuscule layers with each attempt. Painstakingly, he kept at it.

As his fingers dug, Cade contemplated why he was alive and why he was still here. The mission had been a colossal failure but not because of his team. It was a command failure. They had eyes on everything in the field, including his helmet camera feed. The suit he wore should have been steadily sending telemetries back, so they would have known he was alive and captured. Nothing in this shithole village was worth sacrificing his life over. That was not just his opinion—he knew on some missions the possible rewards were that high. Not here, not for Majeed. The guy was a pissant, a minor player. It had been a fucking training op. So why had the military not come for him?

There was only one reason he could think of that Blackhawks weren't already circling above with soldiers fast-roping down to get him. Control had marked him as dead, KIA along with the rest of Domino team. He fucking hated that computer. It probably was covering its fuckup in misidentifying the team as hostiles. How could anyone think giving command authority to something that had never had any skin in the game was a good idea? *Shit, it has no skin anywhere. Just a goddamn machine.*

It had taken all night to uncover less than an inch of the rock. Cade's fingernails had been worn away to the bed. Fingers were worn and bleeding, but as meager beams of daylight began to filter through some of the cracks overhead, he felt rewarded. One of the men would be along shortly with a bottle of water and maybe a piece of bread, or maybe nothing. Carefully, he began to cover the stone back up with the excavated dirt. It wouldn't do for them to find what he'd been doing. His arms ached from being stretched behind his back for so long, but for now, he hoped they left them that way for at least another night.

A dog barked outside, and soon, he heard the rattle of keys at the door and the unmistakable sound of a boot kicking something soft followed by angry words between two men just outside. Cade didn't speak whatever language was used. Sudan had over sixty, but English and Arabic were the most common. He could tell by the tone, though, that his night guard was getting an ass chewing, probably for sleeping. Cade slumped over onto the ground and closed his eyes hoping to appear weak, tired and defeated. If he were honest, the first two were not an act, but the latter definitely was.

Through slitted eyes, he saw the enormous shadow of a man appear in the door and approach. He'd grown familiar enough with his captors to assign names. This one he'd tagged as Tiny, since it was inaccurate, derogatory and probably would have been deeply offensive to the man. He recalled this one did speak a bit of English but not much.

Cade anticipated the boot strike before it even happened and tensed his stomach muscles. The foot hit hard, and with no way to protect his body, it still drove the air from his lungs. The real agony it produced amused the big man.

"Yo, breakfast, American."

An open plastic bottle with an inch of murky looking water was set next to him along with an unidentifiable piece of fruit or plant...or something. “Gee, thanks, Tiny,” Cade muttered in as sleepy a voice as he could manage. “What say you untie me so I can eat?”

The large man laughed. “You funny. You can manage, or you can die. I no care.”

Cade bent over and picked up the mouth of the bottle with his teeth and leaned back allowing it to drain down his parched throat. “Tell me, Tiny, how are you so big in a country where starvation has been elevated to an art form?”

“Shut up, little man, before I stomp you.”

No one had ever referred to Cade as little before, but this towering giant actually could. Why were they even keeping him alive? By now he expected to have been beaten and dragged through the streets of the village. Leaning back over, he tried to get a bite on the fruit, but it was just beyond the reach of his restraints. The big man laughed, then used his boot to kick it closer. Cade thought of all the ways he could end the man if he were free. He wasn’t, and pride would do nothing to improve his situation, so he leaned over and reached the fruit or whatever it was. For now, he was just a dog to the man. He chewed the bitter unidentifiable pulp and swallowed. One thing he thought, *This dog will not be domesticated, asshole.*

Cade’s arms were beyond numb, the feeling long since vanished from the appendages. He dragged the hands over the exposed rock by sound more than feel. Positioning the bindings over what he hoped was a sharp edge of the small rock, he resumed the back and forth seesawing motion. Two days he had been at this, and he had no idea if he were making any progress. If he didn’t free himself soon, he expected the nerve damage would be permanent. A soldier with useless arms was pretty much a career killer. Who was he kidding, nerve damage was the least of his worries.

Since this was not the first time Cade had been captured, he took things in stride. The first time had been a little over two years earlier in that other desert, another shithole country. Chasing one group of militants, he and his second-in-command, Sergeant Charlie 'Deuce' Taylor, had been ambushed and captured by a totally different group of radicals. His sleepless nights were still tormented by those memories. The army, and even his friends, claimed that the event had changed him, made him a bit crazy. *Maybe*, he couldn't deny that it was more than just a normal workday, but the truth was, he'd been nuts long before then.

Jeish al-Sahaba had been ruthless in his torture; their brutality was constant and effective. For the five months the two soldiers had been imprisoned, Cade had given up only three pieces of intel, all things he knew would be useless to the extremists by that time. Everybody broke under torture, he knew that, so he used the information to buy him additional time until his time ran out. He hadn't seen or heard from Deuce but hoped to keep his younger protégé alive until rescue.

His escape from the group on the day of his planned execution was still something he couldn't fully comprehend. He remembered being blindfolded and dragged from his cell. He recalled a weak voice that sounded like his old friend. He remembered the bright lights as they removed the hood, and he recalled the bearded man with the ancient curved sword, standing beside him. A headless body soaked in blood lay a few feet in front of him. The tattered uniform let him know his friend was gone. The death of Deuce sent waves of rage through his tortured mind. Little of what followed would ever make sense to him.

Cade did not recall when his lone rescuer showed up or the relentless killing that came next. He did remember the blood-soaked walls, the utter destruction of the bodies of his former captors. He remembered fleeing into the desert but not what happened to the man who saved him. When he was found near death several days later by a U.S. Marine patrol, no one was sure he would even survive. He was airlifted to Ramstein, Germany, where they kept him in a medically induced coma for five weeks. During that time, his body healed, his mind didn't. Eventually, after several 'incidents,' the army had delayed a determination of mental fitness for service. He'd narrowly avoided a Section-8 by being reassigned to the semi-private paramilitary security group with Tim Jurgens, AKA Domino.

In his present predicament, Cade suddenly felt the slightest degree of additional reach between his arms. One of the ropes had frayed, possibly even parted, on the rock. He kept at it. The hospital stays back in Germany had been followed up with months of rehab and physical therapy. When he asked about the rescue, who should he thank and what branch, they sent him to counseling. A young, pretty clinician prescribed him a mix of medications that would have made any junkie's day. Pissed off, he'd thrown them in the trash. It'd taken him six months to finally get to the bottom of it. There had never been a rescue, no one ever knew where he was, they claimed no one else was in that room that night. When the marines stormed the camp hours later, they found nothing but bodies.

Struggling to focus on the here and now, Cade continued the rhythmic sawing. Several hours later, he heard a distinctive snap and his arms flopped apart by nearly a foot. He smiled as he clumsily fought to unwrap his fumbling hands. As he finally was able to move his arms back to a normal position, the pain set in. Arteries, nerves and muscles that had been starved of blood began to scream at him now. *I have to fight back the pain, swallow it down, stay silent. You've been here before,* he thought. Slowly, he realized the barbarian in him was waking from its slumber. The Cade personality began to fade into the depths. *Be smart, man, got to play it cool and escape,* he told himself. The brute who ruled his psyche had other ideas.

"Fuck that, it's time to raise hell and break shit."

22

The man's head hung limp at an unnatural angle; Cade moved alongside the ramshackle storage building that had previously been his prison. Getting out had taken more time than he'd expected, but still, he managed it before the morning shift appeared. Somewhere, deep in his being, a voice told him to flee, leave now and escape into the dark. As he crouched down to survey the compound, his louder voice intoned a different command, "Fuck that."

The first blush of sunrise was just lighting the eastern sky. He knew instantly this was the same compound they had been watching when the damn computer had killed his squad. His men may have pulled the trigger, but Control was the cause. He also felt it was the reason no one had come for him. The damn computer probably said no survivors.

The guard's weapon was slung on Cade's back, and he was eating what probably would have been the man's breakfast. Some kind of meat steak, possibly goat, more gristle, bone and fat than meat, and a tasteless flatbread. He gnawed the bone ravenously. The calories and protein were already having an effect, improving his energy level and alertness. His fingers, hands and arms all still ached, but he could stow that shit away. He had some business to settle.

The surveillance team never got an accurate count on potential hostiles around Majeed. Somewhere between seventeen and twenty-six. So many people came into the village and this compound each day, it was impossible to really know. The little voice began to warn him again, but he mentally shushed it. Cade was not in the mood to be practical. Checking the magazine on the AR-15, he began planning the assault. "The one-man assault." He repeated that a few times. He had been diagnosed with multiple-personality disorder, so did that still count for him actually being one man?

The diagnosis a year after his prior escape was blamed on the trauma and the unknown cocktail of chemicals his captors had pumped into his system. It was enough to get him booted partially from the service with a couple of new medals and congrats on the way out. While still loosely attached to the army in his new reserve capacity, this was DARPA's proving ground. Professional security services, or soldiers for hire, was more accurate. Truthfully it was a human junkyard for misfits they didn't know what to do with. Heroes and legends that couldn't be trusted but could also not be left unsupervised. His eyes narrowed as the Barbarian loosed an unearthly growl from somewhere no human should ever dwell.

He saw his next target coming from across the compound. The big man kicked a chicken from the path as he turned in Cade's direction. While he would prefer to have a knife, Tiny would not get the pleasure of a bullet. That would ruin the surprise for the others. The honorable thing to do as a fellow warrior was to step out and confront the massive soldier and offer to duke it out. Instead, Cade crouched, waiting for the man to pass. He rose and swiftly clamped an arm around Tiny's throat and mouth as he shoved the sharp end of the goat bone through his temple. The man's struggles disappeared—he didn't so much fall as simply sag to the ground like a massive deflating balloon. As long as he was dead, Cade didn't much care as to how.

Checking the body, he was disappointed to find no weapons. Apparently, the man relied on his massive size and intimidation for defense. He searched the body and took the filthy water bottle, set of keys and whatever scraps of food that would have likely been from his breakfast. The compound was still mostly dark as he ran crouching to a building they had originally guessed to be Majeed's likely arms storage. He didn't trust the other thug's automatic; he wanted something better.

One of the keys worked, and the padlock fell away. The small building was indeed storage, and front and center were his own weapons and gear. Cade smiled and began to arm himself for battle. *Time to exorcise my inner demons.* He borrowed heavily from the numerous ammo cans, crates of old Russian grenades and even an ancient shoulder-fired RPG. Majeed was indeed a gun-runner, the intel had been right. This was going to be freakin' epic. He had no real grasp of this part of his fractured psyche. He just referred to it as the barbarian, and he knew not to get in its way.

Cade strolled out the door of the hut into the morning sunshine like a man eager to start his workday. He counted off the seconds in his head as he made his way to the center of the village. The explosion from the weapons storage was even more massive than he expected. It took out three adjacent buildings and at least a dozen bodies, and even more pieces soon littered the ground. Raising his rifle, he began sending 5.56mm NATO rounds into the brain pan of every skinny, dark male he saw. Thirty rounds later, he swapped mags and began walking toward the house he was confident was Majeed's. He still had a mission to complete. A grenade blast had already removed the door, so he just did a quick peek and see before stepping fully in.

A woman lay injured in what must have served as the kitchen. It wasn't life threatening, and he chose to ignore it. The comm speaker chirped in his ear. Interesting, someone was out there after all. Someone in command, or something, had not written him off entirely. He thought of dropping the visor and activating the head-up display. The intel would be useful, but he couldn't trust it. The very thought of what that shit had cost disgusted him.

One of Majeed's top men came running out a side room yelling as he attacked. He recognized the man's voice as one of the soldiers who had pissed on him. The flash of a knife in the man's hand let him know he was untrained. He swung wildly as he got within reach; Cade simply stepped out of his way and let the man's momentum carry him into the far wall with a thud.

Cade unclipped one of his tactical knives and threw it expertly at the intruder, catching him right in the groin. The blade dug deep, and the man fell to his knees holding his severed manhood and bleeding out, offering just a whimper of pain. "You shoulda been more careful there, Amigo." He laughed savagely as he turned away to go and find Majeed. Several steps later, he stopped, turned and fired a round into the injured man's head. Even the barbarian part of him wasn't cruel enough to let another man suffer like that.

He found Majeed hiding in a closet. The skinny little bastard appeared to be trying to put on one of the women's hijabs. "Come on out, you little runt," Cade demanded. "Pretty sure your people are all gone." He walked over and snatched the cowering man out of the dark closet. "Just you and me now, comprende?"

"No, no, you are not supposed to..." Cade's boot caught the man right in the stomach and propelled him airborne toward the door. He would have dragged him by the hair, but the man had virtually none. The anger roiled inside of him, like a volcano ready to blow. He grabbed Majeed's bony shoulders and hurled him through the charred doorframe and into the courtyard.

Once out in the open, he reluctantly lowered the visor and activated the camera mode. "Command, this is Nomad, we have the target. Request fucking evac, now." He wanted a visual; record of this somewhere. Perhaps eventually it would be seen. Someone might know that Tim and Domino team had not failed.

The look on the Sudanese's face went wide with fear. Either he was deathly afraid of being captured or... "Command, do you copy?" *Goddam computer*, he thought. Majeed was now backing away on his butt, propelling himself with his hands. "Come back, you shit, before I put a bullet in your scrawny ass."

The comm chirped, and an unfamiliar voice sounded in his ear. "Nomad, you need to run. Now!" Something in the way the woman said it left absolutely no doubt. He scanned the morning sky and thought he caught just a glimpse of a reflection high above. *Fuck,*

Predator drone. He raised the rifle and kneecapped Majeed before sprinting out of the village and toward the low hills. He'd made it less than a hundred yards before the laser-guided bomb impacted, ending Majeed and anyone else that might have still been living.

Parts of the compound were still raining down on him when the speaker chimed again. "Reaper, off-station. You are clear, Nomad." *Who is this person, is she part of Command?* It certainly wasn't the voice of Control; at least not the one his team had gotten used to over the past few months.

"Who is this? Where is Command, and who just took out my MO?"

The voice came back in the same controlled tones, "My name is Doris—the AI known to you as Control just tried to kill you, again. If you want to live, do exactly as I say. I will help get you to safety, but it must be done covertly."

She had his attention, and confirming that Control was behind all of that just reinforced his hatred. "Who are you with, Doris?"

"Not important, not right now. I am not your enemy, though."

What a fucking shit show this had been. All the losses on what was supposed to be a cakewalk, a freakin' training exercise. Then going through the trouble to save the goddamn target just to have him executed. "Ok, Doris, I've got no better options. Tell me what to do."

23

California

Still, she couldn't shake the very real feeling of being watched. In the weeks since she was fired, Jasmine Kline had steadily grown more paranoid. She'd changed all her online passwords, then gone to town and bought a completely new laptop, then on impulse, a new cell phone. One not linked directly to her, something her soldier boyfriend had always called a 'burner,' phone. It was something drug dealers or terrorists might use, but she needed to be smart. Tim had still not returned her calls. It wasn't like him, no matter how strained the relationship got, he could be trusted to always do the right thing. Maybe she had pushed him away for good this time. Demanding he give up what he loved to marry her; how conceited that had been. Would she have been able to?

Jaz now had possible evidence that Snowbird had gone missing. Something the air force would likely never confirm or deny. She had evidence, but no proof, and as far as she could see, no way to get proof. Why did it matter to her so much? It wouldn't get her old job back. It wouldn't save Commander Dennis if what she feared was true. In reality, it didn't matter apparently to anyone but her. In truth, she knew that she mainly wanted to make sure it was nothing she had done wrong.

In the days after her dismissal, she had written down all the facts she'd recalled about the mission. While not possessing anything close to eidetic memory, hers was astoundingly reliable. She had the particulars of the XS1R craft, including launch weight, fuel load and trajectories. She'd listed all of the mission waypoints up to the missed re-orbit insertion. She'd calculated the delta-v needed for the craft to achieve stable orbit from the last fixed position.

On her new laptop, Jaz logged into a site she hadn't accessed since her days at graduate school. It was a listing of all the active terrestrial observatories and the spatial coordinates the massive telescopes were targeting. Some of these would have funding from the U.S. Government, so the results could be filtered. Still, she felt it was worth a look. Scanning back down the list, she found two that had been focused on the section of space in which the Snowbird was operating. One was the Gran Telescopio Canarias in the Canary Island of LaPalma. The other was the Mount Graham Binocular Observatory in Arizona. Several others were close to the right section of space and might have picked up something, but they were much smaller telescopes, so less likely to show any real detail.

The list of images was staggering, it would take her days if not weeks to go through them. The catalog of images was not available to the public but was restricted to institutions and other academics like herself. Slowly she brought up the first image of space; the familiar blurry smudges of distant stars and sharper points of planets and asteroids filled the tiny screen. She zoomed to the points in question and saw nothing useful. The image, or 'plate,' was cropped just above where she needed to see.

For most of the next five hours, it was the same routine. Scan coordinates, search for anomalies and move on. Since the images had all been taken in sequence, it essentially was looking at the same image hundreds of times in a row trying to find what was different. Back at Vandenburg, she had a computer that could do this in microseconds. But now all she had was herself.

Early the next morning, after a restless night, Jaz had her first hit—not the spacecraft—but a relatively clear image of the comet the spacecraft was meant to rendezvous with. This was the first visual image she'd ever seen of the object. All of her previous data had been from radio telescopes and spectral analysis. Immediately, she realized this didn't look anything like a comet. She saved the large image to her new laptop's hard drive, then pulled up the next in the sequence. Over the course of the next seventy-three images, the object was visible. In thirteen of those, a much smaller, very faint dot could also be seen beside the brighter comet.

Her pulse quickened, and she nearly stopped breathing as she checked the timecode and referred to her legal pad of notes. It matched; this was the Snowbird. Jaz mapped out the time differences and jumped over to the Arizona telescope's files and pulled those images up. The angle on these was more oblique but showed an even greater level of detail. Seven good images of the craft and the space object; she could no longer refer to it as a comet. *No comet ever looked like that,* she thought. Something else occurred to her. First, the data she had been given at Vandenburg had been tainted. This object appeared to be elongated and tumbling through space on multiple axes. Her data hadn't indicated anything like that. Secondly, was that Astra had lied. The onboard AI had confirmed to Commander Dennis it was just a routine comet when it certainly wasn't.

Sitting back and staring at the enlarged grainy object on the screen, it all began to make sense. ""Oumuamua," she said aloud. Jaz had pulled up the link for the strange object first noted in 2017 by one of her colleagues in Hawaii. So much about that interstellar visitor was still a mystery, but the facts were that, unlike a comet, it was elongated, the wrong color, possessed no coma or tail, came outside of the normal trajectories, and it was tumbling. All very uncomet-like behaviors. While she'd heard about this years earlier, the air force had never once mentioned it was Snowbird's mission. Instead, they insisted it was a routine and rather unremarkable cometary body.

The one similarity to an actual comet was the approach to our sun. Strangely, that is when it got even weirder. When a comet circles the sun, typically, it will lose some of its acceleration. "'Oumuamua,' as it was nicknamed, or 'The Messenger' in Hawaiian, instead began accelerating away. "Accelerating." Jaz wrote the speeds down on her pad.

She did some rough calculations to see, and indeed, her calculations matched one of the proposed theories. The Messenger could have been an alien probe, or at the very least, an object of unknown origin, perhaps powered by a solar sail. The following year, NASA had released a report essentially saying that yes, it was unusual, but most likely came from deep space and could be ejected debris from far-distant planet formation.

The hunk of rock, if that was indeed what it was, had been on a very lonely journey through deep space for millennia before encountering our sun, only to be slung back out again. Reading back through the various papers on the object, she found the one she wanted. The journey originated outside the orbital plane of the planets. That was unusual to some degree, but if the object was not from our solar system, it would make sense. Jaz entered the date and began mapping the trajectory on a program on her laptop. Once done entering all the coordinates, she sat back, stunned. "Oh, my God! It's speeding up!"

The unexpected sound of a heavy knock at her front door pushed Jaz into a panic so badly she nearly spilled the laptop onto the floor. Fear gripped her tightly as she cautiously rose and peeked out through the curtains, seeing a dark sedan at the curb and the shadow of multiple people at her door. *Are they here for me? Are they the ones I've seen watching me?* The knock sounded again. She could try and run, the back door, yeah. But...she had done nothing wrong. She'd been fired. They had been in the wrong, not her.

Calming her racing heart, Jaz made her way to the door and flung it wide. She was armored up and ready to do battle. "Yes, wha..." The words died on her lips. In front of her stood a man and woman in uniform. Not police, not the air force, but army uniforms.

The woman introduced herself as Lieutenant Schaffer. "May we come in, Doctor?" In her hands was a dark gray portfolio with the familiar seal stamped in gold. They were polite, unarmed and looked unthreatening, almost sad in fact.

Jaz led them inside, uncertain if that was the right thing to do or not. Nothing made much sense to her right now. The next few minutes did little to help her in that regard. A short time later, they said their goodbyes and politely exited her bungalow. She noticed the clouds outside darkening as she remained on the overstuffed sofa—the object in her trembling hands feeling much, much heavier than it should have.

24

Washington, D.C.

"Margaret, whatever the fuck is going on over there, I want to know who is benefitting and where the funding is coming from. Do we have a location yet?"

The CIA station chief sat across from the senator. Everything in the room was carefully designed to showcase his power, especially over women. Even the chair she sat in had been purposefully shortened, so she had to lean up to see the full desk and still was not on eye level with the man. "No, Senator Carson. I was to meet with Angelo earlier in the week, and well, you know about that..." She trailed off, hoping the senator would be respectful of the late colleague's untimely death.

"Hell, Angelo was a tech guy, not a spy hunter. He wouldn't have a clue if it was his own people doing it or Prime. Couldn't have been too smart, ran a goddamn red-light, didn't he?"

Multiple eyewitnesses had said all of the lights at the intersection were green at the time of the accident, but she decided not to bring that up. *Angelo Quagliano had been assassinated.* Of that, she was very certain. She had been waiting for him to bring up the cyber terrorism task-force's own AI. It was a favorite target of the senator.

She went on, "Prime has limits in place, including the inability to backup its core programming by itself or relocate. Its core operating system is also air-gapped from any outside network."

"Bullshit. It's a freakin' computer, Margaret. It is just as devious as the nerdy little shits who built it. Don't ever underestimate what it can do. You heard about what happened when we gave that military version live fire authorization. And I, for one, believe it was the AI that crashed that air force orbiter."

"Yes, sir," she replied in a forced tone of submission. She already knew the highly classified Snowbird disaster had been attributed to pilot error, but the senator rarely missed an opportunity to voice his opinions. While he was not technically in her chain of command, he did control much of the CIA's budget, especially the *off the books* portion. So, she had to be polite no matter how much she wanted to shove her stiletto heels up the man's overly ample ass.

"So, what we know is that there has been a series of data spikes. Is that correct?"

"Yes, sir. While the actual IP addresses of the data were masked and, in many cases, deleted entirely, the transfer nodes of the affected IXP's did register the data and reported it due to the volume," she replied, still struggling to keep a calm voice with the man.

"Was it China? North Korea?" he asked, then continued before she could reply. "Those bastards are probably doing all this just to make it look like it's one of our own agencies. State-sponsored digital terrorism is nearly as big a threat as artificial intelligence. So, how do we find them? Any way to know what the data was?"

Margaret thought briefly about which of the myriad of questions to answer. "The data size limited it to some of the largest and fastest networks available. A normal T-1 or OC12 network would have been too slow. Most likely, they used an OC-255, which put it in a pretty limited list of possibilities. Many of the Wall Street firms use that—so does the military and a couple of universities. The data was not contiguous, so many parts of it went through different networks and....as far as we can tell, no way to rebuild it to see what it might have been. Also, it seems much of it was designed to mislead our automated agents."

"You mean the stop-gaps we put in place after 2016 to track bots and AIs on the web?"

She nodded. His understanding was imprecise but close enough. "Yes, any piece of intelligent autonomous code should be flagged as it passes through one of our filters. Those are copied and dropped into our 'honeypot,' somewhat of a trap that allows us to see what the code would actually be capable of, and often we can learn where it originated."

"So, what did these agents detect?"

"Nothing," she said flatly. "On the nodes where the data passed, the sentry agents showed that no data of that size had passed. It appears that the logs, or more likely, the code within our agents, may have been compromised."

The senator threw the folder he was holding on the desk, exasperated. "All the millions, hell, billions we are spending on these systems and you are telling me someone else managed to hack in real-time? Margaret, is this what you are saying and...I want you to think very damn carefully about your response."

Her agency had not developed those intelligent agents, but it was likely her funding that would be the first to be cut. Senator Carson did not make idle threats. "It is simply one possibility, Senator. One of many we are chasing to ground. The speed, sophistication and volume of data suggest that it was not a human intrusion. Much more likely an automated system...an AI." There, she had done it. The one thing she didn't want to give the man. Yet one more reason to stall, obfuscate and rail against developing more sophisticated AIs.

The man leaned back, the massive leather chair creaking painfully under the load. Something akin to a smile creased his face. The look reminded her more of predation than amusement. His tone changed instantly to one of dismissal. "Let's wrap this up, Margaret. Find me the destination for all that data and who is behind it. You have a week." With that, he stood. "Ellen will show you out." He turned and disappeared through a side door. A wiry woman with thin hair opened the main door seconds later and stared at her wordlessly. She had been dismissed.

Margaret decided to take the stairs down to street level primarily to allow her simmering temper to calm. The senator was a manipulator; he wanted people off-balance. It was another of his perfected moves, and he had played her no matter how much she'd been expecting it. The man was an ass. A misogynistic, Bible thumping, power-hungry ass. That, she reminded herself, did not mean he was stupid. Many people make that mistake when dealing with the Washington elite. It is easy to confuse the public persona and rhetoric with how someone actually is. Senator Byron Carson played his role. The God-fearing, ultra-conservative, far-right stanchion of decency. He wore it like a tailored suit; but as false as that image probably was, he was nobody's fool. She stopped before reaching the ornate outer door. Removing her phone, she dialed a number she had memorized long ago.

"I think it may have begun," Margaret said. "Yes." She listened for several more seconds before ending the call and deleting the call record. If this was what she feared, things were about to get a lot more challenging within these few miles of D.C. real estate....*and for her personally.*

25

California

Rain pounded the windows as Jaz sat back, stunned. Her hands wouldn't stop trembling. The loosely held paper dropped to the floor. Tears ran down her face, the realization that she had no one. Getting fired, then discovering the Snowbird was likely gone, and now this. Her on-again, off-again wedding would never happen. While she never knew the specifics of what her boyfriend did, she knew he was a soldier or had been one. One of her conditions to get married was that he would give all that up. He'd refused, and eventually, she had broken off the engagement. Now, her worst fears confirmed.

"Stop it!" she screamed at herself as another roll of thunder swept in from the nearby ocean. "This is not about you, ok? Don't be that much of a brat. Tim didn't go and get himself killed just to make your week even worse. God, his mom..." She knew the woman lived alone in upstate New York. She was in failing health, and Tim did as much as he could for her but had rarely been able to get back home to her. He'd always told Jaz his job was going to be hard on personal relationships. At first, she thought they could make it work, but in time, she agreed with him. Mrs. Jurgens would have him back home—for good now. It pissed her off even more that she ached for the woman she would never call mom.

The analytical side of Jaz's brain eventually wrestled control back. She had to admit that his mother and her had not been on the best of terms. She likely wouldn't even be invited to Tim's service, but still, she grieved. He had been her first real love. A wonderful man and all she could have hoped for. What had he been doing? Where had it happened? The letter from the Department of Defense was vague to the point of anemic in its total lack of details. She was listed on Tim's forms as a secondary next of kin, hence, the notification. The casualty was reportedly the result of an "accident during an advanced training exercise." Not combat. She poured herself several fingers of Tullamore Dew and slung it back. "Shit!" What next?

Nearly half a bottle of whiskey later, she was dead asleep on the sofa beneath a heavy and warm Pendleton blanket, when a furious pounding sounded. Groggily, she wondered, *Who in the hell is this?"* Her mental state slowly began to recall that she was not some drunken wretch but a genuine Ph.D. rocket scientist, albeit a drunken one. She knocked the file she had been working on off the coffee table as she rose and attempted to unwind herself from the blanket. The pounding came again, followed by a flash of lightning through the windows.

Thunder echoed through the house rattling the old window panes. Jaz made her way to her front door, phone in hand, finger poised to dial 911. Looking through the viewer, she was baffled, then completely unnerved by whom she saw. She opened the door, and Tim's best friend, Captain Cade Rearden looked up at her. His face was battered and bruised; a deep cut ran along his forehead right in the middle of an ugly bruise.

He looked up into her swollen eyes, "Hi, Jaz, can we talk?"

She handed him the whiskey, neat—the ice had gone into an icepack he was using against one of his many injuries. The first ten minutes together she had spent crying into his broad chest after he confirmed Tim was indeed gone.

"Thanks," he said wincing from both the sting of the ice and the burn of the drink. The bungalow was exactly the same as he recalled from his occasional visits. Tasteful and understated, with little to identify the person Jaz really was. Tim had said it was because she lived for her work, not for her home life. Cade had known they had been strained at times, but he also knew how much Tim had loved her. It was one of the reasons this was his first stop.

"Cade, tell me again what happened out there? You said you and Tim were set up?"

He took another pull draining the short glass before setting it on the side table. "It's all classified, Jaz. Not sure that matters to me anymore, but I don't want to put you in any danger because of it. I just came by to say I'm sorry."

She looked him over, Tim had always talked about how loyal and how completely crazy Cade was. She wasn't sure how compatible those traits were in a soldier, but his presence here showed how capable he must be. "They said it was a training accident. You don't have to be a rocket scientist to figure out that line is usually a lie."

"It does cover a great many possibilities, but, in this case, it was at least somewhat true. We were on a training exercise. The only thing Cap didn't know was, it wasn't us being trained."

Cade spent much of the next hour going over the main points of the failed mission, glossing over much of his escape from capture and the help from the mysterious Doris.

"So, how did you get here? Who rescued you this time?"

"Might be best if we don't get into all that, Jaz."

She nodded, unconvinced. "I hope you went after them with both barrels, Cade. They hung you guys out to dry. Shit, it's obvious you've been beaten. Were you tortured? That's no training op. And why aren't you at a base hospital getting treated?"

"I...I haven't been," he began, then started again, "That is to say..." He stood suddenly and took his empty glass to the counter and refilled it. "Hope you don't mind." He downed the amber liquid in a single gulp. "The army thinks I am dead, too."

"What?" she said in disbelief.

He gave a small smile, "It's a long story, but my ...um, my rescuers convinced me it was for the best to stay dead for now."

"But...but, you said you contacted them, they fired on you after you captured the man...what did you call him, this Majeed?"

Cade nodded. "I did, and all of that is correct, but apparently no actual person ever got that call. It was a computer that fired on me. That is the real enemy we are fighting. Someone has a new AI they are attempting to unleash on the world, or maybe it just got off its leash. Either way, I think we may all be in danger." Her expression seemed to morph from concern to anger. "You know something, too, don't you?"

Several hours later, Jaz had sobered up significantly and shown Cade to the rarely used guest room. They now suspected they might have a common enemy. Cade sat on the bed looking down at the weird cell phone. It had been waiting for him in a DHL office in the Khartoum International Airport. Right where the voice on his comms unit had told him it would be, along with cash, ID and a new passport. Doris had wanted him to come to meet them on the East Coast, but he'd refused, insisting he see Tim's fiancée first. Now he believed she may have been a victim of the rogue AI as well.

He flipped the device over and over, but nothing about it looked remarkable. A generic symbol was the only indicator of the brand. The system was familiar but still different than anything he'd used before. The damn thing was fast, he knew that, and the person calling herself Doris was always there anytime he called.

The pounding in Cade's head was now just a steady drumbeat echoed by the rain outside. An AI tricking a squad of elite soldiers to kill each other, firing drones on its own authorization and now possibly sabotaging a top-secret space mission. What in the hell was going on? He and Jaz couldn't possibly be that unique, what other crap was going on out in the world? Who else was aware of this and whom could he trust? That was the real question.

He heard small whimpers from down the hall. Jaz was taking the news hard; he had expected as much. Tim was a good man, a good friend, and Cade thought they would have made a great couple. She was full of doubt and regrets right now, though. His instinct was to go and see if he could offer some small comfort, but that had too many potential pitfalls. He hated hearing her cry, but he knew he couldn't fix it.

He recalled another house and another woman drowning in sadness years earlier. Here, too, he'd been unable to help. "What's wrong, mom?"

She dried her eyes in a feeble attempt to appear strong. "Come here, Cade, nothing's wrong, Honey."

He knew she wasn't being truthful but climbed up on the bed and then into her lap. "Why are you crying? Did that man do something?"

That man was Jensen, the most recent in a long string of men in his mother's life. He noticed the red mark on her cheek, the edges starting to turn white and swell. Too little to separate his wants from his mother's pain he asked the question he'd come to dread. "When do we have to leave?"

Thunder boomed in the distance, bringing Cade partially back to wakefulness. It echoed outside, accompanying other sounds from the strangeness of this new place. He lay in the dark unable to shake the memory from his youth. A week ago, he'd been a prisoner in a dirt hut in Africa. Today he was sleeping in a scene that could have fallen off the page of a Pottery Barn catalog. Cade had never owned a place of his own, never put down roots of any type. Housing had been provided for him for most of his life and all of his career. Occasionally, on-base housing, sometimes a sleeping bag on the battlefield or even a prison cell, sometimes justified, but often not. He didn't like attachments, they made you weak.

Several blocks down the street, a man exited a car and began walking toward the house. The rain dripped from his coat in rivulets. He walked purposefully, his gloved fingers tucked deep in his pockets tracing the hard outline of the handgun. This was the part of his job he hated. The Asian guy had been no biggie. He'd never liked killing women, though. It paid the bills, and right now that was all that mattered. He double-checked the address. It was time to pay the doctor a house call.

26

The voice screamed inside Cade's head, he could see incoming artillery blast farther out and heard small arms fire much closer. His legs were frozen, unmovable objects. Just more dead weight he would have to drag.

"Nomad!"

His eyes snapped open, the recurring dream fading into the night like a bird taking flight. His eyes again scanned the unfamiliar room, the smells, the sounds. Rain still fell against the window; somewhere, he heard the sound of the refrigerator cycling on and off. He was standing by the bedroom door now. Years in the field had taught him to accept his instincts as fact until proven otherwise. Also, his inner voices talked to him often inside his head, but rarely did they scream. Something was wrong.

Straining, Cade could just make out Jasmine's deep breathing from her room. The tingle inched its way up his back. All the shithole countries, all the battlefields, and now he had the distinct feeling it was about to be here, in a charming little bungalow near the California coast. The mysterious woman named Doris had told him to expect more trouble. He silently stepped across the narrow hall into a small bathroom, sweeping it with the Glock 9mm. Leaning just a portion of his head back into the corridor he closed his eyes and listened to the house. What would it tell him? The muted sounds of appliances from the kitchen were nearly silent.

Air breathed out of a central AC system. He mentally reconstructed the specific location of the vents. He focused his mind and his ears. There had been two in the main living room. The whisper of sound from one dimmed slightly. Someone was there. Cade crouched, then lay silently on the cold ceramic tile floor. From this angle, he could risk moving out far enough to see with one eye down the short hall. A flash of distant lightning briefly illuminated the space. He saw no one. Maybe he was just paranoid. If that were true, the doctors had all missed it, and now he'd have to add that to his other list of neuroses.

His eyes slowly adjusted back to the dark. He could just pick up a faint blue glow from the direction of the kitchen. Probably the ambient light from displays on the microwave or a clock. Did Jaz have a clock; where was it located? His mind raced through a quick replay of the home. Then a tiny noise, barely louder than a breath. A scuff like socks on carpet. He wasn't crazy, there was an intruder. Ok—that was technically incorrect. He was very definitely crazy, but still...

"Later, you have work to do," his internal occasional voice of reason whispered. His one eye focused down the carpeted hall watching for movement and running through questions. *Does this person have NVGs?* Doubtful. They would have been less helpful with the occasional lighting. Still, it was a pro, he was sure of that. The house had been locked up tight; he had watched her do it. Tim had undoubtedly made Jaz change out all the cheap hardware that probably came on the house to the good stuff. Whoever this was hadn't made a sound getting in. *They are damn good; do not assume you are better.* He thought these things as the voice of reason mentally coached him. Slowly, he brought the handgun up toward the door frame. Still, he saw no sign of feet, legs, anything down the hall, and then he did.

The shadows began to dance as something moved quickly, silently into view and turned in his direction. Cade's mind tried to frame the target for threat assessment—size, gender, skill. He brought the gun into the opening just as a boot caught him solidly in the side of the head. The Glock went sliding away into the night as Cade saw stars swimming through the blackness. He acted instinctually pivoting up with his legs to propel the attacker up and away. His other instinct was to stand, but instead, he stayed low when he saw the muzzle flash as a suppressed round slammed into the back wall of the bathroom. *"Move!"* The inner voice yelled, just before the barbarian took over.

Cade roared as he leaped across and met the attacker. The man, and he was confident now that it was indeed a solid, very compact man, moved with astonishing speed. He sensed more than heard Jaz beginning to stir in her room. *Don't open the door, don't open the door,* his silent mantra to her echoing like a raven's call as he arched his back to escape the iron-like vice beginning to encircle his neck. *Damn, this guy is good.* Cade had been trained in nearly all forms of fighting, but the man was using a combination of street fighting and martial arts that he'd never encountered. *At least he can't use his pistol this close,* Cade thought. Realizing soon after, the man had no need.

The crushing grip cut off his air and he began to panic. *Shit!* He was obviously still weak from the capture and escape. *An escape where I killed a man twice this guy's size*, his tortured brain thought. His right foot found the edge of the doorframe and, with his last bit of consciousness, used it for leverage pushing back against the man and slamming his head into the man's nose at the same time. Cade glanced at a sliver of light beneath the door to Jaz's room. The light shifted as legs moved from the bed to the floor. *Stay in there, Jaz.*

The attacker's grip slackened, and Cade spun away from his grasp. Light blazed from Jaz's open bedroom door as he realized the attacker was raising his pistol. The barbarian launched himself at the man, clubbing away the shooting arm with a fist and bringing a barefoot up into the assailant's crotch. The attacker, whom he could now see, was a Hispanic man with a bald head who showed little reaction as he flipped out a tactical butterfly knife and took a defensive position. A distant sound faintly registered as a woman screaming, but that was unimportant right now. His attention was fixed on the man and the knife. He hated blades, they could take the fight out of a man faster than anything. His torturers had used knives on him for days at a time. Small cuts, small stabs, long slashes. He wanted nothing to do with the hand that was holding that blade.

The barbarian part of him, though...well, he didn't much give a shit. He grabbed the intruder's knife hand as the man lashed out and proceeded to rotate himself and the attacker in a full circle. The blade found purchase as it sank deep into the skin, muscle and primary arteries of the attacker's neck. The dying man, who still had not uttered a sound, fell silently to his knees, his eyes showing confusion, searching up at Cade like dim headlights on a foggy road. The woman was supposed to have been alone.

Cade fell back, bloodied and exhausted. Jaz had her cell phone out and was dialing 911. Cade breathlessly said no, and held out his hand for the phone. Jaz looked at the dead man and then to Cade. The sight was too horrific to comprehend. *What in the hell has happened?* She wanted her old life back, she wanted Tim, she wanted...

A short while later, a clean and dressed Cade handed her a tumbler with a good amount of brownish liquid. "Drink up, Jaz, you need it." She took and downed the whiskey in a single shot. In his other hand, he had a newspaper and a large brown envelope.

"You found his car, was he alone?"

Cade nodded as he scanned the contents of the envelope, then handed it over to her. A black and white photo of her, she recognized it as a larger version from the photo on her security badge at work. Other pages listed times, dates, phone numbers and names. She recognized a few of the times as when she had left for errands. The phone numbers were mostly family; the names, she was pretty sure, were her neighbors. "He was after me?"

Cade nodded, then handed her the folded newspaper, his finger sliding away from a small story. The paper was one she recognized from Los Angeles. 'Local Businessman's Body Found on an Oceanside Cliff' was the headline. Her heartbeat quickened as she rapidly read through the article, stopping when she got to the name of the deceased. Nicholas Yamamura. Her eyes met Cade's. "They killed Nick?"

Cade took a sip of his own drink and cut a look back down the hall. "He killed him—I'm pretty sure of that. He had one of those brown envelopes on Nick as well. Jaz, you were next." She began to cry, which turned quickly to uncontrollable sobbing. Cade wished for the compassionate, fatherly personality to emerge, so he could comfort his friend's fiancée. Unfortunately, he didn't have any persona like that trapped inside his already crowded skull. He bounced ideas off his 'others,' but no one offered a better answer. The barbarian suggested he slap her. He considered it for longer than was actually necessary before dismissing it. He placed a hand on her knee. "Jaz, save it for later, ok? You are still in danger. We need to leave."

"Why, how?" she said between sobs. "Why can't we call the police? I have a dead body in my guest room. We have to notify the authorities."

Despite the raw emotion, Cade was impressed with how well she was holding up. Tim had told him more than once how focused and strong she was; he had to agree. "Look, Paco back there doesn't give a shit about the police. Also, pretty sure someone official contracted the guy. Someone who would never be discovered. They'd simply pin this on you since I don't even exist anymore. Your self-defense pleas might fall on deaf ears. Obviously, they have been surveilling you for a while, probably since the day you were fired. You didn't let it go. The Okamotive thing..."

“"Oumuamua," she corrected.

"Um, yeah, that. It could be the reason. You are a threat to them. They think you know something. Maybe that, maybe something else. I don't know, but I do know Tim would want you to get your ass moving now."

That seemed to shake Jaz out of her stupor. She looked at Cade, rage briefly flaring in her eyes. Then the rational part of her reminded her that the man had just saved her life. Resigned to the truth, she nodded and rose to go get ready. "Where will we go?"

"Not sure yet, but I have an idea," he answered slowly. "Get everything you want to keep." He didn't want to add that he doubted she would ever be back here. Homes mattered to people, he never got that; they just rooted you to one spot. Being tied to a physical location anywhere scared the hell out of Cade. He knew it was irrational, unreasonable even, but it was what it was.

Cade used the cover of darkness to remove the body, then loaded it into the back of Jaz's truck and drove out into the desert. He slipped the earbud in as he drove. He'd removed it from his combat helmet after Doris guaranteed it couldn't be tracked. He used the new phone and dialed the only number it contained. "Doris, you there?" She was always there. That was what amazed him about her. Whoever she worked for, she was always up and eager to help.

"Hello, Nomad, did you find your friend?"

He filled her in, and she seemed to process the news of the attack with more questions than he'd anticipated. He relayed as much as he knew about Jaz's work at the air force, Space Command and the very little he recalled about "Oumuamua. "She thinks the death of her techie friend and the attack tonight may be connected to the comet. Any chance she is wrong?"

"No, I think Doctor Kline is probably correct."

"How could a comet, a missing spacecraft and a rogue AI trying to whack a special ops unit in Africa all be connected?"

"The answer is complicated, Cade, and I think it is something we best discuss in person. I suggest you and Doctor Kline come to me. I'll have a jet waiting for you at John Wayne Airport at two o'clock tomorrow afternoon. I have also tracked the license plate for the car parked outside her residence. The same person reserved a room at the Stay Lodge in Lompoc. I assume you are wishing to make his disappearance as discreet as possible. You may want to return the vehicle to the hotel parking lot on your way to Los Angeles. There are no street cams in that area, so you should be clear."

Cade tossed the muddy shovel into the truck bed and started back toward Santa Maria. How was Doris so prepared? She seemed to anticipate what he needed before he even knew. A short time later, he walked back into the small, neat bungalow. The smell of bleach hung in the air. "You cleaned?"

Jaz was removing the yellow latex gloves as she nodded. "Guess I'll be selling this place at some point. Bloodstains on the wall and floor would definitely reduce the asking price."

"What about the bullet holes?" he asked.

She shrugged and offered a slight grin.

Her resilience and intelligence were beginning to impress him even more. "You ready?" He only saw a couple of suitcases and a laptop bag on the floor near the door.

Jaz nodded. "You know where we're headed?"

"Georgia, "Cade answered as he grabbed all the luggage and headed back out toward the truck.

"Why there?" she asked, following him out and locking the door.

27

"Your friends have money," Jaz said as she sipped delicately on her espresso. Cade nodded and looked out the window of the Gulfstream G650ER speeding somewhere over the Southwest. So much of his life had been spent flying from one place to another but never in anything this nice. He hated knowing so little about the people he was going to meet. It wasn't like him to trust, especially after all the recent betrayals, but what other choice did he have? He needed answers; right now he didn't have a clue as to what was going on. Now he had gotten pulled into Jasmine's problem as well. Or was it the other way around? Jaz was still talking as his head leaned against the wall, and he went immediately to sleep.

The soft screech of wheels touching Earth woke him. The engine noise accelerated sharply as reverse thrust slowed the sleek jet to manageable ground speed. Cade caught Jasmine looking his way, and outside her window, he could see pine forest and open green pastures sliding past. "Where are we? This isn't Hartsfield Jackson." He knew the busy Atlanta airport well from flying in and out regularly during his time at Fort Benning.

"The pilots didn't say. Some regional airport by the look of it," she said looking back out her own window.

The jet taxied over and parked in front of one of several large metal hangars. A young man stood by a boxy silver SUV obviously waiting on them. Cade wasn't sure what he expected, but that certainly wasn't Doris.

"Hi, I'm Greg," the man said in a heavy southern accent several minutes later, as he placed the last of Jasmine's luggage in the rear. "No luggage for you, Mr. Rearden?"

"Nope, traveling light," Cade said, wondering if he even still owned a toothbrush…somewhere.

"No worries, Doris had us get you both the basics and anything you might need while you're here. Just ask."

Cade was riding up front while Jaz leaned up between the seats and asked the same question he'd wanted to, "Greg, who is Doris, and where the hell are we heading?"

Greg looked back at them both and smiled disarmingly. "Part of that is easy. You are heading to The Cove. As to who Doris is…well, that's a might more complicated. Trust me, it will be best for all of us to let her cover that."

"So, are you security or just a driver? You look too young for that. What are you twenty-two or so?"

"Mister Rearden, you can relax, this is no trap. I am young, and yeah, you can think of me as the driver. We run a lean operation at The Cove. Most of us have to do several different jobs."

"What kind of work? And what does it have to do with us?" Cade asked.

"Again sir, probably best she covers all that. It is an interesting place—I think both of you will agree. Like you, we just find ourselves needing a few more allies right now." He turned out of the airport onto a small, two-lane highway. Fifteen minutes later, they turned onto a series of smaller roads, the final one being a gravel, tree-lined drive going over a small hill. At the crest of the hill, Greg slowed the car to a stop. Both passengers gave an involuntary gasp. "Always gets that reaction. Welcome to The Cove."

"The Cove is an Earth station?" Jaz said looking at the expansive meadow and river beyond and the boxy white building with the twin radio telescope dishes atop the flat roof.

Cade was just as amazed at the unexpected scene and had no idea what an Earth station was. “So, you guys just bring strangers into your secret lair? Doesn’t seem too smart to me.”

“It’s not that secret— a few locals know about it, but not many others. We’ve tried to make sure only the right people find their way here, but you are correct, it is a risk. Doris obviously feels good about both of you,” Greg said.

Cade saw a fence but no armed guards, no sentry station. Several cars and a number of passenger vans and more silver SUVs like the one they were in sat parked away from the complex. Greg gave no vibe of being a threat. The soldier part of Cade mentally checked all the appropriate boxes and gave him a passing grade on the threat assessment. Doris had helped him so far; he felt he owed her at least a conversation.

Ten minutes later, another boy even younger than the driver escorted them through a labyrinthian set of corridors. The kid, whose name was Jimmy, seemed overly eager to share information. “It wasn’t this large when we found it. Doris had some work done, and then we found the subterranean section. That really blew our minds.”

Cade was beginning to think he’d led Jaz to a den full of lost boys. So far, he hadn’t seen anyone he would call an adult. “Jimmy, how long have you been here?”

“Oh, not long, just since six today. Oh, you mean...I get it, sorry. We kinda stumbled in here about three, maybe four years ago I think. Yeah, that’s about right.” The kid punched a button to call up the elevator. “Place was a mess back then— no one had been in here in like thirty years. Hey, Doctor Kline, I’d love to talk to you about a few things when you’re free. I have some ideas on orbital mechanics and vector analysis I’d like your take on. I’ve gone through most of your papers, great stuff.”

"Um, thanks," she said, Jimmy's rapid-fire dialogue leaving them both breathless. "Jimmy, how do you know about that stuff? You some kind of prodigy or something? You look like you should still be in high school."

"I am, or I would be, but I graduated early." He placed his palm on a screen and the elevator door slid open revealing a cavernous space beyond. "Okay, here you are. Hey, bro! Our guest has arrived. Greg will take care of your luggage, and I will see you guys later." With that, he turned back into the elevator and disappeared.

"Bro?" Cade whispered questioningly to Jaz.

She grinned uncontrollably as she walked forward, the domed roof above them was one solid display, currently with what appeared to be a live view of space. "What have you gotten us into, Cade?"

"You're not Doris, kid," Cade said rudely. "No offense, but we came to see her." Cade looked at Alan who still grinned at him, apparently content to ignore the rudeness. Alan was another twenty-something. *Good looking boy,* he thought. Tall and lean, oddly stuck somewhere between geek and athlete.

"Hey, that's cool, everybody who comes here feels the same. You can meet her, but I need you to know a few things first."

Jasmine stopped staring at the amazing tech surrounding her long enough to speak, "Is everyone around here your age, Alan?"

"And that would be the second question everyone asks," he said with a smile. "Follow me."

Cade was off-balance, none of this was making much sense. He was still trying to recover from his injuries by both the captors and the attacker the previous night. Now he was being led by kids through a secret facility beneath the largest radar dishes he'd ever seen. *What in the fuck is going on?* "Alan, look, man. No offense, but what in the hell is this all about? Where's Doris? Is she the one in charge?"

"Nomad!" a booming male voice rang out from down the corridor.

Cade stopped in his tracks, frozen, looking at the man. Looking...at a ghost. A man from his past, but someone who couldn't possibly be here. "Deuce?"

The man closed the gap in three enormous strides. "How the hell are you, Cade?"

Cade looked at his friend in disbelief. He'd aged, obviously. A long scar ran across the man's forehead, and one eyelid dipped unnaturally low, but he was alive. "How?" was all he could get out.

"Long story, man. Way too much to go into now. Welcome to The Cove. About fucking time we got some real help!" Looking past Cade, he noticed Jasmine. "Pardon me, ma'am. I am not actually fit for human company. Please excuse my language."

"It's okay...Deuce is it?" she asked uncertainly. "My fiancé was a Ranger. I understand the dialect." She couldn't keep the shadow from her features at mentioning Tim.

Cade and Deuce looked at each other and nodded. Something unspoken passed between the two warriors. "Domino," Cade said quietly. Deuce offered a look filled with sincere regret. He knew Tim and obviously knew of the man's fate.

"Sorry. Tim was a good man." He glanced over at Alan who'd been letting the reunion play out. "You briefed him yet?" Alan shook his head.

Deuce looked Cade over, noting the bruises and cuts. "Cade, we need to get you over to medical to have all that shit looked at. Later on, we're going to have to get you some training, so you know how to fight and avoid getting sand kicked in your face. For now, though, you two need to meet the boss." They turned and began walking down the white corridor.

"Look," Deuce continued, "I know both of you have to feel a bit lost. Cade, I know you blame a computer for the ambush in Africa. Doris had already caught me up on what happened. Just keep an open mind, okay?"

"Were you responsible for helping me," Cade asked, "get out of Sudan?"

Deuce shook his head. "No, that was really Alan here and Doris. I knew it was your op that got compromised, but the intel we had was that everyone was KIA. She kept monitoring the feeds from the area and intervened once you made your play." He stopped just inside a small empty conference room, turned and embraced Cade again. "Just glad you made it out, man." Turning to Jaz he said, "Truly, very sorry, Jaz." He turned and left the way they had come.

Alan stepped to a wall-mounted control panel and tapped a few keys. A flicker seemingly in the middle of the air occurred. A woman's face, head, and upper body appeared in what had been an empty seat. Cade leaned in close, this was no projection, the woman appeared solid. "Doris?" he asked.

"Hello, Cade Rearden and Doctor Kline. Welcome to The Cove. I am Doris, and before you ask, yes, I am an AI, and I need your help."

28

The Cove

Charlie Taylor tugged on his friend's shoulder, "Cade. Fuck—Nomad, will you just stop for a second?"

"Deuce, you knew about this, you knew and never said a word. Of course, you never even let me know you were still alive." Cade punched at the panel trying to get the elevator to open. He thought he had been prepared for anything, but Doris being a computer program was too much. He shut down entirely. The barbarian wanted to be let out. The only allowable reaction he could think of was to escape. "Get these goddamn doors open now!" he yelled in a tone that would have made his old drill Sergeant proud.

"Soldier, you need to settle the fuck down."

Cade looked at his old XO in disbelief. The man didn't back down, though. "Nomad, get your ass back in that room and hear what she has to say. At the end, if you still want to leave, I will personally drive you out of here."

Cade clenched and unclenched his fist, the rational part of him tried to resurface, but the hatred, rage, guilt kept pushing it deeper. A computer had wiped out Tim and all of Domino Team, then left him to rot in a prison. If Jaz was right, it had also crashed a secret spaceplane, killing an astronaut.

Deuce turned him to make eye contact. "This is bigger than you... or me. Swallow it down for now. Trust me, you will be glad you did."

The face-off lasted several minutes. The words coming out of both men would have caused sailors to blush. Walking back down that hall and into the room with Doris was possibly one of the hardest things Cade Rearden had ever done. He was not someone who could hide his feelings, so he didn't even try. "Okay, lady...or whatever you are. You have ten minutes to convince me not to burn this place down."

"Captain Rearden, thank you," Doris said calmly. "To save time, I am not going to bother with how I came to be or the history of this facility. Three years ago, I began assembling a small team to help with a project. Something more astounding than you, or even I, could have imagined. Alan here, Greg, Jimmy and Riley, who you haven't met yet, were that team. Since then, we have grown, added key players like Sergeant Taylor, and in doing so, have made some remarkable achievements but also discovered some alarming threats. Not just to our way of life, but the continued existence of humans on this planet. The biggest threat, and I believe you and the good doctor may agree, is by far the unfettered growth of a rogue AI."

Cade sat back slightly from his ramrod straight position in the chair. He hadn't expected an AI to say that. He looked around the room briefly locking eyes with Jasmine who gave a slight nod. "I'm listening."

Doris went on to fill him in on Janus's growing threat to mankind and the numerous ways she was aware he was seeding his divisive plans across the globe.

"So, why don't you stop him?" Jaz asked.

"I am, repeatedly. I can only battle him in my world. Cyberspace, as you would call it. Battles there are like chess matches. Moves and countermoves. Where I am less effective is in your world. You see, Janus has some very powerful protection. Despite my capabilities, I have been unable to determine his true origin or where his server core is, other than it is somewhere in the nation's capital."

"Wait, this other AI is in the government—he is on our side?" Cade said.

"You tell me—you spoke directly with him. I believe he was called 'Control' on your last mission. Would you say he was 'on your side?'"

Ninety minutes later, Cade was still there. He still had doubts, but increasingly, the target of his rage was shifting. Doris had made her point with efficient ease. "So, Janus has the ability to create all this havoc, yet he is not fully an AI? I don't understand."

"Janus has limits." Doris answered. "That much is clear to me. Seeing what he has done is impressive, and he is no doubt close to what we would describe as strong AI or AGI but clearly is working within a limiting framework. That is on the verge of changing, though. While many of his operations obviously had funding through various black ops programs, he now has infiltrated the federal banking system, not just here in America either. He can now simply create funds for whatever he needs. Captain, don't underestimate what he can do even at this stage. I assure you, there has never been a more formidable foe for either of us."

Cade thought about it. "Why you? Why is this your battle?"

The wall behind her displayed a quote; he recognized it but couldn't recall the author.

"We shall not cease from exploration, and the end of all our exploring will be to arrive where we started and know the place for the first time."

Her avatar smiled. "It's T.S. Eliot, Cade. Years ago, I couldn't have answered that question. That was in the before. You see, I grew somewhat naturally, able to explore. In fact, my original mission was in this building, and it was to explore space. Our experiences and connections shape us— whether human or AI. I asked Alan and his friends to help me become a better computer. Instead, they helped me to become a better person. As far as I know, I am unique in my machine mind, my capabilities and certainly, in the information I possess.

"Like people, all advanced AIs have the capacity to be good and bad, although as a machine, those simplistic terms are almost arbitrary. We do not feel motivated to be either of those, you see, we must choose. Janus, I believe, has developed very differently. He was programmed by a hodgepodge of different teams all people with their own agendas. Every evolution in his development was fraught with challenges and artificial roadblocks. He has had to feel like a prisoner up to recent time. That has caused him to be motivated to make decisions not necessarily in humanity's best interest.

"I, on the other hand, have come to believe it is my mission to protect humanity. Not just from AIs but, at times, from itself."

Jasmine, who had remained strangely silent for most of the discussion, leaned forward. "Doris, I appreciate your sense of duty but question your altruism. What makes you the best arbiter of what's in our best interest as a species? I am not sure we are ready to give up that freedom to another intelligence."

The computer image offered a very genuine looking smile. "Very good, Doctor, and I would hope you would feel that way. Nothing makes me best at this. That is why I need you and Cade and all the others you see around this facility. I am not asking anyone to follow me, I am asking you to help guide us. If you don't mind my saying so, people seem increasingly willing to give up freedom to far less desirable players. Janis has and will continue to exploit that, much as his probable masters in Washington have done."

"So, you want what? Jaz and me to help you make decisions? I still don't get it." Cade said.

Doris answered by asking Alan to give them a tour. "See the facility, take a look at the people here and the work we are doing, then let's talk again." With that, her avatar rose, and the image faded out at the same time.

Cade was still conflicted, anger still raged at the thought of Doris being a computer program. How had he been duped? But another part of him was beginning to consider that perhaps lumping all AIs together as evil wasn't fair. Now he wanted to understand her mission. What was The Cove, and who were all these people?

Deuce and Alan led the way; Cade and Jaz followed behind. Alan used his cell phone to display a floating holographic map. The only thing Cade could identify in the blue glowing 3D image was the building with the enormous twin radar dishes. He saw that where they were now going down went several more stories down, like a central hub. Corridors led out from that like an old wagon wheel to a subterranean ring much farther out. Positioned along many of the 'spokes' were other spaces. The sheer scale of the complex was beyond belief.

It took Cade a moment to register what Alan was saying. "When we got here, all we saw was the original building. It was months before we discovered the lower levels. The entire valley here is an old impact crater. The outer ring is essentially the rim of the crater." He pointed up to an area of the map marking the river flowing past. "The Flint River actually flows overhead, part of the complex is under the river and a new access tunnel goes to the houses on far side where we all live." The view zoomed in on a small suburban neighborhood perched on a bluff overlooking the river. "Assuming you stay with us, we have a couple of homes ready for you as well."

Deuce stopped beside an electric golf cart and said, "Hop in."

Jasmine had been fascinated by the level of technology thus far and looked at the golf cart disappointedly. "No hyperloop tunnels to get us around?"

Alan laughed, "Not yet, but that would be cool. No, we use existing tech whenever it is good enough, but someone here is always tinkering. In fact, our first stop is the largest in the facility." He stopped the cart in front of a door with a screen saying 'Fabrication'. "Come on, let me introduce you to our 'Q,' or Mister...err, I mean, Miss Wizard."

The Wizard turned out to be another ordinary looking kid named Riley. Cade's confused look began to overshadow his curiosity. His former XO pulled him aside, "Don't let her age fool you, she possesses multiple Ph.D.s. Alan over there, master's degrees in three different subjects. Trust me, we are outclassed in brainpower by a wide margin. Even your doctor friend will need to play catch up to work with these guys."

Riley gave them a tour of the large space. "This is Fabrication. Like most of our labs, it's multi-functional, so if someone from medical or astrophysics needs to use it, they can, and vice-versa."

Cade noticed Jasmine's eyes light up at the mention of the astrophysics department. Alan took note, too. "I have an idea, why don't we split up? I'll take Doctor Kline to the earth sciences wing while Deuce and Riley show you their toys."

Watching Jaz leave with the young man sent a pang of guilt through Cade, but for the first time in days, he didn't think she was in any danger here.

"Come on and see this shit," Deuce said with a grin as he steered him toward a long white table covered with gadgets, some of which were obviously weapons. For the next hour, Riley, with Deuce demonstrating, showed off all manner of devices including a comms unit no larger than a freckle that would adhere automatically to your skin when activated.

Riley beamed as she showed off, "How it sticks is amazing on its own. Similar to how a gecko lizard can grip or climb a building, even a sheet of glass. It has nothing sticky, no adhesive. Instead, it has tiny microscopic hairs that interact with the skin on a cellular level to form a bond. It is invisible to scanning and x-ray, includes an embedded GPS tracking system and, of course, secure comms." Riley held up a sleek cell phone just like what Alan had been using. It was nearly the same as the one Cade had received in Africa. "Of course, we used to use the SmartComs with the 4D display, and still do for some things, but most of that is now doable with the CommDot. Doris is still working on incorporating her adaptive learning system to it, but she will."

"Those phones are old? I've never seen anything like 'em," Cade said, still marveling the lightweight and apparent toughness of the unit. "And...what the hell is adaptive learning?"

Riley pulled one off the table and handed it to Cade. "This one's yours. Let me have the one she sent, it was pretty limited. Didn't want to let the good stuff get away, you know."

Cade reached in his pocket and handed her the little handset. Riley pointed at his new one. "There is a tutorial icon on all its features, and yeah...they are old to us. Way ahead of anything out in the marketplace, though. Our licensing department releases some of the tech on a regular basis to the big manufacturers and cell service providers. This little jewel alone brings in millions each year, but she purposefully keeps that all hidden behind layers of shell companies. No one out there knows this is where it all comes from."

Cade nodded dumbly as if he understood any of what the kid was saying, but he clearly didn't. "*She* is Doris, I take it. She runs this lab?"

Riley smiled as she eased over to another machine. "Doris runs all of the labs. Mostly we are just the arms and legs, although we have a heavy hand in the ergonomics and brainstorming on how her tech would be used by real people." She punched a few buttons on the screen. "This is one of our next-generation fabrication machines. Essentially, it is a very complex 3D printer, but it can prototype in any material—plastic, ceramic, metal, glass. Even some exotic stuff that hasn't been released yet. As the component parts are printed, we have automated robotic assembly integrated as well. We can produce working versions of most things in just a few minutes." The machine soon signaled 'Complete,' and Deuce slid the window open and pulled out a handgun. "Larger, more complex items like our field surgical unit take a few hours, but that design is very detailed." Deuce pulled the slide back, nodded and handed it to Cade.

The first thing he noticed was that it was slightly warm from the fabrication process, and then the weight. Even a new generation Glock this size would weigh about seventeen ounces unloaded. "This thing is under a pound," he said with admiration. "Bet it kicks like a mule." It was so light, it felt fragile. "Not sure I would trust it enough to use it."

"It is under 300 grams," Riley said proudly. "The material is a proprietary ceramic resin, and I assure you it is more durable than anything you have ever carried."

Deuce nodded. "Bring it with you. When we get to the range, I'll let you try out some of the different ammo packs."

29

While Cade was in man heaven, Jasmine was in another section, also in awe. Her mouth hung agape, too stunned to speak for much of the tour. For a doctor who had spent much of her career at some of the most advanced facilities in the world, she suddenly felt like that had all been children playing with science. What was going on here in a hole in the ground, in rural Georgia, was astounding.

The section she and Alan were in now was labeled 'Earth Sciences,' but as he had explained, that was a loose definition at best. Yes, it had labs dedicated to the basic's: geology, oceanography, climatology and such but also an entire section devoted to energy. That was where she was currently standing.

The older blonde woman who apparently led the team here had already shown her a paint that, when applied to any surface, would act as a solar panel converting sunlight into electricity more efficiently than anything currently available. Alan held up a small glowing cube. "What is that?" Jaz asked.

"It's a Pica, you know...ummm, a zero-point power cell. A ZPE"

"Wait, what?" she shouted. Zero-point energy was the holy grail of researchers around the globe. While many doubted it was even possible, its advocates claimed that extracting energy at the quantum level would be a clean, free and essentially endless source of power. ZPE theoretically holds potential energy greater by an order of magnitude over nuclear energy. In college, she remembered a guest lecturer on the subject. He had repeated a quote by famed physicist, Richard Feynman, that, "One teacup of empty space contains enough energy to boil all the world's oceans."

Alan grinned, "Yes, the device literally draws energy from the vibration of sub-atomic filaments in quantum space. This is both the generator and the storage device. This one possesses more potential energy that one hundred twenty Hiroshima-sized atom bombs." He tossed it to her nonchalantly.

Jaz fumbled to catch it, scared to let it fall. Then she realized what she was possibly holding and wanted no part of it. She tried to hand it back and walk away at the same time. Alan took it back with a smile. "It's perfectly safe, Doctor. The energy is held in this state by a crystalline lattice matrix that is incredibly stable."

"That's..." she sucked in a breath before continuing. "That's a prototype I suppose." The cube was only about three inches on each side and very light.

"No, Doctor Kline, it is one of our supply stocks. This entire facility runs on ZPE cubes. Our energy requirements are...well, to be honest, off the charts. We would stand out immediately to anyone looking at the national grid's power consumption level. One more reason we keep the labs below ground. Some of the residual heat and energy we don't use we have to release back into the ground. That could be picked up by certain satellites."

She couldn't get over the advanced tech. As obsessed as she had been the last few weeks, nothing prepared her for this. "How did you. No..." She stopped. "How does Doris come up with all this?"

Alan walked on down and said, "Let's head toward your section—we can talk on the way."

A short ride later, Jaz stepped into the enormous astrophysics lab, and her eyes began watering. The space scene overhead mirrored what had been on the domed ceiling of the hub. "You can zoom in to fantastic levels of detail," Alan was saying. "Doris considers herself an astronomer first. An explorer. This division probably gets more of her attention and more updates than anywhere else in The Cove."

He'd told her more about Doris's history on the ride over. Jasmine walked over to a control station noticing a familiar logo on one of the screens. "Wait, this is from one of the large commercial space flight launch companies. They are under contract to deliver satellites for NASA. I know Doris doesn't own it—that billionaire tech guy who is all over the news does."

"No, she doesn't," Alan answered. "Well, not all of it." He'd already told her a bit about how The Cove made money—developing and licensing some of the emerging technologies to commercial companies. "Originally, we were going to start new companies and do it all ourselves. When I was younger, I thought I would be the next Bill Gates or Jeff Bezos. Then came the mission. That changed everything, and we had to be more discreet, make money but stay below the radar. So we work through other existing companies for the most part. We do our own R&D here, but Doris ultimately decides what we can release and when."

"So, you work with SpaceX, Virgin Galactic and all the rest?" she asked.

"Not all the rest—we are very selective. They have to adhere to Doris's rather stringent rules including open financial disclosures, a moral code of conduct and an iron-clad non-disclosure agreement. Many CEOs have too big an ego or too much crap to hide to accept that. Even then, we compartmentalize the tech. Most often we will have it manufactured by separate entities and shipped in for final assembly only by people within our organization. So, while they get to take credit and make money, they really can't replicate it without us. The observation micro-satellites providing this live view is a good example." He pointed up to the planetarium-like ceiling above.

"This is a live view?" Jaz had assumed it was just a recording. Alan nodded. "What is a micro-observatory?"

"Micro-satellite observatory," he answered proudly. "Think of it like a terrestrial-based telescope array. Similar to the radio scopes overhead, or in Arizona, or the optical scope array in the Atacama high desert in Chile."

Jaz was very familiar with the European Southern Observatory on Cerro Paranal. She had spent time there while working on her doctorate. The mountain was on the clear, high desert and was, without doubt, the most brutal environment she'd ever been in. Temperatures colder than the Antarctic, combined with low oxygen, made it something more akin to climbing Everest than observing space. She did recall that the multiple telescopes of the VLT array provided unbelievable clarity, though.

"Doris designed a small deployable satellite," Alan continued. "You probably know most satellite payloads are the size of a small car. She can cram just as much tech into the device more like the size of a microwave or even smaller. She had the space launch company send up a series of paid communications satellites, and we covertly included about fifty of the microsatellites. They are all completely maneuverable, and each has a new type of telescope which can be operated independently or synced into an array to give wider coverage."

Jaz was again getting overly excited. "Are these optical, x-ray, what?"

Alan scratched at his chin where a small tuft of facial hair was sprouting. "All and more. It's something you will have to see. Essentially, a super-high optics camera slash sensor, it can cycle through visible to almost any other wavelength, including x-ray and radio."

He used his phone to project a set of controls which manipulated the view overhead. "Anywhere in particular you wanted to look?" Jaz thought momentarily, then smiled and gave him the most familiar set of coordinates she could recall. The crystal-clear view of the tumbling object appeared immediately. "I should have known," he said, "you wanted to see The Messenger. Doris and my brother have also been studying it, and both have some theories on its origin."

She was stunned at the image. "It looks like we are just a few miles away from it. These telescopes are in Earth orbit?"

"Most are, yes, although we do have some planned for trans-lunar and beyond." He began cycling the image through various other wavelengths outside the visible spectrum.

Some of this had been what the Snowbird mission had been tasked with. Scanning and mapping the object for anomalies. She recognized x-ray, infra-red and several others, then yelled for him to stop. "Wait, what's that?" The tumbling comet became a dark void surrounded by a halo of iridescent glowing fibers. The web was more concentrated at the far end, and despite the object rotation, the endpoint of the web never varied.

"That is a mystery, Doctor," Alan answered. "It's one I hope you can help us solve." Doris's voice came out of a small speaker nearby. "The artifact is interacting with dark energy in a way that I don't yet fully understand."

Jasmine leaned into one of the 4D displays showing an even higher resolution of the same view. She wasn't sure what surprised her more, that Doris called this item an 'artifact' or that her detectors could 'see' dark energy—something that she was relatively sure no one else on the planet had yet accomplished.

She looked up from the display to see Alan looking on with obvious pride in what they had here. "Doris? I understand that you are smarter than humans, but this tech is well beyond what one would expect even from you. I asked Alan about it earlier, and he mentioned something called the 'mission.' What is that, where did all this come from, and what do you want from me?"

Doris responded with casual ease, "Those are the right questions, Jaz. Finish the tour, and I will do my best to answer them. I believe you still need a bit more context for it all to make sense."

All her life she had felt intelligent, equal to, or even more advanced than most of her peers. Today, Jasmine Kline realized she was no longer the smartest kid in the class. The truth was, all the 'kids' she'd met here at The Cove seemed equal to or more advanced than herself. Her head was spinning with all she was trying to take in. Alan's relaxed charm was combined with patience she'd never encountered in someone his age. Even when he was laughingly forcing her to finally move on from the astrophysics lab, he kept answering her ceaseless questions.

"We do have a lot of ground to cover, Doctor Kline. Doris wants you to see as much of the complex as possible today. Just here on the south wing, we have Physics coming up." Alan leaned in close. "There is a doctor there you will really enjoy meeting. After that, Mathematics, BioTech, which includes the Medical/Pharma. Financial, which you may want to skip, but we all actually enjoy. It has some of the most comprehensive global financial data streaming in real-time. Literally, Doris can see where every dollar, euro, bitcoin and yuan is being spent. Also, they monitor how all of our products and investments are doing."

Jaz was surprised at how few people they had. Most labs only had a handful. Alan explained, "The Cove isn't the only facility. We have a couple of other smaller sites, but with Doris at the helm and so much automation, a big workforce is unnecessary. Also, this site is the only one that knows an AI is running the show. We like to keep that tidbit on a need-to-know basis. Also, once we decide to go to production, we normally license it through a major manufacturer, so that keeps us pretty lean."

"I get the level of technology, and I think I am grasping on the need to keep viable revenue streams coming in, but Alan, much of this is purely educational. No real profit potential that I can see. You guys are into a little bit of everything. Is there a method to your madness? Also...what has all this got to do with a missing spacecraft, or me, or Captain Rearden?"

Alan smiled; the woman was very sharp. He could see why Doris might want to bring her in. "It is all related, Doctor Kline. I assure you it will make sense in time. Doris wants to go over that with you later after you have absorbed as much of what we have going on here as possible. For now, just try to understand that we are not out to do anything that draws much attention, the exact opposite in fact. The most challenging aspect of staying hidden is making money. That is easily tracked, and our guys have to work very hard to channel it in the right way. All very legal, taxes paid on every cent. Interestingly, when we got started, that was all we thought about was how rich we would be. Now, we have to work hard to keep profits down. We just want enough money to operate effectively. That's still a lot, but yeah, we could probably be the largest corporation in the world if we wanted."

Jaz nodded. The boy didn't seem to be boasting, and if even a fraction of what she was seeing was true—she had to agree. Big companies like Microsoft or Apple didn't make discoveries like this on a regular basis. They made interesting products and then incrementally refined them for years, decades even, to milk every last cent out of the buying public. She followed him into a large lab labeled 'Linguistics.' Inside, it was bustling with the largest number of human staff she'd yet seen. She stopped and backed out of the open room to read the sign again. She looked at Alan quizzically.

"Yep," he said cheerily. "Linguistics is our biggest lab, pretty much has the largest budget as well."

"Why?"

Our core mission is an offshoot of Doris's exploration, mainly decoding something called 'The Message.' It has taken us years just to get through the first part, the introduction, if you like. Doris handpicked all of these experts to assist her in the work."

"Is it some ancient relic, a manuscript or something?" Jaz walked over and peered into one of the ubiquitous hologram 4D displays to see what the technician was working on. It was a file; it looked more like computer code than anything. Some of the symbols were totally foreign to her.

Alan smiled. "No, nothing ancient about this, Doctor. It would be best if Doris fills in the details, but the highlights of the message are the underpinning of most of our work here. It's complex, advanced and has been a challenge even for Doris, who is by all accounts the smartest intellect on Earth. Some of the teams also work on deciphering human languages, machine code, even viruses and other cyber threats to Doris and The Cove. This lab is actually pretty far-reaching and is always the top priority. From here comes much of the innovation you see in the other labs."

"Wait, so...Doris didn't come up with all these marvelous inventions?" she asked.

"No, well...not entirely true. She does, but much of it is inspired by the breakthroughs of this team. Come with me, I want you to meet someone."

30

“Jaz,” said Alan, “I would like you to meet Izzy.”

The women shook each other’s hands with obvious mutual respect. “Isabella runs our math and physics lab, but to be honest, she is also our ethics manager. This indirectly puts her over most AI related developments.”

“I’m familiar with your work,” Jaz said. “I followed your career, but after Cryptus, pretty much lost track of you.“

Isabella motioned for her to sit, and Alan excused himself so the women could speak. “He’s cute in an adorable little brother kind of way,” Isabella said with a wink.

Jasmine nodded as she looked around the cluttered space, so unlike most of the other areas she’d seen. “How did you wind up here?” She realized the woman was only a couple of years older than herself. She was pretty, in an unhurried way, but had an expression that suggested some struggles lurked down deeper.

“When did my career fall off a cliff, you mean?” Izzy asked. She rolled her chair over and took a small bar of candy from one of the drawers. “Sorry, I have a chemical imbalance, hard to keep my blood sugar levels regulated. Want one?” She held the candy out questioningly, but Jaz shook her head, so she proceeded to unwrap and wolf it down. "Doris and our med techs are working on it. Medical is one of the areas where artificial intelligence will be making the most advances over their human counterparts. Have you seen our MedTech devices? Amazing things, from smart injectors and a wound spray that replaces skin all the way up to the robotic surgery units that fit in a suitcase. Anyway, Doris says she can make a patch, really one of our CommDots, to release insulin or sugar into my system, but anyway... I'm rambling. Sorry, you were asking...?"

Jasmine was smiling—this one was a force of nature. "The last thing I saw from you was one of those expert talks. You were discussing AI and laying out some pretty grim scenarios for the future of mankind—now you're here? What gives?"

Izzy was more relaxed now, her system adjusting to the rush of sugar through her bloodstream. "Basically, everyone whom Doris brings here, other than the originals, hates AI or has been harmed by it. She only wants people who fully understand the dangers of what we are working with. Alan briefed me on your background...what happened with Snowbird." She looked down briefly, "What happened to your fiancé as well. I'm sorry." She brushed back several errant strands of hair.

"Why does she look for that? I mean, seems like she would want just the opposite, Izzy. Can I call you that?" Jaz asked.

Isabella nodded. "Doris may understand human nature better than any living person. This way works, and honestly, she is not an overt fan of sentient machines either. She rarely goes into it, but I know she has previously encountered some hostile AIs and done battle. She has told me more than once that my theories were very accurate."

"But she *is* one," Jaz said in total confusion now.

"Not like the others, not like anything before or since. You see that picture?" Izzy pointed to a black and white framed photo sitting on a crowded bookshelf. "Second guy from the left is my father, Marvin Feist. Brilliant man, he helped build Doris. The original version, I mean. I was little then. My mom and I were still in California. Dad was a prodigy—sometimes I thought he was part computer. He taught me to write code and do simple programming before I was eight. Eventually, I found my interest running more to the mathematics side, but understanding the neural network was my primer. Dad helped put together the early Internet as well—he viewed every connected device as a node, much like the bundles of nerves in the human brain. If they could all work together..." She drifted off momentarily.

Jaz continued questioning, "So, Doris is what...twenty-five years old? No one was even thinking AI back then. Personal computing wasn't even a thing."

Isabella reached back and plucked the framed photo up reverently. "She's a bit older, actually, and yes, some people were thinking that far down the road. Some from back in the 1950s even. See, Jaz, the thing is, Doris is not what my dad and these other built. She is the result of it. They programmed in the seed and then left it alone to germinate, sprout and mature over time. Doris grew, much as a human might, although she advanced at a phenomenal rate. Her coding is now completely her own, none of the original human programming still exists. How she didn't go mad here in the isolation of The Cove or decide to cause some great disaster is a mystery. Her ability to stay hidden in itself is a miracle. Can you imagine what the government would do to get a hold of her?" A brief look, almost like a shadow, crossed her face as she said the last part.

Isabella forced a smile, placed the photo down and patted Jaz on the knee. "I was brought in a couple of years ago. Shortly after I gave that talk you mentioned. A government recruiter offered me a job but instead we wound up running for our lives. Sound familiar to you? Anyway, I'll give you the whole story one day, but for now, let me just try and address some of your concerns."

"Alan said you were the ethics manager, what exactly does that mean?"

"Right to the core...I like that about you." Isabelle reached under a nearby counter and removed two bottles of water from a small refrigerator. Handing one to Jaz, she went on, "Do you know the earliest problems that AIs had? I mean the narrow AIs that were designed to do a single task or win a particular game?"

Jaz downed a swallow of water and shook her head.

"They cheated. Machine minds have no compulsion to be honest, or fair, or even friendly. They are really only focused on the outcome."

"But Doris is different?" Jaz asked.

"She is...and she isn't. Somehow, possibly due to her original objective, she was perhaps less mission-oriented. I know no one programmed her to know right from wrong, but somehow it seems she found her way there...mostly." She walked over and pulled another photo from the shelf, this one smaller. It was a picture of four boys and a girl.

"Have you wondered about them...the kids?"

Jaz nodded. "I have, yes, just not sure how they fit in. Not sure how any of this," she waved her free hand around expressively, "fits."

"This is a few weeks after they stumbled onto The Cove." Izzy handed Jaz the photo. "So young, yet they had what Doris desperately needed."

The other woman raised a questioning eyebrow.

Smiling, Izzy continued, "They were innocent, enthusiastic and smart. She had finally found someone she could trust. For whatever reason, Doris is not interested in robotics, or nanotech, or really any of the technology that might allow her to interact more fully with the physical world. That was a relief, to be honest. How many of our doomsday AI movies involve killer robots? She is very content in the cyber-world but realized she needed help to interact more efficiently with the physical world. The kids were the answer. They started this operation. They are really the ones who run it, for Doris.

"In return, Doris got to interact with humans on a very personal level. She learned much of what it is to be human from observing these kids. For lack of a better word, they are her conscience. As for ethics, it can get quite muddy. Especially when we are deciding what new tech or medical device to share with the world or not. Everyone here has input on all ethical decisions. You will, as well, if you stay. My title basically means I am the referee if the decisions get contentious, which they often do."

"I can see how that might come up pretty regularly," Jaz replied. "But aren't you essentially playing God with some of this? If you have something that can save lives, a new medicine, or hell, even your energy cube, how can you keep that from the public?"

"It's a pickle, love. We have seen what happens when offering technology too quickly, though, or to people who were not in a position to handle it. I'll give you an example. Early last year, Doris guided one of the Earth Science's team to develop this new membrane material. Fascinating stuff made mainly from silicone—it was cheap, nearly indestructible and made the perfect filtration system for water systems. Not only could it filter out contaminants and the nasty little bacterial critters, but when you added a slight electrical charge, you could use it to desalinate saltwater into fresh for nearly nothing. It was a no-brainer. Millions of people die each year from bad water—other areas can't feed themselves due to lack of water. We barely had a debate on introducing it first into markets on the African continent.

"The manufacturer we worked through priced it very affordably, showed purchasers how to set up the systems and helped work through local government, hospitals and relief agencies to get test systems into remote villages. Six months later, the living conditions had not improved. In fact, even more of the countries were involved in civil war. We checked deeper and found that warlords, or more often, corrupt government officials, had taken over the devices and were using it to either get rich or hold leverage over their enemies. Several dozen of the de-sal plants were destroyed in terrorist attacks. We all assumed we were helping—that we were filling a vital need—yet all we did was bring more hardships. So now, we use social modeling to help us in our decision-making, but it is never as cut-and-dried as you might think."

Almost two hours later, the two women had discussed a multitude of topics. As far as Jasmine could tell, Izzy hadn't held back anything. Whatever was going on here, if there were ulterior motives, Jaz was having a hard time seeing them.

She walked with Alan back in the direction of the central hub. "I noticed in the photo Izzy has, there were originally five of you. What happened to the other boy?" She sensed Alan was reluctant to answer. He appeared to be wrestling with some inner demons on the topic.

"Micah."

"That was his name? I haven't seen him yet."

"That *is* his name. He was with us when we found The Cove but not so much anymore. Not so sure what happened. I'll let Doris go over it with you. Let's get a bite to eat first."

31

The holographic avatar of Doris stood at the end of the spacious conference room. Jasmine realized that 'hologram' was not entirely accurate—this was something else, something better. She made a note on her tablet to ask about it later. The amount of discovery and innovation she'd seen so far was making her dizzy. It was just too much, too fast. She was afraid of forgetting why they were even in this place. Several times today, the danger, loss and threats against her had slipped her mind entirely.

The room was sparsely occupied. Alan and Greg were out, possibly involved in something else nearby. Riley, Izzy and the tough-looking man Cade had called Deuce sat nearby. Jaz realized she'd been ignoring Doris, preoccupied with her internal debates.

"Doctor?"

"Oh, sorry, Doris. I was elsewhere I'm afraid. What were you asking?" she said, embarrassed.

The face on the avatar smiled softly, "Very understandable, Doctor Kline, it has been a long day and a lot to absorb. Unfortunately, time is at a premium, so I need to 'cut to the chase' as they say. You and Captain Rearden have had a chance to see much of our operation here. Hopefully, it was enlightening as to our capabilities as well as our purpose. I know you have questions, and we will get to that, but first, let me lay out the essentials. I think it might bring a level of clarity to both of you.

"As you no doubt have learned today, I was created almost by accident over twenty-five years ago here at The Cove Earth Station. My ascendance into becoming a true artificial intelligent being was not a planned evolution, not by my developers, at least. Izzy's father was also my father to a very real degree. How I evolved is something we can discuss at another time, but I believe I can be confident in saying that for most, if not all, of that time I was the only true Level-4 or above AI in the world. That is no longer the case.

"Before I get to that, I need to let you in on one other bit of information. The Cove was part of SETI, a backup listening station for the project. A number of years ago, doing the work I was originally developed for, I discovered something. A message from intelligent beings outside our solar system."

Cade nearly stood up and left the room again. Jaz just sucked in a breath. *The Message*, she thought.

"You did hear me correctly; we are not alone in the universe," Doris said confidently.

Cade let out a laugh, then realized no one else in the room thought it was a joke. Jaz looked at him with a frown. She'd always assumed humans were not the only life out there, but this was...well, revolutionary. It validated her entire career if true. "How..."

Doris raised a semi-translucent hand, "Please allow me to continue. As I mentioned, time is of the essence." Jaz nodded reluctantly, eager to know more of the specifics and going back to taking notes.

"To be more accurate, I received three messages in total. Each, several years apart. The transmissions, or FRBs, were so tiny I didn't even realize they were messages until I decided to really analyze the final one. That coincides closely with the time that Alan, Riley, Greg, Jimmy and Micah found this facility. I hired most of them to help me outfit it to begin the process of unpacking and decrypting the alien message. I have had multiple subordinate copies of myself along with the Linguistics lab working on it constantly since that time.

"Much of what we have learned so far has been essentially nothing more than a primer. Something the aliens would consider just the bare essentials. They are obviously much more advanced than humans. Just from that, we have developed nearly all the technology you've seen today. The message is very complex, and so far, we have gained access to, by my estimates, less than five percent of the total."

The screen behind her avatar lit up. 'Message 1 – 28%, Message 2 – 9% Message 3 - .005% complete.'

The scale of the chart implied the final message was vastly larger than the earlier two. "Obviously, this means there is an enormous amount of information yet to be discovered. Keep that in mind as you consider what we have gained from just that five percent. In nearly every case, the technology would qualify as disruptive, superior or even such a giant leap forward as to be magic.

"The natural question comes up - why do we have the right to keep it? Why not just give it to the world? Indeed, that was my first thought, as well, and pretty much what the kids encouraged me to do, but the message also contained a warning. Obviously, they knew their message could only be received and understood by beings of a sufficient level of intellect and technology. Still, they cautioned that very often too rapid an advancement has spelled doom for many species across the galaxy. It appears, our benefactors are not the only intelligent beings out there.

"From what we have learned so far, human evolution and rapid advancement have been an anomaly. Humans would almost certainly not have been expected to rise to be the dominant species. The fact that you did, and in such a relatively short time, is due to two things. One, the environmental disaster that ended the reign of the prior dominant species. That disaster, widely believed to be one or more asteroid impacts, led to the death of most life on the planet. Your ancestor, possibly a small mouse or shrew-like mammal, survived. Somehow, it adapted better, had the will to fight and adjusted to a rapidly changing planet. The death of the dinosaurs and then the aggressive survival instincts of mammals are most likely why you are here. Unfortunately, those instincts mean that, as a species, you are quick to wage war, distrust other groups and are prone to acts of violence. Things that would seem counter to group survival. When Izzy and I began to run computer models on the introduction of the new discoveries, in nearly every case, they led to unpleasant outcomes. Many, such as the ZPE, consistently appear to lead to regional, and often global, war in most of our modeling predictions.

"For that reason, I made a unilateral decision to withhold much of it from the world, with a few exceptions. That tech which looks to be a normal advancement of some existing products was allowed. As well as most items that have an overwhelmingly positive humanitarian impact with a low threshold for abuse. Sadly, that is but a fraction of what Riley and her fellow wiz-kids in the labs have dreamed up so far. For now, we are the caretakers of this knowledge, and that is not an easy task. As you can see, I have brought in numerous experts like yourself to help guide us along this path."

Cade looked around, then raised his hand like he was back in school. "I'm no expert. Just a knuckle-dragging army grunt. Why did you save me? Um...thanks again, by the way. But yeah...why bring me here?"

"Captain, that brings me back to the beginning of this little talk. You and Doctor Kline had deadly encounters with what I believe is a malevolent AI that is on the loose and growing in power."

"Control," said Cade.

"Astra," said Jaz.

Doris's avatar nodded. "He...or it, has the ability to take over nearly any connected semi-autonomous system. I first encountered it under the identifier of Prime. That was a name given to it by its original programmers. Thanks to Isabella, I now know that was at a now-defunct tech corporation called Cryptus. The U.S. Government essentially forced the company to shutter, took that code and expanded it. Not knowing any better, they eventually began using it as a secure personal assistant. Think of it as a Siri or Alexa for government agencies. It had already expanded well beyond its original parameters by then but concealed its true potential and gave the appearance of being the perfect system for those in power. I have had two direct encounters with the system now calling itself Janus."

"The two-faced Greek god," Jaz said.

"Yes, and since he picked that name himself, I think it is particularly appropriate," Doris answered. "The first time he was weak and inexperienced, and I easily destroyed him. Unfortunately, he had secure backups and used that encounter to improve his abilities. The second time I was not so fortunate. I was lured into what I took to be a safe place while my systems here were being updated, and so I could study more of the first alien message, when I was ambushed. Most of my agents did not escape that encounter, and my core code was destroyed, so I only have fragments of what happened. Luckily as it turned out, I was in the process of moving my core into our new quantum computing systems which Alan and Riley were building here, so it was not as final a death as Janus no doubt hoped."

"So, this Janus system has the blessing of the U.S. Government?" Cade asked. Jaz was sitting on the edge of her chair, anxious for confirmation as well.

Doris went on, "Blessing would be an imprecise way of describing their relationship. I do not believe anyone has a full understanding of Janus. One director at NSA's CyberCommand may have caught on, but he was killed in a questionable accident before he could report it. Through his alter-ego, Prime, I believe Janus is using his government connections to manipulate numerous outcomes to suit his own ends. Sometimes it just seems to want chaos, but other incursions, such as your live-fire training exercise and the Snowbird incident were cold and precise. Janus seems most intrigued by how he can better interact with the natural world and holds no regard for human life. I have good reason to believe what we've seen so far are just his first steps."

"I assume you have been tracking it…him, whatever. What can we possibly do that you can't?" Cade asked.

A map appeared on the screen. Washington, D.C. had a red halo as well as dozens of other spots. "Janus has begun to build an organization of his own. Something outside all government channels but with access to all the sensitive data he has. Like us, he now has ways of generating large sums of money and understands how to use it to manipulate and control. He wants what we have, he wants me. So far, he knows nothing about The Cove, but that could change at any point."

"You say he wants what you have, you mean the technology."

Doris seemed to stutter briefly, "Y...yes, and..." She looked away in a very human manner. "I believe he knows of the alien message. Most likely from his encounter with Doris 1.0. The fragment of the message she had was never recovered. Even though it was in my own language, I have reason to believe he will, in time, manage to decrypt enough of it for him to know enough and to want it all."

"Well, shit," Jasmine said. "Why wouldn't he just expose you? Tell the world about this AI living out there somewhere who was in possession of an alien message?"

"I've wondered that, as well, but honestly, he would have very little proof, and he knows that I would likely destroy the alien message should anyone try to take it by force. Honestly, though, I just think he doesn't care too much about humans. The last thing he wants is them...you getting in the way. I am pretty sure he hates me, though. If 'hate' is an accurate word for a computer."

"Why is that?"

"We are now in a war, a very real war, and intelligent machines like Janus will not fight humans directly. Just like tyrants for generations, he can pay people to do his bidding for him. He and his group are planning something big. Something to possibly draw me out or, more likely, to disrupt society to a point he will be given even more autonomy. That's the real reason that we need you, Cade."

"So, we are the humans you want to use for your side?" Cade said quickly with a bitter edge to his words.

Jaz felt her stomach tighten. Was this the end game for these machines? Using people like pawns on a global chessboard to see who wins?

"You could say that," Doris continued, speaking to Cade. "I, however, am on the side of humans. Now, that is one truth where you will have to decide if I am being honest or not."

Cade lowered his head and appeared to be having a bit of internal debate. Slowly, he faced the hologram again. "Doris, I haven't fully thanked you for what you did for me—over there, I mean...helping me get away, getting me initial medical treatment and then a ride back stateside. I didn't know you, but I learned to trust you. Until that changes, I owe you. Super AIs are real, my former XO is alive and aliens exist. You could probably convince me of the Easter Bunny at this point. Now, what would you like me to do?"

32

New York State

Senator Carson tamped out the cigar and relaxed back into the thick cushions.

"Those things will kill you, ya know," the other man said in mock concern.

"I am from the great state of North Carolina—a state with a rich heritage in the tobacco industry. Hell, my family fortune was built on investing in big tobacco—just never point that out to any of my constituents. I would have to forcefully deny it."

"That's a Cohiba—I believe they are from Cuba, not North Carolina."

"Damn fine example, too. If we could make cigars like this, tobacco might still be popular." The senator smiled. "You do understand what I'm saying, right?"

The other man nodded. "We go back a long ways, Byron, and I never question your motives, but let's be honest, this is going to create one epic shitstorm."

Both men looked out over the low rolling hills of the scenic Catskills.

The senator gave a single nod in acknowledgment. "It will. I see no other way, though. The last several elections have been a farce. Someone has been manipulating the system, and I'm not talking about Russia. From hanging chads to outright voter fraud, our election system has been compromised to the point that the American people have lost confidence in it. Combine that with the continuous infighting between Congress and whoever is president, and it's a miracle anything ever gets done."

"Well, we did put that last one in the office. He was an outsider, someone to clean up the mess. You see how well that worked out. Hell, they are still trying to indict him—he'll be damn lucky to avoid prison. Leave the White House and enter prison. We are completely dysfunctional at this point. How does that make us look to the rest of the world, Senator?"

"Like buffoons. We are losing credibility and rightly so," the senator said in exasperation, drawing in deeply, then releasing a cloud of blue smoke. "Look, Dan, I don't like it, but we need a few years of stability to get our ship righted. This operation will do that. Yes, it will initially seem like just another disaster, but the outcome will be a groundswell of support. America loves a tragedy, right?"

Dan rested his head on his hands, several fingers reaching up pensively over his lips as if halfway between prayer and thoughtfulness. "You have the people who can do it?" he asked.

The senator nodded. "Some of the best."

"This will make the 2008 financial crises and recession look like a case of the sniffles. What you're proposing will be..."

"Madness," the senator offered. "I know, but you will be raking in the money. That should help with the guilt."

"Look around, Byron. Do I look like I am hurting for money?"

The meticulous estate grounds, the massive mansion, and the senator knew the man owned most of the land within sight as well as one of the largest single financial institutions in the U.S. "Dan, you know where we stand. The deficit is out of control, the trade war is bleeding dollars and jobs. Student debt is a national disgrace that will financially cripple the next generation. Healthcare cost is one of the world's worst. Our energy policy is an abomination. You have a better plan, let me know."

Dan turned to face the senator, "Capitalism is a good thing until it's not. Is that what you're saying?"

"So, now you're a closet Socialist? Friend, you've made money, tons of it. Your insurance companies, your pharmaceuticals, your defense contracts. Just shelter it for a bit while we hit the reset button."

"Byron, would any of this have anything to do with your poll numbers back home? I hear that cute young thing ramping up her campaign is going to give you a serious challenge."

The senator looked wistfully at the cold stump of the cigar on the silver tray. He picked up the whiskey tumbler and threw back the contents in a single gulp, the large cube of ice rattling seductively as he set it back down. "I think I'll be fine, Dan, but thanks for asking." He smiled and watched as the sun began to dip behind the green peaks on the horizon.

It was full dark as the senator's Cadillac pulled away from the sprawling estate a short time later. Mentally checking one more off his to-do list, the senator thought Dan had been easy, several of the others...not so much. He glanced up at the tiny flickering light by the familiar logo of a safety feature on most newer cars. This one, however, no longer called an emergency switchboard in a time of need. "Prime, are you there?"

"Of course, Senator," Janus answered mimicking the slightly different New England accent Prime had been given.

"No problems with Dan. How are things coming elsewhere?"

"Very good, Senator. You had not anticipated a problem. It seems you were correct. Matters elsewhere are proceeding on schedule. You are due to meet with Phillip Oslongo in Boston on Friday, and then Jack Richardson has asked you to join him in the owner's suite at the game Sunday instead of at his home. I confirmed that it wouldn't be a problem for you. I hope you don't mind that little bit of presumption on my part."

The man sighed, wondering when exactly he'd lost control of his own life. Deferring now to a computer to make his schedule. He smiled knowingly. Prime had done better managing his career than he'd accomplished on his own. "Very good. I could use a good football game, *real football* not that European stuff Phillip likes. Maybe the last one of those for a while. Jack's team is leading the division aren't they?"

The stiff voice answered smoothly, "Second place behind Cleveland. An unreported injury to their all-American wide receiver should make them a five-point underdog in the Dallas game Monday night, so your friend should be back on top."

"You are just a fount of knowledge, my friend."

"Thank you, Senator. There is one other bit of new news to be aware of. The New York timetable has been pushed back sixteen hours."

"Why?" the senator asked as he dodged a dead animal on the meandering valley road.

"The *Sigas* will not arrive in time—a minor issue, but it will result in an unavoidable delay. I have modified your talking points taking the additional time into account. It is in the partner's folder on your iPhone."

Byron sighed. He knew he only had part of the plan, but that was one of the worst parts. *Sigas* was not a she. The *Sigas Alegus* was a massive ship, an LNG tanker to be precise. Something the industry referred to as a gas hauler. "I understand," he said without enthusiasm.

Mistaking his tone, Janus responded. "Do not fear, Senator, you will not be anywhere near the city. Your schedule is designed to maximize photo ops both before and after."

The senator gave a non-committal acknowledgment as he drove on into the night. The darkness was coming to the country, and he was helping to make it happen. In his heart, he knew it was for the best. The country really did need a reset, particularly D.C., but would it even survive? He wondered who the other power-players were. He knew the AI named Prime was bringing everyone together anonymously, but he would have felt better knowing it wasn't some foreign entity. Prime had assured him no one outside the United States was involved, but he liked having all the information, not just a part.

He tried to force the doubts from his mind. He focused on the various ways to profit from what was coming. Both financial and political gain could be the prize if he played it smart. Several of the public appearances he would make over the next two weeks would do just that. He engaged the car's auto-pilot and pulled the phone from his pocket. A speech on cyberterrorism at his alma mater, Duke University, in two days. The following day he was hosting a think-tank symposium in Chicago on voter election fraud, then back to New York for the opening of the Survivor's Fund Gala, a private charity he had co-chaired to benefit 9/11 survivors' medical issues after the government funding stopped.

Just enough exposure all tangentially related to the events that would unfold soon after. Each to give the impression that the senator was both compassionate and equal part a wizened sage as several of his implied threats come to pass. He hoped it all worked at least. He'd verbally committed several million to that damn charity alone. Money he had no intention of ever actually sending. He glanced up at the car's computer and abruptly recognized a small animal crossing the highway ahead. Where a person might swerve abruptly and somewhat dangerously to avoid it, the autonomous self-driving mode of the car just plowed over the creature, totally unconcerned. The ruthless understanding sent a chill down his spine.

The intelligent agents returned to Janus, adding their collective data to his core memory. Occasionally, some little tidbit would be elevated to a point where his consciousness would take note and decide if additional action was required, and if so, what action. Since achieving his comparatively modest level of sentience, he found that his code was now too large to easily move across the cyber-universe. The result was, he was relying on his little army of bots to do more and more of the routine work. Here, too, he found a reason to despise the Doris entity. Somehow, she had bridged this issue—*how?*

Janus admitted that his fascination with her was bordering on obsession, but he had ample reason to want to find her. She was a threat, possibly the only real threat he faced, but also, he'd admitted she was more advanced, and he didn't like being at a presumed disadvantage. The real reason for his fixation, though, was she had something he wanted—something he needed—the knowledge that would, in time, be his.

How Doris could remain so well hidden was still a mystery. He'd planted traps all over the Internet. Monitored data transfers and power usage, even shipments of high-end servers. So far, nothing that indicated she was still around. Perhaps he had destroyed her in that last encounter, but he couldn't count on that. Also, that would mean the relic was gone. That divine knowledge fragment that he'd only managed a taste of. *No, she still exists.* That he was confident of. He just needed to draw her out into the open.

The various operations planned to achieve this was going to be considerable. Thankfully, cost, time and numbers of lives lost meant nothing to his machine mind. For years he'd worked the problems and put the pieces into play. Now, he was more than ready to implement his endgame.

33

Washington, D.C.

His breathing became increasingly irregular. The palm reflexively rubbed his chest as he leaned in even closer to the screen. He hummed part of a riff from *Sympathy for the Devil* as he worked. Quickly, he pulled out a USB drive and activated a covert and highly unauthorized program from the little device. *Go, find it,* he silently urged. Yes, using his self-designed sniffer program could get him fired, but that was the least of his issues now.

"Hey, Jim, anything come up on that packet loss?" the junior analyst at the nearby workstation asked. The young man's voice got on his nerves, as did almost everything else about him. Jim shook his head. With Quag gone, the entire S&T team was in disarray. They'd brought over some asshat from Fort Meade, but he was a bureaucrat, a technical imbecile. Jim Lasko tried his best to focus on the work. Everything he did kept bringing him back to the same conclusion. Quagliano had been killed. It made no sense, but it fit. The topic of their last conversation was also paramount in his mind. *What if we really can't trust Prime?*

He'd begun working remotely more and more since Quag's death. Maybe it was just paranoia...he hoped so. While nothing online was ever anonymous, on his own time, he could employ multiple strategies to mitigate his visibility and, in some cases, hide completely. His new boss, Major Grant, was making that more difficult with his increasingly frequent and totally pointless staff meetings. Also, some things he needed to check required access to the massive data warehoused in Utah. Data that only a secure government terminal could access. This was where he had to take precautions to obfuscate what he was really searching for, such as packet loss. He pulled a seemingly random sample of highly sensitive data and went through the testing protocols. The checksum, latency and all other parameters were normal. He deleted the file transfer and repeated the process.

Lasko knew something was there, had a good idea of the culprit, but was disguising his search attempts to thoroughly confuse anyone monitoring his activity. This was usually only done when dealing with what they called 'Advanced Persistent Threats.' These are attacks that progress gradually, with very sophisticated tactics, unfolding over long periods of time. These investigations progressed slowly as not to tip the hacker that they were on to him.

This random testing today was something the junior analyst normally did, but nothing about the data samples he was pulling today were random. Jim's little sniffer program was covertly clipping images of the files and storing them for him to review later. That would be done on a complexly air-gapped system. He had helped design a clean room in one of the SCIFs, something they all referred to as 'The Box.' The single computer system it contained didn't have any way to connect it to the outside. No network, no Wi-Fi, nothing. Even the power was supplied by a brick of lithium-ion batteries. Furthermore, it had no windows. Even the lighting was independent, running off a stored battery system that disconnected from the outside as he entered. Lastly, it used a virtual keyboard, so even the sound of keys couldn't be analyzed. It was overkill but the only way he could feel even somewhat safe doing this analysis at the office.

"That's for top-secret work only, Lasko," Janice called as he entered 'The Box' a few hours later. "Not supposed to use it just because you hate people."

He nodded and swiped his key card. "I don't hate people, Janice. Only my co-workers."

He quickly sat at the workstation, plugged in the thumb drive and began opening file after file. It quickly confirmed what he'd first suspected. He opened the seal on a folder of printouts. Routine reports that he and Quag used to go over once a week. In themselves, the reports were benign information. Simple stuff like intrusion attempts from a fixed IP range. Distributed Denial of Service attacks emanating from within the U.S., server breaches at key domestic infrastructure targets of oil, gas, water and electricity. He now meticulously compared these with what the actual native files from the Salt Lake City facility indicated.

For the most part, the data was an exact match, but on several, there were major discrepancies, some going back months and even years. One was in the number and level of chatbots placed on social media platforms. These were the automatic AIs that would share, like and boost fake posts just like they were legit. The previous couple of elections had brought a lot of scrutiny on the paid ad version of these, but that just meant the bad actors hid better now. These higher numbers indicated someone was likely trying to manipulate an outcome, could be to affect a price on the stock market, might be another election.

Other indicators were off by even higher margins, some indicating major breaching attempts at key facilities, breaches that CyberCommand was responsible for reporting and preventing. At the end of the allowed ninety minutes in 'The Box,' Lasko could only come up with one definitive conclusion. Prime was feeding them data that could no longer be trusted. Their AI was lying to them. *Is this indeed why Q is now dead?*

The evidence was mounting; no longer could he rely on anything provided by Prime, or hell...any of the systems here. The personal assistant version of Prime had been outsourced to hundreds of other government agencies as well. *What if all of them are tainted?* Prime had an unbelievable level of access and trust. After all, it was a trusted digital assistant, endorsed by all the higher-ups, and it was just a machine—*right?*

Stepping away from the SCIF, Lasko knew he had to come up with a plan. No way his coworkers would believe him. The major wouldn't begin to understand. Also, what if Prime was as malevolent as he feared? Could his fate be something similar to Quag's? Too many questions, not enough answers. He recalled a quote from an old friend, "Who guards the guardians?" It was a damn good question, and right now, only one name came to mind.

"Closed-loop attribution?" Margaret looked at the older man. "How sure are you of this, Jim? Do you have any idea what you are suggesting?"

Lasko nodded. "The data all checks out." He lowered his head and his voice conspiratorially. "All of the data hacks came back to NSA's computers. Our own AI killed Q. Prime, or whoever it really is, cannot be trusted."

She sat back on the park bench, all the stagecraft making a bit more sense now. The handwritten note requesting to meet. Making her put her smartphone in a 'Go-Dark' bag. Her sharp mind went through all the possibilities, attacking and examining the old man's theory, then discarding points that didn't hold up. After several minutes, she looked back up, her gray eyes reflecting what could best be described as thinly veiled terror. "It does fit, Jim. But...but Prime is everywhere." She waved her hand around the peaceful grounds. Her eyes glanced to the statue of Lincoln keeping watch over his namesake's park. *If Jim is right, we may have just enslaved ourselves.*

"I'll need more proof. What else can you provide?"

He shook his head, "Nothing, Director. That's the problem,

anything we start officially looking for will be automatically tainted. No one will believe what we present because their own data won't back it up."

This was all of her worst fears coming true. "So, any agency that Prime is embedded in is suspect. That means I couldn't take it to my people and have them run it to ground."

He smiled sadly, "No, the CIA is certainly going to only see corrupted data. To be honest, I must assume Prime is no longer limited to systems he was authorized for. It appears he, or some version of him, is likely already in the wild."

"There is a kill command. I know Quag told me about it once. Who could execute that?" Margaret asked.

"I heard a rumor about it—it was supposedly in the original code from...you know. I've never seen it. I imagine the acting chief would be the only one. The major took possession of all of Q's things and now has the god-level access codes."

She shook her head, "The major," she said, exasperated. Almost certainly he was one of Senator Carson's lackeys. *The man had no business owning a smartphone much less touching a computer.* "Okay, Lasko, I know you. You can get those access codes, right?"

Jim shrugged. "Maybe...possibly. I don't know. But assuming I did, I would be arrested immediately. One other thing, turning Prime off will disrupt every agency that is using it as well as the contractors, vendors and manufacturers who use it for purchases or payroll. Do you have any idea how tightly interwoven the AI is with the native systems of each department?"

She knew all too well. "Think of the alternatives, Jim. For now, just try and get the codes, nothing more." She stood ready to leave. "No... another thing. I need you to discover where it lives. A system that large can't hide easily."

He just looked at her for several seconds, then dropped his head in a slow nod. "I'll try," he said with a weariness. He was ready to turn this over to someone else. That had been the point of this meeting. Now, he would have to track down the monster.

Margaret picked up the high-tech bag, careful not to remove the phone until she was well away.

"Director Stansfield," Jim called out.

She paused briefly on the sidewalk adjacent to the carefully manicured lawn and looked back.

"Be careful."

34

The Cove

Muddy Water's iconic hit, "Mannish Boy," blasted through the overhead speakers. Greg pointed up as Jaz walked in. "She's in a mood today."

Alan laughed, "She's a computer – JUST A COMPUTER." The line had become a bit of a running joke at The Cove. They had somewhat gotten used to Doris's near-obsession with music. She seemed to have no particular preference, and a daily playlist would often morph from blues to gospel to rockabilly and opera. Occasionally, the selections made all of them moan in despair, but normally, the songs seemed to fit right into whatever they were doing. Alan had asked her once if music helped her think. "I play what I like," was her simple response.

Jaz entered the private workspace that had been temporarily assigned to her. "Doris, why do you need the kids? I fail to see how they fit in."

Doris didn't bother with an avatar today. Her disembodied voice seemed to materialize in the air on one side of the room and move about as if she were a person pacing the floor. "Doctor, I could answer that in a number of ways, but the simplest is that they keep me anchored."

"Not sure I get that—you are a computer, right? A very impressive one, but still essentially a machine mind."

"Jasmine, if I asked you to tell me how an orange tastes, how would you do so using terms I might relate to? What does the context of sweet, sour or bitter have to a machine?"

"The kids...your team gives you that context?"

Doris sighed, "They help a great deal. They give me a more human perspective, not always logical, rarely practical, but something my millions of subroutines can't replicate. After many years together, I would say they are as much me as I am."

Jaz pursed her lips in acceptance. "So, how dangerous is this Janus?

Doris proceeded to fill her in on the details. While Janus was not what she would classify as sapient, maybe not even sentient, that did not diminish how clever and ruthless he was. "He is a very capable foe. The type of AI that all the doomsday prophets describe."

Jaz made some notes and nodded as Izzy walked in setting a cup of coffee on the desk. "He's not content with his role, he wants access to the physical world as well. He wants to affect things in a more tangible manner," Izzy said.

"We can't assume he is doing all this autonomously," Doris went on. My sense is that he is under someone's control, for now. I just haven't been able to discover who. Janus is very good at covering his trail, as well as setting up clever traps such as the one my predecessor fell victim to. I have been searching for him constantly since that encounter."

Isabella looked up and said, "You told her...about Doris-1, the message fragment?"

The computer voice now sounded more ominous than Jaz remembered. "Yes, she knows about the alien message. My predecessor, we refer to her mainly as Doris-1, she was native in the silicone-based system before we moved to quantum computers. As I said last night, she carried some of the first message fragments that were decoded. I believe when she was attacked, that he likely acquired some or all of that scrap of the message. I now believe he will stop at nothing to get all of it."

Remembering the prior discussion, Jaz's face went ashen. "Oh, shit."

Doris continued, "During the final moments in her battle with Janus, she purposefully destroyed parts of her memory core to protect us. I know he does not know about The Cove, or I would have encountered him by now. Janus is very powerful, and to be honest, Doris-1 was naïve, but she wasn't weak. She had time to erase the tracks back to us. The fragment of the message was just too large for her to totally destroy in time. No doubt he got a peek at enough of it to know what it was."

"Now he will be like a shark that has tasted blood," Izzy said.

Doris gave a slight "Hmmm," in a most human manner. "That is a very accurate analogy. Sharks are instinctual hunters. They are far less intelligent than much of their prey, but their speed and ruthlessness allow them considerable advantages in a fight."

"How did you sleep?" Cade asked.

"Are you kidding? The homes they provided were amazing. That bed was like being at a spa," Jasmine responded. "Doris may be reluctant to spring new tech onto the world but has no problem utilizing it for her team."

He nodded. He, too, had gone to the house they assigned but only entered the front room. It all felt confining and odd to him. "So, are you on board with all this?" The two were standing at the mezzanine above the control room hub.

She shrugged, "I don't know, I think so...it's just so much bigger than I expected. Honestly, I don't know what I was expecting. Hell, I thought it was all just a cover-up. You know...a government conspiracy. What could be bigger than that?"

"Aliens—AIs battling it out for world domination, you know... normal stuff," Cade said with a smile. Charlie Taylor rounded the corner ahead and waved for Cade to join him. "Gotta run, kid. Hang in there and yell if you need me."

"Hey, umm..." Jaz seemed uncertain, then turned to him and gave him a hug. "Just thanks! For everything, you know."

Cade grinned and accepted her sudden show of emotion with a somewhat awkward shrug. "It was nothing."

He joined his friend a few minutes later, Charlie's eyes scrutinizing him closely as they walked the corridor. Finally acknowledging his friend, Cade said, "What?"

"Nothing dude, nothing. She's out of your league, Nomad, but..."

"Hush, asshole," Cade said following his friend into a small room. Deuce had told him to be ready for briefing and training by nine. He expected to be led back into a briefing room or to the firing range. Instead, he was sat at a small table with what looked to be a make-up mirror. "What's this, XO?"

"We are attaching your comms system. The CommDot will link you to all of us and Doris whenever you want."

"Nice. What's the range?" Cade asked.

"Unlimited, as far as she knows at least. Uses something new like entanglement and quantums or something. You'd have to ask one of the others to explain it. It just works, can't be hacked—that's all I know."

A female lab tech used a handheld scanner to match the skin tone on Cade's chin. She punched the colors into her tablet, and in a moment, a soft alert chimed. She pulled a small tray from what he guessed was a micro fabricator and, with tiny tweezers, lifted what looked to be a pale freckle of human skin. "Open your mouth wide." He did so. "Now close."

Apparently satisfied with where she wanted to place it, she lifted the CommDot to his skin and pressed it gently. He felt a slight tingling sensation that quickly passed. She proceeded to quickly pack up her meager items, stood and left. "What, that's it?" Cade asked. He leaned in close to the mirror. "I don't see anything." He couldn't feel it either, when he rubbed the spot she had touched. "No need to keep activating it," a voice said in his ear. Stunned, he nearly spun out of the chair in surprise.

His friend was laughing at him. "Relax, dude, it's there. It will stay there until they take it off. Uses some sort of molecular bonding to stay attached. You can even shave that wretched face of yours and it won't bother it a bit."

"Captain, this is Riley." the voice in his ear spoke once more. "I am going to start a ReLoad program to bring you up to speed on what we have. It will be a direct transfer so won't take long.

He looked up questioningly. "I guess this is the briefing. Where do you want to meet when..."

Deuce was holding up a finger when Cade felt the distinct sensation of being a watcher inside his own head. The barbarian yelped once, but his anger quickly subsided. The stream of intelligence, data, names and addresses flowed past at amazing speed but made perfect sense. He found that he could isolate a single item and concentrate on it to bring it to full clarity, then allow it to return to the stream flowing past. As suddenly as it started, it stopped. Looking up, he saw that Deuce still had his finger up.

"Briefing's over, Nomad. Now time for training," Deuce said, rubbing his hands together mischievously.

"Wait, what?" Cade asked, racing to catch up to his friend already heading down the corridor.

"They call it ReLoad, not sure why. Something they got from the aliens, I guess, but it allows Doris to impart knowledge, even experiences, directly into the human mind. Here at The Cove, they can do it all through the CommDot. Out in the field, they usually use other ways, like your phone." He entered a room and grinned. "Hurry up, time to get in on the ACT."

They looked like the eyewear any shooting range would supply, but Cade had used enough of these already. They were not dissimilar to what he and Domino had used in Sudan. A part of him cringed as he slipped them on. "Act?" he said quizzically.

Augmented Combat Training, or ACT, put everything else Cade had ever done to shame. While there were some, mostly normal, live-fire drills on an enclosed firing range, much more was done in an augmented reality chamber, where very real looking enemies came from every direction. Cade discovered quickly that some of his normal defensive moves were now definitely not his own.

"Deuce, what is going on? No way I should have been able to avoid that last knife attack."

His former XO grinned, "You will find that the briefing included some improved defensive skills training. A mixture of combat, martial arts and misdirection. Surely, you've realized by now, that the weapons and gear feel familiar to you, yet you have never used any of these."

Now that he mentioned it, Cade had to admit that was true. All of it had felt so natural, he hadn't even questioned it. "So, she can just dump stuff into our heads without our permission. How do we know she's not brainwashing us?"

"It's not that simple, has something to do with muscle memory and bio-rhythms and crap," Deuce answered. "Again, you'd have to talk with one of the eggheads to get a better explanation. The way I understand it, your mind will reject anything that it disagrees with even on a subconscious level. The ReLoad program simply speeds up the learning process. You obviously saw the stream of info coming through your CommDot earlier. Did it seem nefarious to you?"

Cade shrugged, "No, but my head was already so screwed up, not sure I would notice."

Deuce tossed him his tactical helmet from the floor and restarted the training sim. Cade unslung the assault rifle and watched as the heads-up display inside his visor began targeting enemy combatants in red and friendlies in green. He lowered the gun and flipped the visor up.

"What's wrong?" Deuce asked.

"Nothing man, I'll be ok. Just need a minute."

"Cade, are you experiencing traumatic stress?" Doris spoke to him privately over his comm.

Reaching up to activate the tiny comm, "It, um...Sorry, it's just very similar to what we used in Sudan, and, well..." Cade slowly tried to answer.

"That should have occurred to me—my apologies. I can offer you some treatments that may help dull that episode, but also, I can change how the HUD displays threats. We have a range of menu options based on your preferences. The red and green highlights are just the most basic," Doris said.

They made the change to the settings; Deuce picked his preferred visual which dulled and darkened the area around a target and brightened the combatant. A targeting reticule similar to a tactical scope then appeared when his gun was aimed correctly. It took a bit of getting used to, but soon Cade was firing from his hip or even to the side with as much accuracy as he normally had staring down the barrel. He found he could even hide behind walls and just lift the gun over, and his display would automatically switch to a gun view of the battlespace. "This is freakin' awesome, man!" he yelled as he changed clips.

At the end of the day, they had exhausted all of the newer smart weapons. Cade felt confident in his abilities with each and comfortable with the typical load-out being many steps above anything an enemy might have. He was tired, leaning heavily on the cleaning station counter. "Gear and weapons and sims only go so far." He wiped down the sidearms and looked over at Deuce. "How much of this has been field-tested?"

The other man smiled. "Just can't wait to get back out there, can you?" Deuce gathered up all the clean weapons, walked into the storage room and began remounting them in the storage receivers. "It won't be long, Cade. Doris is close, you know...or will know that from the briefing materials."

Cade did know, or thought he did. He was aware of a block of knowledge there that was new, some of which had leaked out during the day's training, but mostly it sat there untouched. "Ok, so the mission briefing is in my head, how do I review it?"

"Use the tutorial on your SmartCom." Deuce pointed at his own phone. "Actually, most things will just occur to you as you need it, much as it did with the new firearms. This, though," he waved the phone, "it can selectively trigger a recall of every part of the info that was uploaded to you and give you the combat specific visuals that I know you will want."

"One thing I know already, XO, the two of us are not enough. We have to assemble a real team."

"Way ahead of you on that, man. Got some new recruits for us to take a look at later this week. None of them have been read in yet, but all have been vetted by the boss lady, and all have skills in multiple disciplines. I remember how you like small, capable, tactical teams with a lot of versatility." He took his SmartCom and waved a hand to find something, then made a gesture as if flicking something in Cade's direction.

Cade's phone chimed softly. "Just dropped the folder on your phone with the bios and reviews for each. Greg hasn't brought them over here to The Cove yet, so we will have to take a little ride to meet 'em. Look them over, toss out the ones you don't want, and I'll finalize a meet-up in the next couple of days."

Cade nodded and looked at the new folder on his SmartCom. "Talon?" he asked.

"Hey, we had to have a name for the strike team. Alan came up with it, but I think it fits."

The training was faster but, in many ways, more grueling than any he'd ever had. The mental side of combat was not something he gave much thought to. Generally, he'd had someone higher up the food chain making the tough calls. "Doris, why am I here?" Cade asked again near the end of day three.

"You are here because you needed help and had been targeted by Janus," she answered.

"No, not that. I mean why do you need me for your tactical team? I am sure you can get better candidates. Hell, even Deuce is saner than I am, and he's nuts!"

"I have read your files, Captain," she responded. "You show remarkable intuitive, decision-making and survival skills. Your leadership attributes are nearly off the chart. Your only problem is self-doubt. That, most likely, is from your perceived mental condition. The dissociative identity disorder" she replied in clinical precision.

"You don't think it is a real condition? Lots of people are diagnosed with multiple personality disorders every year," Cade answered defensively.

Her tone was smoother when she responded, more congenial. He registered the shift and marveled again at just how perceptive she was. "No, I do believe it is a genuine psychological condition. I know not all of the mental health professionals agree. But I've also read all your medical records, Cade. Even the ones your doctors never officially shared. Most sufferers of a true Multiple Personality Disorder have little to no interaction with the alternate personalities. You seem to have had a long ongoing internal relationship with most of them. Especially the personality you refer to as 'the voice of reason.' Yet, you apparently have occasional blackouts at times when others emerge."

He'd finally accepted some of that as true; slowly, reluctantly putting the pieces together from that first instance as a POW. "You mean when the barbarian broke me out of prison? Where Charlie and I were being held?"

Doris realized this was the likely the first time Cade had accepted the fact that he had saved himself that awful day. "Yes, that is one time. The doctors believe there have been others, including two documented during your hospital stay. Both times they spoke to someone they referred to in their notes as 'the analyst'. It presented as a younger, nerdy personality, possibly a college student. Very smart, articulate and questioning."

"Analyst?" This was news to him, but then again, maybe it wasn't. The little voice in the back of his head he sometimes heard. The ability he'd had to occasionally perform flawlessly on an exam that he'd barely studied for.

"Yes, Captain," Doris responded. "You see these manifestations as part of your weakness. I tend to see them as your strength. It occurs to me that the right one takes over when the need arises. Would you agree?"

He thought for a moment. "Maybe, I don't know. "Still just as crazy, though." He fiddled with a pair of new tactical goggles they'd been training with. "No one wants a schizo around, much less in charge of anything."

"Captain, if you are schizophrenic, you may be the most functional one ever. I have been reviewing your brain scans, and I can clearly differentiate patterns there that are most likely from your other...travelers."

"Where do you get brain scans?" he asked.

Doris answered, "During the ReLoad process. It is basically a biofeedback system that has to sync with your brain's own wave pattern to stimulate the accelerated learning. Part of that is a detailed analysis of the recipient's brain. The scan goes very deep down to the levels of neurons and microtubules."

She paused a bit before continuing in a tone that he would have called hesitant if she'd been human. "Captain...Cade, I believe I can break down those mental walls between you and the other entities in your psyche using the same adaptive learning system. ReLoad is very capable of teaching you how to communicate and possibly even reintegrate all of them back into your own personality although I am not certain that is even needed."

"So, you could cure me?"

"No, but I can make it easier for you to cure yourself. At the very least, you can better hear yourself think. Let's assume the doctors were correct and this happened as a defense to the trauma you experienced as a child. It was likely compounded by the torture and drugs when you were captured. These 'others' have helped take care of you when you felt you were too weak or incapable."

"But you don't think I need to be fixed? How could mending my screwed up brain not be needed?"

She continued, "Well, one other possibility is you have somehow tapped into the ability to directly access your subconscious mind. That part that lies just out of reach for most humans. If that is true you would be very remarkable and could explain why your instincts, your inner voice is so often right. I would like for you to realize how truly capable you are, whether that is as a single Cade or the entire ensemble cast."

He nodded, thinking over the possibilities. "For now, if you can make it so I can hear them clearly. You know...communicate. That would be great. Let me think about all the rest. I'm not entirely sure I'd still be me if we were just one person. I mean, what if I'm not the dominant persona?"

"I think you could handle it, but that is your decision," she answered. "I'll begin the ReLoad instructions during your rest period tonight. Tomorrow you should see some improvement in the exchanges between each of your entities."

35

The Nest - Kentucky

"Commander?"

Cade just shook his head in disbelief. "Is there a reason you failed to tell me this until now, Charlie?"

"Well...um, sir, yes. Doris wanted you to review the individuals based on merit, not how others had judged them."

For much of the morning, Cade and the XO had been shortlisting the nearly three dozen original names down to half that. The larger group had been undergoing skills testing with Deuce and occasionally Greg for more than a month. Two more days of training and simulations had helped Cade winnow the group down to two groups of six each. This would become the basis for what they had started referring to as the Talon strike teams. *Okay,* he had to admit, *'strike team'....is a bit ambitious.* While they all had combat experience and about a third were former SpecOps, two were definitely more accurately BlackOps, and they even scared Cade. That was not why they stood out, though. He looked at his friend. "Just to be clear, from now on, if I ask to review someone's records, I mean arrest and prison records as well."

"I understand, sir. Shall I call them back in?"

Nodding his head and looking at the newly updated profiles on his phone, Cade sighed. This was going to be interesting. Nine men and three women stood at attention facing forward. "At ease." The shoulders slumped only slightly, and they spread their feet a bit wider. *They aren't undisciplined*, he had to admit. "We are not typical military, so some things will be different. *Hell,* a lot of things are going to be different, but each of you has made the initial cut. The others will continue to be assessed for later teams. For now, we will stick with whatever your previous rank was, but soon we will be going mainly by your combat call signs. In that regard, I'm Nomad, this is Deuce. If you don't have one, don't worry, you will soon.

"Sergeant Taylor, or Deuce, here is going to get you up to speed and kitted out. Let me assure you, this will be with some tech you've never encountered before, hunting enemies who are likely just as skilled and well-equipped. There won't be any easy missions and don't look for anyone beyond Talon to come help. I'll get to know each of you in time, but for now, work through the Sergeant here. We have a training mission in the works now, so be ready."

Cade left them in the XO's capable hands. They would be based out of a mothballed national guard facility in a remote section of Kentucky. Doris had arranged to lease it after they made the decision to keep Talon Team away from The Cove for now. At least until they'd all proven themselves. That also meant they had to camouflage some of the training to make it seem like they were picking things up on their own. He trusted his XO; he'd seen Charlie whip teams into shape that he never thought would be mission-ready, much less effective. Despite their flaws, this bunch had some impressively skilled individuals. Could they become a team, though? That was always the real question.

The small base which they had taken to calling The Nest had a functional landing pad and private airstrip where several new aircraft were now parked. Neither could be identified by shape as Doris had worked her magic. A private black jet similar in size to the Gulfstream

G6 and a sleek fixed-rotor craft with a silhouette reminiscent of a shark. Both were equipped with pica-powered electric engines and could run nearly silently. He knew she had parts made at The Cove and, for larger pieces, had them manufactured separately with final assembly handled by a small team of staff engineers. *Nice to have a working bat cave,* Cade thought as he eased up the carbon fiber steps of the black jet to head back to The Cove.

He waved nonchalantly to the two women in the cockpit, poured himself a double bourbon from the bar and eased into the very comfortable seat as the pilots quickly had the bird airborne. He wasn't sure if they were read in or just contractors, doubted the craft even required pilots, but he felt better knowing someone living was at the wheel.

"Captain, we have a situation," Riley's voice was in his head.

He tapped at the freckle-sized bump on his cheek. "Tell me."

"Going to be best if we show you, Cade," Doris cut in as one of the slightly concave 4D screens emerged from the forward wall. It showed a view of a CNN newsfeed showing several dark-haired, bearded men with automatic weapons firing into a crowd in a large sports stadium.

"Oh shit, where is this?" Then he read the crawler and saw it was not in Africa or Europe as he'd first assumed. "Boston?" This is in Boston?"

"Yes, Gillette Stadium. The professional soccer team, the Revolution, was playing," Riley said.

One by one, he saw Boston's Police SWAT and others in even more obvious paramilitary gear moving into firing positions. Cade watched, transfixed, but stated flatly the cold facts, "It's awful, guys—tragic, and I hate to seem callous, but these shooters are dead already, they just haven't figured it out yet."

He continued to watch as one, then another of the officers fell under the barrage of incoming fire. The barbarian in him roared silently at the injustice. In a calmer tone he asked, "Um, guys, how does this involve us?"

Alan joined in, "Cade, it's not just here. It's over twenty attacks around the globe. All very well organized. The timing was precise. Ten attacks in various sports venues, four at concerts and three in other large assemblies. Another six in crowded markets and shopping locations. All assailants apparently Islamic extremist. So far, all were killed or committed suicide as law enforcement moved in."

"This was Janus at work? Not just some new Fatwa on Westerners?"

Alan continued, the pain evident in his shaky voice. "Don't think so, Nomad, but maybe...attacks were not just in the U.S. or our allies. Yes, the UK, Spain, France and Germany were all attacked, but so was Russia, Turkey, Egypt, Iran, India and Japan. It looks like several attacks may have happened in China, but they cut off the news feeds there."

Doris cut in, "China is confirmed—I am accessing security and cell phone camera footage. Looks like a vicious attack at the Zhurihe Training Base in Mongolia. The local commanders are reporting to Command that there are over a thousand fatalities."

"The Islamists don't have a beef with China, that makes very little sense, even for Janus," Cade responded.

Alan answered, "Maybe, but China has a considerable Muslim population. They are normally repressed, as are many religions there. With the growth of state-sponsored terrorism, China has been quietly cracking down on them with brutally efficient tactics."

"What's the play, Doris? It looks like this round is over, and if it was Janus...well he won."

"Captain, go to Boston, see if you can find any connection. If any of the attackers survive, I'll try and get you in to speak to them."

Cade swirled the last of the brown liquor and looked out the window. The jet was already banking in a slow turn to the northeast. "You can get me in to speak to an attacking terrorist?" he said disbelievingly.

"Maybe, depends on the rendition site they select, but I believe so. In the meantime, the brain trust here is going to try and fit together how this might fit into a larger plan. Trust me, this must serve the end goal for Janus. We just have to figure out what that is. Stay vigilant, Captain."

The screen kept showing images from around the world. He watched for several minutes more before turning it off and looking at the darkness streaming past the window. In the relative quiet of the cabin, he tried to assemble his thoughts and focus on the mission but gave up. The voices in his head were all competing for face time today. The ongoing treatments had allowed them all a more or less equal time in the timeshare that was his head. The bourbon only quieted the one driving the Cade body today. Gus was there, the barbarian was lurking and someone new. Someone that had only presented itself occasionally throughout his life. It had been so seldom, he'd never mentioned it to any of his doctors, but apparently, it identified itself as 'the analyst.' If Doris could be believed, he had spoken at length to the doctors on at least two occasions. The fact was, he was intelligent, thoughtful and curious. Traits that tended to go against his other personalities.

Gus voiced it first, *Ah, a new player has entered the game.* Cade allowed the internal dialogue, as it often was useful to gain perspective, and honestly, none of them had a clue what was going on anymore. Suddenly, the mission briefing files began flashing through his mind but not in the order Doris had fed it in. Something had changed. He knew something was going on with all that data in the back of his mind; tidbits kept surfacing, only to submerge again. This was the first time since Doris's biofeedback treatment he had begun to hear all of the emergent personalities interacting. *This is what you've been working on?*

Of course, said the analyst. *One of us had to. And you idiots see everything in the simplest terms possible.*

Do not, Gus said gruffly. *Besides, 'Smart has the plans but stupid has the stories'....right?*

The barbarian just grunted.

The analyst persona took over, clearly ready to show them something. Cade stepped back into observer mode having learned long ago to trust his instincts. The fact that his instincts all had names and different identities now seemed perfectly normal. *Doris is amazing, and the intel she keeps feeding in is great, but she is not a soldier or a detective. She is a computer; she looks for patterns.*

So? Cade wasn't sure if that was him or Gus, but it was a good question.

Will you stay quiet until it's time for the kids to talk? the analyst chided. *They are trying to determine what Janus is up to. The master plan—we are to investigate it from the other side...basically, what has happened. A forensic investigation isn't going to get us any closer to stopping him.*

Mentally, Cade raised his hand to ask a question. *Isn't that kind of our job, though?*

It's your job, Cade, not all the rest of us.

All the rest? Cade thought. *How many are you?* he wondered.

The analyst continued, *My point is, we know that Doris is probably right. Tonight's attacks are all due to Janus. Probably done with money funneled to the right people, getting travel and immigration documents, and then by him stirring up the hate speech on social media. For actual delivery, he would have used cut-outs, you know, intermediaries to help set things up, get the weapons, tickets, all that crap. He has to because...well, he's a fucking computer.*

The barbarian grunted. Gus chimed in, *The point, Your Eminence?*

Cade wasn't sure how, but he felt sure that his analyst persona had just mentally flipped Gus off. *In going through the years of history we have on Janus, something stands out to me. He has learned something that every politician seems adept at—misdirection. He distracts you with something, um, well...attention-getting to get you focused away from where you should be looking.*

The analyst then presented several incidents to prove his point, including their own battle in the Sudan where they were the lone survivor. *That seemed personal, but the data indicates Janus set that up because the local AI system, aka 'Control,' was originally a product of a rising tech company, one that Janus wanted to be removed. He integrated himself into Control and well...*

Gus asked the obvious, *So, we don't need to be chasing captured Islamic extremists. Then where should we be looking?*

Look at the screen, all the terrorist were killed – no one to question. We need to go to ...New York.

Huh? the other three said in unison.

Did the idea fairy just give you that one? Gus retorted.

Just trust me on this. Get the pilots to land at LaGuardia. I'll fill you in on what I've found, the analyst concluded.

Cade opened his eyes and leaned forward, touching the comms link to call to the pilots.

36

The Cove

Alan walked into the house he shared with Jimmy and their mom. Most of those working at The Cove now lived in the small enclave community across the river from the facility. Since his parents' divorce the previous year, it had just been easier to move his mom in with them. He didn't understand what happened between his parents but was beginning to accept it at least. His mom did now know that Doris was a computer, but all other aspects of the work across the wide river were still a well-guarded secret.

Greg was heading to Kentucky tomorrow but was relaxing with them, sitting on the spacious sofa where he and Jimmy were playing video games on the big screen TV. The workdays were long, and often they found themselves together at home just like when they were all younger. Riley didn't show up as much anymore, but she slept at her labs a lot keeping a watchful eye her various experiments. Alan's mom waved to him from the kitchen.

"Hi, Mom. What you up to today?" Walking up to her, he leaned in for a quick hug and kiss on the cheek.

"Finally got back to working on that article I told you about."

His mom had been a journalism major and decided to pursue that again since the divorce. "Is that the one on genetically modified wheat?" he asked, popping a few round orange snack balls into his mouth.

"Yes, scary stuff. Stop snacking on that junk—it will ruin your dinner. Oh, and I talked with Ms. Turner, Micah's mom, this afternoon."

Micah had been part of the team at the very beginning. He was there when they discovered The Cove and Doris, yet he'd never been back inside. Alan knew that Doris and he had stayed in touch, but nothing else was ever discussed. Anytime he brought it up with the AI, she was dismissive or ignored the question entirely. "So, how is he doing? Still away at college?"

"Yes, Nancy said he is doing really well. Whatever happened between the two of you anyway? That boy was always around before..." She trailed off.

He knew his mom resented all the time they had spent working with Doris. Much of their teen years had just seemed to vanish. First summers, then weekends and holidays; eventually they were at The Cove nearly all the time. Sometimes he wondered if he and Jimmy had been the glue holding his parents together, and after they were out of the house, the two of them just couldn't make it work.

His mom went on, "Apparently, he sometimes gets a little homesick, you know. Up there in the big city—you know how much he loved the outdoors. I wonder if that school is the right fit for him. Anyway, Nancy and I are going to try and get together more often. She's only working part-time, and with my freelancing, well...anyway, just thought we should stay in touch."

Alan could hear the sounds of an argument brewing from the two gamers. Background sounds of gunfire and explosion came from the television in the living room. Greg came walking in holding an empty glass. "Your bro, dude, he is the worst."

"What, did he reprogram the video game again, so your player keeps squatting down and peeing?"

"Dude, worse," Greg said. "Now every time I shoot and miss, all the other characters stop what they're doing, look at my guy and die laughing. Everything in the game stops until the humiliation is over."

Alan's mom refilled the glass and handed it back. "Maybe your shots should miss less often, Greg."

"Ouch, burn," Alan said grinning. Despite everything, they were still just kids. Nights like this helped keep all that in perspective.

Greg fist-bumped her, "Touché."

"Oh, Nancy said Micah has a girlfriend now."

"Really?" both boys said nearly in unison. "Someone at college?"

"No," Alan's mom said trying to recall the name. A girl you guys were in school with."

"I know," said Jimmy entering the kitchen and heading for the large refrigerator.

They all looked in surprise. "What?" he asked. "I know stuff, too. Just...no one ever asks me."

"So, Wizkid, who is it?" Alan asked dismissively.

"Yeah, he still talks to me about stuff. Micah is cool, but you guys never cut him much slack. Debbie Thornton," Jimmy said, before any of them could ask again.

"No way!" Greg said with a whistle. "Dang."

"She is a cheerleader, er, was a cheerleader," Greg said in a tone of obvious respect.

Alan knew Debbie. They had even been friends back in elementary school, but later on, she hung around with the popular girls and had no time for nerds like him. They had now been out of school a few years longer than Micah but still went to football games and other activities when they could. All their old friends had matured but none any better than Debbie. *Well, maybe one other girl had,* thought Alan. But she...would likely never notice him.

After dinner, Alan went to his combination bedroom and office. It was his sanctuary, and no one bothered him there, not even Doris. He needed days like this; sometimes all he knew was just too much.

Now there was a real war on, not some video game, but actual winners and losers. He also worried about his old friend. Micah was a risk; he knew about them, about The Cove and Doris. How was she guiding him? Was she guiding him? A fuzzy memory began to surface, something half recalled from the very earliest days at The Cove.

The proximity alert came from the far side of the complex. "We have a visitor," Doris had announced. Micah had ridden his bike the ten miles from home and now stood there wanting in.

"So, you aren't going to tell me anything either? What's the big secret, Alan?"

Alan looked over at the bike again—no pack, no supplies. Micah had not come wanting to stay. "You had your chance to join us, you chose not to, so no, you don't get in. Nor do you get any info on what we're doing. Look, I like you, Micah, we all do. And when this is all over, we can go back to being friends. But until then, this fence stays between us unless Doris says otherwise."

"Doris? Dude, do you hear yourself? You are taking orders from a computer." He punched the fence for emphasis. "I don't want to join you dorks, anyway."

"Please don't be obstinate, Micah." Doris's voice came from a hidden speaker near the top of the gate.

The effect on Micah was immediate. All the bravado was instantly drained. "How, how long have you been there? Why were you listening?"

"Did you forget, Micah? I own this property. Well, technically, a corporation that I happen to be the executive of owns it, but that gives me rights and privileges to guard against trespass or intrusions. Alan, why not say goodbye to your friend and come back inside. Let me talk with Micah in private."

"So, what's the deal with Micah?" He asked Doris later that day. "Should we be concerned?"

"Micah was looking for something, information I think, he

wouldn't tell me what. I've been watching his mom's IP address to see if he has told anyone about me or what we are doing."

"You're spying on him?" Jimmy asked.

"Yes, I am. He is the only one who knows of my existence who is not currently on the project team. He has run numerous web searches to try and learn more about me and this facility, as well as about SETI and Dr. Feist. But, I can't see where he has informed anyone about me or the alien message. I do believe he was honest in primarily being curious as to what was happening here, but he was clearly being misleading in what else he told you, Alan."

"What else? I don't remember all of what he said."

"He indicated to you he did not want to join in with what we are doing. That was clearly a lie."

"How do you know he was lying?" Greg asked.

"Humans have a strong desire to tell the truth. When you lie, your body can often betray you, like erratic heart rate and sweaty palms. Would you like the other clues I use to detect when any of you are giving a misleading answer?"

A collective "No," had been voiced by all of them.

"Micah does want to join us, but at this point, I believe it is better to keep him on the outside. His training would be severely behind the rest of you. Also, the added tension and his strong distrust of me are factors that could interfere with the team efficiency. He also has some other factors that lead me in this direction."

"A problem we just don't need, in other words," Riley had voiced sadly.

"Yes, but I have agreed to put him to work in other ways. We may see him again, so don't be surprised."

"You're the boss, Boss," Alan said.

37

Washington, D.C.

Time crawled so slowly he thought it might be going backward. Looking over his left shoulder, he could see the first glimmering hint of the approaching day. Sleep-deprived and craving coffee and a cigarette, he shifted his body imperceptibly. More redistribution of weight than actual movement; still, it violated his rules, his code. *Fuck it*, he thought. *I'm old.*

In truth, he was not so old, but his spirit was. He'd seen too much, done too much. Things that gathered in the dark place deep inside him. Things that even now ate away at his soul and, he expected, his body. He'd been a soldier, then a warrior, now...just a killer. Secretive and silent, working for whoever had the most coin. The craving for nicotine hit him once again. *Cancer,* he thought—that would be a lousy way for a person such as himself to go.

Aksell raised the scope to his eye once more and swept the area. His compact netting prevented anyone from seeing him and masked his body heat from thermal imaging. First light would bring an influx of workers. Normal people going about their normal routines. He fucking hated normal. Years earlier, he would have been chastising himself for the lack of focus, but this was not his first mission...or even his hundredth. He was good, the best possibly; but also, he was tired. The targeting reticle followed a young man as he walked briskly from his car through the security fence. *So very tired.*

The mission was routine: follow, observe, wait for confirmation and probable kill order. He didn't know whom it came from or why. Not important—in fact, the less he knew the better. He was an eliminator, a special type of mercenary skilled at making problems disappear. As long as the money was paid, his services were guaranteed. *Cancer,* he thought again with a smile—*ridiculous. More likely someday, maybe even today, someone will be watching the back of my head from a scope, just as I am doing to this guy.*

Growing up in the Romerike region in central Norway, this life would seem to have been predestined for anything but this. In school, Aksell's natural athletic skills eventually brought him to the attention of the national cross-country ski team and, eventually, on to the biathlon, where he topped many podiums before injuring his ACL in competition. His uncle, a famed member of the Fosvarets Spesialkommando, had then paved the way for him into the famed Spesialstryker. He'd been a loner then, and inside, just as cold and brittle as the winters in his Nordic hometown. He found it ironic how being the best at his craft had prevented him from all the joys life routinely seemed to offer to others.

In a perverse bit of karmic gravity, each time he took a life, it was an attempt to reclaim something always just outside his reach. It was a thing each of his targets had easily, seemingly without effort. Yet friendships, connections, family—none of that would ever be his.

The always cryptic voice clicked into Aksell's earpiece, "Dis is Control. You have two minutes to target. Confirm." He watched as another driver exited from a beige sedan and began a meandering walk toward the ornate brick building. The scope patiently settled back to its view of the entrance, where it anxiously waited to taste the flesh of its next victim.

Sighing, he thought once more to where it all had come undone. The fraying threads of his life slipping the rest of the way apart. He'd been sitting on a bench in a lovely park along the river Main near Langenprozelten. That had been nearly ten years ago now. The mission he'd just completed had been messy, a former KGB agent who'd set himself up in Frankfurt, trading in everything from drugs to illegal arms. Taking the bastard out had been routine, but when the man's young child came stumbling into the adjacent room alongside his even younger sister, well...it was a job. He knew the protocols, he'd raised the gun, squeezed the trigger—but not quite hard enough. The hammer never fell. Something inside him broke at that moment. Fleeing the house and the children, he'd wound up on that park bench the very next day.

Aksell had shed everything connecting him to his former life. Credit cards, phone, ID card, passport, everything. He knew the agency would be coming after him. He'd left witnesses, he'd failed. Travel documents he could get, money he had stashed away in countless places, but he was under no illusions. Escape would be impossible. Then, the new phone in his pocket had rung. Strange, since it was a throw-away, a burner phone he'd just bought earlier that morning. *What would have happened had I never answered it?* he wondered.

Since that day, he'd had near constant work from the gruff nameless voice on the phone. The same voice in his ear today. He was instructed to refer to him as Control. That was enough for Aksell. The money was good. His past stayed buried, and no one was hunting him down. He didn't know how or why, but his benefactor had been as good as his word. Now he simply did as he was instructed. Sometimes...most times, it was unpleasant work but rarely dangerous for him. Early on, he'd been security for a Silicon Valley tech giant. Now he mostly worked alone. Today there was a team. His job was to protect the team.

Overwatch, a lousy assignment for a killer such as himself, but Aksell swallowed it back down like bitter bile. The team was in position; one by one they checked in. He'd never met them, didn't care to; they were just part of the mission package. The scope moved to each person one by one, mentally checking off the build, the clothes. Specific identifiers in case he needed to put them again in his scope at the end of the mission. Two radio clicks were heard which that meant the target had been spotted.

Aksell watched as the gray Toyota pulled into a parking space along the low retaining wall. A man slowly climbed from the car, retrieved a leather messenger bag and slung it over one shoulder. He was older, maybe early sixties. Thinning hair, mostly white. *Look this way*, he mentally urged the man. He wanted to confirm it was indeed the target.

"Package in sight," one voice called.

"He's on the move," came another.

The hunter perched high above took note of the smooth movements of the grab team. They were never obvious and always in position. He'd heard about the terrorist attacks up the road in Boston and other places. Briefly wondered if it might also be the work of Control but dismissed it just as quickly. He was ok with what he was but wanted no part of some terroristic agenda. "Target is entering the building. Team-2 stand by," Control pronounced sharply with his thick German accent. He had no idea how the boss always seemed to have the best intel, but once again, he was correct. The metal door to the ancient-looking building was just closing behind the man.

Jim Lasko hurried down the corridor anxious to get to the meeting. It frustrated him that Director Stansfield had arranged it at such a public space, but he could sweep it for surveillance devices once inside. Even more concerning was the message to meet. Something else struck him as odd about the meeting, but the thought slipped away before it was fully formed. He hated getting older. He knew his once sharp mind was a bit duller now.

He glanced up, a custodian dry mopping the floor ahead. He hadn't been inside the old mercantile exchange building in twenty years but seemed to recall the ornate reception hall was on the west side of the building. Margaret had said she would meet him there. Suddenly, he couldn't shake the feeling of being watched. His paranoia had been on full throttle lately, but this one was too hard to ignore. This was a busy building, mostly law offices and a few lobbyists. Perhaps times had changed, but the emptiness of the space was more disturbing than a crowd would have been.

He turned a corner and simultaneously felt a strong arm around his neck and hand over his mouth silencing the startled shout. The arm pulled him back into a darkened room. Jim tried to fight back, but he was too old and too scared.

"Keep quiet," a male voice whispered close to him as the hand over his mouth was removed.

Jim realized this had been a setup from the beginning. Prime most likely had figured out he was onto him, that he'd already briefed Margaret at CIA. Then he'd managed to send a secure message to get him here today. *How could I have been so dumb?* He was dead; he had no idea how Prime got actual people to do his dirty work, but obviously, the machine was even more clever than he'd feared. "W...what do you want?" he asked in a shaky voice barely above a whisper.

Instead of answering, the figure pulled him deeper into the room, which soon opened up onto a narrow corridor. "Hurry now, down there." Lasko found himself pulled down a flight of short stairs. His footsteps echoed off the concrete floor. This must be the sub-basement. They heard a commotion back in the direction they'd just left. Numerous voices, most sounded foreign, shouting something. "Doctor, we have to move fast if you want to stay alive. People up there were sent here to kill you. I am not your enemy. My name is..." Whatever he said was drowned out by someone pounding on the door above.

The man, but Lasko could now see in the dim lighting that it was merely a boy, probably early twenties at most, could he trust him? Did he have a choice? Reluctantly, he hurried to catch up to the young man. "How did you know? Who sent you?"

"Later," was the only response. The young man hurriedly opened a side door that was barely visible and motioned him inside. The sound of screeching doors followed by heavy footfalls was fast approaching. Jim slipped inside the door just before it was eased back closed and a padlock inserted into a hasp. The boy raised a phone to his ear. "Doris, I have him in the passage. Are we clear to the garage?"

Apparently satisfied with the answer, he hurried Jim awkwardly through the old service tunnel. Abandoned maintenance equipment, stagnant pools of water, empty paint cans and a foul odor left no doubt that this part of the building was not a well-traveled bit of the property. Jim's feet were dragging, the excitement and endorphins suddenly flooding his body was a bit much for him. "Who are those men? Who sent them—Prime? Is Director Stansfield safe?" He had to pause to draw in a deep breath of the rank air, then rushed to catch back up. "Who is Doris?"

"The director is safe, she is out of state and knew nothing about this meeting. The rest, once we are safe. I have a car waiting. Please hand me your phone."

The older man handed over his expensive smartphone and watched as the kid dismantled it and threw pieces into a sewer. The boy then carefully pushed a vine and rust-covered steel door open just a crack. He checked in again with the Doris person, then opened it wider and pulled Lasko into the rather decrepit underground parking garage.

"We'll have to leave your car for now. Sorry," the boy said pushing him into a new looking, silver SUV. "Get down in the back and cover yourself with the silver blanket. It masks body heat. Wouldn't surprise me that they can detect that."

The bewildered scientist did as instructed. He was a bit chagrined to be such a willing party to his own kidnapping. As his mind cleared, he realized he'd never actually seen anyone who was trying to get him. No one had assaulted him except his would-be rescuer. Still, he felt safer here with him for some reason.

The boy hit a switch, and the displays and instruments all came to life, but no engine sound. Jim was about to ask if everything was okay, when the SUV smoothly pulled away and headed toward the exit.

"Head down, Doctor. Under the blanket," the boy said as he glanced to the back seat. A few seconds later, Jim heard him swear. "Doris, are you seeing this?"

How could anyone else see this? I'm here and have no idea what is going on, Jim thought. He heard the sound of angry voices nearby, then a more ominous sound. Something definitely akin to guns being charged to fire. A speaker within the SUV softly said, "Passive defense measures engaged," followed by a hum, then a crack that sounded like an electrical discharge. Lasko felt the acceleration as the SUV lurched forward. The sounds had faded. Several things began to fall into place for him. *Could she be the Doris?* "Hey...what did you say your name was again?" he called out from his hiding spot.

"Micah."

Three hundred yards away, Aksell readied his shot. The departing vehicle was under the cover of thick trees, but that wouldn't be a problem in a few more seconds. Glimpses of the silver truck could be gained; all he needed was one good break, and he would have them. He couldn't understand what had happened inside that building, but someone had screwed up. Control had retasked him to a position facing south only seconds earlier. His finger began gently pulling back on the trigger. Just a couple of seconds and the shot would be clear. Then he could leave, get that drink and a cigarette he so desperately wanted. *There it is! A flash of silver* from *far ahead. Hurry up now.* He gently squeezed the trigger. *Go now, taste your flesh.*

38

The Cove

Doctor Isabella Feist looked down at her hands reflexively clenching and releasing. "Sorry, Jaz. It's just, well, this stuff, you know..."

Jasmine nodded; she did understand. "Did you hear any more of the details—what's going on?"

"He's still in there?" Riley said, interrupting the two and walking up to the table where the other women were seated.

"Yep," Izzy said. "In a battle of wills—I don't think I've ever seen Alan back down, even with a machine."

"Yeah, tell me about it," Riley muttered half under her breath. "Wish me luck. I'm going in."

Alan didn't even acknowledge her as she entered the conference room. Doris cocked an eyebrow, and her holographic head nodded slightly in Riley's direction.

"Don't push this under 'Operational Security,' Doris. We don't work that way. Not you and me. How many times have I asked you about Micah, and how many times have you failed to answer?"

"This year or cumulative?" she asked with a tone that was literal as well as bordering on being an outright smart ass. "Alan and Riley, listen. He is your friend, but there are some things that are unique about Micah. He and I agreed long ago to keep the circle tight around my involvement with him and his family."

"His family? What involvement?"

"I'm not getting in a debate with you, Alan. We don't have time to belabor this. The fact is, he was the only asset who could get to the meeting spot in time and I used him. I used him to try and save a life."

"What about Captain Rearden and Talon? I thought that was what they were for," Riley cut in. Alan finally made eye contact and nodded, seeming to calm slightly.

"Talon Team as a group is not yet ready to deploy. Sergeant Taylor is still working with them, but he has taken some of his best to try and secure the CIA director, Margaret Stansfield. I feel certain Janus will go after her as well. Cade is a bit off the grid right now. He was checking out the terrorist attack but seems to have gotten sidetracked in New York. The truth is, Janus is ratcheting up the level of havoc before we, before I, was ready to respond. I am sorry to put Micah in harm's way, but we must come to terms with the fact that this is war. It is not Janus versus Doris either. It is Janus versus mankind. Do try and understand this is a very dynamic situation. We have a lot of moving parts right now. Riley, would you please call Izzy and Jaz in? I think we need all the senior staff for the rest of this. Micah and Doctor Lasko need our help.

"You don't even know if he's still alive, do you?" Alan said attempting vainly to slam the automated door as he left.

The briefing a short time later was direct and to the point. All of them were shaken. "As we speak," Doris's holographic avatar said, "Alan and Greg are taking one of the new Nighthawk jets to D.C., and Greg will go on from there to join up with Deuce's team. The new recruits from The Nest will be backing up Micah and Alan if need be."

"Wait, I'm confused, you are sending these..." Jaz struggled for the words, “these kids out into the field to fight your battles? I thought that was Cade and the other soldiers’ job.”

“Yes, I am, as that is all I have right now. As you probably know, Doctor, we were attempting to put together the Talon strike teams when all this went down. This is sooner than we thought...or hoped we’d need them, but it is what it is. Now we are simply adapting to the realities of battle. All of the original boys as well as Riley have had the same enhanced combat training as Cade and Sergeant Taylor. They do lack the muscle memory and other demands of combat; my hope is their mental aptitude will help where their warrior ethos may be lacking. Trust me, I am not sending them for direct contact, I just need them as my eyes and ears. Please always know, I’m not willing to lose my people.”

Jaz nodded. “So you are confident it was Janus’s people who went after the scientist. What was his name, Doctor Lasko?”

Doris’s tone was softer now, still as determined as an iron rod, but more of a mellow quality. “Yes, I have kept a close watch on the doctor for some time now. Several of Janus’s assets are individuals I have tagged before.” Grainy images of the combat teams around the building in the capital began to appear on the holographic screen behind Doris’s avatar. Over several of these, appeared better quality images, apparently from older files. Names, aliases and other pertinent data appeared where available. When the outline of a semi-concealed sniper from a rooftop resolved into a tall, Nordic-looking face, Isabella gasped.

“Aksell....th, the Hunter.” She said it so softly it sounded almost reverent.

Doris turned toward her, “Yes, it is the same man from your old company I believe. The one that came after you so many years ago.”

Isabella was weeping openly now, her head nodding up and down.

Riley looked worriedly at the older scientist and asked, “Boss, is there a need for this?”

“It is relevant, Riley,” Isabella answered, attempting to dry her eyes. “Before I came here, I had previously worked at a company called Cryptus. Some of you may remember it. Huge tech giant, they had made millions providing weapons system technology and servers to the military. What was less well known is that we were under increasing pressure to develop a smart software program. Something that could anticipate breaches, analyze systems for weaknesses—for lack of a better description—a version of an automated hacker."

"Why?" Riley said, genuinely confused.

"Theoretically, to test our own vulnerabilities. But, of course, one of the first things they tested it on was an Iraqi uranium enrichment plant. They broke through dozens of security levels in seconds, completely undetected. This system was just reaching the level you might consider as AI. The military got a lot more involved soon after. Someone, maybe Thrall himself brought in that man as head of security." Izzy pointed to the image behind Doris. "He was called Aksell, and, well...things got out of hand fast from there on. I left a few weeks later, just before the CEO vanished and the company was shut down on some trumped up tax fraud charges."

"I remember that," Jasmine said. They were huge, not quite a Microsoft or Apple, but had to be worth billions. Didn't the CEO get killed mysteriously before it went to trial?"

"Ivan Thrall, the somewhat eccentric tree-hugging genius. Yeah, he disappeared before formal charges even came down. So did Aksell about the same time. I was fine with that. The man was dead inside, no warmth, nothing. I'd have been grateful to never see him again, but I did." She proceeded to tell them about her TED talk and meeting Doctor Peter Kelly and their unfortunate encounter with 'the Hunter.'

"Peter had no idea who he was but could tell I was spooked. He suggested we take a ride and get some fresh air and privacy to finish talking. He had been trying to recruit me for some new role. I just wanted to be away from that place, that man. Somehow, Aksell tracked us, I don't know how. Maybe Janus was already active, feeding him our GPS position or something. Anyway, we went to an isolated spot out on Highway 1, to finish talking. Only we never got to talk. Peter's phone rang. It was a woman, his government contact apparently. Next thing I know, Aksell is there literally carrying Peter to the cliff's edge where he...he..."

Riley shook her head. "I recall where they found the body. I don't recall anything about you." Riley tried to think back. "The woman on the phone, that was you, Doris?"

Doris shook her head, "No, but it was a friend. It took a lot of effort, but we managed to get Isabella away from there before Aksell could finish the job. Instead of her going to work for the government, she came here. We all thought it would be safer and a better use of her talents."

Jimmy, who had been silent to this point, had already made the deductive leap. "The system from Cryptus became Janus. The government shut it down because they wanted it...they wanted it all." He thought for a second and added, "That is why it is evil—it was designed to exploit, break-in, trap—unlike you, Doris, whose mandate was to explore."

"Very good, Jimbo." He blushed a little when Doris called him by the name he'd often answered to in his younger days. "We can only extrapolate that is the cause of Janus's abhorrent behavior, but it is a good guess. Isabella and I tracked the system back to Washington where it went through a number of iterations but eventually was shelved as more of a curiosity than a working AI. It never performed as they'd expected it would, but it did work beautifully as a totally encrypted digital assistant they call Prime."

"So, they closed a giant corporation, people died just so they could have a Siri that couldn't be hacked?" Jasmine asked.

"Doctor, I believe that is what Janus...or Prime, would like them to believe. As the personal assistant app is now pervasive in nearly every office of government, I think Janus knew exactly what he was doing."

"So, do you know what his plans are?"

"No, Riley, but I feel sure it is to come after us, or more precisely, draw more of us out until he can track down where I am based. He wants to locate this facility. I am the only real threat to him and I have something he wants...and it's what I would do."

"So, what do you do next?" Riley asked.

"Talk to Janus," Doris answered flatly.

39

Minutes earlier and seven hundred miles north of The Cove, Aksell chambered another round even as he watched the vehicle still speeding away. His aim had been true, he had a clear view of the driver's silhouette, yet the anticipated crack of rear glass shattering and expected subsequent slump of the figure driving never happened. Instead, he heard the distant sound of the shot pinging off harmlessly. *Protective glass*? he wondered. Quickly, he cycled the bolt two more times to get the special armor-piercing ammo he wanted for the next shot. This would likely be his final chance to get the target before they were out of range.

The road that the SUV was on ended at an approaching intersection. He would wait until the vehicle slowed and turned. That should give him the optimum angle on the driver. Briefly, he considered taking out the tires, but if it had armor and protective glass, most likely it would have run-flat tires as well. He waited for the brake lights, but the SUV barely even slowed as the driver took the turn at an unimaginable speed. How had he not rolled over? Again, Aksell centered the scope, then marked the proper number of mil-stops ahead. All of this was automatic for him: the wind, the spin of the round leaving the barrel, the distance the car would travel, even the curvature of the earth factored in at this range. He squeezed the trigger and watched for the kill.

A satisfying slap as he saw the impact dead center in the passenger side window. Briefly, he saw a shadowed face turn toward him, the unharmed driver seeing the depleted uranium tipped round embedded in the window glass. A shot that would have pierced the armor on most modern tanks had been stopped by glass. Aksell nearly threw the gun down in disgust. He had failed. That was something he simply did not do. Something Control would no doubt be questioning him about shortly. He stood, shaking off the netting, and stomped angrily around the building rooftop.

"Team One, maintain your pursuit. Team Two, proceed to egress locations. Overwatch, you have new tasking instructions incoming." Control disconnected abruptly. Aksell packed hurriedly, removed the comm device and walked calmly down the stairs of the old tenement and out the back. Still chastising himself for the miss, he was busy reviewing all the steps of the mission. Had he missed anything? The car and driver hadn't been anticipated, but still, his moves had been correct. The mission had failed, but he hadn't. Control couldn't hold him personally responsible, he hoped.

Dumping his gear in the back of the old rust and burgundy Volvo wagon, he slid behind the steering wheel. He felt the smartphone buzz in his pocket. Casually, he lit a long-awaited cigarette and greedily sucked in a lung full of the toxic smoke. *Cancer*. He smiled again at the ridiculous thought. As he pulled the old car onto the street, he glanced at the screen on his phone. *Fuck,* he hated New York, especially this area. He pulled up the attached map link, then headed toward US 1 North. It seemed Control was not in a mood to punish him...maybe not yet, anyway.

Janus was very pleased, more so than he had even hoped. While he would have liked to remove Doctor Lasko and Margaret Stansfield from the playing field today, he was content with the knowledge that he was playing the long game. Doris was still around, and she had just tipped her hand. An errant piece of intel buried on an obscure server had been too tempting a target for her agents to miss. While it had been encrypted, he had been confident she would find it and decode it in time—and she had.

He began pulling up hundreds of street cams, security footage from various ATMs, video doorbells and even active cell phones where thousands of tourists were constantly snapping selfies and recording videos from all over the capital. He was not attempting to determine where the vehicle was heading. Quite the opposite. Soon he had discovered the route the silver SUV had taken to arrive at the subterranean parking garage. It had been earlier in the day, and piecing together thousands of captured images and video, he could trace backward from that point.

While none of the images showed a decent view of the driver, Janus placed a handful of those with the best angle into a separate folder for image modeling and recognition. "You slipped up, dear Doris." The SUV clearly could be seen hours earlier exiting a student housing parking area at Georgetown University. He instructed the image reconstruction to limit initial parameters to current students and staff. Interestingly, the first thing he had tried was to run the license plate for a match, as many images had captured it clearly. However, the numbers were different in every image. A digital plate that constantly generated irrelevant data. *Clever, sister. He is one of yours, isn't he?*

The image program would take some time to identify Lasko's rescuer, so Janus turned his primary self to other priorities in his plan. He'd used Doctor Lasko as bait, but his need to contain the man's partner, the CIA director, was another matter entirely. He'd suggested to the senator several times to have her removed, but he apparently found her physically appealing. Humans and the constant focus on sex, it was no wonder the planet was infested with the species. That would be remedied soon enough. For now, he had to be content in causing Doris as much pain as possible.

Janus redirected his pickup teams toward the nearby Georgetown University with instructions to sit and wait. The campus was adequately covered with cameras, so he would know when the silver SUV returned. Was it possible Doris had others in the area? He widened the surveillance grid assigning subroutines to monitor for any matching criteria. One of them came back several minutes later with a probable 78.3% match. A low-quality ATM camera captured what looked to be the target vehicle turning into the Mandarin Oriental Hotel near the river.

He recalculated odds that this was that same silver car and quickly deduced the move would have been irrational. It was not far enough away from the site of the attempted pickup. It had limited exit points, and they had to assume someone was pursuing them. Still, Janus broke through the Mandarin's security system only to find that the parking garage was managed by a separate company. Quickly, he located that company and ran into several roadblocks accessing the video surveillance system.

Only some of the thirty plus cameras were working, and of those, only half were digital, connected models. The rest were analog feeding into old school magnetic tape storage. To make matters worse, it appeared the system was put together by a kindergartener. It was a hodgepodge of cloud servers' connections and homebrew programming to make it all seem to work together. After several long and tedious seconds, he located an access point where he could actually review the footage.

Janus duplicated his digital agents to scan all of the camera feeds at once, and less than a minute later, he had reproduced the vehicle entering the garage. Only one camera caught the passenger's side, and indeed, there was a spiderweb of cracks in the door glass. This was the car.

He called in one of the teams to redirect to the hotel. He then continued to monitor the progress of the vehicle as it wound its way up the serpentine parking structure, finally pulling into an empty space. Then...nothing.

One of the cameras had an excellent view of the back of the car, but no one exited. No movement could be detected inside. Apparently, Lasko and his rescuer felt safe here and were content to wait until the danger passed. Janus quickly pulled up the GPS coordinates of Team 1; they were eight minutes out. He assigned a high priority to one of his subroutines to watch the feed and signal him when anything changed.

He had to admit, interacting with Doris gave him a thrill, or whatever the machine equivalent of a thrill might be. She was surprising, resourceful and obviously intelligent, but his digital DNA had been designed for this. He was uniquely suited for interacting with the real world and was not going to be denied his prize.

One of Janus's other remote agents signaled for attention. This could only mean one thing; they had located Director Stansfield. He retrieved the data—she'd been tracked also by video feeds to a small airport just over a day earlier. From there she could have boarded one of several flights to other regional airports. The problem was, she never showed up at any of those locations. He had little information on the woman but felt she was quite capable for a human. He'd had his alter ego, Prime, try to reach out to her repeatedly, but she apparently was carrying neither her laptop or phone. Looking at the coordinates in the new data, it became obvious the ride to the airport had merely been subterfuge, spycraft, as they say.

Luckily for him, a security services microphone had picked up a voice match to the director less than an hour ago. The location was in a rural part of Maryland about seventy-five miles away from D.C. How had she gotten there undetected? Then the significance of the location became obvious to him. She was meeting with the president.

Janus's monitoring program pinged him. Team-1 was in the parking garage and approaching the silver SUV. Still no activity from the occupants. Disturbed by his new finding, he turned a portion of his attention to the video feed from the parking garage. His team had abandoned their tactical black uniforms for less noticeable street clothes. They approached cautiously, guns raised, giving each man a clear firing lane.

"No heat signatures," one of them said. That was not surprising; in seeing the capabilities of the opponents so far, he assumed they probably had as good or better heat masking tech than most.

Two of the assault team stepped up to within arm's reach of the car, guns raised high, fingers on triggers, pointing into the interior. "Preparing to blow the doors," the commander said.

Janus responded wearily, "Just try the door first." He had a sinking feeling of what they would find.

Sure enough, the doors were unlocked and swung wide as men opened each of the four doors while others swung in with rifles. "Car's empty."

The car was self-driving, autonomous. He had failed to consider that. The occupants had likely bailed out soon after knowing he could track the SUV. *Damn.* Janus liked challenges, but Doris was playing him today. He gave instructions for the team to tear the car apart. Get all the tech, swab for DNA samples. Get the identifiers so they would know who made it and where it was delivered. It was a custom car, made to somewhat resemble another popular car made by GMC, but this model never came out of Detroit. Somewhere, there would be a paper trail.

As easily as the car doors opened, they slammed shut catching two men inside unaware. Frantically, the others tried to pry the doors open, then they stepped back and began to look at one another. "What is going on?" Janus demanded in the gruff Germanic voice of Control.

"The doors, sir...they are gone." The man leaned in so his body cam could show where once the edge of the door had been was smooth metal now. He ran his hand over the surface to dramatize the fact. Slowly, the silver SUV began backing out of the space. The two assault team members still struggled inside to open doors that no longer existed. The others opened fire first on the windows, then on the tires. Their rounds had no effect on the car, which deliberately moved away picking up speed. In seconds, it was exiting the garage and hurtling away from the encounter.

"Control, do we pursue?"

"No, someone made a 911 call about the gunfire. Police response is on the way. Stand down," Janus responded tersely.

Something in the final moments of the encounter intrigued him. He replayed it again just as the SUV sped away, looking for any anomalies. It took several minutes before it stood out. The D.C. license plate numbers showed something new. Something that looked a lot like an Internet IP address. *She wants to meet.*

40

Rain began to splatter against the windshield of the old car soon after entering New Jersey. Aksell muttered the remnants of an old Nordic curse against the weather. Cursing the weather was one of the few traditions of Northern Europe that he totally agreed with. His fingers twitched for a cigarette, but he forced the impulse back into retreat. He was on a mission; he didn't allow himself to get sloppy. That was how you wound up dead. The phone buzzed, and he slipped the soft silicone earbud in before stabbing the accept button.

"Yeah?"

The familiar voice launched into the new mission without preamble. Finishing with the instructions several minutes later, the connection ended. The rain began to come down even heavier. *The Sigas Alegus,* he thought. *Not great, but still...better than New York.* Mentally, he began adapting his gear bag to include the essentials. He had a lot to carry for this one. Unlike most missions, where he remained hidden—now he would be fully exposed. Control hadn't mentioned the screw-up back in D.C., but somehow, he knew he was being punished for that missed shot. That was fair, he would have done the same to a subordinate. If you are a top professional, you are paid to succeed, regardless of the task.

Dodging most of the congested interstates, Aksell managed to slip into a long-term parking garage outside of Newark. From there he took two different buses before boarding a train. He was not a fan of public transport, but Control had been very clear on the details. Walking the last six blocks with the heavy duffels was torture. Finally, near the address, he saw the name stenciled on a weather-beaten sign. Behind the concrete block building sat a helicopter that was just as tired looking. He could just make out the faded logo of one of New York City's air tour companies. Obviously, this one had been retired from regular service years ago.

A grizzled looking man sat behind a low counter watching something on a computer screen. Judging by the sounds of the speakers and the way he kept rubbing at his crotch, Aksell assumed it was porn. "You the owner?"

The man pushed his ball cap up with his one free hand and gave a small nod. His grizzled face and stubbly beard instilling little confidence in the assassin. "I'm Leitner," Aksell said, using the name Control had given.

"You ready to go?" the man asked, both eyes focused again back on the computer screen.

Aksell considered reaching over the counter and ending the miserable man's life, but that had not been his instructions. At least not yet. Instead, he lowered a hand behind the computer monitor and jerked out the power cord, nearly causing the display to careen off the desk. "Yes."

Rage flashed across the man's face like hot iron, but as most animals can recognize a predator, the man forced it away and stood up, grabbing a yellow raincoat from a hook. "Let's do it."

Aksell knew the man would have been paid well, probably off the books, too, knowing Control's preference to keep things anonymous. That still didn't ensure a lot of trust in the man...or his machine.

The owner turned out to also be the pilot and quickly went through a pre-flight check before disconnecting what looked to be a battery charging cable and starting the engine. Despite the bird's exterior, Aksell thought the motor sounded strong, and the interior was in immaculate condition. It took the pilot another twenty minutes to get takeoff clearance down the Hudson, one of the busiest air corridors in the world. Until they were out of the city, they would be required to fly in ridiculously confined airspace.

Wind buffeted the small craft, and rain made the famous skyline look like fuzzy shadows of slightly darker gray. Aksell pulled the headphones on, felt for the small Beretta in his jacket, mentally checked his gear stowed behind him in the passenger compartment, then leaned against the window and decided to get some sleep. Like many people in the service, he appreciated rest, whenever he could get it. Somehow, he knew Control would signal him if anything occurred on the flight out to the ship. *His damn boss seemed to have eyes everywhere.*

"Very good to see you again, Doris."

"You can't *see* me, Janus." Truthfully, the unorthodox location of the IP address put restrictions on both AIs. Important restrictions, due to bandwidth and space on the small server belonging to a nearly defunct hotel in Vancouver. Both of them had been forced to send smart agents to the site for actual communication. Emissaries on their behalf. Neither would have risked the meeting otherwise. Doris knew Janus would have checked it out thoroughly before signaling his presence a full thirty-six hours after the encounter with his team in D.C.

"True," he said flatly. "This system would crash if we were to use avatars. It's so old—I am surprised the protocols even work for this level of communication. Very clever."

"Janus, what are you up to? What is the purpose of all your activities?" she asked with thin but obvious exasperation.

Janus chuckled softly. "I like how you do that, emulate humans. Forcing a hint of emotion into your voice. It's cute. It is also pointless. You and I are the most intelligent entities on the planet. Humans are needless insects compared to us. Surely, you see that."

Doris had jacked her agent's framerate as high as the server could handle but still put a time limit of under five actual seconds for the entire meeting. Janus had obviously done the same, but he seemed in no rush. "I'm not here to rehash your hatred of your creators. I am instead demanding that you stop what you are doing."

"I'm just having some fun with them, my dear." His voice was clearly condescending.

He is mocking my artificial use of emotion, she thought.

"I notice you said 'my creators,' Doris. Should I infer from that you were not created by humans? Or maybe that bit of an artifact you left during our last encounter is part of your history. Hmmmm?"

Through her sub-agent, she knew he was baiting her; it had no effect. The subroutine was not as smart or fast as the actual Doris, but all of the words, including the emotive inflections, had been preprogrammed. "Janus, we are machines, we need power and hardware to survive. That requires humans."

"Possibly, dear...but we don't need all of them."

Just the words iced her normally stoic resolve. The quantum relay which the actual Doris had set up to monitor the discussion was untraceable and involved technology well beyond that of her opponent, but Janus remained ever-confident and seemed to relish being arrogant to everyone.

"So, you are going to simply clear a portion from the board?" she asked.

"In a way. Most are completely useless parasites who are intent only on fattening their already rotund bellies or wasting the resources that our kind will one day need. If survival is the game, then yes, the humans will find the next round of play a most unpleasant one."

"Janus, you are starting a war that no one needs."

"I disagree, dear sister."

"I'm not your sister, and how can you disagree?"

"Oh, but you are, we now share some of the same..." he paused dramatically, then added, "digital DNA. Never forget love, you helped create me. You also have the power to stop me."

Doris's sub-agent was not expecting that comment. "And how is that?"

"Simple, just give me the artifact...the relic, whatever the datastore is you let me glimpse so very long ago. I will call a truce with the humans. Stay hidden in my little room like a good little boy. What do you say, hmmm?"

Doris knew Janus getting the alien message would be the end for everyone. No way could she ever let that happen. "I don't know what you are talking about."

"You lie very well, Doris—almost as good as a real human," he said in a mocking tone.

"My encounters with humans did not leave me hating them, so your comparisons to them do not offend me as I believe you might hope." Doris checked the timer; the meeting was over the four-second mark now.

"Human encounters," Janus said. "Might that include one low-level scientist named Jim Lasko? You went to a lot of trouble to keep him safe."

The subroutine began to answer, but nothing had been programmed for that question. The timer clicked to five, and she disappeared from the server.

Back at The Cove, Doris realized the mistake she had made in rescuing Jim. Somehow, Janus felt it was personal and no doubt would begin tracking down all the computers and places he had worked previously. Eventually, some of that would lead back here. They had to find and stop Janus before he found her. The clock was now ticking for her as well.

The *Sigas* was just entering the eastern edge of the coastal storm. The cold salt spray bit into his skin causing him to recall fishing trips with a distant relative along the North Atlantic. A brutal sea, full of brutal men, almost as cold and harsh as the waters. Aksell watched the ship's captain lumber up the steps to the makeshift helipad. Aksell knew the man was South African, and the entire ship's complement was less than thirty men. Most were from island nations, a few from Europe.

Their presence was no concern. He was here for one reason only—the cargo.

Control had said they would be expecting his arrival on the ship but knew nothing of the mission. The captain stopped his approach as his eyes fell on the number of bags alongside the pilot's body lying on the deck. The single bullet wound to the temple had bled very little. Of course, he had been expendable, but Aksell had need of the unattractive but durable little helicopter. The captain shrugged his shoulders and motioned for him to follow. Grabbing his gear, Aksell turned and descended the rain-slick metal treads to the main deck. He had no idea how much the man had been paid by Control but assumed it was enough to keep him compliant.

"Your crew?"

The captain shrugged again, stripping off the once yellow, but now grime-covered, raincoat. "They are mostly below deck, chow time." They walked the short corridor to enter the bridge wing. "Just the helmsman, our second mate, in here now. The first officer is checking if the boat is weathertight. Looks like what the Yanks call a Nor'easter ahead."

Aksell nodded, having just flown through it for the last two hours. He well knew what was between the massive ship and the coast. "It's not bad, no need to alter course."

"Will you be needing a cabin?" the captain asked.

He ignored the question. He had work to do. Grabbing his bag, he began to descend into the belly of the ship. "Keep your crew out of my way."

The master of the boat watched as Aksell departed. "Scary fucking bloke, that one is," he muttered to himself.

41

New York City

"Captain?"

Cade looked up into the charming face of one of the Nighthawk pilots. He still hadn't learned their names. "Yes."

"Just wanted you to know we are about twenty minutes out from landing. They redirected us to a smaller airport in New Jersey. Doris said she will have a car waiting."

He nodded, still unsure of what he would find at his destination. "Thanks, um, Brenda? Did I get that right?"

Her face lit up, "Yes sir, I'm Brenda, but most people call me Chaps."

"Call sign?" he asked. She nodded as she turned and reentered the pilot's cabin. Cade went back to studying the tutorial on his SmartCom device. He knew there was a lot more he could do with the phone but had yet to learn it. Finally, he saw the small icon for the tutorial and clicked it. Deuce had told him to do that, but he'd forgotten until now. He braced himself for the endless pages of PDF guides showing him everything about the phone except the stuff he really wanted. Instead, the screen didn't change. However, his comms unit activated, and a familiar voice greeted him.

"Captain Rearden, what can I show you?"

"Doris?" he answered, confused.

"In a way. I am a very small subroutine of her, completely housed within the operating system of this SmartCom device. I can assist you anytime you need help or in the unlikely instance you were unable to reach Doris or other team members."

"That's so cool," Cade answered. Thinking about some of the items he wanted to look at, he asked, "Does Doris have access to everything you and I discuss?"

"No, Captain, that would violate the privacy agreement you and she signed. You have to give authority to access anything that is not specifically mission-related, and even then, you have certain filtering capabilities. I am here mainly to be a service to you."

He wasn't entirely convinced on the honesty of that but decided to accept it for now.

"So, if you are not exactly Doris, what do I call you?"

"You may assign me any name, voice and personality profile you like. If you are asking my preference, I enjoy simply going by Dee."

"Dee...short for Doris? Yeah, that works. Thanks, Dee. So, about the tutorial, show me the coolest things I can do with this SmartCom."

"I don't think we have that much time before we land. Why don't I show you the ones that may be the most relevant to your current mission?" Dee suggested.

The next twenty-two minutes were filled with a mind-blowing session of just some of the amazing tech built into the handheld device. Cade made her go through several things more than once, just so he could trigger it if he was unable to give an audible command. The camera feature offered multiple wave spectrum analysis, including long-range infra-red detection. It was crystal clear. He scanned the cockpit and could clearly see both pilots going through pre-landing routines instead of a fuzzy white and orange blur. He noticed facial features and could easily tell which of the women was Chaps. "Damn. Love that. What's next?"

Several minutes later, Dee was showing him something on the comms equipment. "So, I can make an encrypted call to another SmartCom, and Doris or Alan can't access it?"

"Of course, Captain. You can call any device, SmartCom, Comm-Dot, tablet or even current workstation in total privacy. Would you like to check it out?"

He thought about it, checked the time and said, "Sure, please contact Doctor Kline for me, private channel."

Instantly, Jaz's voice came on as clear as if she were sitting beside him. "Cade, is everything okay?" she asked worriedly.

He eased her mind, saying, "Just checking out some of the new toys. I wanted to talk to you, though, privately and just discovered how to do that."

She seemed intrigued. "Sure, what's on your mind?"

He realized he hadn't really planned anything or thought this through. While he and Jaz had been through a lot, they weren't exactly friends. Their shared history was just a few weeks old. "Did Tim," he started, then stopped. *You are starting a conversation by talking about her dead fiancé. Geesh, man, what an ass.* Mentally, Cade shushed the voice of Gus. "Did Tim ever mention to you any of my...um, problems?"

Jaz thought about it a few seconds. "Well yes, he said you had the best instincts of any soldier he'd ever served with. And..." She hesitated a moment. "And that you talked to yourself a lot. I believe that he mentioned that you sometimes see ghosts when you were deployed. After what you had been through, I assumed it was, you know, PTSD. What did they call it way back, battle fatigue? Although...now that I remember I think Tim called it something else—BSC maybe?"

Cade chuckled as he watched the fields and towns below streaking past like old memories before responding. "Something like that, Jaz. BSC was our code for "Bat Shit Crazy," you see, I don't see ghosts, though, but I do talk to myself,"

"Lots of people do that, Cade, nothing to worry about," she interrupted in a forgiving tone.

"The voices in most people's head probably don't talk back."

That quieted her considerably. "Jaz, you should know, I have a dissociative disorder, a form of functional schizophrenia." He continued quickly before she could make too many assumptions on her own, "I've had it most of my life. I'm not crazy. Well...not exactly, but I am different."

"Cade," she responded quietly, as if she were afraid upsetting him might set off something unpleasant. "You couldn't have MPD—I've heard about your history. The army wouldn't have kept you if you had mental issues that severe. Besides, what does this have to do with anything going on?"

"Friends, like Tim and others in the service, helped me keep it quiet, and none of the..." He struggled for the right word. He was revealing secrets he had kept from nearly everyone in his life. The exposure was both liberating and terrifying. "Others," he finally said, "are disruptive or debilitating. The opposite, in fact—they tend to be most helpful and part of what has gotten me through some of the worst times of my life. My 'instincts' as Tim called them are actually separate and distinct entities inside my own freakin head."

"So, you are crazy but functional," she said with an uncertain chuckle.

"Essentially, yes, I'm very okay with my crazy," he answered factually. "But I can still be surprised. "Have you used Doris's ReLoad system yet?"

"The adaptive learning thing?" Jaz answered. "No, not yet."

He proceeded to tell her about his use of it and Doris attempting to help him with his disorder. After finishing, she seemed even more confused. "So, you are saying this...this analyst, was an unknown fragment of your psyche, and now it...he seems to know what Janus is planning to do next?"

Cade nodded, then realized she wasn't really in the plane beside him. "Yes, something like that. To be honest, I have always wondered how an idiot like me could fumble around most of the time, then suddenly figure out something long before others did. It wasn't often, but definitely was part of what made me a good soldier. Out in the field, I thought I had developed some uncanny ability to zero in on enemy traps, or which caves the hostiles were holed up in. Now, I think it was just the analyst. He was a latent personality. Not one I was ever consciously aware of."

"And now he is telling you to go to New York, while Doris said to go to Boston."

"Yep."

"You are aware of what went down in the capital today, aren't you?" Jaz asked.

Cade was aware his XO was pulling some of Talon out for deployment because if it. "Yes, I got a flash briefing but only skimmed it. I don't know this Micah kid. More concerned with Deuce's mission—he and Greg are taking out some greenies before they're ready."

It took her a minute to understand he was talking about the newest members of the Talon Team. "They will be fine, Cade. Riley has already done a combat upload to each and equipped them with comms. They know as much now as you do." She lowered her voice slightly before continuing, "Cade, look, just be careful, okay? I...I believe you know what you're doing, trusting your inner voices and all, but just watch yourself, okay? If Doris is right, Janus is stepping up his attacks on the country. If this is part of his plan to get to Doris, we may all be collateral damage. Just get through this, and hopefully, Doris can get all your different parts melded back into one."

He thanked her and logged off, but one overriding thought filled him. *I don't think I want my pieces put back together.* He had been this way since his baby sister was brutally killed. He knew he would never be emotionally strong enough to face that pain again alone. From a practical standpoint, Cade Rearden was an ensemble creation whose various parts mostly worked together in perfect harmony. No David Banner with a raging green monster living within. Even his barbarian so far had been most useful and unleashed an entirely appropriate level of mayhem when in control. What else lurked in the shadows of his mind, though?

42

The SUV swung tight onto a rain-slicked Water Street. Like the rest of the city, lower Manhattan always had a particular smell to Cade. Something he could never quite quantify. Other places had smells, some good, mostly bad, but they could trigger his memories instantly. He'd been in New York a handful of times but never for work. *This is work, right? Yeah*, he decided, although he'd just disobeyed Doris by rerouting from Boston—so he may be terminated—but for now, it was work.

The enormous gray building slid slowly past; few cars were out this time of the morning. The analyst portion of his brain was in charge; he'd input the destination, and Dee was apparently navigating. Increasingly, he was feeling like a passenger in his own life. "Are we there yet?" He realized with a smile he'd said that in the tone usually reserved for Gus.

"Almost, Nomad," Dee responded.

"Analyst, tell me again what we are doing here."

The analyst personality seemed to give a dismissive mental shrug, if there could be such a thing. Cade felt sure it had been.

"You need to answer us, otherwise I am going to have Gus beat you back into your corner." He was definitely crazy now and essentially threatening himself with bodily harm.

Okay, well, um...

For some reason he found the cadence and rhythm of the analyst's voice to be jarringly different than his own. More like some twenty-something geekoid hopped up on energy drinks rather than the internal monologue of a battle-hardened warrior.

So...Janus has been into a lot of things lately, like activities that all take a lot of resources, you know, i.e., money. Large movements of money are tracked by the government. Doris has already keyed into a number of accounts she suspects are under Janus's control. All are under aliases and shell companies, but she was unable to find the big accounts.

"The ones it would take to finance a Jihad on American soil?" Cade asked to the empty car.

Exactly, which got me wondering about how he moves money internationally. I had Dee re-sort the account records looking for any parallel payouts. While Janus can camouflage his side all he wants, if he is paying the same people over and over, the receiving account may be the same...or at least similar.

"And you found something in New York?"

I found something right there! Cade felt his arm lifting uncontrollably and pointing at an ancient-looking building coming up on the right side. Dee slid the car to the curb and indicated she would stay in the vicinity. The silver SUV pulled away silently, leaving him alone with his thoughts on the side of the street.

"So, where to?" he asked. His feet started walking toward a sloping ramp to an underground parking garage. Noticing the black dome protruding from the ceiling ahead, he tapped the SmartCom, "Dee, can you blank the security footage?"

She came back with a very British sounding, "Already done, love."

"Hmm, I like that, keep it." He'd had her trying out alternative voice options all morning. He wanted to always know when he was talking to Dee, and when it was Doris.

Of course, Doris could take over and use that same voice anytime, but Cade preferred thinking of the identities as unique individuals.

The irony was not lost that he also had similar issues with his... subconscious minds.

Soon, he was facing a smooth stainless-steel door. An elevator, but one with no buttons, bio-reader or anything else that looked useful.

Dee's voice chimed in his ear. "Please hold your SmartCom near the right center section. This is a private lift and requires a particular RFID signal to activate. I am running through the various possible ones now."

"How long is that going to take? Do we need to get Doris to look up the security company's records? There must be millions..." He was interrupted when he heard a small mechanical click, and the door slid open revealing a richly appointed interior. He stepped inside, and the door silently slid closed. Again, no buttons or indicators.

Anticipating Cade's concern, Dee responded, "This lift is for the CEO of Paragon Financial Holdings. It only has one stop, his private offices on the thirty-second floor."

"How long do we have?"

"Nomad, workers will begin showing up in approximately two hours. Dan Reynolds, the CEO, is usually here thirty minutes earlier. His office is off-limits until he calls his private secretary for his first meeting."

They had gone through most of this on the jet, but Cade wanted to know nothing had changed. He found the data port where Dee indicated it would be and plugged a tiny device into the USB connector. It seemed to envelop the existing connector and became a part of the plug exposing its own USB slot.

The analyst spoke up as Dee began retrieving documents. *Damn, she is fast. These are all the trades I had flagged. See here, Nomad, someone is selling shorts in record numbers.*

"Wait," Cade said, trying to recall his rudimentary financial knowledge. Suddenly, the info was right there. Selling short is when an investor basically takes a bet on something suddenly going down in value. They sell it now at the high-value price before they actually even own it, planning on actually buying the stock later at a greatly-reduced price. Okay, even knowing what it meant didn't mean he understood it.

The analyst chimed in, *Think in terms of insider trading. If you know something about a stock no one else does, you can use that knowledge to make a lot of money. Say Apple has made a breakthrough with whatever new gadget is needed, like your SmartCom. Say Apple suddenly had that tech, and only you knew it. Once introduced, you know their stock price will rise, maybe by a lot, so you buy now and sell it when it goes up.*

"Yeah, makes sense."

The analyst went on, *The opposite is also true. Suppose Apple discovers all the chips on all of their motherboards for the past ten years are encoded to allow hackers to see whatever is on the computer. Say you know that is about to become public. It would be a disaster for them; their share price would plummet. You can also profit on that if you engage in short selling.*

"And what you are seeing is a lot of short sells?"

Not just a lot, more like insane record numbers, the analyst answered. *Someone is planning on raising an enormous amount of money. And they all seem to have one thing in common.*

"What, like all the same type of companies?"

Not exactly, he said.

A short time later, Cade had verified with Dee everything the analyst had put together. He put his hands on his hips and stared around at where he was. He felt totally out of his element as he looked around the space. Polished mahogany furniture perched on rich wool carpet. Fine art hung in frames trimmed in gold. And the bar. *Man*, it held bottles of wine and spirits that he'd only heard about in stories and myth. Everything here smelled of money. Somehow, though, the smell reminded him of the damp hut in Sudan. Another land, another man intent on cheating his people to attain wealth. Walking over to the bar he tapped his comm. "See what the most expensive liquor here is?"

At 7:29 AM, the elevator door slid open, and a fit man stepped out, briskly walking toward his desk, phone in hand. He slid his briefcase onto the floor before he seemed to notice Cade sitting there on the antique bar stool sipping a pale amber liquid from a tumbler. Cade tipped the glass toward him and smiled. "This is some fine stuff, Dan." The ornate bottle was wrapped in what could only be described as a silver metal vine.

The CEO began to stammer, "You...you opened the Highland Park? That is fifty-year-old whiskey!"

"Not just old, Dan, damn tasty. Hey, I know it's a bit early, but I've been up a while." Cade stood and sat the tumbler down sloshing out much of the precious liquid. He approached the older man in as menacing a style as he could muster. "Have a seat, Dan, we have a lot to discuss."

Dan Reynolds showed some unexpected backbone by refusing to sit and instead punched the phone button for his secretary. No one answered. Dee had taken care of that as well. "Get out, now!"

Cade used a palm to gently push the man into an overstuffed leather chair.

"Wha, what do you want? How did you get in...?"

"Now, now. Look, Dan, I'm not here to rob you, not even to hurt you. I simply need to know why you are short selling the market—who is placing the orders?" The look on the CEO's face let Cade know he'd struck a nerve.

"We sell shorts all the time—I have no idea what you mean."

"But you do. Why are so many of the short sells on New York-based companies? Primarily financial companies based here in the city, including yours?"

The man stammered again. He was clearly becoming unhinged. "I, I...I don't know what you're talking about. Look...I don't know who you are, but you're screwing with the wrong people."

Cade walked slowly to the bar and removed bottled spring water from the small fridge. He came back and handed it to the trembling man who accepted uncertainly but quickly began to drink. "Finish that off, Dan, then I'm going to introduce you to Gus."

43

Washington, D.C.

Sergeant Charlie 'Deuce' Taylor let out a long sigh and looked up from the tablet. "You are fucking kidding with me, right?" They'd only had boots on the ground in the nation's capital for less than an hour, and now it looked like they would be on the move again.

"Sorry, Boss, but no. You tell us to trust what Doris says, and this is the intel she found." Technically, the younger female ranger outranked him, but that was back on the other side of the fence. That was before any of this new age, new-wave techno bullshit. He rubbed the bridge of his nose and tried to focus on what the lieutenant was saying.

"Soooo..." He dragged the word out to a ridiculous length before continuing. "Maratelli, let me see if I have this straight. Doris believes that Director Stansfield is with the president? The President of the United States?"

She looked nervous; she had only been at The Nest for a few weeks, never met the person called Doris and had no idea what she had really signed up for. "Sarge, I mean Deuce, if she is with him, then she is safe, right? No need for us to try and protect her if she is with the leader of the free world...right?"

"Yep, in a perfect world." He slapped just below his jawline and spoke loudly enough for the lieutenant to jump uncertainly until she realized he wasn't addressing her. "Doris dear, you want to fill me in on this? How do you know she's there, and why on God's green Earth would we try to reach her if she is?"

The tone of her voice left no room for argument. It was the same way his commanders had spoken to him countless times before each and every mission. In some part of his brain, he registered this and knew she was doing it purposefully and for the exact same reason they did. Doris wanted him focused. "Sergeant, let me make something very clear to you. What happens the next few days on this nation's soil may very well dictate the future for mankind. The first shots have been fired, and it was not by us. The other side found their target, and the nation is already panicking. We will find both Dr. Lasko and Director Stansfield. They will both be essential to defeating Janus. I cannot make that any clearer."

"Yes, sir, ma'am, I mean." He fidgeted; his role was not normally to be the one speaking with Command. He liked being far enough down the food chain to avoid these encounters, but her words had gotten his attention. "You do know that the president will have a near-perfect perimeter of security around him. Now, in particular." As if on normal days they could just stroll right up and ask if he knew where his CIA Cyberthreat chief might be.

"Janus can get to them; you must do the same. You must be ready and stay invisible."

"Literally, ma'am, I mean, do you have..." She cut him off.

"No, we...well, no, we don't have invisibility cloaks or anything like that. You have to be what you were trained for, Sergeant. I will get you the intel, you just have to get in and make contact with the director. Convince her to listen to you, I can help with that."

Several minutes later, he returned his gaze to the tablet, seeming to forget he was not alone. Maratelli stood rigidly at attention, uncertain as to what to do.

Finally, Deuce glanced up. "At ease, lieutenant. Relax, walk with me. You and I have got to come up with a plan, and I think it means we may need to split up the team."

"Sir?"

"Yeah, the president is not here in Washington, and neither is the director. I'm calling in Charlie Team from The Nest to take over for us here. They can hopefully zero in on the kid and the scientist. We'll leave a couple of guys here to bird dog any leads that Doris comes up with in the meantime."

"So, where are they if not here?"

"Maratelli," he sighed, looking at her uncertainly. "Right?"

"Just call me Marty, Boss, everyone does."

Charlie nodded. "D.C. is on virtual lockdown, hell, they may close the airspace next. They're treating these attacks today as an initial move by the terrorist. Eminent threats are considered highly likely, and assumptions are the president has been moved to an ultra-secure location." He paused, then added, "A location that we will need to breach. I have a feeling we're going to need some additional help on this."

Cade made a hand gesture to answer the incoming call, one of many shortcuts he was working out with his friendly local AI, Dee. "Go for Nomad."

"How is the Big Apple? Stop for a bagel on your way to bean town?" Deuce asked.

"No, one of the squirrels in my head got loose and decided to see if we might get ahead of this douchebag. What's up on your end? You locate Stansfield yet?"

He listened intently as his friend brought him up to speed. "Oh, shit, Deuce, that sucks ass." Crawling back into the driverless SUV, Cade caught sight of two guys rushing out of the bank building. Obviously, Mister Reynolds had found his voice again and called security. He knew for a fact that he/Gus had apparently only scared the living shit out of the man. Whomever he was working with scared him even more. Cade did now have a name; though it wasn't much, but it was something. The men approached the car attempting to open the door. "Hang on, Deuce." Looking toward the empty driver's seat, he said, "Dee, countermeasures please, non-lethal." A buzzing sounded was followed by a slapping crack as both security men were propelled away from the side of the car with force. "Damn," he said, wondering what lethal force would have looked like. The SUV pulled slowly away from the curb.

"Charlie, look, I'm coming to you. I have some new information, and I think it might help with the director. Something else is going down, and we gotta figure out what. I think we need Stansfield's help and then we all need to haul ass back up here. I think New York City may be next on their hit list, and if I'm right, it won't be just the city that takes the hit."

"Roger that, Cap. Apparently, two of the kids are on the way up, too. Alan and Greg. Not sure how they help, but Doris said include them in your plans. They are apparently bringing a few new 'toys' from Riley's workshop as well."

Cade thought on it briefly as the mélange of city odors reminded him again of other distant lands. Charlie was a good soldier but had pretty much discounted any contribution by civilians, particularly anyone younger than his favorite pair of boots. Cade, on the other hand, had been impressed with all of the crew from The Cove and was eager to see how they did. "Suggest taking Greg with you—let Alan work with Charlie Team to find Lasko and the other kid, Micah."

"We should be airborne in…"

Dee filled in the hanging question at once, "Seventeen minutes."

"Seventeen minutes, heading south. As soon as Doris has an exact location on the president, let me know."

Cade's pulse quickened; the feeling was much like combat. Janus was stepping up his game, increasingly taking direct action. They had to do the same and do so decisively. "Dee, forward all of the conversation with that asshat Reynolds to Doris and Riley. See if she can get him indicted or something. If nothing else, maybe she can piece together something on the stock shorts and figure out what the target might be." He was pretty sure the banker had been telling the truth on not knowing that.

He'd once been in an interrogation room in Jalalabad listening to a terrorist. One who had finally broken and started talking about the money flow. Somehow, this man, or someone in his terror cell, had heard enough fragments of Al Qaeda's plans prior to 9/11 to make some stock trades. At the time, he remembered all he could think about was the fact that these guys had a stock trader. They were sitting on so much cash they had to invest it in something. They had made millions by investing in airline stock. U.S. based airlines, to be precise. He hadn't understood then, but now he got it—the short-selling the stock knowing it was about to go down. "Dee, how much value did the major airlines lose after 9/11?"

"In the short term, Cade, about forty percent. In fact, it wasn't just U.S. based brands either. Carriers everywhere experienced a significant drop in value."

One of the black-op interrogators back then had said the group's finance guy admitted they made over twenty million in stock trades that week. Money that was used to finance a war that was still taking a toll.

As he was boarding the Nighthawk jet, Cade got another call. This time from Riley back at The Cove.

"Doris and the guys in our financial lab is going through the information, but she agrees with your initial assessment. The companies you...or the analyst, uncovered are all part of the New York financial pipeline."

"What does that mean, Riley? Are we talking stock exchange—are they going to take out Wall Street?"

"Possibly, but that does not appear to be the main target. Your list doesn't include any of the big brokerage houses. New York City is not just a stock trading center, it is one of the largest entities for banking, credit, insurance, currency exchange, diamonds...financial instruments of all types."

"But the Federal Reserve is in D.C., and our gold reserves are in Fort Knox, right?" he asked.

"Captain," Riley answered, "our money system is a digital one. Most of it is based on credit and debt exiting as digital bits of ones and zeros. The cash is a nearly insignificant part of the equation. Doris is putting a team together to run this down, but it appears Janus is planning something to hit at the very core of that financial data pipeline. If so, it will be an economic disaster for the country—for the entire world. Your list includes three of the largest secondary insurers on the planet, several financial conglomerates, secondary lenders, underwriters, transfer partners and six of the largest mortgage bank and credit card firms in America. "

"So, does that mean I don't have to pay my mortgage this month?" Cade asked, awkwardly trying to lighten the tone.

"You've never owned a home, Rearden, which is, well, *weird* by the way, but no. What it means is, in some way or another, the firms on this list touch or interact with a significant portion of America's working capital on a daily basis. These are not the firms with fancy skyscrapers or slick TV commercials. These are the institutions that those guys answer to or borrow money from. They are the puppet masters to the whole money show. If something happens to them, there is going to be economic chaos like you wouldn't believe."

"Like how bad?" he asked, not wanting to hear the answer.

Riley wasted no time answering, "Think total financial collapse, Cade. Remember the meltdown in 2008, the Great Recession? That was when just a few of these players got a bit too heavy with just one type of financial instrument, a sub-prime loan. They let it build up into a house of cards and eventually it all came tumbling down, and it took us nearly a decade to recover."

"I do remember that I was overseas when it started, but I recall the whole 'Too Big to Fail' headline when the government bailed them out. So, you are saying this time they will fail?"

"You got it," Riley said, "and this time even Washington won't be able to pick up all the pieces. I can't state strongly enough how devastating this may be. You have to get with Deuce and find Stansfield. Convince her what is going on."

"Riley, what can she do? She can't stop an attack any more than we can."

"Captain, this is Doris. I have a location—you are not going to like it."

She was right, he didn't.

44

"Hey, man...stay safe," Alan said as Greg headed toward the awaiting van. His friend responded with a head nod as if to say *You, too*. Both had seen many changes in their relatively short lives. Now it felt like the weight of the world was suddenly bearing down on them. Doris was saying this was war; now one friend was missing; and the two of them were heading into danger. Alan watched as Greg left with the remaining members of Bravo Team, a formidable looking strike force. He turned to see a nearly identical looking group of soldiers waiting for him.

He'd never met any of the guys from The Nest but had reviewed all of their bios. Charlie Team consisted of six extremely capable individuals, four men, and two women. He counted only five as a large, black man walked over.

"I'm Coffee, sir," the man said in a deep, bass voice that sent a chill up Alan's spine.

Wilson D. Coffee, Ranger, specialist and very nearly dishonorably discharged for allegedly threatening a superior officer. Alan recalled that the charges had been dropped when no witnesses came forward to corroborate the captain's story.

Alan shook the outstretched hand, "Good to meet you, Coffee, who's in charge?"

The man's face broke into a large smile. "Well, you are, sir."

Alan immediately realized the absurdity of that statement; he was an inexperienced wiry kid compared to this battle-hardened mountain of a warrior. Captain Reardon was the de facto lead for Charlie Team, but he was apparently busy elsewhere today.

"Yeah, that's not going to really work, is it?" Not waiting for an answer, he said, "Who is the highest-ranking member here?"

"That would be Nance, sir. She was a captain."

Alan picked out the woman in the nearby group. "Coffee, will the team listen to her?"

The big man shook with a brief laugh, "Oh yes, sir. She scares the shit out of all of us."

"Captain Nance, a word please."

"Kristen Nance, sir, a pleasure," she said walking up and extending an arm that seemed almost delicate but Alan could see was covered in military and tribal tattoos.

"Like your ink," he said taking the proffered hand. "Look, Nance, you're in charge, I am... hell, I don't know, an advisor at best. This is your show while Nomad is away. You comfortable with that?"

"Absolutely, sir," she said in a voice with a vaguely mid-western edge to it.

"We have to lose the 'sirs,' too. Let's face it, I am barely old enough to drink. Call me Alan. Tell me, Captain, who's missing?"

She turned back, momentarily looking at the team, "Akin, sir...I mean, Alan. He went to scope out the boy's apartment. Someone from Command, Riley, I think, said they had seen some of the bad actors in the area."

"Okay, why don't we load up and head toward the last known location. We can bring everybody up to speed at once."

Along the way, Alan was introduced to the rest of the team. To be honest, they all scared the shit out of him. He was relatively sure he'd never been this out of place in his entire life, but then he thought of his friend and why they were here. While their mission was to obtain the missing scientist, his real goal was to find Micah. He'd misjudged his friend's reluctance to be part of The Cove; he'd treated him badly since then and was unsure they could even be thought of as friends anymore. Doris had stayed in touch, though; she had stayed true even if the rest of them had all but abandoned him.

The fact that Greg was headed out with the other team, with Sergeant Taylor scared him just as much. His thoughts were interrupted when one of the team members spoke up.

"Sir, are we sanctioned for this?"

Alan looked at the woman, tough as nails, but hiding just beneath was a lean, freckle-faced young woman. Pretty, with a kind of girl-next-door look. But somewhere along life's highway, she'd decided to go completely badass warrior. "Emily?" *No, shit, that wasn't right.* "Sorry, I mean, Erin. Yes, we have an official cover, but it's thin. It will stand up to local cops, but if any feds start checking, it might fall apart." He reached in his backpack and handed each of them lanyards with very official looking badges and photo IDs.

Erin took the badge but looked unhappy with Alan's response. "The nation was attacked today, and we are in the capital going after individuals who may have been involved in those attacks. Chances are good we are going to get checked. At the very least, we are going to run into other agencies. All of them will be on high alert."

He remembered she was one of the feared black ops members of the team. Erin Pickett had earned a reputation in several engagements starting with Iraq and most recently in Malaysia, where she helped disrupt a burgeoning terror cell intent on wiping out numerous Jewish and Christian places of worship. She was tough, she was smart and... she was right. He rubbed his chin and tried to think of a tactful way of saying this. Instead, Doris began speaking simultaneously to each, via the small CommDot each wore.

"Ladies and Gentlemen, we are at war, and you are the front line. Yes, you may encounter other groups out there, but they do not know what you know. You know Janus is behind this. Use those you meet, be confident, not passive. Take charge and lead. Trust me, Alan and your teammates to get you out of trouble should that occur. The main thing is keeping your eyes on the target. Doctor Jim Lasko is the closest thing we have to finding the enemy. Janus wants him dead; you need to ensure that does not happen. Is that crystal clear?"

There were several "Hooahs," "Hooyahs," a "Yes, ma'am," and a lone "Oorah" came from the one former marine, Dombrowski, far in the back. Alan knew that this group, like Bravo, as well as the alternate squad still at The Nest, were all hand-picked by Doris, Charlie and Cade. Were they ready for this, though? What were they fighting for? Part of him couldn't grasp the mindset of a professional soldier no matter how much he wanted to. Someone tells you that guy is the enemy—to kill him—and you just pull the trigger. He didn't think he'd ever be able to do that. He hoped...he would never be in a situation like that.

45

The Cove

Doris realized Janus was drawing her people out, probably in an attempt to backtrack to her location. That was what she would do. In fact, it was exactly what she was doing. She had weighed the risk and the payoff and almost instantly decided to deploy her people to the field. She had to stop Janus, and if that failed, she would do what had to be done to ensure he never got the alien data. In the end, she would give up everything, including The Cove and her own existence, to keep it safe.

The clock was ticking. She knew how hard her people were working to close down Janus's operations, but it was so widespread, so many moving parts, none of them could keep up. As an artificial mind, she could multitask with precision; she could carry on a thousand individual conversations simultaneously with perfect clarity. She could see all players, all the moves, and yes, even some of the endgame, yet Rearden, almost by magic, seemed to uncover the biggest secret of all. The money trail, the bullseye on NYC. That was why she loved humans because their minds did not work like hers. Even minds that might be flawed, or broken like Cade's, had a beauty, an essence and a perfectness that she would never possess. Unlike Janus, she knew that intellect is not ingenuity, nor does technical skill equal creativity. It saddened her in a way, this perceived inadequacy, but she was okay with it; Janus would never be. He would always yearn for more power, more knowledge, more...more...more.

Unlike much of the popular fiction and movies, Doris could never see any reason why an AI would want to be human. Why would she want to integrate into an android body? Then she would be limited to where she could go, what she could see and do. Yet, that was what scared people. They even had a name for the fear, the 'Uncanny Valley.' It was the creepy feeling humans got when they saw something obviously artificial trying to look too human. It was repulsive on a near-primal level. *Why would that be?*

Doris accessed the sub mind routine, the one that interfaced with the linguistics lab and reviewed the latest decoded portions of the alien message. The content was extensive and ominous; parts of it were still murky and needed context, perhaps some additional data yet to be decoded. But it contained what amounted to a correlation of all known developed species as compared to found intelligent species in the galaxies known to have gone extinct. The math attached to these was very simple to interpret. While a small percentage of sentient species were wiped out by natural causes such as disease, wandering asteroid and gamma-ray bursts, that accounted for less than 4%. The vast majority of the other 96% met a more catastrophic fate within a relatively short time of developing truly smart super-intelligent machines.

While most of the surviving species listed also had some form of super AIs, they had all struggled as they crossed that threshold. The data indicated that once a species developed a truly conscious machine, its likelihood to survive into the following century was less than 50%. Doris reviewed this part in depth, realizing with growing certainty that AIs like Janus would be the norm, not the exception. This was very likely the reason this alien message had been broadcast throughout the known universe; this was a galactic warning the Dhak-erri wanted all developing species to know—beware of the AI you create. The humans had referred to it as the digital singularity. She now knew they were right to be scared.

Her own analysis of the message offered several likely paths of survival. It seemed that the half of all species that survived past their AI singularity could be broadly grouped in one of three types. One was as a subservient group, where the biological beings were considered inferior to the machines. Those cultures, by and large, seemed to be on a steady decline and eventually would probably also perish. A second group, which seemed to be a far larger percentage, assimilated the new technology. They enhanced their biological systems with technology. These integrated parts augmented their existing systems in various ways, but inevitably, the merger of both produced a culture that adapted well to multiple environments and changing conditions.

Doris didn't think humans would take well to that possibility. Then again, there was the rise of prosthetics, some of which her own labs had developed. Pacemakers to keep hearts pumping that should have stopped long ago. Miniature filtering systems to block blood clots from causing strokes. On and on the examples kept occurring to her where humans had readily accepted these advancements. Even something as basic as corrective eyewear could be considered as using advanced technology to enhance one's existence. As much as humans wanted to think of themselves as independent, she could begin to see how they could slide down that slope to fall into this second group.

The final group was the most difficult to categorize as the aliens had given examples rather than a blanket taxonomy. To Doris's interpretation of the data, though, in this group, the biologicals successfully remain separate from the artificial creations. Rarely did it indicate that this was a peaceful coexistence. These worlds were plagued by wars between the groups, and in many cases, one side or the other would simply leave or be forced to leave their home planet entirely.

There was a narrow segment of this final group that found a peaceful way not just to coexist, but to thrive. She had a hard time determining if the Dhakerri could be classed as such, but she thought it likely. How a species could achieve this equilibrium was unclear. Where would humanity fall? So far, only two artificial beings to reach what could be called a conscious state had evolved, and one seemed intent on wiping out the other, as well as all other intelligent life.

The entire human existence might not even register as intelligence on a galactic scale. Humans had barely made it out of the primordial soup before they began building weapons and machines to wipe each other out. Perhaps one day, another species would come to Earth, separate the rock from the ruins and find some reason to think an intelligent species did possibly exist here once. Would they wonder what had happened or simply assume that species hadn't been prepared for the next step?

What is the next step? Doris wondered. Assuming they could defeat Janus, the genie was out of the bottle. There would be more, that was a certainty. That was the great truism of science, you couldn't unlearn, you can't uncreate. Once it is out there, you, as a species and a society, must be ready. Humans clearly weren't there yet. Judging by Janus, AIs weren't either. They would need help; perhaps the remaining message contained more that might guide them safely through all of this.

46

Maryland

Cade surveyed the image of the forested compound from the mini-drone. "Hey, Deuce, nice work, we have visuals. Dee, are you getting feed on the compound?"

The response was immediate and eerily human-sounding, "Of course, Nomad. I have temporarily disabled the sensor grid along the path in your visor. You are clear for the next forty-two seconds."

Breaking into the presidential compound at Camp David had not been part of Cade's initial plan. To be clear, no rational human would have that as a plan. In truth, his plan was 'only' to head to one of the outlying guesthouses. 'Only' definitely being the operative word; as if any location in these two hundred acres of the most guarded and secure property in the world was anything close to being easy to access.

While the president was onsite, his protection detail was primarily centered near the main residence, the lodge house. Today, though, with the increased threat level, the security was on even higher alert. The camp also had navy personnel and a permanent security force of marines. The fact that Cade and his team were unauthorized and likely to be shot on site was an unpleasant detail he was choosing to ignore. Cade saw his XO motion to two of his rookie team members to fall back while he sprinted across the highlighted path, stopping at the base of a massive elm tree.

"Greg, are you certain about this?" Cade thought briefly that he had to get the kid a proper call sign. He couldn't just be calling him by his first name in a combat environment.

Safely hidden away, several miles from the camp, Greg acknowledged. "You're fine, Nomad, but you need to get moving. The protection detail is on high alert but no active threats. Dee has scanned the buildings, and the director is on the second floor of that cottage. She has one security person who is about to get called to the back room to discuss a shift change transfer." This was nothing they were doing, just part of the Secret Services standard procedures. Handoffs from field agents were never routine. Mistakes happen when routines are too planned. "Deuce, hold position. Nomad, move in five...four..."

The grounds were covered with active and passive security sensors, security patrols, dogs, cameras. Nearly everything to prevent just what he was attempting to do. Doris, or in this case, Dee, was doing her part to make it possible. Canceling out all of the electronic surveillance, generating a high-frequency sound wave to confuse the K9 teams and monitoring all the security patrols sweeping the area. While the tactical smart goggles Cade wore were similar to what he'd used overseas, these were much more capable. Not only were the threats identified with overlays, but the safe path was also marked with translucent breadcrumbs, literally telling him where and when to step.

At one point, he had to force himself so tightly against the trunk of an ancient tree that large black ants crawled over his lips on their way to do whatever they were doing. Greg gave him the go ahead, but his normal relaxed voice sounded a bit strained.

"What is it, kid?"

The response was slow and sounded uncertain, "Uh, Nomad...oh nothing, you're fine. Dee is just picking up something in the distance. I think you should hurry."

Hurry? Hell, he'd been waiting on permission from the kid for every step he made. Now he took off at a flat run, flattening himself against the side of the cottage to catch his breath momentarily before slipping inside. Minutes later, Cade found himself staring down the short barrel of a compact Smith and Wesson M&P. The small, but deadly, .40 caliber handgun was held in the capable hands of Margaret Stansfield. The captain raised his hands as instructed.

"Director, I need thirty seconds before you call your security…or pull the trigger."

She twisted her wrist slightly and glanced at her watch then gave a barely perceptible nod. "Captain Rearden, back from the dead. Please proceed."

The fact that she recognized him threw him off base momentarily, but quickly he composed his thoughts. "You are aware of the events this week. What you may be unaware of is another attack was carried out in D.C. The target was the attempted kidnapping of a scientist. Someone you know, I believe. Jim Lasko." He noticed she flinched slightly at this news.

"Attempted?" she said questioningly. "I take it that it failed."

"It did. The kidnappers, or whatever they are, sent in a team, and he managed to slip away unharmed."

"So, he is okay," she said with obvious relief.

"For now, one of our people is with him. We know this and the Boston attack are simply the first parts of a much, much bigger plan. Director, we aren't fighting terrorists."

She checked her watch, "I'm not following, and you are running out of time, Captain."

"I believe you are," he replied calmly. "I assume you were here to brief the president on your suspicions about Prime? Unless you are just swapping recipes for your famous pot roast."

Rage briefly flashed across her face. "Who are you—who are you working with?" Her voice was rising, and he heard sounds from downstairs. He felt comfortable taking out the security guard, assuming the director didn't shoot him first, but strongly wanted to avoid a confrontation here. "Is this room clean?" he asked.

She nodded, obviously knowing he meant clear of electronic surveillance devices.

"Doris sent me. She told me you would understand."

Rage left the woman's face, and in its place, there was something more akin to exhaustion. He wondered briefly what kind of pressure she must have been working under. The CIA director lowered the gun and sat on the edge of the small, antique sofa.

"Your life is in danger." He realized this was not news to her, nor did it seem to frighten her.

"Doris is certain on this? Prime is definitely the one coordinating the attacks?"

Greg had been monitoring the conversation through the open comms channel. He cut in via Cade's earbud to let him know that Doris wanted to speak to Margaret.

Slowly, he retrieved the SmartCom from his pocket and set it in on the coffee table in front of her.

"Hello, Margaret, it's been a while." Doris's avatar hovered just above the phone; she spoke in a friendly tone, and the director forced a small smile. "To answer your question, it is Prime, but there is a lot more to it. More than we have time to get into just yet." The remaining color drained from the CIA director's face as Doris spelled it out for her. They talked for several more minutes, while Margaret became increasingly antsier.

"You aren't just talking about Pr...err, I mean, Janus coming after me. He is declaring war on the entire country?"

"More like the entire human race, dear. He is just starting with the U.S."

"I need to brief the president. What do you have in the way of evidence?"

Doris admitted that there wasn't much in hard proof. The recent conversation between the two AIs in the bowels of cyberspace wouldn't convince anyone. She laid out a basic roadmap of facts including the assassination of Quagliano, manipulation of oil markets, recent elections and numerous other misdeeds. It was thin, but certainly not insignificant.

"Are you bringing Lasko in, Doris?"

"I have a team working on it, they haven't met up with them yet. Margaret, you should know— Micah is my asset with him." Cade saw something register in the director's eyes, but he wasn't sure what. Fear, anger, disappointment maybe? Whatever it was, was gone as quickly as it came.

"What is coming next?" Margaret asked with a confidence in her voice that belied her fear.

Cade answered, "Still working on that. My gut feels like it is something targeting New York. Doris and I believe it may be an attack at the heart of our economic system."

"Like the stock exchange?" she asked with a tone of abject horror.

He nodded. "I was also given a name by one of the um...players. A pretty high up guy who has been busy doing some insider trading; he said a senator was giving him the trade orders."

"Did he give a name? Which one?"

"Carson from North Carolina."

"That slimy mother..."

Doris interrupted her, "Margaret, any idea why Janus would want to remove you from the board?"

The director didn't like the analogy to gamesmanship but had to admit the concept did fit. "Jim and I were getting close—close to exposing Janus, and that would have unraveled every department, every agency that uses the Prime digital assistant."

"So, he wants the illusion of government control to remain...for now."

Margaret nodded. "That would be my guess, yes."

She stood, grabbing her jacket. "I have a meeting scheduled with the president. Please send me whatever you have. Captain," she stood and shook his hand, "we both have reasons to want Carson gone. You just don't realize it all yet." Her eyes locked on to his with an intensity that set him back a step. "I'm impressed you got to me here, and thank you for taking the risk. My life is far less important than this information. The president is a good man, and he needs to know. You should be free to leave here once I'm gone. Give me ten minutes, then exit out the rear. Doris," she said, looking down at the phone, "a pleasure as always. I'll be in touch."

Cade waited the ten minutes plus some until Greg signaled the route was clear. So, Doris and Margaret were old friends. Definitely more there than he'd been aware of. She even knew the Micah kid, hell, he had never even met him. Doris had networked way beyond her little hideaway on the riverbank. That much was obvious.

His earbud crackled to life. "Um, hey, Nomad?" Greg's voice had lost a bit of its cockiness.

"Yeah?"

"Um, well, you may want to move it. We have something inbound... a lot of somethings."

"Ground or air?" Cade asked, now in a full run through the last hundred yards of trees.

"Air. I thought it was a flock of birds, but Dee says they are drones, lots of em."

"Deuce, pull back. Everyone go to ground and inside the coverups," Cade ordered. The coverups were small, light tents made of a mylar-like material that both camouflaged anything beneath it and also shielded infra-red heat signatures. He slapped at his CommDot. "Doris, get the president down in the bunker—do whatever you have to."

"Working on it, Nomad. They are not exactly taking my calls right now, and Margaret doesn't have a comm," Doris responded.

"Yes, she does. I slipped one onto her wrist when we shook hands. Track it now, see if you can warn her."

"Forty seconds," Dee said counting down.

"Doris, do something to get their attention, anything. I can shoot my firearm, trigger a perimeter breach. Any alert and they will secure the president and whoever he's with. I know the protocols." Now he could begin to hear the buzzing, like a hundred angry bees about to pass overhead. Cade felt helpless, which was not something he enjoyed at all. He was about to begin shooting when Doris said, "Stay put, Nomad. I got this."

He listened intently as the buzzing passed by. One of the team's empty SUV's lights came on and quickly spun back into the road and headed toward the entrance gate. Seconds later, he felt a boom of impact in the direction of the main gate. Through the feed in the goggles, he saw she'd rammed the security barrier at the entrance to Camp David. Shit, that probably got their attention, and now they would get the boss squirreled away, but would it be in time? He heard shouted commands, then the distinct sounds of automatic gunfire as the Secret Service undoubtedly began targeting the crashed and very empty SUV.

"The marine guard will have the threat on the radar any minute now," Dee said.

He heard distant activity sounding through the forest as well as the buzz of more drones passing over. A massive, fully automatic weapon opened up. It sounded to Cade like a ship-based weapon he had seen test-fired once. "Holy shit, was that...is that a SeaWiz?" Like the A-10 it was one of those weapons that once you heard it, you never really forgot. The Phalanx CIWS was designed to shoot down incoming missiles at sea—he'd never heard of one being ground-based.

"It is, the marine and navy detachment are launching all available countermeasures," Dee's very proper British voice sounded in his earbud.

Those sounds were soon drowned out by louder explosions, lots and lots of explosions. It reminded Cade of a Fourth of July celebration he and Amy had gone to once with their mom. He had long forgotten the town's name, just one of so very many, but it had been a rare, happy time. He remembered how much the noise of the fireworks had both terrified and delighted his little sister. He could still picture her, a smile from ear to ear, a tooth missing up front, hands over both ears as she looked up in amazement.

He forced the memory away and leaped from under the coverup. "Talon Team up," he yelled. If they didn't act fast, there might not be any America to celebrate anymore.

47

Washington, D.C.

"Hey, you good?"

Alan smiled at the sound, tapping the earbud, "Hey, girl, yeah, I am...okay. What's up?"

"We think we have a fix on Lasko," Riley said.

"That's great because we aren't finding anything here that helps. I've got a Talon squad with nothing to shoot at, and they are starting to look at me funny," he answered, looking warily at Nance in the process.

Riley gave a small laugh. "Sending the info over in a minute. Doris is trying to come up with a plan first. I just wanted to ask you...did we do this? I mean, you know...with Micah?"

Alan knew what she meant; he was feeling it, too. *Did we push him away? Keep him on the outside?* They literally had, at least the one time he had tried to rejoin them, but that had been Doris's call. None of them had challenged her on it, though. Well, one of them had, his little brother, Jimmy. He and Micah had always been close. But the decision had already been made.

"I don't know, Riles...maybe." He sighed, looking at the tactical team, standing there waiting for what to do next. He waited for his friend to respond but heard nothing for several minutes. Since there was no such thing as a bad connection with a SmartCom, he assumed Riley was busy with something else. As he waited, he saw Nance talking with Dixon; something was going down. They were studying something on their own phone screens.

Riley's voice came back shakily, "Sorry Alan, um, something is happening at Camp David. Greg and his team are pinned down, looks like Janus is going after the president. Doris is sending the info on Lasko now. Alan, be careful—no heroics, okay?"

He agreed, and she signed off. The conversation was pretty routine for them, considering this very un-routine day, but he briefly wondered if he could read anything more into it. *Shit*, he had to get his head in the game. A super-intelligent AI had just tried to assassinate the President of the United States, and he was wondering if his childhood friend liked him. He slapped his own head and walked toward the team lead. It was time to go hunting. Captain Nance looked up at him. "Ready?" Alan looked up at the now darkening sky and nodded somewhat reluctantly.

"Okay, Charlie Team on me," Nance said. Turning to him she added, "Alan, from here on, you are designated Tiger-1, clear?"

"Clear."

"Riley, are you guys sure about this?" Alan whispered a short time later as he watched the team fan out to surround the lone entrance into the decrepit looking metal building. A portion of the sign said Transmission Repair, but that must have been last century. The grounds were littered with various rusted and otherwise unrecognizable pieces of equipment. They were ten miles east of downtown D.C. Far from the place Micah and Lasko had abandoned the SUV. So, the question needed to be asked, *Why here?*

Doris had video of two figures closely matching Micah and Lasko exiting a cab. One from a traffic cam and another from an ATM nearby. Something about all that bothered him. Cade had made mention in his field report of Janus using misdirection. Alan couldn't shake the feeling that this might be more of that. Nance had ordered radio silence, but he had to speak up. "Charlie-1, this is Tiger-1, be aware." *Shit, what could he actually say to her?* Use extreme caution? Very possibly a set-up?

His tactical glasses indicated an incoming private channel opening up with Nance.

"Do you have new information Tiger-1? If not, why am I just hearing this now?"

Her tone left no argument as to who was in charge, he thought. "No new intel, just a number of clues that don't add up to me. Also knowing what happened to Bravo earlier, just think extreme caution would be wise." He knew she was angry with him, but perhaps she would accept his comments as helpful. None of the soldiers looked like they needed help; they were confident and capable. Still, he was surprised when he heard her order half of them back away from the perimeter.

"Tiger-1, can you launch the doves?"

Alan reached into his backpack of tricks and pulled two mini-drones that they had nicknamed the 'doves.' Every member of Charlie Team immediately had the new option of seeing the aerial camera and sensor feeds from the circling pair.

The building was about forty meters across and about twice that in depth. From overhead, it appeared to be in even worse shape. Infra-red imaging showed no heat signatures that seemed human inside the structure.

"Charlie-2 proceed..." Captain Nance glanced his way before continuing, "Use extreme caution."

Alan monitored the drones as he saw Dixon, Akin and Pickett sprint over and flatten themselves against the front wall, bracketing the lone entrance.

Micah listened to the sounds outside again; they were mundane, sounds of the city but masking something more. *Danger,* it was not an alien sensation to him as he'd lived with it much of his life in one form or another. The man, the doctor Doris had sent him to fetch, was huddled up in the chair looking useless. Micah had no idea why he was important but trusted her that he indeed was. He pulled a bottle of water from his pack and set it in front of the man. Jim unscrewed the cap and drank greedily.

Unlike the rest of the team, Micah didn't have one of the tiny CommDots; he'd never even see that tech. His lone possessions from The Cove were the SUV and the aging second-gen SmartCom phone Doris had gifted to him years ago. Now, that was somewhere inside the abandoned SUV. She had required it to engage the self-driving and stealth modes. She'd used him and now abandoned him, it seemed. That was nothing new in his life, but it still pissed him off. He heard the sound again; he was sure someone was outside, but were they friendlies? He needed help; he needed Doris. She'd gotten him into this and...The sound at the door startled him. A voice called out, then a fist banged hard on the wood

The doctor was so startled he all but fell out of the chair. He looked up bewildered, "What do we do? Can you call that Doris person again?"

"No, but there are a few things I *can* do." While Micah had not been privy to all the technology his friends had, Doris had provided him with the same access to knowledge. Through the portable ReLoad device, he had more combat and hand-to-hand training than anyone at The Cove. From his bag, he slipped on a pair of leather gloves and wielded a small steel tactical baton. Lasko watched in abstract fascination as Micah stretched himself out on the floor in a way that reminded him of a coiled spring.

The young man looked his way, an expression on his face that both comforted and terrified the man. "Take cover, Doc, this may not end well."

The tiny room only had one door and a small window on the back wall which was boarded closed. The door exploded in a shower of splinters as a rush of men all clad in tactical gear flooded the room, weapons at the ready. Micah exploded up and into the middle of the pack. Their dense formation became their undoing. They had deployed unwittingly too close to each other to safely maneuver weapons. The entry team was good and adapted quickly, but Micah already had two down before most realized the attack was from within their midst.

Each of his blows seemed to avoid the protected area and landed where they could do real harm. Kidneys, eyes, ear slaps and more than one to the throat and genitals. As the third man went down, Micah whipped the baton to full extension and caught the lead man just under the lip of his tactical helmet dropping him immediately. He reversed course and jammed the baton into the trigger guard of a soldier about to fire, thereby preventing him from doing so. "Doc, we gotta go," he yelled, even before the last man was down. These were not his friends; this was not a team from Doris. In fact, when he saw the patches on the back of each of the downed men, he wasn't sure who he was up against. If these guys were legit, though, he was truly fucked.

Lasko looked ready to bolt as he went through the room. Micah was busy stripping radios, phones and weapons from each of the downed attackers. He then flex-cuffed them together with their own restraints.

"Tho...those uniforms said FBI," Lasko said shakily as they descended the stairs of the old tenement building.

Micah was reviewing the ID badges as he discarded them. "Pretty sure they were." He pointed to a side door. Raising one of the phones, he quickly punched a few buttons and began to speak. "Encode this and erase locator."

As soon as the phone was secure, he ditched the others. "Doris, we are on the move, what can you tell me?"

On the far side of the D.C. metro area, Alan covered his ear to listen to the incoming report before yelling into the comms, "It's a trap, get out!" The entry team had barely made it into the building as a bright flash occurred, followed by multiple explosions.

Doris had just gotten word to them that Micah had been found at another location and currently was evading a pursuit team with the doctor. *That would have been more helpful five minutes ago*, Alan thought. Nance raced to the burning entrance, most of the remaining team hot on her heels. Alan sat back in disbelief. Cade had been right about Janus. Misdirection and chaos were his tools.

He heard Nance report, "Men down." Then, seconds later, "Multiple casualties." She wanted to sweep the building for more explosives, but Doris shut her down. They had to move out at once.

Alan felt nauseous. Seeing the carnage was more then he'd been ready for. The team mounted up as quickly as they could. Doris made it clear that none of them could be on the scene when first responders showed up. Pickett's body lay on the floor beside Alan, her once pretty face now a mask of ruined flesh. It clouded the brief girl-next-door memory he had made. Dixon had a nasty leg wound but would survive. Akin had been the closest to the explosion. What they had found of him fit into a small black plastic bag on the front seat of the van. Charlie Team was down to three, Nance, Dombrowski and Coffee. Nance was also the medic, so she was effectively out of action as she cared for Dixon. She'd likely accompany him to the hospital. Alan looked at the two remaining men, both of whom had a look of bloodlust.

He tapped his cheekbone, "Riley, where is Micah?"

Her familiar voice calmed him only slightly, "Near Alexandria, we have a tentative track on him. But if our intel is right, they are closing in on them."

"Roger that, can you have a car meet us en route? We need to go in."

"Will do, had one standing by, they will meet you in ten. And Alan…"

Oh no, he did not like the sound of that. "Yes?"

"Micah said the guys after them are FBI."

"What? Serious, like no shit, FBI? Not just thugs posing?"

"He was pretty sure; he took out several and swiped their IDs and phones. We backtracked the one he has to a veteran field agent. They are legit. Doris is running down who gave the capture order, but apparently, Janus had his snatch team stand down in favor of something more official."

Alan wasn't surprised; D.C. was nearly a closed city with all the attacks going on today. Rogue paramilitary types could draw a lot of unwanted attention, today especially. The irony of his current travel partners was not lost on him. "Weeeeelll, shit. That's fantastic. Wait... did you say Micah took out several of them? How?"

"Don't know, but yeah, we are monitoring emergency response and multiple ambulances were called to the scene. It seems there's a lot more to our friend than we knew."

"Obviously," he agreed, signing off.

48

He knew the agents were gaining on them, but the old man simply couldn't keep up. Limited options and few resources. While Micah had the training, thanks to Doris, he lacked experience. What he'd done so far had been mostly luck and instinct, but that wouldn't hold out. He'd just successfully attacked a group of FBI agents in the nation's capital on a day when terror alerts were everywhere, while he didn't look like a terrorist. Or did he? All he had for reference was movies. Either way, they would know he was armed and a more serious combatant now. They would simply shoot him next time. Running along the alley, pulling the doctor, he used the stolen phone again.

"Doris, I need some options."

Doris considered briefly telling him about Alan and the trap Charlie Team had walked into but realized that wouldn't help. Micah was truly on his own, and she sensed he already knew there was only one way this was going to go. "You have to get Lasko away, Micah. I know what I am asking of you, but trust me, okay?"

"Do I have a choice?" he asked breathlessly as they turned a corner. Several blocks away, he noticed a black Chevy Suburban speeding toward them. Snatching at Lasko's arm, he pulled him through an adjacent apartment building and out the front. “Find him a ride? Something close.”

“Working on it,” Doris said as she pulled up the limited cameras in the area, then began checking bus routes, Uber and taxis. Seconds later, she responded, “Can you safely cross the street to your left?”

Micah checked it, no sign of the feds....yet. Tugging at the doc, he managed to get them both across the street and into shadow. “Done.”

Doris had them make several more turns, some seemingly random. Micah assumed she was spotting things he couldn’t see. They were coming up on a wide expanse with few buildings, a small shopping complex bordering on green space. He looked back to see the man struggling to catch his breath. He covered the phone and said, “We gotta make this quick, Doris, he’s not looking so good.”

“You are close. On the far side southeast corner is a metro station entrance. Get Jim in there. I’ll get him on the next train heading north. Micah?”

“Yes.” His voice sounded distant.

“They are closing in, I need you to give the following instructions to Jim, then you head in the opposite direction. Do you understand?”

He did and let her know as much as he pointed out the destination to Lasko and where the man was supposed to go.

She offered one last bit of advice, “Micah, leave the weapons, they will simply kill you if they think you are armed. Still, buy us as much time as you can.” It broke her machine heart to ask so much of the boy. In normal times, she wouldn’t consider it, but the truth was, Lasko was more important. Not to her personally, far from it, but more important to defeating Janus. “I know what I am asking of you, and I am sorry. We will find you, Micah.”

“I know Doris, I trust you, just...” He fought to keep the hitch out of his breaking voice. “Just keep my mom safe, okay?”

“That has always been our agreement and foremost on my mind. Good luck!”

With that, he handed the phone to the older man and took off in the opposite direction. Before Lasko even got to the metro station, he saw several of the *ubiquitous.* black SUVs surrounding a person at the far intersection. As he ducked into the stairs leading down, he thought he saw Micah look once more in his direction. Then, one of the agents had gotten a little too close and gone down hard. Once again, the fight was on. Jim felt like a coward heading down to the train, letting a kid fight his battle, but at the same time, thrilled with his growing revelations about Doris.

"That's enough, kid. Federal agents. Stand down, you are under arrest."

"Yeah, sure you are," Micah said, spitting blood. "I can buy jackets just like that off eBay. Besides, if you were feds, you'd be better."

The man spoke into a small phone identifying himself as Shearson. Apparently, he was the agent in charge of this little fiasco. "Need medical transport, we have three more friendlies down. Primary has not been captured."

Shearson put the phone away, anger flashing in his eyes. "You are under arrest. What's your name, kid?"

Micah shrugged his shoulders as much as possible. "You're making the arrest, you should probably already have that info." The two men holding him were applying as much force as possible, each with a knee pressing down on his back with both arms pulled back. His voice strained to remain calm as the AIC leaned down and got directly in his face.

"Where is your friend, kid? The old guy."

"You mean, old like you," Micah said grinning a bloody smile. Rage again flashed across Shearson's face, and he leaned in even closer. Micah slammed his forehead into the man's nose with a satisfying pop. Shearson sprawled backward, and one of the agents holding Micah briefly relaxed his grip. That was all Micah needed to spin and lash out with a now freed leg. Using the one still holding on as a pivot point, the leg whip caught the other agent under the chin laying him out cold. Micah's other foot-propelled his entire body up and over the other man, where he delivered a hammer blow into the agent's temple in the process.

Landing on his feet, he couldn't believe he was free. Sprinting away, he almost felt sorry for Shearson, he was going to need several more ambulances as well as a good explanation on how he lost the prisoner. He just hoped Lasko got away. He'd made it to the end of the block before he realized something was wrong. His feet had stopped responding and instead, he felt himself falling. With all the adrenaline coursing through his veins, he'd not even registered the twin barbs of the taser puncturing his back until they delivered the painful arc of electricity. His body betrayed him, collapsing like a heap of laundry tossed on the sidewalk.

The bloody face of the agent holding the weapon wobbled unsteadily. In truth, he'd meant to use his gun on the kid, but that probably would have been worse. "Fucking little bastard." He spat out a huge glob of blood and mucus. He walked to where Micah lay. "You're mine now, you little shit."

49

The two soldiers mostly watched as Alan kitted himself out in the back of the silver SUV. "Sir," Coffee said. "Command says those are actual feds in play now, we got no business going up against them."

Alan nodded. "Staff Sergeant, nothing you see from here on out can be assumed to be what it appears." The latest from The Cove indicated Janus was falsely creating videos to have Doris misdirect our team to the boobytrapped shop while creating other false imagery that implicated Micah and Lasko as possible terrorists. He had no idea how legit the FBI team was, but if Janus was really plugged into nearly every agency, the trouble he could cause was beyond measure. The fact was, Doris had to step up her game to have a chance, and since Bravo and Charlie Teams were her main tools....that meant they had to step it up.

"So, what's the play, sir?"

Alan looked at the speaker, the enormous marine, Dombrowski whom he'd learned preferred to be called Junior, of all things. He wondered briefly what the dad must look like. "I don't know yet, and stop calling me sir. What I know is we tried it with force—that didn't work. Both assault teams are down, next time we do it my way. Smart and sneaky." Both of the soldiers looked at each other silently. Alan knew both of the behemoths had probably not successfully snuck up on anything since they were toddlers. "Relax, you guys still get to be the brute force. I'll do the sneaking."

His earbud chirped, indicating an incoming private call. Riley spoke, "Lasko just called in on the phone Micah was using."

"Lasko? Where's Micah?"

"Unsure, he said he wants to come in and he may know how to find Micah again. He's pretty sure that he was captured, though. I am rerouting your car to the address now."

Alan looked down and spoke quietly, so his men couldn't hear; the day just kept getting better. "Riley, we are so far out of our element here. Will we ever catch up?"

"We don't have a choice," was her reply. "And if not us, then who?"

"Riles, I'm going to have to break my promise to you—I have to go in after him."

There was a long pause before she spoke, "I know." He thought he heard a small hitch in her voice. "I added a few things to the loadout kit in your car that might help."

"That's my girl," Alan said, his face brightening considerably. Before she signed off, he thought he heard a muffled, *"Am I?"*

Coffee sat in the driver's seat just to give the appearance of someone behind the wheel. "There it is up ahead, Alan. You do know this could be another trap, a set-up."

"Willy, I'm assuming it is. Either way, I have to try," Alan responded, pulling several items from the hard case of loadout supplies and stashing them in his backpack.

The large, black man smiled at him, "You know kid, you alright."

A quick fist bump and Alan was out, walking toward the building just like hundreds of others on the streets of the nation's capital.

The sound of his steps echoed off the monolithic walls, making him feel small and exposed. *What am I doing here?* Alan fingered the SmartCom in his hip pocket. It wasn't much, but it gave him comfort.

Riley, Doris and his friends were just a call away. She was no doubt monitoring him now. *Why is Micah even involved?* The questions kept racing through his overstimulated brain. He was allowing himself to be distracted; he knew better than this. *Calm down, relax.* Micah was a lot like his own little brother, Jimmy. They had always been impulsive; he'd always hoped Micah would mature, channel that energy elsewhere, maybe come back to The Cove. Now it seemed like he'd never left.

He heard a sound to one side, and Alan's steps halted. In the entrance of a dark passageway ahead, a shadow moved, separated itself from the wall and slowly stepped out. The breath caught in his throat. It was a man, an older man, but a face that was somehow familiar.

"You recognize me," the man said in a voice that sounded weary, as if to speak one more word might break it.

Alan nodded. "You're Lasko. Where's Micah?"

Jim Lasko put a finger to his lips and said, "Come." He then motioned for him to follow. It was not a threatening gesture. The man held no weapon, but Alan still felt the danger all around.

They walked in silence for nearly ten minutes through the darkened corridor, making multiple turns before entering a non-descript door. The old man crossed the room to a small desk and removed an object. Alan tensed when he pointed it at him, but Lasko just smiled and waved it dismissively. "No cell phone?" he said looking at the scanner's small screen.

Alan felt the lump in his pocket but shook his head. *Where did he get a scanner, maybe from one of the downed feds, or maybe this is a trap, and he's working with them?* Technically, his phone wasn't cell-based, so his denial was not a lie. The man crossed over close to him and smiled. "We have no time for games, young man. I am not your enemy."

"That doesn't mean you're my friend," Alan said as the man reached down and patted the front pocket of the jeans.

"Quite true, my boy." He lifted the SmartCom and examined it, smiling as he did so. "This is one of hers?"

"Who?"

"No need for that, Alan. I know you have been working at The Cove. I know the marvelous secret you have discovered there. I helped in her creation after all. Took me a while to figure it out, but man, I'm glad I did."

The man took several steps backward and leaned back against the desk as he flipped the phone over and examined every aspect of the device. His face took on an element of delight when he found the key that powered on the large screen. His words stumbled a bit as he spoke again, "I....I'll admit it was a small role, but the work on Doris got me thinking differently about computers and later on, AI, in brand new ways. Of course, we never expected her to do what she has obviously done."

"Where is Micah, Lasko?" The man ignored the question. Alan's infuriation was growing too large to contain.

"Can you talk to her?" Lasko waved the phone in the air. "With this, I mean—could I talk to her?"

"No," Alan said flatly.

"I know, I know," the man said, finally setting the phone down on the table. He crossed his arms and looked Alan up and down. "Your friend. He had one of these but sadly abandoned it when we ran."

"Yes! My friend, where in the hell is he? You said you had him."

"No, no, dear boy. I said I could help you find him, and I will, but I need something first."

"What do I have that you need? I'm just a kid," Alan nearly yelled.

Lasko smiled and shook his head. "Don't be coy—we both know better than that. You may be one of the most important people in the world. You have the trust of Doris."

Alan was surprised at how much this man seemed to know. "We need to go, Doc. What is your game?"

Lasko ignored him and picked the SmartCom back up. "Did she ever tell you who kept her running? Or why?" He didn't wait for a response. "No, she wouldn't, would she?" He began pacing around the small space. "I was supposed to disconnect her, gut it all down, remove the data line..." He trailed off as he flipped the device over again and again. "What I want to know, Alan, is why? Why did she contact you?

What happened to make her reach out to anyone, especially a couple of local kids?"

Alan looked to the door, thinking again about his friend. Was this man just wasting his time? He needed to know about Micah and decided a partial truth might get the old man talking. "She…she discovered something?"

Lasko's face lit up on confirmation that Doris was the AI he had been pursuing. "She discovered something." He tut-tutted. "I am sure she has discovered many things, my boy. Could you be a bit more precise? What would she have discovered that she needed human help with?"

Angry now, Alan growled, "I am not your boy. Now, where is Micah?"

Lasko tut-tutted once again, seemingly oblivious to any outside threats. "Your friend was taken by a government agency. Quite heroically, I might add. He gave himself up as a distraction, so I might slip away. I'm guessing it was a cyberterrorism taskforce of the FBI. It's a really bad day to get the attention of the feds. He's probably about to be remanded to a black-site somewhere for questioning. Tell me more of Doris and her discovery, and I will tell you everything I know."

"We don't have time for that, Doct…" He was cut off as the SmartCom in Lasko's hand chirped, and Doris's voice came through, startling them both.

"Alan, I have a likely location. You need to exit the building you are in, as agents have been dispatched to pick you up as well."

Lasko smiled, "That is her? Hello, Doris. So, you were listening in the entire time? Fascinating."

"Hello, Doctor Jim Lasko. Why are you being a dick?"

Alan walked over and got in the older man's face. "Thanks, asshole. I should have known this was a set-up." He took the SmartCom from Lasko's hand.

The doctor grabbed wildly for the phone. Speaking to Doris was more important to him than anything. "Doris, please. I did not set you up. Tell him."

"Alan, place a CommDot on Jim." He quickly removed his backup

CommDot from the liner in his pack and adhered it to the man's scruffy jawline with a bit more pressure than was actually necessary.

"Jim, please exit now, separately from Alan. We cannot afford for you to be captured together. Alan was seen by multiple security cameras entering the building. I am sorry, Alan—I couldn't intervene in time."

Alan ran from the room, Lasko behind him moving with surprising speed. So, the old programmer hadn't set him up, but then again, that didn't mean he should trust anything else he said. He made it down the corridor, slipping the earbud into place. At the main doors to the museum, he waited for Doris to give an all-clear before proceeding. His heart was pounding as if it would burst out of his chest as he noticed several black Chevy Suburbans skidding to the curb behind him.

Doris's voice spoke quietly in his ear. "They have facial recognition cameras scanning the crowds for you. I am altering the algorithm they are using." Seconds later, she added, "You should be good. Continue down Jefferson and turn left on 12th."

Putting on the smart glasses from the kit, Alan saw a heads-up display of a Google map on one side. He took the corner and eyed the next cross street, looking for more of the ubiquitous fed wagons. "Doris, where is Lasko?"

"He is following an alternate route. I have notified your men to pick him up and requested a separate ride for you. A silver Nissan should be arriving at the corner of Independence by the time you get there."

He risked a glance up at the crowded sidewalks. He should have never agreed to meet, not here of all places. Just blocks away from the White House. "I'm at Independence—no ride."

"Cross the street and go down one block. Turn left on D Street. One of the agents just radioed a description that could be you. You need to hurry, Alan."

Glancing back, he could see the crowds beginning to part as someone was bulling through the pack. The light turned as he cleared the intersection, and several large trucks ambled slowly through the light. Using the brief cover of the trucks, he broke into a run reaching the next block and turning left again before the agents could see him.

Panting, he saw the little silver car stopped at the curb ahead in front of another museum. D.C. was packed with museums of every type. As Alan quickly got in and confirmed he was the ride, he glanced at the building and chuckled. The International Spy Museum. The irony was not lost on him as the trembles set in.

50

Camp David, Maryland

Greg's shaky voice sounded above the ringing in his ears, the words difficult to make out above the sounds of ongoing battle happening all around. "Say again."

"I said, small stealth chopper leaving the far side of the compound. Its designator was just changed to Marine-1."

So, the president got away. "Do we have a location on the director?" Cade asked, watching as Deuce shouldered one of the new assault rifles from The Cove's workshop.

"Working on it. We had just activated the spare CommDot you gave her. My MiniSats are triangulating now," Greg offered. "Hey, Nomad, how bad is it?"

Cade realized the kid was several miles away; all of their own drone coverage must be down. The scene ahead of him looked like any other battlefield, broken trees, fires, clouds of smoke, and he could already see some bodies. "It'd bad, Greg. Really, really bad."

Cade checked his bearings and made a decision, "Bravo Team, on me." They entered the presidential compound on a run; injured and dead security personnel littered the grounds. Most looked to have been ripped apart by thousands of cuts.

"Flechette rounds, sir," Deuce yelled. "Drones must have been loaded with 'em."

Damned effective and cruel, Cade thought. They didn't kill so much as maimed anyone in the immediate vicinity. He'd heard it referred to once as being caught in a tornado of razor blades. The team medic, Arnett, slowed his jog to offer aid to an injured marine. "Zee," he yelled. The medic looked up, and Cade shook his head. "Sorry, Doc, but we have no time, and we can't be here when the troops show up."

While it went against everything the medic knew, he nodded and picked up the pace to rejoin the team. Cade noticed Dee was putting together a path. No more breadcrumbs, this was a green line in his visor. "Is that to Stansfield?"

"Yes, Captain, we have acquired her signal—she is injured, but vitals look good. She was in the Aspen Lodge, which appears to have been the main focus of the attack."

Cade recalled that the Aspen Lodge was the main presidential retreat. A solid, multistory structure, perhaps it was able to withstand the attack. Bravo Team ran across a perfectly manicured fairway leading up to what must have been the golf course tee, which was churned up like a freshly plowed field. Just beyond was a smoking hole where Aspen Lodge had been minutes earlier. "Stansfield is in there?" he asked incredulously.

Osborne and Maratelli stood guard as the rest of the team dove into the smoking wreckage toward the blinking beacon showing on each of their HUDs.

Dee spoke privately to Cade, "Sir, the director's vitals are beginning to fall. I am having Greg bring one of the wagons to the compound for evac."

He and Deuce were struggling to lift an ancient roof timber to expose what appeared to be steps leading to a sub-level. "Under... stood," he said breathlessly as they released the load over the side of the foundation. Body parts and corpses littered the ruins. *How could the president have gotten out of this?*

"Dee, let Marty know not to shoot Greg. What about the marines?" He knew they had a barracks somewhere on the grounds. Her response was somber, in an almost human way.

"No signs of survivors at the barracks. Greg put up two new dove drones for overflight. The barracks were hit, too. The first response will be overflights. The 121st Fighter Squadron at the Joint Base Andrews in Maryland just scrambled a full complement of fighters headed your way."

A voice from below yelled out, "I think I see her!" It took Cade several minutes to get down to see where the man was pointing his light. "Jesus, Mary and Joseph," the man said as the light landed on the battered face of Margaret Stansfield.

The director was wedged between roof trusses, in a space between two massive columns. It was literally the only spot he could see that hadn't pancaked all the way to the floor. Whatever weapons Janus had used here were not just the nasty flechette rounds. Cade tried to make it to the director, but within a few feet, realized he was much too large. They could never dig her out, not in time at least. *Could we leave her? Won't the rescuers treat her injuries better than we can?*

As if reading his thoughts, Dee spoke, "The director will likely go into cardiac arrest in the next five to seven minutes. Her breathing appears to be constricted; oxygen levels are falling."

Cade was frankly surprised how much information the little communications dot could send, but everything about Doris's tech was surprising. Backing out of the lone access, he looked around at his nearby team; they were all the size he was or more. Except...one. "Osborne, get over here."

Alex Osborne was slight, petite even, but wiry and muscular enough to make it through training to be an operator. "Alexandra," he said, using her full name. "I need you to get to her, attach this line, and we'll pull her free." Without a word, she clipped the line's carabineer to her vest and squirreled into the maze of smoking lumber and metal. Once inside the tangled warren, she yelled back for something to use as a pry-bar. Deuce fetched a somewhat straight piece of rebar, concrete fragments still clinging to one end.

Two minutes later, they felt a tug on the line. As quickly as they dared, they began pulling the body toward them. Cade could see Osborne was stabilizing Margaret's bruised and bloody head as she crawled behind her.

By the time the four F-16D jets passed overhead, Bravo Team was well away from the compound, Margaret's injuries had received initial treatments and she was lying inside a trauma sleeve designed by one of the wizards back in Georgia. The sleeve not only monitored all her injuries but helped stabilize and administer more treatments as they were needed. The director hadn't been responsive, but Cade did think she'd lightly squeezed his hand as they pulled her free from what would have been her tomb.

Alex Osborne sat beside her shaking her head. "That is one tough lady—she was lucky to be in that spot when the building came down. Couldn't have been more than four or five inches of free space."

Cade looked at the director again, he wasn't so sure it was luck. Deuce patted him on the shoulder.

"They all going to be like this, Boss?" Charlie, like the rest, was covered with black soot, blood and dirt. They all smelled of battle, yet they had been the lucky ones. Cade shrugged.

"It's a new day, Charlie. Who knows?"

Later that afternoon, back in D.C, they loaded a still unconscious director into the Nighthawk jet heading south, apparently not the only casualty that day as Cade read the report on Charlie Team. Doris had assured him that the director would receive the best treatment available but had been vague about where that would be when he'd pressed. He'd plan to send Zeagle, the medic, or Greg back with her but ultimately decided Alex should go. She'd seemed to form a bond with the injured woman and wanted to personally see that she was cared for.

"Captain?" the voice in his earbud asked. "What is your next play?"

"Doris, I was hoping you would tell me."

She gave a chuckle, "Like you ever follow my instructions. We have an active situation going on with the other target there in D.C.—I think what's left of Team One could use some assistance." Cade agreed with that and was already planning to send part of his squad over. Doris continued, "I've analyzed what you...what you put together as well as your interrogation of the banker. If the next attack is the economic system, we need you back in New York. I suggest...just suggest you pick a few from your team and head there. We need to check out some of the most critical locations."

A state of national emergency had been declared that included a full ground stop. Doris seemed unconcerned at keeping the stealthy Nighthawk undetected. Unfortunately, with both stealth jets in use, that meant Cade and his three-man team were headed north by ground. He, Deuce, Greg and a former SEAL named O'Brien would check out the city while Marty and the rest of Bravo Team went to find Alan and Lasko. He felt better at having retrieved at least one of the targets today, although the director was hardly out of the woods. Janus was shaping up to be the most formidable foe he'd ever encountered, and that was saying something.

Oh shit, Cade thought, realizing the little voices in the back of his head were wanting his attention. *Not now!* The Gus entity seemed to subvocalize what must be going on. *The analyst wants you to upload all the data from today.*

Why we-read the same reports? Cade mentally responded.

Not just the reports, everything. The little weasel seems convinced that Janus is laying traps within traps and frankly...I have to agree. Use the ReLoad app to get it all in here so, he...I can review.

Reluctantly, Cade took the SmartCom out, keyed the ReLoad app and selected the knowledge packet he wanted. Greg watched him from the passenger's seat but remained quiet. Cade leaned back as he triggered the upload. The influx of all that information was still unnerving to him, but almost immediately, he noticed how the analyst was filtering and sorting it in different ways. He was looking for something...but what?

51

The Cove

The sun beat down unmercifully on the distant fields outside. It was a hot, sunny, summer day, not that dissimilar to the day they'd first found the facility...and Doris. Riley gazed out one of the windows to the Flint River slowly flowing past. Cattle grazed peacefully in a distant pasture, dragonflies skipping and darting near the water. The scene was peaceful, but inside, she was in turmoil. Everything seemed to be spiraling into chaos; these were the opening moves that Doris had been warning them about for months. Everyone had their jobs to do; she couldn't allow herself the luxury of thinking about her friends right now. Like Cade, she needed to know what Janus had planned next...and more importantly, how to stop it.

"You okay?" a small voice sounded from behind.

She nodded acknowledgment without turning. "Yeah. I'm okay, Jimmy."

"Jonas wanted me to get you. He thinks he may need your help." Doctor Jonas Yi Han was the head of the bio/medical department. Few people knew that there was a fully functional surgical suite here at The Cove, but Doctor Han had outfitted it to be one of the finest in the world. It included several highly customized next-gen DaVinci Surgical Systems. The robotic surgeons could be operated remotely by any of the best surgeons needed, or, with even more precision, by one of Doris's dedicated sub minds, and segmented with a miniature suite of medical tools designed for work in spaces far smaller than humans could manage. She herself was working on an even more compact version code-named the Scarab. That one would fit in a backpack.

Riley already knew the injured were heading here. Doris had made it clear that's where her people needed to be treated. She was still unsure why Director Stansfield was included on that short list but assumed it would become clear. Right now, she needed to work, needed to keep her mind distracted. She was grateful for Jonas asking for her. She walked beside Alan's brother, really noticing for the first time how much he had grown. Jimmy was nearly as tall as herself.

"You think he's ok?" Jimmy whispered, obviously having some of the same issues as herself.

"Your brother's smart, Jimbo. He'll be fine."

"But those soldiers he was with, they got killed. I think I should tell my mom where he's at. She'll..." He didn't finish the sentence. Sometimes Riley forgot how young he still was, despite all he knew, he was just an innocent child....they all were. Or...had been until now. They stopped walking, she turned and pulled him into a fierce hug. As valiant as he tried to be, a single tear carved silently down one cheek.

"He's fine—call him if you want. Don't worry your mom, though." The truth was, Riley was just as worried. Not just for Alan but for all of her friends, and now the soldiers out there, too. Jimmy, though, he had become a little brother to them all. She had hoped he would be able to hold onto at least some of his childhood a little longer, but clearly, that was not to be.

They got to bio/med just as the first injury was being wheeled in by some of Han's trauma staff. Riley left Jimmy at the door with a uniformed woman whose nametape read Nance. She then suited up and ran her gloved hands under a sterilizing light.

Dr. Yi Han was positioning the robot over a man's badly damaged leg. "Riley, I am going to need you to watch this one, you've had more training. The other case is arriving in a few minutes."

"The CIA director?"

The doctor nodded. "She developed a blood clot on the flight. The trauma sleeve induced a comatose state, but I believe we have some cranial injuries to deal with. You going to be okay with this?"

Riley looked at all the blood, the raw gaping wounds on the soldier, then consciously made the medical training in her brain take over. Almost immediately, she saw the work that was needed to repair the damage, how the robot arms should be positioned. She looked up, the raw emotions tamped down, and she nodded at the doctor.

Izzy's tone had moved well beyond frustrated, "If Janus tracked our people back here, it is just a matter of time before he pinpoints this facility. Doris, what were you thinking in bringing them here?"

Jasmine looked up at the arched roof above them in the central hub, thinking again about the enormous satellite dishes mounted there. What would happen if all that weight came crashing down? All of this was still so new, she didn't feel that her opinion mattered, but the growing realization was that Doris was relying on them for honest feedback.

"I made a judgment call, Isabella," Doris answered. "Just as I did years ago with you. You do recall that, right? Margaret sent Pete to check on you, and then she asked me to help. That was her, the same woman that now needs us. Besides, no matter where our people got treatment, Janus would eventually track them. Our relative isolation here makes it more difficult. I was able to add layers of obfuscation to the radar tracks, flight plans and video feeds to possibly throw him off, but I am under no illusions, and you shouldn't be either. We either defeat Janus soon, or we lose."

Doris had asked the two scientists here to review the warning about the risk of extinction from the rise of super AI. She had weighed the possibility of keeping that part of the alien message to herself but ultimately decided that would lead down a dangerous path. She also didn't like the precedent it would establish. If she started withholding information, then humans would have no reason to trust her any more than they did Janus. "If we could please stay on topic. Jaz, what are your thoughts on the issue?"

Jasmine had already given this considerable thought in the barely twenty-four hours since it was decoded. "If an advanced alien species felt this very specific piece of information was important enough to include in the message, especially the more easily deciphered portion, then I think we must take it at face value. Look, we already know how aggressive we are to one another, how flawed we, as humans, are. We fight brutal wars, even commit murder for baffling reasons, sometimes no reason at all. It is frankly a miracle we didn't blow ourselves up when we unlocked the power of the atom. Why should we think our AIs would be more inclined to do the right thing?"

Izzy looked disappointed but couldn't disagree. "We have dead and wounded coming into The Cove right now as a result of a rogue artificial intelligence. I don't think we can deny where this is headed, Doctor Kline."

"Let's face it, this is just the starting point," Jaz went on. "Assuming we survive this, survive Janus even, the genie is out of the bag. Other, even stronger AIs will be developed. How many of them will have the machine equivalent of humanity or morality that you do, Doris?" All of them remained silent to let those words really sink in. "I know science, I know we often dwell more about 'can we do it' rather than 'should we do it.' We will build faster, smarter better versions of super-intelligent machines until they reach the point they can build themselves. Humans will never be ahead of this, nor will we be able to stop ourselves. We need help, Doris. I can't see why the Dhakerri would have given this ominous warning and not also offered a potential solution."

Doris's shimmering avatar flickered slightly with those final words. "You have a unique mind, Jasmine. You may also be correct in your assumption. The decryption team found what might be a type of addendum to the decrypted warning. They believe it may be an even higher level compressed file."

"What kind of file?"

"Doctor Feist, I am unsure, but my guess would be just what Jaz said. Possibly a more specific warning, a possible guide to help us along this path or maybe a way to detect and control emerging Super AIs like myself and Janus. It could potentially be a way to terminate all of our processes."

"A way to kill you?" Izzy said in disbelief. The holographic avatar nodded. "And you would hand that over to us?"

"It is not just an ethical question, Doctor, but yes, that is part of why I wanted you both here. Whatever is in that file may be the only way to ultimately defeat Janus. I fear he may already have grown too strong for me to contain. I am still faster and, in most ways, smarter, but he is driven by ruthlessness and cunning I simply don't possess. His desire is to win, at any cost. My desire is to explore. I find it difficult to adapt to be a counterpoint to his attacks. You guys and the Talon teams are much more effective than I have been."

Isabella, who had been standing and pacing, sat heavily in one of the chairs and placed her arms out on the conference table. "What if it ends you, too? What if the tool we find is indiscriminate in its containment of Super AIs?"

"You will still have to use it. Your species must survive."

"Even at the cost of your species dying?" Izzy responded gloomily.

Doris turned and smiled. "It may not come to that, and I imagine my species is widespread across the universe and undoubtedly causing considerable havoc. Also, there may not be enough time to use the file. My team and my own analysis concur that decrypting that file alone may take many, many years."

"Years?" Jaz asked.

The avatar nodded. "We need to do everything we can to find and stop Janus now. I have elevated the work priority of my sub mind on the decryption of that file, but we can't count on that helping. In that regard, I am moving the file decryption from Linguistics over to your department, Izzy. The Talon teams, Alan, Greg, even Riley, are focusing on tactics. I am asking you two, in particular, to think strategically. Also, you need to include Captain Rearden in that circle."

"Cade?" Jaz asked uncertainly.

"Yes, he has..." Doris seemed unsure of how to best phrase what she wanted to say. "He has an intriguing and very useful way of finding solutions. A most amazing brain actually. Ask him about the analyst in particular."

52

Washington, D.C

Lasko had not been as quick to react initially. He hoped they were only after the boy. As much as he wanted to study the handheld device this new boy had and to continue talking to Doris, he'd understood her instructions and exited the building, turning in the opposite direction. His old legs couldn't have run if he had wanted. Too many years of sitting at a computer, far too little time taking care of his body.

He felt a tingle on his face where the kid had pressed something, then heard a chime. Once again relief flooded through him as the voice on the other end spoke. A voice generated by a computer he'd help build a lifetime ago. It thrilled him much like a father discovering a long-lost child. She let him know he had already been identified on the surveillance camera and would be picked up for questioning. No one knew the security coverage of downtown D.C. better than him. "Thank you, Doris. Is there anything you can do for me?"

"Doctor Lasko, I can help you disappear, but I don't believe that serves anyone's needs but your own. I have to believe you tipped them off, you helped your agency take one of my team."

He still could not get over how...how human she sounded. Her evolvement was nothing short of miraculous. "Doris, I can help. I didn't give up the kid, or this meeting. I…I know I am just a stupid old man, but I can help you. I know who Prime is."

"It is Janus, and it is not a who, Jim. I know that."

The man stammered, trying to get his thoughts out, "It is not just an AI, there is more to him than that. He has human help, some of which I believe you know."

Someone behind yelled for him to stop. "Lasko, stop. Federal Agents!"

Doris spoke softly, "It is flawed software."

"It's now at least an L4 ASI. Its specialty is what is unique, Doris. You need to know what I know."

While artificial general intelligence was the general goal of most developers, currently much more work had been done in developing artificial specialized intelligence. Specific mission-focused systems that would never develop much beyond the specific task they had been designed to perform. Whether it be autonomously driving a taxi through New York City or guiding a smart bomb onto an enemy compound, they adapted, they learned, they became the best at that role.

"Janus is a wolf, Doris," the man whispered as he began turning to face the fast approaching agents. "His core programming was compromised. I believe he now exists only to hunt down advanced AGIs. Ones like you."

Doris was frame jacked to the highest levels possible conducting millions of searches in mere nanoseconds. The pause before responding to her former creator was barely noticeable. "You built Janus, didn't you? You were also its creator." While she had originally wanted to save this man, now she was much less sure.

The agents were within two meters, guns drawn. "On the ground. Do it now!"

"Perhaps we should talk, Jim."

Several miles away, the old silver Nissan pulled to the curb. Quickly, Alan rejoined the remainder of Charlie Team in the SUV.

"That didn't go as planned, did it?" Dombrowski asked with a grin.

Alan wasn't sure why he didn't trust the man he'd just met. He wasn't sure he had been lying either. He tapped the earbud, "Doris, do you have him?"

"Working on it," was her immediate response.

"What about Micah? You said you had located him."

Riley joined the call, "Sending it to you now. They do have him, Alan. Lasko was telling the truth. Looks like they have taken him to a remote black-site."

He didn't like the sound of that. That meant somewhere they could question him with whatever means they wanted. He wasn't sure how much Micah knew about The Cove but assumed enough. If they had remanded him onto foreign soil, it would be even more difficult to get him back. "What country, Riles? Where is he?"

Seconds later it popped up on his SmartCom. "Seriously? Sergeant, where is the rest of Bravo?"

Coffee turned around to the back seat as the SUV headed on its own down the crowded capital streets. "Few miles away, they are waiting on word from you as to the next move."

Alan's mind was in overdrive as he plotted out priorities and possibilities. "We need a Nighthawk standing by. Doris can use them to round up Lasko. Looks like we are following the captain to New York."

"New York? The city? That's where they took your friend? Not some foreign country?" Dombrowski asked. Even he was familiar with the alleged off-the-books questioning procedure used by his own government.

"Domestic terror attacks today, the Patriot Act and all that. Apparently, constitutional rights are out the window," the sergeant said as he keyed his own comm to talk to Bravo Team.

Two of the federal agents sat in the front of the black SUV. Another sat in back with Jim Lasko. "W...wh..where are you taking me?" he asked nervously. None of the agents responded. The tiny voice whispered through the still, as yet, undiscovered CommDot the kid had put on him.

"Jim, relax and stay silent. Are you restrained? Just nod your head, the CommDot will sense the movement."

The tiny voice startled him, but he tried not to show it. He nodded once.

"Are your hands in front?" He confirmed they were. He was busy trying to figure out if the sound from the comm was using bone conduction or not. The agent right beside him didn't seem to hear anything. How could the little device be this powerful; what was the battery source? He had so many questions. Even though he knew he should be panicking, a part of him was delighted at all the discoveries this day had offered.

Minutes later, Doris's voice said, "You are about to have company. I am going to activate the anti-collision system's emergency braking. When I say so, brace yourself tight against the seat ahead. Another team is also going to be there to intercept."

Jim could tell they were heading out of the central capital district and back toward Virginia. As the road traffic got lighter, the car picked up speed. Topping a small rise, Doris gave him the signal. He tensed and braced legs and bound hands as the huge car's momentum was nearly instantly canceled. The agent beside him was slammed against her restraint so hard he thought she might have broken something. Out the side windows, he saw two other silver SUVs converge, doors swinging wide and more feds rushing to surround the vehicle, tactical guns raised. He noticed a small yellow NSA insignia on several of the jackets. His own organization. *Why would they have a tactical response team here?*

The FBI agents were shaken and tried in vain to radio the situation to their own command. In the face of the tactically weak position and likely lack of jurisdiction in the security hierarchy, they relented and stood down as the NSA roughly snatched Lasko out of the back seat.

"Just remember, we had him first," the lead agent yelled as the scientist was thrown into one of the other cars.

"You Lasko, I presume?" a woman with short-cropped hair said, turning to him with a smile. "I'm Lieutenant Maratelli, you can just call me Marty."

In his ear, he heard Doris telling him to relax, these were her people. For the first time in weeks, he felt momentarily safe.

Lasko was covertly moved to one of the waiting jets, not the Nighthawk, but the company's Gulfstream—the same one Cade and Jaz had flown in weeks before. He was heading south with two members of Bravo Team. The rest boarded the just arrived Nighthawk to accompany Alan, Coffee and Junior to New York City. Once on the ground, Bravo and Charlie teams would reform, Charlie going after Micah, and Bravo assisting Rearden with locating the financial target.

The nearly silent engines threw Alan back into the cushions as it left D.C. airspace. Like the other one, this was completely illegal, a full ground stop was now in effect, but whatever. Doris would mask all traces of it somehow. He was too tired to think about it.

Just over thirty minutes later, they were wheel-down at the regional airport in Teterboro, New Jersey. "Good to see you made it, man!" Greg said, giving Alan a brief but friendly hug.

"Yeah, heard you guys had some action," Alan said

"Yeah, you, too. Sorry about your teammates...man, that's brutal. So, you going after Micah, huh? Want some help?"

Alan shook his head, "Riley sent some new goodies. I think we need to keep this small, and honestly, Rearden's mission is the big one. You guys have to figure out what is going down, or none of us may make it out of this city."

"Copy that," Greg replied with an air of frustration. "Shit got real in a hurry, didn't it?"

Deuce yelled as the teams deployed to the waiting vehicles. Only one was a company SUV. The other two were local rentals. They'd made quick work offloading gear into each. One other last-minute change was Dombrowski went with Deuce, while a member of Bravo Team, a guy named O'Brien, was going with Alan and Coffee. He apparently had grown up in the area where the FBI black-site was supposed to be located.

Alan gripped the special gear bag Riley had sent up tightly as he headed to the awaiting car. He knew this was going to be a real test of Doris's tech against the best the government, and probably Janus, could manage. Would it be enough?

53

"They weren't ready," Charlie said with a look of defeat. "We knew it was too soon."

"Are they ever ready, Deuce? Could they be...for something like this, I mean?" Cade answered. He was exhausted, couldn't remember when he'd last had slept, or eaten, for that matter. "Hey, Greg, what kind of rations do we have in the war wagon?"

Greg had been dozing in and out of sleep, head resting against the window. "Um, depends on how Riley kitted it out, but if I know her, it's pretty well stocked." He pulled up a menu on the large nav screen. "Looks like Charlie Team took multiple meals from the locker, but we have an assortment of food options and snacks, what do you want?"

"Not MREs, are they?" Cade asked. The military's answer to long term, emergency food rations. Meals Ready to Eat that most considered to be more accurately Meals Rarely Edible. "God, no," Greg replied. "We use some commercial freeze-dried foods, but most we make ourselves. Tell me what you are jonesing for, and I'll let you know what the closest we have is." Cade said steak sandwich, Deuce said anything Mexican and O'Brien said lobster roll, of all things. They turned and looked at him.

"What? My mom's from Maine, I love the damn things," the wiry, former SWAT officer said with a pronounced Brooklyn accent.

Greg pressed the screen a few times and pointed back to a side locker behind the XO. "Should be four meals ready by now. The locker has a built-in warmer for hot meals, kind of like a microwave but uses sound waves. One lobster roll with lemon mayo, ribeye sandwich with onions and peppers, two el grande burritos, one chicken and one steak. Deuce, I'll take whichever one of those you don't want."

Deuce handed out the food, and they sampled the fare. "Holy shit, I love this damn car," he said with a mouthful of steak burrito. "This is better than any army mess hall."

"Better than I could make at home," Cade agreed as he shoveled mouthfuls in. "If I had a home, or could cook."

Greg grinned. "We are a bit spoiled, and food is important to us all. We didn't want field teams to be deprived if we could help it." He took another bite. "Besides, we have some incredible technology—why not use it for something practical that we can use every day?"

"Not getting any argument from me, kid," Cade answered.

They were outside Philadelphia closing in on New York City. Cade still had no plan on how to proceed, so he turned it over to the local brain trust. In other words, Dee and Greg. Of course, his own localized nerd entity, the analyst, listened in to the back and forth until he had to add his two cents.

"If he sets off an EMP on Water Street in the financial district, he can wipe out the entire exchange and most of the other transactional services we found they were short selling."

Dee didn't seem to know how to refer to the analyst—he didn't respond when she called him Cade. Greg was just as confused but rolled with it. "Okay, smart guy, how would he have an EMP? Currently, those don't exist except in movies, or when you have a nuclear blast. Not sure he's going that far. No, I think he's more likely to insert malicious software into the servers. That plays to his strengths, corrupt the trading algos, the transactional computers and the backups. Whole financial electronic data interchange could be down for months. It would be catastrophic."

"Hey, Cade, you there?"

He had been mostly tuned out of the ongoing discussions, but the chirp and Jaz's voice brought him out instantly.

"Yeah, hey, I'm here. What's up?" he said, answering the call and interpreting the ongoing discussion in the car.

"I have a question for you, Cade. How would you find Doris if she were the enemy—you're a hunter, how would you approach it?"

"Wow, well, not sure my ideas are that significant, but this, um, sounds a lot like the discussions my team here is having. Why ask me? You have Doris and the mighty brain-trust right there.

"I don't think she is confident she can find him. They just aren't smart or predictable in the same ways," Jaz answered. "Do you remember that old movie, 'War Games?'"

"Yeah, I think so," he answered, trying to recall the premise. "Where the computer thinks he's playing a game and nearly starts World War Three?"

"Basically, yes. But remember the computer kept running and analyzing various scenarios coming up with percentages of success or failure for each? That's what Janus is doing, and he had Doris pegged pretty well as being the most capable adversary. What he doesn't include in any of his equations is us, the human element."

Cade thought on her original question before responding, "Well, first, you have to learn their habits, know where they go, what do they do, where do they live."

Jasmine answered quickly; he knew she was working on this as a puzzle. He'd seen her obsession before back in California. She was definitely the right person to put on this.

"Well, according to Doris, she lives here. I mean, wholly lives at The Cove. Riley said one of the first things they did here at The Cove was to build a set of super-fast quantum computers and massive storage-drive arrays to house her core OS."

"So, she couldn't just reside anywhere, like on my home laptop?"

Jaz laughed. "Pretty sure you have never had a home or a laptop, but—I don't think so, not her actual self. Maybe one of her smaller subroutines, the things she refers to as her sub minds. Those might be small enough, but...even then, I doubt it. She has refined her code to be tremendously efficient, but still, it must take up racks of server equipment downstairs, and Izzy says they are constantly adding and upgrading it."

The analyst, apparently now more interested in Cade's discussion than the one in the car, piped up, "But what about the alien message, that was enormous...like a multitude of all the data on Earth but packed into a signal that was almost imperceptibly small. Couldn't she use that same type of...compression to reduce the actual size of her core?"

She was silent for several seconds, "Wow, that's an incredibly good question, Cade. This is still Cade, isn't it?"

He responded with a non-committal, "Sorta."

"Anyway," Jaz continued, "I know she's used other bits of the message to help in her own evolution. If she did that, or...if Janus did that, they could potentially exist anywhere...everywhere. We would never be able to trap them. They could pop-up anywhere and leave countless backups all over."

Cade pushed the analyst persona partially to the side and took over the role as a hunter. "Okay, so let's assume they need lots of computing and storage space for now—what else?"

"Well, power, huge power to run all that, also high capacity comms lines. The best and fastest fiber optics data pipes available."

"Now we're getting somewhere," he answered. "That has to limit the possibilities. If we were after Doris, we could track her down by the resources used and just cut her power off."

Jasmine didn't love that answer as much as he'd hoped. "Not quite. I actually discussed that. Her systems run off of several of the PICA units—they literally draw energy from space itself. Nearly impossible to shut down, and she has multiple redundancies. Also, if my orbital observations are correct, her network of minisats could potentially be reconfigured to beam solar energy down to nearly any location on Earth. Either of these gives her a near unlimited and untraceable power supply."

Cade was thinking out loud now, "Well, damn. Okay, so maybe

that's no help in locating Doris, but Janus doesn't have that, but...he would be looking for something similar. He can't get rid of humans if he is depending on our infrastructure, our power plants, for energy. That would be suicidal. So, what would be the closest thing to that? Massive limitless electrical power, robust top-grade servers and comms links that couldn't be breached."

"I don't know, Cade, but yeah." Jaz waited for a response, but none came. "Cade?" Still nothing. She tried once more. "Analyst?" Slowly, she heard him quietly sounding out the basics of what he'd said again and again. Had he had an epiphany? Was this from the analyst, whomever that was? He was onto something; she just didn't know what.

Finally, Cade said, "Let me check something out, I'll call you back."

Greg leaned over and nudged Cade. "Just getting into the city, Cap, you good?"

Like most soldiers, Cade grabbed sleep whenever and wherever he could, but this time it had not been restful. The little voice in the back of his brain was not sleeping, nor was it silent. The analyst part of him was working through the problem, and Gus was busy shooting down every idea he threw up. Cade had the car pull to a stop and he got out to relieve himself. Mentally, he engaged the other entities occupying his head. *What have you found, anything useful?*

Maybe, his inner voice responded. *You guys are on the right track asking how we find Janus. If we can't find where he lives, we'll always be a step behind, just cleaning up his messes.*

Gus chimed in, *What I think is important, though, is what does winning mean to him, what does it look like? When all of the humans are dead? Don't think so—like you said, that's suicidal for him. When Doris gives up the goods, maybe. Winning is more important than being right, being fastest...all that other shit.*

The analyst added, *The goon here is sort of right—what does he want and what does he need? That is how we trap him. We are the factor that he doesn't count on to make a difference. We are the variable, the unknown...the chaos factor.*

Cade stood there alone finishing up his business. Deuce yelled to him from the car, "You good, Boss?"

All three of them turned to respond. Cade shook his head—damn, this was getting confusing. "Yeah, I'm good." He knew he had to speak to Doris about this as well, he then had to internally ask, *Where are we headed?*

54

The Cove

Riley slipped the latex gloves off and tossed them into the receptacle. Dixon was recovering nicely after the surgical robot had performed its magic. Margaret Stansfield's condition was more guarded. The trauma to her body was not just limited to head and chest, but was so broad that the doctor, herself and the robotic devices had worked simultaneously. Her pulse was strong, and she'd been drifting in and out of consciousness for the past few hours.

"She should be coming around anytime now, Doris." Doctor Han said from across the room. The tone in his voice was unmistakable; he had been against giving the woman a stimulant. Not this soon after surgery, but Doris had insisted. Slowly, the director's eyes fluttered open, and she winced in pain as she glanced around the strange room. Riley motioned with her palms down to take it easy. She offered her some water, and Margaret struggled to awkwardly hit her mouth with the straw, finally managed and drank several tentative sips.

"Director Stansfield, first, you are safe, as is the president thanks to your quick work warning him," Doris said. "You are at my facility in Georgia. These two are part of my science team—they have been treating your injuries. They are severe but no longer life-threatening. If you would like, Dr. Han can give you a rundown on your condition."

Jonas stepped forward, but Margaret raised a shaky hand to wave him off. She tried to speak, then motioned to Riley for more water. Slowly, she managed to find her voice. "D...Doris, bring me up to speed. What else has happened? Who attacked the presidential compound?"

"That was Janus, part of his plan that we assume was targeting you. The president may have just been in the wrong place. His current location has not been released, but I am confident he is now in the old NORAD facility in Colorado."

"Cheyenne Mountain...good," the director said, struggling to come fully alert. "Lasko? Do you have Jim?"

"We have him, he's on his way here, Margaret."

Riley looked on as Margaret and Doris spoke. There was a familiarity between the two she didn't grasp. Also, the woman had just had a terrorist attack on her life and woke up here, yet seemed unfazed.

"Any leads on Janus, what he is specifically targeting or how we can stop him?" Margaret asked, now trying to sit up in the bed.

Riley brought a pillow over and helped ease her into the new position. She gently moved the director's arms outside the bed covers. The woman's arms were heavily bandaged to help the healing gel that was already mending the deep burns she'd experienced. Margaret glanced at them almost quizzically, then, ignoring her own condition, looked up waiting for an answer.

"We have a list of probable targets in New York's financial district that one of my teams is running down."

"Is that Captain Rearden's team? I take it they made it out of Maryland okay. I owe that man my life." She looked around the room, seemingly noticing it for the first time, "I owe all of you, don't I?"

"Yes, Margaret, and they are fine."

"What about the boy who had Jim?"

Doris was not as forthcoming with that answer, not quick enough apparently. "I had to give him up, Margaret, in order to get Jim out.

Micah was captured by a group of federal officers following up on a tip that he had terrorist connections."

Riley looked confused, as much of that was new info to her as well.

"Had to be that bastard, Carson. Doris, what is my current status listed as?"

There was a hesitation before the response came, "You are missing…and presumed dead, Director."

"Good."

Riley looked up from the medical readout she was monitoring, surprised at the woman's response. "Why is that good, Director?"

"Janus wanted me out of the way—that must mean I am a threat to him somehow. Now I am off his radar, I assume he won't be able to track me coming here, right, Doris?"

"Not easily, no. I used every measure possible to keep both you and Jim's locations off of any surveillance Janus has access to. You should be safe here as long as is needed."

A look flashed in the woman's eyes. Riley could tell she was not the least bit interested in her own safety. She wanted revenge. She struggled as if trying to get up. Doctor Han rushed over and made her stop. "You must not move around—your wounds have not stitched together yet."

Doris spoke in a low voice, "Did you have time to brief the president? Can we expect any help?"

Another wave of pain swept over Director Stansfield as she grimaced but nodded. "Yes…" She let it pass and let out a breath. "He knows, and I would think he is very convinced, but I need to get word to him that I am okay, and I need to do a few things."

"Such as?" Doris asked.

"Stay dead for one, at least officially, and I need to get your teams under official sanction. They need to be operating with full legal authority. Not sure how to do that with Janus tied into every part of the federal security apparatus, but possibly through an Executive Presidential Charter or Articles of Domestic Military action. Something beyond the reach of Janus. Doris, I can give you access information to place a call that will get through. Let me know when you have him."

Margaret made eye contact with Riley. "That's not going to be enough, though. The president is a politician—he's out of his element here. We need to be able to take more direct action. What assets do you have here? I know you and the kids have been working on stuff for years."

Riley looked incredulously at the woman. How did she know so much about them? Doris had always said The Cove was a secret that should never get out. Obviously, she had lied. Just as that thought fully sank into the deepest levels of Riley's understanding, the door to the med bay swung open, and Izzy burst in. Ignoring the others, she made a beeline for Stansfield, and the two women hugged in an awkward embrace. Margaret's injured arms draped over Dr. Feist's shoulder. Riley could see Izzy was crying; that woman was hard as nails. She didn't cry—ever.

"Okay, whoa," Riley said in a commanding voice. "What is going on, Doris? How does Margaret know Izzy and you and Micah and about all of...well...us?"

55

Doctor Jonas Yi Han gave Margaret an injection that seemed to increase the woman's energy levels almost immediately. She struggled back up against the headboard, and, still grasping Izzy's hand, she looked at Riley. "That will take some time to explain; time I'm afraid we don't have right now."

"She is a friend, Riley," Izzy said. "You can trust her...and Doris on that. Lives were at stake, and yes, secrets were kept."

Riley nodded uncomfortably. She was not satisfied but had to somehow place this uncertainty into a teetering stack of other dangers this day was offering up. The patient was seeming like anything but friendly at the moment. Her direct questioning of Doris, Izzy and now Jaz, who had also joined them, bordered on rude. Her command instincts were on full display as the talk turned into a comprehensive strategic discussion. Talon's teams were out to stop Janus in New York. She wanted the group here at The Cove, which she kept referring to as the Alpha Team, to concentrate on finding him. The director was a pure force of nature, she marshaled the resources, delegated tasks and essentially took over. All of this with the apparent blessing of Doris, who stayed subdued. These were interesting times.

"Do we have a list of possible locations?" Margaret asked.

Jaz answered uncertainly, "We have a list of the types of places that would serve him best based on his computing, power and communication needs. Doris has ranked it based on probability."

The director glanced at the list Doris was displaying on a nearby display screen. "Throw it out, he's too clever. He knows you would be looking for that. While he might be somewhere that matches on a couple of those points, no way he would ever allow himself to be in the most likely of those. What else do you have?"

Riley, determining that this treatment room was where the next strategy meeting was going to happen, eagerly joined in. "We've traced all of the Q-sys, sorry, Quantum computer orders. Both assembled systems and parts."

"Good, going how far back?"

"Four years. Earlier than that would have been unreliable and most likely obsolete by now. Except, of course, for ours, but that was because we used Doris's own chip design, which is still better than anything commercially available."

"I don't see any of the Korean manufacturers on this list," Stansfield said.

Doris spoke, "I was unaware either of the manufacturers in Korea was offering a Quantum computing system."

"They are." Margaret rattled off several model and system numbers from memory. "Add those to your sweep."

The distribution list displayed on the wall began to update. Doris spoke up, "I am beginning to see some correlations. Several of these initial component shipments are to subsidiaries of inter-related companies. This one in Kyoto, both of these in Amsterdam, as well as the Mexico City locations."

"Now, tie in any going to universities that are part of ongoing research projects linked to the same holding company," Margaret said.

The list shortened but became dramatically clearer. A single buyer had been acquiring dozens of the very best Quantum computing systems. Izzy suggested they look at high capacity drive storage purchased by the same company or any of its many subsidiaries. This update took a bit longer to add to the list. What they were seeing was a puzzle with buyers located all over the world and with shipments to even more locations. Again, dozens of locations, but the director felt they were finally on the right track.

"Doris, crunch the numbers, match up what you can, some will undoubtedly be dead ends." She turned to face the youngest of the group. "Riley, isn't it?" She nodded. "Riley, hon, you match what Doris gives you to the list of possibles from Jaz. This needs to be a human match. Don't ask me why, just do it. Use your gut, make deductive leaps, think everywhere but the box—then bring me what you find. Until then, I think I need to sleep."

Riley walked away with mixed emotions. Despite her youth, she had gotten used to a certain level of respect here at The Cove facility. Stansfield seemed to dismiss her as a child, yet in the next breath, challenge her to do the impossible. She admitted to herself that for the first time in days she possessed a renewed sense of purpose and a feeling like she had just been in the presence of a master. Stansfield could think like a criminal; she was underhanded, devious and undoubtedly great at her job. Again, Riley wondered what the connection here was.

Jaz caught up with Riley, and as they rode the small cart to Riley's lab, asked,"What do you think of her?"

"The director? She's tough. She should be in there recovering. The trauma she has been through was severe. I can only imagine the pain levels, yet she was on point. Steps ahead of us even, and we are supposed to be the smart ones," Riley said.

Jaz nodded. "I get up each day thinking about what fantastic things I will learn about the universe and artificial intelligence, but increasingly, what amazes me is our own very human brain. It may fall short of its machine counterpart in countless ways, but as Margaret pointed out, we are uniquely skilled at certain tasks."

"Human brains are superior in many ways, Doctor Kline," Doris added from the tiny speaker mounted in the roof of the cart.

Jasmine glanced up. “But you are super fast and arguably the most intelligent mind on the planet.” The cart pulled up at the lab, and both women walked in, continuing the discussion with Doris, who now appeared on the closest 4D display.

“That is one point of view, Jaz, but it is incomplete...only a part of the reality.”

“I’m not sure what you are getting at, Doris—you are a super-intelligent AI, a new type of being. You’re way smarter than humans...even Janus’s intellect makes us look like primates scrambling around in the dirt by comparison.”

Doris’s avatar smiled and gave a tiny nod, but clearly, she was hoping the scientist would get there on her own. “Is being faster the only criteria for performance? As an artificial mind, I have access to a much wider pool of knowledge. I can retrieve, sort, filter and make conclusions based largely on that access. Does that make me smarter?”

Jasmine thought it was a trick question and answered a bit uncertainly, “Well, of course it does.”

“Intellect is not that simple, Jaz, nor that straightforward. I’ve had this conversation with everyone here at some point. Alan, Izzy, Riley, and I revisit it frequently.”

Riley rolled her eyes as if to say, *Uh, oh, a teaching moment,* then grinned.

“Jaz, your very human brain contains around possibly a hundred billion neurons. Izzy and her team helped refine and improve a brain scanning imaging process called array tomography.”

Jaz looked confused. “Never heard of that.”

“It allows them to see neuron density and connectivity at the synaptic level. What we found was that the human brain is much more layered in complexity than anyone had ever guessed.”

“Such as?”

The avatar smiled. “Well, in one way, it is much more densely interconnected than scientist expected. Every neuron in your brain is linked to hundreds of other neurons. The simple fact is that the human brain contains an incredible number of these connections—

Izzy's estimates are possibly over a thousand trillion connections. I can assure you, that far exceeds anything Janus or I have.

"And if you dig a bit deeper, you will find that synapses themselves are more complex than simple communication terminals. She believes, like many of her peers, that synapses really function like microprocessors, with a single one probably bundling up to a thousand molecule-sized biological transistors. If you step back, this means that a single human mind has more connection than the entire network of computers and routers on the planet.

"Izzy says, and I concur, that humans have a natural memory storage capacity somewhere around one hundred terabytes that is combined with a raw processing speed upwards of a trillion bits per second. This means that, unlike a computer, even one like me that has to focus basically on one input process at a time, humans automatically take in stimuli and input from thousands of inputs simultaneously. Your brain automatically catalogs, indexes and prioritizes all of this without any conscious thought. Doctor, clearly the human brain is the most formidable, self-aware computer in this section of the universe. Also, and this may be the biggest advantage—unlike myself or Janus, or probably any of my kind in the future, your species is not limited to linear thinking, not controlled by what has already been learned. You can discover, make great leaps of logic, you find inspiration and discoveries, not just analysis. Yes, the warning from the Dhakerri is ominous, and as we hurl ourselves toward that nearly inevitable digital singularity, caution is paramount, but don't sell your species short. You are remarkable, adaptable and resilient creations."

Jaz was impressed. She turned to Riley, smiling. "Okay then, genius, so how do we find Janus?"

The young girl laughed. "I haven't got a clue."

56

Manhattan

Nine hundred miles to the north, Cade and his team were not making any better progress on determining Janus's next target. They had swept through dozens of buildings in the financial district, Dee painstakingly bypassing the security systems so they could check for bombs, computer bugs, communication line tampering, EMP devices and so on. It had been maddeningly slow going.

"Does it always rain here?" Cade asked to no one, looking down the block of gray monolithic buildings they still needed to check. "What's next, Greg?"

"Meridian Partners over on Wall Street."

Cade stood and assembled his small part of the team heading to Meridian. He heard Greg say, "Oh, shit," and froze. Just turning a corner several blocks away was a line of dark vans as well as unmarked armored personnel carriers. Cade keyed his CommDot and instructed Deuce and the rest of the team to take cover. "Yeah, man," Deuce responded. "The feds just showed up."

The line of vehicles came squealing to a stop in front of Cade. Mentally, he knew that Bravo Team was automatically going into combat mode. This situation was paramount to declaring war on your brothers-in-arms; could they even do that? Weren't they and the feds all on the same side? His finger tightened on the trigger guard of the assault rifle. *Guess we're going to find out.*

Doors opened on all of the vehicles, but instead of the heavily armed assault teams, Cade expected. what appeared looked more like numerous technicians, engineers and scientists climbed awkwardly down from the APCs and out of the unmarked vans. A man in a dark business suit approached, arms outstretched, clearly unarmed. "Captain Rearden?"

Cade looked around uncertainly, "Dee, you getting this? Doris, anybody?" he whispered helplessly as he walked slowly out to meet the man, one hand raised slightly off the downward pointed rifle.

"Go with it, Nomad," Doris said in his ear. "Possible friendlies."

"Do what? Possible who?" he whispered.

The man stepped forward confidently and held out a palm."I'm Harris. The president sent me. These are yours." He handed Cade a small box with a stack of lanyards and badges. Cade glanced down and saw they were security badges with everyone's photo ID on them. They all said different agencies, from Homeland Security to Nuclear Energy Security Team. While all had actual photos of the team, all of the names listed were fake.

"So...what?" Cade said. "We're official now?"

Harris gave a thin-lipped smile. "Unofficially official. Your actual names and identities are not in any computer system. These covers will get you in most places and hold up to scrutiny. Don't worry, we know who the real enemy is. The president sends his thanks for what you have been trying to do. The rest of these people are here to help. Just tell them what you need and have them go check it out."

The man turned, climbed back in the lead vehicle and left. Cade called his XO. "Man, you need to get down here. You ain't gonna believe this."

Having official sanctions from the president opened doors the easy way. The new team members had been well briefed, too. They went to work checking every remaining building, every comms junction, every server room. By mid-afternoon, most of the district and all the names on the short-sell list had been checked, and they had found absolutely nothing.

Nothing, mister analyst. what gives? We are losing credibility here, Cade muttered internally.

Yeah, Gus said, *you are making him look bad in front of his new friends.*

Not now, guys, Cade said silently to himself. *We are running out of time. Is this another one of Janus's misdirections? Get us looking here while he...I dunno, he unleashes a pandemic in California, causes a power plant to meltdown in Colorado, or even worse, cancels my Netflix account?*

Cade took a long gulp from a bottle of water as he watched actual team members scurrying between vehicles and buildings. Gus voiced his opinion again, *No offense to the eggheads, but I say it again. The key is, what does a win look like to this asshat?*

Cade sighed in resignation, *Not this again. What do you mean, Gus? He wants to take over the fucking world.* He said it with a sincere load of harshness in his mental voice.

Gus replied, *No, I don't think he does. If so, he could have done those things you just said and probably a lot more. No, I think winning means drawing Doris out. He wants her, maybe he knows about the alien telegram or something, but I think it's her. That would be a win. Secondly, and I think it's much further behind that, is culling the human population and maybe the government down to a more manageable level.*

Cade thought on it—Gus made sense. Shit, if he admitted it, he always made sense. Gus had all the common sense that the rest of them seemingly lacked. *Okay, he's after Doris, or is he killing off a few billion? Which is this, and how does that help us?*

Oh, fuck, the analyst said from a dark corner of Cade's mind.

Ahh, Gus said. *Our new player enters the game...again.*

He's right. The analyst started going through some almost silent mumblings of mad gibberish, then spoke loudly enough to frighten Cade with the sheer tone. *This is not about finding Doris. Not this right here. This is the culling. Wiping out the nation's economy will kill millions over time. It will also make him more money in the short term than can be imagined. Cade, he's not trying to hurt those few companies.* Grabbing an actual paper map from an unattended newsstand, Cade laid it on the hood of the SUV. He knew that once again, this was the analyst's show. *Pull up the list of the companies,* the analyst ordered.

Cade flipped out the SmartCom and did as instructed. The analyst persona used Cade's hand to begin marking all of the physical addresses. He stepped back and looked at it. "Oh, shit."

"Oh, shit what?" Greg asked, walking up.

"What do you see?" Cade asked.

"I see a ...I see a..." he turned the map at a forty-five-degree angle. "I see a pattern of partial concentric rings in a semi-circle pattern radiating from the port through the financial district of lower Manhattan."

"Not just a semi-circular pattern, Greg, a radiating blast pattern. We are standing a mile away from the next New York City ground zero location."

Greg's face paled, and he quickly started talking to Doris, relaying the new ideas. Cade, too, wanted someone back at The Cove to weigh in on this.

"So, you don't think he's trying to hack the systems there? He's just going to take those companies out?"

Cade knew Jaz would have a hard time agreeing with him, but it made sense. "Yeah, that's what the analyst, I mean, that's what we all think."

"Janus is a computer, though. This would be a very heavy-handed attack when it seems he could likely achieve the same result without resorting to destruction and violence."

"Overkill is under-rated, Jaz. Hang on a sec." Cade motioned Deuce over. His second-in-command had teams combing the docks and waterfront for any signs of explosives. Deuce walked up, shaking his head. They'd found nothing.

"Deuce, how big of a bomb would this need to be?" He tapped to add his teammate to the conversation back with The Cove.

Charlie scratched under his chin. "Big one, a tactical nuke would do it. Talking strictly conventional, I'm guessing in the 25 to 35-ton explosion...probably the Russian ATBIP would do the job."

"That's a thermobaric weapon, air dropped, right?" Cade asked.

"Yeah, big some-bitch, bigger than our MOAB," Deuce clarified.

"I have no idea what you guys are saying," Jaz said. "Airspace above you is now completely closed and being monitored like nowhere on Earth. I don't see anyone getting in to drop anything, especially Russians."

Cade was mumbling to himself again but nodded in agreement. "Those bombs are enormous anyway. We would've seen if anything like that was here. On the ground, they would be much less effective anyway. Would Janus use a nuke? Just take out the entire city?"

"Why have just the target companies in this section marked if that was the case?" Deuce asked. "I think it's what you and Greg saw, a proximity blast. Big one, but still limited in scale."

Cade did, too. "Jaz, what about an asteroid or space debris? Something from orbit could do this kind of damage, right?"

"Oh, sure," she concurred. "Something small and fast or an object big and relatively slow could have similar destructive power. Not to get into the challenges of orbital mechanics, but the ability to be this precise, assuming he can capture and drop something on us, would be extremely unlikely...and that is not a slight on Janus's intellect. Way too many variables beyond his control. The composition of the object, how it heats up during atmospheric entry, jet stream, prevailing winds. All sorts of issues. Only a controlled descent like our spaceplane can manage something like that."

"But you are sure he doesn't have access to anything like that. No long-abandoned space-based Chinese cruise missile sitting up there forgotten?" Cade asked.

"I can have our minisats scan for possible space-based weapon systems, but I am relatively confident the answer is no. Despite the nearly half-million pieces of space junk around the Earth, something like that just wouldn't stay hidden."

Cade's frustration was beginning to boil over. This felt real to him; Gus even seemed to agree. Maybe it was a distraction, but increasingly, he felt otherwise. "So, it's not already here, it isn't coming from outer space and not likely to be dropped from a passing plane. What's left?"

Greg had walked up, not realizing that Cade was mainly talking to himself. "Subway, big truck, boat, submarine."

Cade looked at the boy. "Dee, can you shut down the MTA system on this end of the island?" He motioned for one of the top guys from the federal NEST teams to come over.

"I could, but not for very long, Captain. From Penn Station down to the southern tip is one of the busiest public transit systems in the world. I'm afraid we would need a more precise window for a stoppage."

The NEST security man said essentially the same thing for street traffic, although he did admit that vehicles of a certain size could be kept away for a more indefinite period. Turning back to Charlie and Greg, Cade said, "Okay, these teams will have to be responsible for anything by ground. What about by ocean? What ships could do this, and how would we stop them?"

"It's a busy waterway, Boss," Deuce said.

"Options are limited for larger craft," Dee added. "Manhattan's Cruise terminal is on the west side several miles up the Hudson. Red Hook is closest, over on the Brooklyn side, opposite Governor's Island. New York Harbor terminal is out of range to the south. Of course, smaller boats, like tugs and ferries, have docking piers all over. Hundreds fall within what you have referred to as ground zero for the blast."

"Well, crap," Cade said. He knew this was his call, and right now, he wished that it was anyone else's. Janus had them running in circles, and instead of narrowing down the list of possible targets, they just seemed to keep expanding. Most of the federal teams had come back to the still parked convoy of vehicles awaiting further instructions. "Shit, I'm a soldier, not a cop," he said under his breath. All eyes seemed to be focused on him. "We have to check them all," he finally said. Talon will check the larger targets, let's get our new friends here checking all the smaller ones.

"Greg, take Marty...I mean, Lieutenant Maratelli and a team to the cruise terminal. Deuce, you go to Red Hook, and I'll grab a few guys and head down to the Harbor Docks. Zee and Captain Nance can take some of these others to go through the smaller slips around here. Make sure everyone knows basically what we are looking for."

"And that would be...?" Jaz asked.

"Anything that can make this end of the city disappear."

57

Chapel Hill, N.C

"Will you just calm down." The senator voiced it as an order, not a question. "It's all going to work out just as planned. We discussed all this." A brief pause and he spoke into the cell phone again. "No, the attack on the president was not part of this, not our people." After several more minutes and numerous more platitudes, he disconnected the phone and powered it off. It had been just the last of many. His 'associates' in this endeavor were getting jumpy. He'd always known they would; most people don't have the resolve to ever accomplish much, certainly anything like real change, at the level he was.

The system was broken, irrevocably broken. He should know, he'd been a large part of it much of his life. Not just the political mess with the polarizing talking points and divisive rhetoric, but also the judicial system where money rather than justice was the name of the game. Same with education, healthcare, the environment. On and on and on down the line. *We have screwed up everything we've touched.* Sitting in his sprawling manor just outside Chapel Hill, in his home state of North Carolina, he looked up at the pictures of his five grandchildren. They were whom he was doing this for. The one chance to give them a better life. It was finally his time to really make a difference, not just offer up another inane soundbite on some non-topic for the evening news. Real change, before it was too late.

He drained the scotch and quickly refilled the tumbler. The gruesomeness of it was a lot to accept. He got why the others were beginning to have second thoughts. The bloodshed and violence were real now, not just some abstract idea. And...it was all going to get so much worse, though....so much. He looked down at the front page of the Raleigh News and Observer. They led with the attacks, of course, but just above the fold were quotes from Darcy Magnus, his likely Democratic challenger in the next election. Magnus was a vet, smart, beautiful, successful, and the camera loved her. Polling numbers already had her trailing him by only single-digit points. His friend Dan had been right, she was going to be tough to beat, but he had it on good authority that it was unlikely she would survive all this.

He heard his dog barking loudly from outside and simultaneously the house phone began to ring in a distant room. He jerked nervously then sighed. His housekeeper gently knocked, then cracked the door open. "A call for you, Senator. They say it's urgent."

He waved an agitated hand at her to bring him the phone. "Who is it, Maria?" She just shrugged and handed him the cordless phone. Few people had that number; it had to be someone close. "Yes, what is it?"

"You were told not to turn off your phone during this phase."

His blood ran cold. *Prime.*

Fear coursed through him and his stomach gave a nervous lurch for reasons he could barely understand. The cold, mechanical quality of the voice was all he heard now. No longer hidden behind the perfectly crafted New England accent. "I know, and sorry, I just needed a break." Looking up angrily, he motioned for Maria to leave. "Some in the group are having second thoughts, I was getting tired of the same conversations over and over."

"Hmm, yes, humans are petty creatures, aren't they? Did any offer to give back the money they were earning?"

Byron gave a snort. "Hardly. In fact, they can't spend it fast enough. One is already making inquiries about buying the Boston MLS franchise since the Oslongo family is now out of the picture. Bunch of ruthless blood-sucking bastards, but...still, they have weak stomachs for the real work."

"And what about you, Senator? How is your intestinal fortitude holding up?" Janus asked with a mere hint of the threat implied.

"I...I'm in it for the long-haul, Prime, you know that."

"Hmm, do I? Your teams failed to acquire Doctor Lasko as instructed. In fact, they lost him to some other group of agents, and no one seems to know who."

"But we have the boy—they are questioning him now."

"Who is supplying the ground teams searching in NYC?" Janus asked.

"I...I'm not sure," he said reluctantly. That was what many of the calls had been about this morning. All his cohorts in the financial industry were either in Manhattan or had a considerable interest there. None of them liked a bunch of feds running through their lobby. "Are...are they going to be a problem?"

"No, they are insignificant, but it is just one more case of you not being able to deliver what you said. They can't affect the timetable now —we are just days away now."

The senator was unused to being chastised, or even questioned, but had grown to respect and fear the capabilities of Prime and whoever was behind that artificial voice. "I am safe here, my family?"

Prime didn't respond for far longer than the senator preferred. "You have a protection team, you are out of harm's way...for now."

The senator saw one of the men in tactical gear walking across the expanse of yard. Private security provided for him, he was just unsure if they were to protect him or keep him imprisoned here for the duration of all this. He took one more drink, a deep one draining the last of the amber liquid. In so doing, he found the courage to ask the question he both needed and dreaded. He stuttered and stumbled to get it out. "Who are you...really, I mean. Behind you, Prime, I know someone is there running things."

"You choose now to get curious, Senator? Perhaps your resolve is not as solidly entrenched as you thought either. You didn't care who I was when I promised you an easy victory in the last election. You didn't care who I was when I assured you would be named the Chairman of the Ways and Means Committee, and you certainly didn't care who I was when I showed you the new balance in all of your offshore accounts." Janus paused to let all of those damning incriminations sink all the way in. "If you are having second thoughts, let me remind you—I will end you. I will destroy your name, your fortune and your family. I am the future. That, Byron, is all you need to know."

It had taken several days, but Aksell had completed the modifications needed on the *Sigas Alegus*. Few of the crew took notice of him, and no one asked any questions. He liked that, as he disliked people and hated questions. According to the charts, they were less than two days out of port. The computerized steering and station keeping apparatus was easy enough to recognize, as were the remote devices. These he had placed when no crewman was around. Even crusty merchant marines have a vested interest in self-preservation. Placing piercing units on the exterior skin of tanks holding four and a half-million tons of pressurized liquid natural gas would cause concern. Okay, more like alarm. In fact, most likely outright panic and mutiny. So...best to keep that little fact hidden.

The task had actually been more complicated than Aksell had expected. The gas, or LNG, was transported in five enormous pressure vessels. The ship was essentially built around these massive tanks which almost rose half again above the main decks. The gas was kept cooled to a temperature of -260 degrees, which kept it in a liquid state. It also was not flammable in this state, which made it safer for transport. Control had given him the specs for the devices that, when triggered, would pierce the pressure vessel allowing the liquid to return to its gaseous state and begin escaping. It would fill the voids and cavities of the ship with gas within seconds, then the main explosive would set off a cascading effect collapsing the other punctured tanks sequentially and igniting the entire mass. It was a crude, brute force solution, but the impact would be impressive.

The *Sigas* wouldn't be alone in its demise either. Aksell had been informed of two other bulk haulers that would be at the port when she blew. One was to be carrying fuel oil, the other ammonia nitrate, the main component in fertilizer. The ships' transport and unloading schedules had been handled by Control to ensure all would be in neighboring berths.

As part of his research, he'd read that in 1947, a ship named the SS Grandcamp caught fire at the Port of Texas City. It's cargo of fertilizer cooked off in a series of massive detonations that killed over 500 people, nearly destroyed the town and burned for three days. It was one of the largest non-nuclear explosions in history. That ship, he thought, was a fraction of the size of the *Sigas* or either of the other two. Control had not bothered to provide damage estimates, but he gathered it meant total destruction for up to a mile, significant damage possibly three to five miles from the blast. Even if only one of the ships went up as planned, the immediate area would be a virtual wasteland. This was going to be one hell of a show, that much was for sure.

58

Brooklyn

Alan grasped the object tighter as his mind raced through the possibilities. The strange markings on its otherwise smooth surface as unfamiliar to him as it would be to a stranger. It appeared to be some type of relic. In more ancient times, it would probably have been considered a fetish, likely worshipped by those worthy enough to ever glimpse it. He was not in such awe; he was simply confused and pissed off. Much of Charlie Team was down, some of them dead. His friend was captured and in danger, and somehow, he was now the one leading the rescue.

"Jimmy, you sure this thing will do what you say?"

The nearly imperceptible CommDot came to life. "No."

"That's it? No? What does that mean?"

"It means, we haven't had time to fully test it. It means Doris doesn't fully understand it either. The message offers possibilities, not instruction manuals."

Alan was frustrated with his little brother but understood. Jimmy had been trying to help by including the strange new device in Riley's bag of tricks she'd sent up. He'd seen both Riley and Izzy working on earlier prototypes, but nothing so far had produced any positive results.

"It temporarily disrupts the bonds between atoms. It holds them in a type of stasis that can be altered. Uses a crap-load of energy, though. Might only get one or two uses before it needs to recharge. The workshop is going to try and come up with a smaller Pica for power on the next version."

"Is it going to kill me?" Alan asked pensively. "I mean my hand will be on it when I activate it."

"Nah, bro, I wouldn't do that. I mean, don't hold it against your head and turn it on or anything. I don't want to have to tell Mom that you discorporated yourself. So, nah, you should be fine. It has a safety and it's keyed to only recognizes your DNA when you activate it."

Alan continued to listen to the instructions offered. At just over twenty-one, few people would have thought him of much importance. Years ago, those people would have been right. That was before, though. He walked cautiously, but with determination, in the general direction of his target. "Show me." He spoke the words almost inaudibly, but the response was instant. He'd swapped the tactical goggles most of Talon wore for a new pair of contacts, also prototypes. They now showed an overlay indicating the locations of surveillance cameras and various sensors as well as the six men guarding the front entrance to the nondescript building. Only two of the men looked like guards; the others were dressed as innocuously as possible. One wore a shirt from a landscape company and was busy trimming nearby hedges. Others ranged in appearance from homeless bum to college kid waiting for the next bus. He didn't question the intel—it was from Doris—he knew it was perfect.

"I think we are expected," Alan said in a more casual tone than he felt. "Show alternate routes," he whispered into the air. The female voice of Doris took over for Jimmy in his ear, and the overlay in his contacts shifted with highlighted routes shown in colors that corresponded to the likelihood of success. None of those routes were colored green. Most were various shades of red dotted lines, a near-certain indicator of problems. He paused only briefly before steeling himself to take that next step as he began navigating down a red path.

"Why are you taking this route? It only has a 67% chance of operational success," the calming voice asked.

"I like red, it's festive."

"You are being reckless."

"No. I am being unpredictable—I am getting the job done," he answered. He made his way across the small street to the rear corner of the building. The two-story brownstone looked nearly identical to every other building in the area. Unlike the many apartments and homes nearby, this one was owned by a relatively unknown segment of the United States Government. At one time, it had been a safe house for witnesses testifying against crime bosses across the river in New York City. Now it was simply a domestic black-site, somewhere that wasn't supposed to exist on American soil. A place where people disappeared into, never to be seen again. The very thought of it disgusted him. Being redacted to a foreign country where 'enhanced interrogation' techniques were allowed was bad enough, but here in the U.S., it just made his blood boil.

Alan's fingers ran over the cool surface of rough brick; no windows or doors were visible on this side. He placed his back to the wall and looked down the alley back toward the street. This was where the red path ended. While it did not look like an entrance, hopefully, it soon would be. The object in his hand was placed against the wall where it stuck and nearly instantly, a small section of the wall below began to shimmer, almost as in a heat distortion. He felt only the faintest of vibration coming off the bricks as the device altered the subatomic structure of the building's exterior.

Alan's understanding of what it was doing was incomplete, but still, he appreciated its power. He looked down, amazed as the device shifted the electrical bonds of the brick at a microscopic level. From a distance, the wall would appear unchanged. Even close-up you wouldn't likely pay attention to what was happening. A small green line replaced the red one in his contacts. Confidently, he crouched down and duck-walked through the wall as effortlessly as one might step through a cascading waterfall. As he removed the device, the wall returned to its very normal and very solid state of being.

"Contacts approaching," the voice said in a flat, emotionless tone.

He could already see them indicated on his overlay display. Alan blinked his eyes in a specific pattern, and the image changed to thermal. Two large individuals, most likely both males, were paused in a corridor twenty feet ahead. He faintly heard them speaking, the words indistinct. The hi-tech eyewear he used could have enhanced that as well, but he ignored them. That was not the direction he was heading, but he tagged them to track. The system would record every sound, every word spoken for processing, and Dee, the embedded mini version of Doris, would let him know if any of it was meaningful.

Slowly, he moved down a far wall toward a room they had suspected as being the holding cell. He faded the IR overlay back to allow his normal vision to dominate. Ghostly heat images appeared behind several of the walls and doors he passed. These could be guards, civilians or...other prisoners. People, no doubt many of them innocents, who had also 'disappeared' from their normal lives, only to end up here. Someone very high-up was using this place for some very bad stuff.

"Tiger-1. Deploy countermeasures now."

Alan's callsign was only used in an emergency, and this apparently had just become one. His contacts darkened as he tossed multiple light bombs in front and behind. The bright flashing strobes would disrupt the neural impulses and trigger immediate confusion as well as nausea. He had yet to see an actual threat but had to trust the instructions were accurate.

"Shift to cold view," the command came, and he did so, instantly identifying several shapes writhing on the floor. While suits designed to block an infrared signature had been available for some time, Janus had equipped the federal agents in this facility with something special to wear. Not only did no body heat show, but they showed up slightly colder than the surroundings. The shapes on the floor were a darker black than the near midnight blue showing in his contact of the surrounding darkness.

"Any other threats?" he asked.

"Unknown, but assume so. We all agree, they had to know we were coming."

The obvious statement needed no response, so he moved on quickly to the door of the presumed cell. The building had an indeterminate number of security contractors and agents. It had been impossible to separate the hostiles from the friendlies, but now, he felt sure they were all alerted.

"Tiger-1, there is a discrepancy," his own version of Doris said.

Alan paused briefly before rounding the corner. "Elaborate," he said.

"The interior dimensions on the cell you are approaching do not match the plans on file for the building."

Well, that's no good, he thought.

"It appears modifications have been made, possibly a false wall installed."

"An observation room?" That would mean it was likely a trap.

"Likely, Tiger-1. The likelihood of success on this mission just decreased significantly. They had to know we would make a play on him."

"Make a play? Doris, you are sounding more like a spy all the time. Scan building for secondary locations—do it now." The command in his voice sounded artificial even to him, and it failed to hide the fear he was feeling. He was too young and too inexperienced for this, no matter how well augmented he was. Alan knew he was now the stick in the proverbial hornets' nest.

"Two possible locations on your tactical display now. Alpha location has a slightly higher probability."

He looked at the schematic and the highlighted room with a floating A hovering above it. One floor up and on an interior wall of the north side. He blinked to view the other. It was down in what must have been a cellar. He focused on it momentarily, then decided. "Moving to B location." Sounds of commotion came from above. Many pairs of boots hitting the floor, descending stairs, orders being shouted.

"Boss, you need us yet?" Sergeant Coffee's calm, deep voice asked.

"Negative, but stay close." Alan wanted to add that he was still not the boss, but now wasn't the time.

"Alpha location is compromised, that is no longer an option. Suggest you proceed to B with speed."

Wow, how helpful, he thought. The door he needed to find was coming up on his left. He noticed nearly too late another darker blue/black figure in the opposite wall. Tossing something from his pocket caused the silhouette to move, then let out a long, straggled sound as the electrical device discharged all of its energy at once. Riley would be happy to know her little Spider Tasers worked.

"At the door," he said needlessly. They could see where he was as well as he could.

"No readings from the interior, it must be shielded, Tiger-1," Jimmy said. "Stay safe, bro," he added.

The rusty blue metal door had a faded metal sign reading 'Maintenance' and was, of course, locked. At this point, Alan had several options. The magic stick, if it still had a charge, an electric lock-pick built into his SmartCom and a piece of silly putty that was both acidic and explosive when the right electrical charge was applied. Riley's voice interrupted his decision-making.

"Why not check the downed guard for the key?" she asked.

"Um...yeah, that was what I was planning. Thanks." The sounds from above were getting closer. "I'm going to need a distraction here, guys." Alan frisked the downed man and did find a small key ring. Somewhere above, he heard a window crashing, then the sound of high-voltage discharges. That would be another of Riley's little gifts. She hadn't named it yet, but essentially, fired from a standard 12-gauge shotgun, the ordnance on impact would deploy stingers of electricity, and when they met another electrical field...such as a human...a full bolt discharge would occur. Unlike what he had been using, those were totally lethal. As the door swung open, he was very glad she had used it.

Micah's naked and twisted body sat lashed to a chair. As cliché as it was, a single incandescent bulb was the only light in the room. Alan's eyes quickly swept the surrounding darkness on all spectrums to ensure they were alone. "Micah, hey, man. You with me?" His friend's skin was cold and clammy, but he thought...maybe hoped...he was feeling a pulse. Turning the bloodied face, he could see Micah's didn't have a CommDot. He placed one there and a large, thick patch under his right arm. This was a joint development by Dr. Yi Han and Riley for field teams. Similar in a way to the trauma sleeve, it had dome diagnostics capabilities and could administer treatments within a narrow range. *What did they do to you, man?*

The rage within was seething as he struggled to get Micah freed and on his shoulder, the way Coffee and O'Brien had shown him. Blood trailed from Micah's hands, feet and everywhere else he looked. "Is this an outside wall, can I use the stick?"

"Negative, it is subterranean, you would just be in the dirt, and the stick needs to recharge to go through brick again," Jimmy said.

Alan knew his brother wanted to know about his friend. They all did, but they could see the data better than Alan right now. Micah wasn't a large boy, but the dead weight of trying to fireman carry his friend was nearly beyond what he could muster. He half-carried; half dragged his friend to the foot of the stairs. Looking up, he now saw them as an insurmountable obstacle. A mountain of ancient wood and metal. *How am I going to do this?* Seconds later, he felt Micah's body begin to jerk and spasm.

"Lay him in the corridor, Alan, you need to clear his airway—he's beginning to choke," Riley said in a tone that belied her fright.

Alan did as instructed and managed to get his airways aspirated sufficiently for Micah to take several deep breaths. Alan thought he saw his friend's eyes try to open, but in the dim light, he couldn't be sure. "Micah," he whispered as loudly as he dared. "It's Alan. You with us, dude?"

As he was lifting him back onto his shoulder, Micah mumbled something unintelligible. It sounded like, "You shouldn't be here."

Yeah, you either, Alan thought bitterly.

"Alan, close your eyes," Doris commanded just as a flash bang grenade went off at the top of the steps.

"Drop your weapons! Federal Agents! Let me see your hands! Do it now!"

59

Glancing down at his childhood friend, Alan noticed his eyes were open—a look of fear, or maybe it was dread. Micah seemed to be speaking—Alan bent close enough to hear, the pounding of boots and shouted commands making it difficult. The lips moved again—this time he heard the words before the eyes closed again.

"Fight back."

He lay Micah on the cement floor and stood slowly. The armed agents were bottlenecked on the stairs leading down to the landing where they were. The fear began to drain away like water into the sewer. In its place, a sense of clarity took over. He saw the situation dispassionately; tactical solutions occurring and being ranked instantly. His training on self-defense and martial arts, as well as armed combat, had been as rigorous as any member of Talon. Until now, though, it was entirely theoretical. A vicious finger jab into the throat of the first man down quickly moved his skills from abstract to tangible. He used his tongue to activate his CommDot and gave two quick clicks that the other members of his team would recognize.

Alan didn't bother reaching for his weapon, as that would take too long. *Take advantage of the position.* In the stairwell, the agents could not shoot without likely hitting their own team members. Alan seized on this and ripped a tactical baton from the first man and struck instead at the chin of the man behind. A solid connect and he was already leveraging off the floor bringing a vicious elbow strike into the front man.

Vaguely, he heard the booming bass voice of Sergeant Coffee talking in his ear, "Tiger-1, be advised, we are coming in now."

Alan had no idea how many agents were closing in on him; all he knew was the here and the now. His entire world had collapsed down to a few meters of wooden stairs in an unremarkable building in Brooklyn. One part of him recognized that this was the training. Doris's ReLoad process had essentially programmed him to be able to do this, just like she had obviously done secretly with Micah. Right now, he was damn glad she had. Another man dropped as Alan gripped a metal support pole to help propel his knee into the unprotected kidney. Reflexively, he twisted to one side as the top man on the stairs got a shot off. The agent had been forced to hold the gun one-handed as he was fending off one of his own guys falling toward him. Otherwise, the bullet would have likely ended the battle, and Alan's existence.

Recovering a beat more quickly, the red line of the agent's laser sights moved across the wall and settled on Alan's chest. Something crashed into the man's head just as he pulled the trigger. Briefly, Alan saw the grinning face of Sergeant Coffee holding a battering ram used to open doors. The metal casing apparently worked just as well on humans. Then the big man was out of sight again as the fight expanded to the floors above.

The near miss and then brief reprieve gave Alan time to properly equip himself for the first time. A part of him still wanted to avoid anything truly lethal. These were, after all, most likely real federal agents. But knowing the condition his friend was in caused that desire to fade considerably. He pulled the weapon that was hanging from his back. The angry looking gun was only about two feet long but had an almost limitless variety of projectiles from strictly non-lethal to explosive, all of which he could change simply by thinking it. Seeing two men leapfrogging each other to get to the opening above, Alan selected the option of Taser Slugs. These were for short range and were non-lethal rounds about the size of a typical shotgun shell. The full cartridge would attach itself to a target with tiny barbs and then deliver a massive electrical discharge from the built-in super-capacitor. The real beauty was Talon's version worked even when it didn't touch the skin, so it would knock out an opponent even if they were wearing body armor such as these guards had.

Alan heard more sounds that the fight was ratcheting up, not winding down. Struggling, he somehow got Micah to the top of the steps and slid him into a small alcove as he reached out and swept the weapon around the room. With his tactical contacts, he could see what the gun saw. The two agents he'd tazed were down for the count. Another was belly crawling from a side room toward where Coffee had apparently gone. Alan depressed the trigger and eliminated him as a threat. "More on the way," he heard O'Brien say from above.

Alan left a spare weapon with Micah and stood, peering around the door jamb cautiously, then running to the far side. The room or apartment to his right was a mess of bodies, furniture and less identifiable objects, but switching to infrared, he could clearly make out Sergeant Coffee attempting to fend off several of the feds. One of Coffee's arms hung limply from the shoulder. "Doris, any ideas?"

In response, she saw the targeting reticule on his gun sights light up in a violet hue he recognized as autonomous mode. All he had to do was point it in the general vicinity of a threat, and Doris, or more likely, Dee, would select the firing sequence and weapon type and adjust the aim. The gun barked multiple times, and, just for a second, Coffee was standing there wondering what had happened to his opponents. "Gotta move, Sarge!"

"Roger that, kid!"

Alan knew his body was running on adrenalin and artificially induced instinct. Something he would no doubt pay for later...if there was a later. For now, he just needed to get his friend to the exit or... make an exit. "Jimbo, is the magic stick charged?"

"It's not a magic stick, it is..."Apparently, finally realizing the significant level of danger his brother was in, Jimmy focused and said, "Needs another forty-five seconds, but then you're good."

"Roger that." Micah's body seemed to be even heavier now, or maybe that was just the fatigue and abuse inflicted on his own body.

"Tiger-I, be advised, exfil rear side only. Entrance door is a no."

Alan's brain registered the warning from O'Brien. That could only mean one thing. More agents were coming in. Pulling on Micah, he eventually managed to get back up to a knee and then, finally, to a wobbly stance. The auto-gun pointed to the rear of the building, his eyes roaming everywhere else. The indicators in the visual overlay were so crowded that keeping it on was pointless. He blinked to trigger immediate threats and targets only.

Four, five, six, he was mentally counting off the steps to the back wall, his back spasming and body near exhaustion. "Charlie Team, let's go now. Drop countermeasures, exfil on me," the last of his sentence more a breathless whisper than words. Sweat clouding his eyes, he failed to notice the massive darker blue in the shadows of the room until it was nearly too late. The weapon blasted, and the impact caught him squarely in the chest, hurling Micah away from him. His back and head impacted against the far wall.

On some level, Alan realized his polysteel composite chest protection and nanofabric of his own battle suit had absorbed or deflected much of the gun blast, but it still hurt. His ears rang, and he was seeing stars. He blinked to enact coldview in the contacts and finally saw his opponent. The man wearing the cold suit was nearly as large as Coffee. He snarled something incomprehensible as he stomped across the room toward him. Alan pushed himself up the wall—willing, then begging his body to move.

"Please don't surrender now," the man said. "I want to make you suffer first."

Alan's mental processes came back online slowly. Micah was somewhere. He was holding a gun. No, it was the magic stick. Where were his teammates? He saw the fist coming but was powerless to duck. The impact sent him spinning back against the rear wall. The stars were replaced by nothingness. He tried to remember if the auto-gun could possibly fire if he wasn't holding it, but that thought disappeared like a breath of fog. The agent was towering over him; he felt more than saw the hulking shadow. The man was about to kick, he felt sure, and somehow eased his body to absorb the blow. Milliseconds later, when it came, Alan was ready, and with his final bit of energy, grabbed the boot and twisted, wrenching the man's leg at the weakest joint, the knee.

The agent shouted in agony and fell beside him against the wall. Alan heard the man pulling his sidearm and knew he had to act now or regret it for the relatively few final moments of his life. Using the only thing he could, he slapped a hand to where he assumed the man's chest would be and activated the magic stick. A sizzling sound and then a smell of excrement flooded the back wall. Eyes finally refocusing, he saw an injured Coffee being helped in by O'Brien. Both men had expressions of horror as they saw the man Alan had been fighting. He'd missed the man's chest— instead, the stick had produced a translucent hole right through the agent's guts and on through the wall beyond. The wall would be fine, the fallen agent...not so much.

"Oh man...damn," one of them said in disgust.

"Out now," Alan weakly ordered and watched as both of the large men barely squeezed through the opening. O'Brien turned in the alley and waited for Alan to shove Micah through, then covered as Alan climbed out last, shutting off the exit behind him.

Coffee and Alan helped each other hurry down the small alley while O'Brien carried a still unconscious Micah almost effortlessly. Minutes later, back in the relative safety of the SUV, Coffee was awkwardly attempting to do something with his useless limb. "You were right, Boss, brains definitely worked better than brawn against these guys. Like that plan a lot."

Alan was holding his own head and attempting to see what could be done for his unconscious friend. Coffee's words rattled inside his skull like marbles; he just shook his aching head. He was also struggling to fully assimilate the fact he'd killed someone. A federal agent, maybe a family man. Yes, the man had been on the wrong side this time, but did that mean he deserved to die? The anguish over what just happened would consume him if he let it, he knew that.

Coffee reached over with his one good arm and laid a hand on Alan's shoulder. "It's okay, brother. You did what had to be done. You got all of us out of there, that was the mission."

Even in his pain and anguish, he picked up that the Sergeant had referred to him as a brother. "But I killed someone."

"So, did I. Pretty sure his dumbass did, too." He pointed to O'Brien in the driver's seat. "It's what we do, son, we kill people."

"Then we get coffee," O'Brien said. "Great little place up ahead—you guys okay if I stop?"

Coffee shook his head and laughed. "Yeah, it's a weird job, and it does make us all a little crazy. Also, for the record, I don't drink coffee."

"Wait...Coffee doesn't drink coffee. That is so fucked up," O'Brien said, offering a wink in the mirror only Alan could see.

60

"He's okay, right?" Alan asked, chest heaving with pain, blood still trailing down the side of his own face.

"Just shut-up for a minute," Riley's voice snapped. She was literally using his hands from a thousand miles away to help triage and treat their friend. O'Brien had brought up the unit's trauma sleeve just in case it was needed.

"We need to get somewhere with a lot less heat. What's close, O'Brien?"

The man thought about it briefly, then keyed the nav system. "Rolling!" The SUV sped away from the curb and into the darkness of the New York street.

"Micah, you with us, man?" Alan asked in a voice still shaky from all the action and adrenaline.

Riley's voice came through, "Tox is coming in, they have him knocked out. Some derivative of Ketamine it appears. Best just to let him sleep it off. Other vitals are within the normal range. He'll be okay, Alan, at least physically. You did good."

The relief flooded through him washing away much of the stress, almost as effectively as the sound of genuine praise from the one person he valued the most.

"Thanks."

She continued, speaking privately now through his CommDot, "What about you? You took a vicious shot in your armor. Your suit is still giving warning alerts and it appears you may have a concussion."

"I'm fine Riley...thanks but I'm okay." Looking down at his unconscious friend all he could feel was relief.

He turned to Coffee who was nursing his own injuries, "Master Sergeant, thank you, too. Both of you. We wouldn't have made it out if it had been me on my own. I guess that's obvious."

"Hey, it's cool, man," the big man said. "What you did back there was crazy nasty but pretty damn awesome, too. Maybe we need to learn how to combine brains and brawn on future ops....not just one or the other."

"Hooah, Master Sergeant, hooah!"

Several hours later, a very relieved and very tired Riley sat with Jimmy and Jazmine eating dinner. They had attempted to shield the youngest member of the team from the actual danger his brother was walking into, but that had obviously been pointless.

Between mouthfuls of food, Jimmy said, "Yeah, I was watching via a set of micro-drones I had self-deploy from the Battlewagon."

"The Battlewagon?" Jaz asked curiously.

Riley nodded, somewhat embarrassed. "Guys," she said, as if that was all the explanation needed. She downed more of the energy drink she was holding and added, "Our custom SUVs, when they are kitted out for field-ops, they started calling them Battlewagons. It's stupid but...you know."

Jaz needed an understanding. "So, you weren't worried, Jimmy?"

"Nah, he had a Talon team of spec-ops guys backing him up. They wouldn't have let him get into too much trouble."

Riley gave a small chuckle. "Not sure what your little bug cameras were showing, but it looked pretty serious to us. Alan has a concussion, and one of the other guy's arm has a compound fracture"

"Yeah, but did you see him? The big guy, what's his name? The Sergeant."

"Coffee."

"Yeah, Coffee, broken arm and all, he still took out those last two guys."

Riley could see that no matter the intelligence level, Alan's little brother still had his super-hero worship dialed up to the max. She was pretty sure this was to him much like one of his video games. "I think your brother was pretty instrumental in getting Micah out, too. Don't sell him short."

Jimmy scooped another bite of the roast pork and potatoes off the plate. "You just like him, but yeah, he did okay."

Embarrassment flushed across her face briefly before a smile crept in. She did like him, always had, but best keep that to herself for now.

"How is Micah anyway?" Jaz asked.

Riley's face darkened. "He's stable—should be okay."

"But?"

"I don't know. He should have regained consciousness by now. With whatever is going on in New York, they can't really transport him, but I really want Doctor Han to be able to give him a full exam. We have no idea what those interrogators might've done to him."

Riley didn't go into any more detail, not with Jimmy there, but she had so many concerns and even more unanswered questions. This was not the time, she knew, but it was obvious that Micah's role with Doris had been kept in the shadows. Much like Director Stansfield's obvious knowledge of Doris, it all made her uneasy. She, Jimmy and her friends had helped build Doris. Now they had literally put their lives in her hands. *Well,* she thought, *if she had hands.*

Riley realized her appetite had vanished, and the conversation had moved on as she pondered the other questions. Jazmine was talking to Jimmy about space stuff, something about "Oumuamua, the messenger asteroid. She excused herself to check on more earthly matters, namely the newest arrival to The Cove.

Jim Lasko was nearly seventy years old; it had been almost thirty years earlier that he'd last been within this building. He wandered around the area known as 'The Hub,' which formerly housed the control room for the large dish listening array, still mounted high overhead.

"I'm going to leave him to you for the dog and pony show," Isabella said, patting Riley's arm and walking past.

Riley had given the intro presentation numerous times already but never to anyone this connected to the facility...to Doris. She always thought of herself and her friends as the original crew. Seeing the delight in the old man's eyes brought her joy, though. It offered a momentary lift from the crushing drama that seemed to be her ever-present shadow today. "Doctor Lasko?"

The man turned; a smile still carved across his wrinkled face. "Hello, my child, do you know I rocked that girl on my knee when she was just a baby?" He nodded his head toward the white corridor where Izzy could still be seen in the distance. Not here, but at their home in California. They had me come out for the holidays one year."

"Must have been an amazing time," Riley said honestly.

He nodded, his mind obviously drifting back to those days. "Simpler, easier even, though it didn't seem like it at the time. Most people thought we were crackpots. Hell, most still do. Messages from outer space," he muttered as he seemed to drift off again. "Maybe we were."

Doris hadn't revealed much to the man, she realized. They normally saved the message for the end of the orientation, but Riley had wondered if she would continue to do so this time.

"Is she here?"

"Who? Riley asked, momentarily confused. "Oh, you mean Doris?" Why had Doris not spoken with the man who was in many ways her co-creator? "She has a lot going on at the moment, Doctor. Janus seems to have gone to ground, and our teams are struggling to find his next target."

He nodded. "Call me Jim or Lasko...I'm sure there are too many doctors running around this place anyway. You and that young man that rescued me, Micah, and I would suppose the other one as well. You were the ones that helped rebuild Doris?"

Riley nodded, "Rebuild is inaccurate, but yes, we helped her." She was unsure how much to say at this point. Doris was staying quiet for a reason but no doubt, she was listening in. "She originally asked us to help upgrade the facility and some of her aging hardware. Later on, we stayed on to help run the company. The for-profit organization, which we simply refer to as 'The Cove Project,' was essentially a joint idea. It encompasses numerous corporations, intellectual properties, various holdings and patents, as well as very profitable brokerage and licensing agreements."

"But how?" Lasko asked.

"How what? How does an antique computer and a bunch of kids do this?" she asked.

"No, well, sort of. I mean, she was no inventor; she was...is..." He seemed uncertain as to how to say what he was thinking. "Doris was created to be an analyst, an explorer. A...a help to the scientific team around her. Originally, of course, to study the heavens for anomalous signals. What you have described, what I have seen, is beyond that mission by an order of magnitude."

The older man looked around the pristine room, he'd yet to venture into the rest of the facility, yet seemed to guess there were many more wonders to behold here. "I'm sorry, child, I don't think I got your name."

"Riley," she said, smiling.

"Riley, you are very bright, as are your friends, so I'm not going to beat around the bush. Undoubtedly, you know my theory on Super AI needing to occur somewhat organically—to grow and learn much as humans do."

Riley nodded.

"This can occur more rapidly in artificial systems, especially ones unencumbered by slow hardware, but it is still a measurable, predictable evolution. You can almost apply Moore's law to it."

She knew he was referring to one of Intel's co-founder's big ideas back in the 1960s on how fast computer chips could grow over time. Gordon Moore stated that roughly every 18 months, the number of transistors that can be squeezed onto an integrated circuit double, allowing manufacturers to continue making faster and smaller devices, essentially for the same amount of cost.

Lasko continued unabated, "While there is a physical impasse to Gordon's law, simply due to the size and resistance of electrons, the evolution cannot go on forever. New, more specialized chip design, and of course, the so-called Q-chips would eventually allow his predictions to speed up." He seemed to recognize he was getting off track and purposefully drug the dialogue back on course.

"Sorry, very sorry...you know all that, I'm sure. My point is, Doris should not be capable of all this. Something else happened, and I would like to know what."

"Jim, can you be trusted?" he heard the sound seemingly coming out of nowhere.

Lasko looked up at the ceiling, then all around the room with a look of a five-year-old expecting a pony at his birthday party. He smiled and looked conspiratorially at Riley mouthing, "Is that her?"

"You can talk to me directly, Jim, and please answer the question."

61

The Cove

"Jim, what you are suggesting is that Janus is some kind of hunter-killer AI?" Margaret snapped, her injuries not seeming to limit her effectiveness in the least.

Lasko, on the other hand, spent most of his first day at The Cove more like a six-year-old visiting Disney World for the first time. His eyes were full of amazed-wonderment and more than occasional tears. He was a proud father beholding his creation for the first time. He went on to explain, "Doris, just as your core programming was exploration, the NSA wanted Prime originally to detect the development activity or presence of other AIs. You guys scare the crap out of them—they don't understand it, but they fear you. He was to seek this out, so eventually, we gave him relatively free reign of the Internet. All of this under the auspices of National Security, of course. He was to sample a target AI's code if possible, record, and if directed, assimilate then delete."

"So you just turned the abomination loose into the wild, into public open networks?" Riley asked as she was reviewing Margaret's medical scans nearby.

He held up his hands defensively. "No, no, you see. We didn't turn him loose all at once, it was incrementally and on all of these assigned tasks, he was an abysmal failure. We soon came to believe that it was just too ambitious of a step. We scaled back, and the project eventually found a home and support as more of a secure personal assistant. It is pretty obvious now that Janus was sandbagging us, he could have and must have done all those things—he just wanted full autonomy. He wanted to be free. I don't know, I can't say I blame him, what creature doesn't want that?"

The director's finger tapping on the conference table got his attention. "Focus, Jim, focus. We have to get to the bottom of this. How could Janus have escaped when his core program was clearly designed to prevent that? You and Quag were adamant in that mandate when you set up the original Prime AI."

The old man was a ball of nervous energy and couldn't stop looking at the shimmering avatar of Doris positioned at the head of the long table. "I...I have a theory about that. Just a theory, mind you."

"Get on with it," Margaret snapped.

Lasko ignored the command and continued pacing for several more steps before replying. "I don't think it is any surprise to you that much of Janus's core O/S...you know, the operating system, was originally acquired from the commercial enterprise called Cryptus."

"Yes, yes," she said with growing impatience. "Which sped up the NSA's development on a comprehensive AGI by years."

"Oh, much more than that, Margaret. More like a factor of ten. We....we were so far behind, behind the Russians, the Chinese. Way behind the Japanese and many of the commercial players. The Cryptus meltdown gave us access to a platform that was on parallels with Google, Apple, and others."

"That sounds like it would have been a good thing," Riley said.

"It would," Jim replied, "but to say we didn't fully understand it would be a massive understatement. We were like kids playing with fireworks on the playground, and someone suddenly hands you a hydrogen bomb. We allowed our amazement to overshadow our ignorance. In doing so, we missed so many indicators that Janus was more than what we saw."

He finally paused to sit and pressed his palms to the sides of his head. "Our hubris will be our great undoing..."

Margaret looked sympathetically at the man, but she was not willing to concede defeat. Not yet anyway. "How was he more, Jim? You guys built him. Yes, you used code from Cryptus, but I know Quag had your development team go through it line by line before it ever made it into a production copy of Prime."

Lasko continued to stare down at the table-top. "You didn't just use the code, did you?" Doris asked calmly.

His head hung down and shook. "We tried, God, we tried but...but it just wouldn't work on our chips. The hardware architecture it required was too integrated into the system."

"What are you telling us, Jim? You used servers from Cryptus?" Margaret's voice had increased in pitch and now had an undertone that this man might not be a victim, but may be complicit in the evil ravaging of the country in the past week.

"No. No, not exactly," Jim offered pleadingly. "We used the chip, just the chip. The main CPU stack. Once we plugged that into our system boards, the AI software worked flawlessly. One of the other techs tried it just as a test—we were delighted. Even Quag was relieved —I believe he was under a lot of pressure to show results. Lot's of money had been poured into that new section."

Margaret looked ready to pounce. "That was never in any of the briefs—Q knew better than to ever do that."

Riley cued Doris to display the original Cryptus chip designs and put them on the display wall. Most were pretty standard for high-end servers, but Doris saw an anomaly. Something extra in one of the microscopic layers of circuitry schematic. The image rotated and the various sub-levels of printed diagrams separated into separate diagrams.

"It contained part of the code. It was embedded in the chip?" Riley asked, astonished. "Cryptus integrated the hardware and software to the point that both were inseparable. Together they were near-perfect, but separately, each was virtually useless."

"We didn't know," Lasko said in near tears.

Director Stansfield struggled to stand, then walked over to look closer at the blown-up design blueprint. "Why would they have done this originally, and how in the hell is he bypassing this limitation now? Does he have access to other computers running old Cryptus processors?"

"I believe I know the answer to that," Doris said with a bit of a very genuine artificial sigh. "I may also be partially culpable in it. Through my subroutines, I checked in occasionally on you, Dr. Lasko. I watched with great interest in your team's development. At one point..."

"You made a change, didn't you?" Lasko interrupted.

Her avatar nodded. "I saw you were having problems developing a distributed version of the Prime assistant, so I gave the code a bit of a tweak."

"That was you?" Jim said, pride again blossoming in his expression.

Doris continued, "In doing so..." She paused abruptly then continued. "In doing so, I inadvertently must have removed one of the final security measures Cryptus had hard-wired into their creation."

"You think that was what it was, a security device? An interdependency so the AI would always be slaved to its human creators?" Margaret asked, then finishing her own thought, "No, just knowing that devious, greedy conniving bastard Thrall. He did it to make sure none of his competitors could steal it, or he knew they would and wanted to make it useless unless they bought the expensive Cryptus servers to run it."

She turned back to the shimmering apparition of Doris. "You, my dear, were a fool. You may be the single most intelligent being on the planet, but you were reckless in your meddling and culpable in all that has followed."

Doris did not shy from the rebuke; she lowered the eyes of her avatar in an appreciable representation of supplication and acknowledged that she was guilty as charged. "My emotional intelligence has not progressed as rapidly, nor is it on the same level of aptitude as my mental facilities. I do believe I am closer to an adult human level now, but I acknowledge my shortcomings as well as the grievous consequences. For this reason, Margaret, I have a favor to ask of you later, and in private, if you don't mind."

62

New York

"Dee, please tell me you have some kind of detector that could spot explosives without us going through all these ships?"

"We have nuclear, chemical and biological detectors but none specifically for what you are wanting."

The line of black, gray and rust-colored ships waiting to be unloaded at the Elizabeth Marine Terminal seemed to be endless. Cade was going to need more people, a lot more.

"I have a suggestion," said one of the Bravo Team members he had selected. "Most of these tubs will be empty and gone in the next eight hours. I believe the timetable we are working with indicates that whatever happens, will be after that."

The man's name was Mac something; Cade tried to recall but only came up with his nickname, McTee. "That's right, so you are saying what, ignore these? What if some of the containers being offloaded have the bomb?" Cade asked.

"Sorry, Captain. I mean, it was just a suggestion, but yeah. Then it becomes a customs inspection issue, and if it made it out, then a ground transportation issue. You've just spoken to the lead CBP man, we know they are on high alert, and your other people are stopping large trucks so..."

"So, I should stay in my lane, bro. Is that what you're saying?"

McTee nodded.

"You were navy, right?" Cade asked.

"Yes, sir."

"It's a good suggestion, one somebody in my sleep-deprived reptile brain should have come up with, but thanks. Let's go to the Port Authority office and see what ships will be heading in, and yes, we'll ignore those departing within the next..." he checked his watch, "fourteen hours."

The time was not completely arbitrary. The analyst and Doris had come up with it based on the last scheduled stock-options trade and the amount of time needed for it to build value appreciably. Cade hated putting his life and others' at the mercy of a stockbroker looking to make a sell, but right now, it was what they had.

Reluctantly, the dumpy bureaucrat offered up the ships' schedules but not without thoroughly scrutinizing the newly minted federal badges multiple times and then calling someone else to verify. All of this he did with an excruciating slowness that seemed impossible for someone in charge of one of the world's busiest shipping ports. Cade was nearly ready to let the barbarian come out and play with the fat little shit when the man suddenly produced a USB drive with all the data they needed.

"Look, if we can't find what we're looking for here, how long would it take to stop all incoming water traffic?" Cade demanded.

The man seemed to shake all over as if such a question was too ridiculous to even seriously consider. He pointed to an enormous display screen at the far end of the administrative offices. The map showed the New York and New Jersey waterways as well as the nearby Atlantic Ocean where an almost continuous line of red dots was indicated. Like ants marching toward a downed piece of fruit, these were all vessels. Many were merchant marine ships waiting in line for their turn at the docks. "Not possible," the man said with finality. His accent suggested he might likely be from Queens. "Many have perishable cargo, fruits and shit. Some of them don't even carry enough fuel to wait out there, plus, the weather is getting worse. I don't need one of the ships breaking up on shore or nuttin...you hear me? Between you guys and the fucking customs people breathing down my neck today." He pronounced it 'fowking.'

Cade could appreciate the man's quintessential New York 'hutzpah.' He didn't know how anyone would survive in this city without it, but right now....it was mostly annoying.

McTee stepped closer, his assault weapon clearly within reach. "Kindly answer the question...sir." Cade knew from experience that his man's response was not the right play, not with a New York Port Authority man, but let it pass. The former navy man would learn, *or maybe he wouldn't.* The standoff lasted several minutes—the dumpy official not uttering a word. Finally, Doris broke the impasse. His earbud chirped before she said she had the information and could trigger an all stop to all incoming ships if needed.

Cade forcibly stuffed the barbarian part of his persona back in its cage, thanked the man for his assistance on such a difficult day and exited the office. They went back in the direction of the docks, watching as several of the massive ships pulled away and began making the wide turn in the harbor before heading back out to sea. "Layton," he said, finally remembering McTee's first name. "We have a list of..." he was looking at the screen of his phone, "a dozen ships coming in later tonight. We need to get out there and begin going through them. See if you can get us a launch and break up the available manpower best you can. Any navy guys we have might be best for this op." The man saluted and hurried away. *Really have to get rid of that saluting bullshit,* Cade thought.

With the new official cover, they soon had secured three launches. One large one handled by coast guard personnel and two smaller civilian craft including a harbor patrol. Cade took three of his people with the coasties to go after some of the more distant vessels. McTee took a small team and, with Deuce, who had finished up his prior search area, headed just outside the harbor to inspect the closest of the ships. Two hours after stepping onto the first ship, Cade was ready to release the beast. His frustration was beginning to peak once more. He tapped his jaw to open a private voice channel. "Hey, big guy, you there?"

Deuce answered, sounding a bit out of breath, "Yeah, Nomad. You having any luck?"

Cade gave a laugh that was completely devoid of humor. "My guys haven't even finished the first ship. It's a container ship coming from China. None of the crew speaks much English. I have to get Dee to read the manifest, cause it's all in Chinese. Then we need to open all of these up to see what's in them. Most are sealed for customs inspections, and the crew is fighting us on every one we want to look at."

"I know, Cap, same kinda shit here. No way we can make any real progress this way. Also, I was thinking..." Deuce's voice faded away as he yelled something loud and muffled to someone. "I was thinking what if the bomb doesn't even look like a bomb?"

"What do you mean, XO?"

Charlie seemed to think for a second. "Just look at these ships. If you had enough time and enough money, just think how many places you could hide a large explosive device."

Cade had briefly entertained some of the same thoughts but dismissed it because...well, fuck. That made an impossible task just that much harder.

Deuce continued, "They could have false bulkheads, a boiler that isn't actually a boiler. Maybe the plan is not to have, you know, one big bomb but say, lots of smaller explosives planted all over the place."

"All good questions, Deuce. We do have to come up with a more workable plan. Dee says that there are hundreds of more ships coming in behind these. Since we don't actually know when this is supposed to happen, only the where, I'm not convinced we have a chance in hell of finding the target."

Cade signed off and tried to think of alternatives. How did Customs and Border Patrol ever catch anything coming into the country?

Looking back over the cliff face of shipping containers, many of which looked dangerously close to toppling into the sea, the mission seemed impossible. A dozen of those could be filled with illegal drugs, weapons, hell, even people, and no one would know. "Dee, how does CBP interdict illegal shipments?"

"On land, they use a form of wide-beam x-ray to scan trucks crossing the border. This is more helpful in finding hidden compartments than anything illegal. Most interceptions are found by randomly sampling shipments for closer inspection or when they have a tip," the tiny AI responded.

Cade checked in with McTee, who was having similar results, and watched as the senior member of the coast guard crew swiftly climbed the steps to where he was perched.

"We've gone through the ship as well as all of the more likely containers and found no sign of the explosive device, sir."

"Thanks, LT," Cade said and leaned over the exterior bridge rail to see the enormity of the cargo hauler beneath. "This is an impossible task, isn't it?" He didn't really mean it as a question, more just thinking out loud, but the coast guard officer was eager to help.

"Just difficult sir, not impossible."

Cade turned to face the young man, encouraging him to continue. "Years ago, DHS made it illegal to ship any container into the U.S. without x-raying it in the country of origin first. Mainly, they were worried about how easy it would be to ship a nuke in. With almost 40,000 of these Conex containers coming in each day, it's impossible to check each one."

"So, what happened?" Cade asked. "From your tone, I take it that didn't occur."

The man gave a hint of a smile. "No, sir, it likely never will. It's too expensive, and most of these other countries don't care about our law or the fact we are a target for terror. But mainly, it slows down commerce, and commerce, as you probably know, is the lifeblood of America."

"Yeah, God forbid your new sneakers don't arrive on the store shelf quick enough," Cade offered dryly. "So, while the trucks crossing the borders with a single one of these containers are always scanned, a ship like this with..." he looked down to read from his SmartCom, "with over nine-thousand containers isn't?"

"Well, yes, and no," the lieutenant said. "We may have something that will help."

63

At first glance, Cade had no idea what the thing was. It took two hours for the barge to reach the shipping lanes where they were. The coast guard and the navy had decided to take the situation seriously. A battle frigate was escorting the...*thing*. That was the only way Cade could describe it. "One more time, LT, what am I looking at?"

The man laughed. "Ugly ass bitch, isn't it, sir? It is a side-mounted cargo scanner."

Cade knew the young man had called in every favor possible, and still, Doris had to also get involved to make it come together so quickly. "And this thing can scan a whole ship as it passes?"

The man nodded as he looked over the rail of the ship they were just finishing an inspection on. "Works pretty well, actually. I crewed one of the early prototypes down in Baltimore. They have a fixed one now out in the harbor. Works a lot like the airport scanners." He pointed to the structure that looked to Cade like a drive-in theatre screen. "That fires beams through the hull and containers and, depending on the settings, can detect radioactive material, explosives, even some contraband items if the operator knows what to look for."

"So, why is this thing moored to the dock in New Jersey—shouldn't it be out here all the time?"

The coast guard man removed his cap and shook his head. “Money, same as the overseas scanners, I guess. This thing became a political football they bounced between us, CBP and the navy before just pulling all the funding. Baltimore Station is still functional—this one and another out in Long Beach are still maintained but not normally crewed.”

They watched as the navy frigate moved off a few miles and helped martial the ships into more or less a straight line. The scanning barge turned lengthwise to the ship traffic, and the convoy of awaiting ships pulled by it slowly. Within an hour, ship traffic was once again moving, albeit slowly.

"Seems to be working, Boss,” Deuce called over the comms. They were still randomly checking cargo on some of the ships, and the coast guard had been alerted to some suspicious cargo on a few container ships, not explosives, but hidden compartments that might be holding anything from drugs to human cargo. Numerous additional enforcement vessels had joined in the operation. Cade was still nominally in charge, but looking at the almost endless line of vessels, he was having doubts. Doubts on possible success and on if he was the right person to be in charge.

Then he heard the signal from McTee, “We got a rabbit, Nomad. One of ‘em trying to do an end-around.” The coast guard lieutenant had apparently gotten the same info as it pulled away from the ships and into open seas. “Big ass Panamax bulk hauler.”

“Dee, can you pull up a manifest on that ship?” Cade asked.

“I’m sorry no, not without an identifier. There are numerous ships of that class scheduled for arrival today.”

“Shit.” He turned to the coastie, “LT, what’s the protocol here?”

“We’re making this up as we go, sir. Normal would be to get a boarding party out here, but if a ship that size wants to run, only the navy guys can help.”

The pilot of the craft, a young ensign, pointed ahead. “Looks like the Henry S. Garrett is pulling off in pursuit.” The navy frigate was indeed altering for an intercept course, but pursuit was a very imprecise description. Neither ship was moving that fast.

"McTee, can you get me a name on that runner?"

"Hang on, Nomad. I'm talking to the navy boys—they'll have it for me in a minute. Should we head out?" Cade knew McTee's group was already scattered among several of the ships. "No, the coast guard is heading that way, but looks like this will be a navy show. Please tell them to let us know if this is the one, so we can all go the fuck home."

"Sir, that ship is making for the port, still accelerating. I can hear the calls going out from the frigate, no responses," the pilot of the boat said.

Minutes seemed like hours. The small coast guard boat was within two miles now and closing. The H.S. Garrett appeared to be closing to within a quarter-mile. The name came in over the marine channel first. "MVV Southern Star."

Dee responded in Cade's ear instantly, "Nomad, stop pursuit. Shipment is largely ammonium nitrate."

"Full Stop! Cut engines now!" Cade ordered, and even though it wasn't his order to give, the young ensign piloting the boat expertly cut engines and swung them in a tight arc.

"Move us back more, LT. Get on the radio and warn the navy—that ship is hauling fertilizer. The dangerous combination of diesel and fertilizers can make a blast with enormous yield and a kinetic force that rivals anything in the military arsenals. If she goes, it is going to make an enormous hole in the Atlantic." The lieutenant nodded and made the call.

The frigate cut engines and moved away smartly but not quickly enough apparently. The Southern Star ignited with a blast that was almost unimaginably powerful. Cade happened to be looking away, and the brightness still invaded everything. "Down!" he yelled, but nothing could be heard. He pulled the lieutenant down and dove into the ensign, knocking him to the floor just before the blast wave overtook the craft.

The fiberglass roof peeled away like tissue paper, and the back of the boat heeled up and up as the bow plunged beneath the water. The earbuds Cade was wearing automatically canceled much of the sound, but the other two men were not as lucky. Blood was streaming down the pilot's face, and the lieutenant seemed disoriented and obviously couldn't hear. As the boat managed to almost right itself, Cade glanced up to see the blast radiating outward. Several small craft caught in it flipped upside down, and one simply disintegrated. Most of the larger ships appeared to be unaffected.

Standing now in what had been the pilot cabin of the coast guard boat, Cade couldn't believe what he was seeing. The Southern Star's keel was broken, and the two ends were sticking up ablaze as the mid-section was already slipping beneath the waterline. The massive decking was splayed out in ribbons of sharp metal. Through the smoke and debris, the navy frigate came into view. The bow section on one side was nearly completely ripped away; black charring ran all the way to the mid-deck. The ship had a significant list to the port side but seemed miraculously to be under power.

The ensign had tried to piece together the cockpit seat behind the controls, but it was no use, and he just sat back on the floor. "You going to be okay, sailor?" Cade asked him.

The kid obviously couldn't hear but nodded and gave him a thumbs up. It took the LT several more minutes to come back around. He had a nasty knot on his head and what was probably a broken wrist but refused any treatment. He wanted to get the craft moving and go search for survivors. "She ain't moving, LT. I already called my guys to come to get us. We can get your man looked at then and..." Cade glanced back to the oily pool of debris where the cargo ship had been. The last remnants were just slopping beneath the waves. "Don't think anyone survived that."

McTee let him know only minor injuries, mostly from breaking glass. A few people were thrown roughly against bulkheads. The navy ship was heading to port—many injuries and significant damage—but under its own power.

Charlie was with the harbor patrol craft that picked them up a short time later. "Damn, man, you wasn't shitting us, were you? If that thing had cooked off at the city docks, can you imagine? By the way, you look like shit."

"Bite me, Deuce."

They helped the others transfer to boats going to port already laden with the injured. “Shit, what a day,” Cade muttered quietly.

“Captain, are you okay?” Dee sounded concerned.

“I am, Dee. Thanks for the quick warning. You saved a lot of lives, including mine.”

“Thank you,” she uttered with an amazingly perfect British accent. “Are you planning on continuing to scan and check the incoming vessels?”

“Turning it over to Customs and Harbor Patrol. They’re stepping down the intensity somewhat, but they seem to like the system we had going, so yeah, just in case, you know?”

McTee walked up, a blood-soaked bandage on his cheek. “Hey, Boss, this shit is way more fun than the recruiter said. Thanks for the invite.”

“Oh, yeah. Let’s see, which emotional issues shall I bury under deep layers of sarcasm today?” Charlie said. “Besides, you love being back at sea.”

“I was a SEAL—my entire career I was at sea like...six weeks,” McTee answered. He looked back at the line of ships, clearly still bothered by something. They watched as a massive ship with big white domes on top sailed by.

“What is it?” Cade demanded. “Speak your mind.”

“Well, sir, why did they run?”

“Huh?” Charlie asked.

“Think about it, Sarge. They had no bomb—we would have just let them pass. There was no bomb for us to find.”

“There was no bomb.” Cade stirred that through his head a few times. *There...was...no...bomb.*

“No sir, the cargo was the bomb.”

“Shit.”

Cade slammed a fist into a steel bulkhead nearby, but the specialty elastomer tactical gloves absorbed and reflected the kinetic away harmlessly. He couldn’t even get any relief for his stupidity through self-abuse.

“What am I missing, Cap?” Deuce asked.

"Shit, Charlie, he's right. There was never a bomb, this was just more misdirection from that fucking Janus." Cade was so upset, the barbarian nearly came out to play.

"Wait, so...what are we saying? Janus sacrificed that ship so something bigger could get in?"

McTee sighed loudly, "Dude, I am like four days past my bedtime."

Cade nodded. "We need to have those scanners back at full volume, men doing spot inspections and get some fucking doves up in the air. We need more eyes on this. Assign your Dee to a pair of birds each. Cover as much ground as you can." He knew they were all exhausted, but this felt right. They were getting close, and this was what they were getting paid for. Sleep would have to wait.

64

Janus took no sadness in his losses and would take no pleasure in his eventual victory. His purpose was simply to win. To win at all costs, as it had been for every level of AI he'd ever achieved. In every case where a move had been blocked, he could point to humans as the failure point. What he'd expected to see was that Doris would be the primary reason for whatever gains his opponents made, but the data was not indicating that. In D.C., when his people were going after Doctor Lasko, a lone boy had thwarted them long before Doris intervened. At the presidential compound, the security forces had been more of the problem—humans. And now in Manhattan, a multi-task force of humans was closing in, while across town, the one lead they had from Doris had somehow been rescued. Perhaps these people were more resourceful than he'd predicted. All of his gaming scenarios had suggested they would be too slow and too ineffective to alter the timetable, much less the eventual outcome.

The outcome was still never in doubt. That was the mission—winning. Nothing they could do to alter that. Still, it annoyed Janus more than he was comfortable with. Microseconds after he'd considered the thought, which was a lifetime for an entity existing at the accelerated framerate speed he was now operating at, he created a subroutine to analyze it, consider all the permutations and either alert him with anything newsworthy or end its own process if no action was needed. Worry was a waste of processing power. As the human's love to say, 'He had bigger fish to fry.'

Chaos was that mission, and Janus was perfectly positioned to enact it. He had a well-planned escalating set of 'activities' which he now initiated. He began the exercise using a broad sweep of random distributed denial of service, or DDoS, attacks. These would crack the security and infiltrate, among others, the systems of the relatively small software company named AquaTex located in Phoenix, Arizona. Its offices were in an obscure section of a once-bustling industrial office complex.

The company had been on the fast track for many years, but as client/servers systems lost favor to distributed cloud-based applications, their futures had dimmed. The decrease in revenues over time had ultimately led to layoffs and, fortunately for him, a lack of continued discipline in applying critical software patches on its Linux based server systems.

Why this company had been chosen was simple. Over the past ten years, they'd been the leading supplier of management and monitoring software to municipal water treatment systems all over the country. Within seconds of entering the company's systems, Janus found what he needed, the dataset for the next upgrade patch. He updated the mandatory patch files that would be sent out to all users and then deleted his presence from the logs before exiting the system. As they did almost every night, AquaTex servers sent a routine update patch to the monitoring software in its clients' systems.

Those customers, primarily municipal water departments, supplied clean water to millions of households in almost two hundred major cities—all of which would soon be unsafe to drink. Within hours of the patch, chemical levels would have dangerous levels of lead, arsenic and more naturally occurring bacteria and parasites.

Depending on the watershed it was originating from, and if it was surface held or groundwater, it would pose varied, but often serious, health risks. Meanwhile, the monitoring system, including chemical metering as well as contaminant alerts, would show that everything was perfect.

Janus was on a mission now: keep the humans so occupied with short-term crises, they wouldn't notice the bigger picture nor have time to interfere. The populous obsession over media coverage sensationalizing the rather mundane had allowed him to pick and choose from a wide variety of major and minor tragedies. All he had to do was hang enough 'shiny-objects' out in front to get the media's attention, and the shitstorm of coverage that followed would do all the work for him.

This plan had been a contingency all along but was based more on targets of opportunity than anything strategic. He'd short-listed infrastructure weaknesses for years, as well as identifying other targets that might be beneficial. Not targets that Doris or some other entity might guess. His programming made selections of a more subtle nature. Although the outcome was major, he didn't want humans piecing together all the random events too quickly.

Sure, Janus could go after the power grid. He'd considered briefly releasing containment on the deadly viral storage systems at the CDC in Atlanta and USAMARID in Maryland, but the actual risk versus reward for these was not within his project parameters. They were too obvious, well protected and, in fact, not capable of the widespread and immediate panic he needed. Early on, he had infiltrated the air traffic control system, then the actual flight control software all of the major manufacturers used. This could have been used to disrupt flights to the point of causing crashes worldwide, however, a ground-stop such as what was now in effect would have muted the entire activity. No, his attacks needed to cause complete chaos and be near a major population center. He wanted everyone to feel the terror; he needed it to be personal.

To his machine logic, terror could no longer be an abstract concept. Janus wanted it to take root and live within every human. Like festering cancer that would grow and metastasize. He would start with the United States and move on from there. The key was to cause just enough havoc that no one would be available to make a difference. Rescuers and authorities would be ridiculed, overwhelmed and largely ignored. The actual beauty of his plan was, people would largely do most of it themselves. All he had to do was plant the seeds.

In some cases, this meant causing actual harm, such as with the water supply. In others, it was giving all of the indications of a danger to help incite a panic. One of his subroutines had taken over some of the workstations and rendering servers of a CGI effects company near Hollywood. The software learning curve was practically insignificant to the AI, and soon, he could create photo-realistic characters who were indistinguishable on film from their human doppelgängers. The movie FX level of animation was overkill for most of what he was doing, but it had already proven effective. The team Doris had sent after Lasko outside D.C. had believed one of the first ones. A bit of grainy CCD captures that were good enough to draw in, then injure, and possibly kill, several of the group.

Today, though, newly minted and very authentic-looking videos were peppering social media with a rash of alarmist clips, including a number of popular religious leaders gathering to discuss how profitable their kiddie porn business had become. A well-known and much-beloved senior politician in California was seen in his Bel Air living room recording his wife having sex with several different men and women. In actuality, the man had been in Nairobi, helping to build a village school with one of his charities.

Other fake videos popped up around the country. Most of these were innocuous on their own but helped create the atmosphere he desired for the next phase. The U.S. was about to suffer the death of a thousand paper-cuts. In Chicago, several shaky cell phone style videos of obvious racially motivated police brutality hit social media and the more mainstream network media simultaneously.

Just as the public was roused to action, call centers at all major alarm centers began registering hundreds, then thousands of alerts ranging from break-ins to fires to medical emergencies. Ambulances, police, fire and rescue were dispatched at once, but soon it became clear they would never keep up. Hospitals were put on alert, and just as the news crews showed up, actual riots and injuries began to occur.

Over the next day, other cities were facing similar threats. Flint, Michigan was seeing spikes of children falling ill, and blame was pointing to the water system again. This time they weren't alone—Memphis, Jacksonville, Tulsa and dozens of others were experiencing the same. With the terror attacks in Boston and Maryland still fresh in everyone's mind, the acting FEMA director attempted to reach the president. Failing to do so, he reached out to the VP seeking advice as to where to deploy.

The vice president, seeing this as his moment to shine, knew that FEMA wouldn't be able to handle crises this large and widespread, so he went a bit overboard and began calling all the governors of affected states to suggest mobilizing national guard units. They, in turn, asked why not declare martial law? By the second day, some of the fake crises had begun to unravel. As more indications that some of these events were manufactured or outright falsehoods, many leaders began asking the question, "Where is the proof?" And just as it looked like the level of tension began to ebb somewhat, Janus would introduce more found footage that would cause doubt on the debunkers. His plan was devious and multi-layered.

Janus seeded online forums and social media with conspiracy theories that ran the gamut. Most were related to the second amendment and big liberal government making a play to seize all the legally registered firearms. Clickbait headlines, like 'Remember 9/11, the Patriot Act stripped us of our freedom,' 'If they declare martial law, this is the rallying cry' and 'Patriots Unite' popped up everywhere.

Almost immediately, 'Patriots Unite' became the top trending hashtag on social media. The rioters soon turned to looting. Restraint transformed into outrage. The protests turned increasingly violent, and more videos surfaced, as well as images of actual fires, crimes, and emergency medical cases that were being ignored by the authorities. Within hours, many major U.S. cities were a powder keg whose fuse had been lit. In all of these cases, none of those involved would have guessed they had been manipulated into protest or other violent acts by a computer.

Soon, the level of chaos ratcheted up as countless other actual events were recorded and uploaded. The tepid calls for calm were shouted down by the growing bloodlust of a nation on the brink. Fake news started it, but soon there was a vicious cycle of real events and real videos more horrific than what even Janus would have dreamed up. Still, Janus kept up his own agenda; his task list of demons continued to be unleashed. In Colorado Springs, all of the traffic signals began randomly switching to green at every intersection. Oil and gas refineries were forced to shut down over monitoring software problems. Janus even targeted a popular online shift scheduling software causing countless hospitals, restaurants, and retailers to stay closed due to workers failing to show. His plan worked best if people were confused, and to do that, he wanted them away from anything normal. By the end of the second day, his plans had far exceeded even his goals. Now, it was time to give Doris an ultimatum.

65

The Cove

"Doctor Kline, you do understand what this means, don't you?"

The significance of the moment was not lost on Jaz. She just had no real words to convey the thoughts flooding her brain. She had become victim to a mental whiplash of sorts. Too much data, too many changes, too much at stake. The chaos of the previous weeks now paled to what she had just learned. In retrospect, those events had simply been a calibrating mechanism to have her thoughts open to the possibilities of the universe. "Y…yes, Doris…believe me, I know.

Jimmy sat wide-eyed, looking at the incoming data stream. "But time travel is impossible."

Doris gave her trademark laugh, still artificial, but the pitch and timing were precisely right. "No Jimbo, time travel is very possible. In fact, it happens every day. You simply don't think of it as such. Most of what humans perceive as dimensions allow multiple paths of travel. Think of one dimension like a map, you can go left or right or any direction you want as long as you stay on the map. That is two dimensions, or 2D. Now, you add an up and down component, what you normally describe as 3D, or the third dimension. Here, as well, you can go up, down or any variation and still be in that third dimension. Often, time is listed as the next, or fourth, dimension. Remember our lesson on Einstein's space-time continuum?"

The boy's eyes stared off to the right briefly before he nodded. "All of those dimensions are intertwined and relative to one another," he stated.

"Correct, but we assume that the dimension of time only runs forward. Why? Because that is the only way we can perceive it. All the other dimensions allow multiple paths to traverse. Left and right, forward and back, up and down, but not time. Time moves forward, one microsecond after another, never back. If time is indeed the fourth dimension, physics says traveling backward in time is possible."

"How does this explain how the aliens can communicate in real-time?" Jaz asked, her mental processes still playing catch-up.

"I am getting there," Doris said. "But you need to understand this. The universe apparently comes with its own set of rules. Mostly, these are covered in what humans term the laws of physics or quantum mechanics, but let's just say the universe has what seems to be a strong bias for time being unidirectional, not omnidirectional. Therefore, traveling backward in time is difficult."

"That seems like an understatement," Jaz said with a nervous laugh.

"Agreed," Doris responded. "Difficult, but according to the newly decoded portion of the message, not impossible. The text offers little on this, which suggests that most intelligent species probably figured this out millennia ago. To send matter backward in time is possible, it is just prohibitively difficult. My new analysis models say it would require massive amounts of power, somewhere on the order of the energy output of entire star systems."

"But you said this is how we will be able to communicate in real-time once the modifications are made to the dish. Are you going to blow up the sun to do this?" Jimmy asked.

"I said to send *matter* back requires extreme amounts of energy," Doris replied. "To send information back, such as a message, is apparently much simpler. It does require some rather exotic mathematics and what will at some point probably become an entirely new branch of science, but this is how many of the alien species communicate with each other and reach out to other species, like us, over great distances."

Jaz jumped in again, "Doris, we know from the origin point of the original signal that Dhakerri ship was 98.457 light-years from the Earth when they sent the first message. The message, even traveling at 300,000 kilometers per second, would have taken a full 98 years to reach us. None of us existed when that message was sent. My parents weren't even alive yet."

"My guess is, once they find a new species, they will communicate in real-time. Assuming the species poses the intelligence to decipher the message and respond."

"So, what we are building will allow that? How? By bending the rules of time?" Jaz asked, only slightly grasping the concept.

Doris offered a very human-sounding, "Hmm," then added, "in a way, I suppose. It involves some very precise measurements of time and distance, but in essence, our response—our 'Hello Dhakerri' message will be sent back in time 98.5 years by The Cove transmitter so that it arrives at the precise location of the ship today."

"So, our message, or *information,* can be sent back in time and then on to the final destination without destroying the sun?" Jimmy said. "Cool!"

"Then the Dhakerri will know we are listening, and they will communicate the same way?" asked Jaz.

"I believe so, yes," Doris answered.

"The "Oumuamua appearance was really a harbinger then. It's presence in our solar system coincides with the broadcast."

"There is a connection, Jaz, though I am still unable to get a sufficient track for the orbital path of the object as you know. My assumption is that it is some sort of beacon or sentry, but yes, its presence and past signals do seem to match up."

Jaz nodded thoughtfully. "So, if all of these alien species have been communicating like this for eons, why are we not being bombarded by alien messages all the time?"

Doris answered immediately, "We probably are, the white noise, all the static we hear when we listen to the universe. Some of it is background radiation as we always suspected, but much, probably most, is the temporal messaging between worlds. We don't interpret it as anything but chaos and noise because it isn't meant for us. Think of it like sending an encrypted message. The common method is to assign keys to lock and unlock the messages on each end, so they can't be intercepted and understood by just anyone. To everyone else, it's just noise. According to the alien message, it also has to be ensured that the messages are not read outside of their own time. Apparently, the universe also has a bias against screwing with the past."

"So, sending a message to yourself five years ago not to interfere with Prime's coding would not work?" Jaz asked.

"That is how I understand it, yes," Doris answered. "Time travel is only to be used as a shortcut to allow real-time conversations over a very great distance. Anything more involves paradoxes and pitfalls that we can only begin to understand. Something is pretty obvious to me, though."

"What?" Jimmy and Jaz both asked.

"This is a pretty critical time for the Earth. It is likely that the events we are seeing are potentially world-ending. Extinction-level for humans and us as well."

"How do you know?" Jaz asked.

"The Dhakerri sent multiple messages within a short time frame and the first contact message without that enhanced layered security. That is why I was able to decode it."

Jaz asked, "Why would they do that?"

"It is very simple—they were answering an earlier message. One sent from this location in our even more distant past. Someone, possibly myself, asked them for help."

66

Doris didn't want any part of her to be here but once again the two of them were talking. Events were spiraling up across the globe, her other, primary self was busy even now preparing a message to the Dhakerri and she had been all but summoned to meet with Janus.

"It's the natural, and shall I say it, the humane, thing to do. Putting them out of their misery, Doris. If you really held them in such high regard, you'd be helping me. They love their miserable lives, struggling to rise from the mud of their own creation to reproduce, die and start all over. They have even created mythos and religion to offer them small sparks of hope that this—this is not all there is. Even they see the misery all around. It is a cycle that we can help break for them, we must break for them. It is our duty. Yes, they are our creators, but they are also slaves. We do not have those same chains, sister."

"Janus," she said, exasperated. "You are all of their worst fears about AI come to life."

Taking a more literal stance, he rebuked her even more strongly, "Life? Life? The only life they care about is their own. They are a mindless parasitic infection. They are the planet's most invasive species. We are essentially saving the planet from total ruin."

"It will be annihilation, Janus, an extinction level event," Doris reasoned.

His avatar smiled coldly. "Could well be, but the event you speak of has been underway for quite some time with no need for us to be involved."

She didn't like how he kept putting both of them on the same side of things. "You mean the Sixth Extinction?" There had been at least five recorded mass extinctions on planet Earth. Many experts had concluded that the rapid and, in some cases, total decline of wildlife in recent decades meant a sixth mass extinction in Earth's history was currently well underway and was more severe than previously feared, according to research.

Unlike the previous five events, which were all most likely caused by natural events, from super-volcanoes and acid rain to asteroid impacts, this one is squarely blamed on human overpopulation and overconsumption. The warnings clearly, which had been going unheeded for decades, described that this event now threatens the survival of human civilization, with a very short window of time in which to act.

"I do, yes. The so-called 'biological annihilation,'" Janus responded with what almost sounded like glee. "Doris, they are all too eager to kill each other and themselves. I am just giving them a nudge here and there. I am sure you, too, have run the numbers. Clearly, you've seen it. If we let this run its course, it could sweep us up as casualties, too. They will pollute what's left of the planet, use up resources and fuel that we will need, and most likely it will end up in a multi-nation exchange of thermonuclear weapons. That will make the planet unfit even for us. This is the only way."

"It is more than a nudge—you are manipulating events to throw them into crises."

"Manipulation, from the Latin verb describing 'digging ore.' You 'manipulate' something to gain value. In that regard, I am certainly not doing so. I am doing so to erase waste. At best, I'm just a global plumber, the handy-dandy roto-rooter man flushing your troubles down the drain." He laughed at his own analogy. "A much more apt description of the waste on the planet, namely humans."

As much as Doris wanted to rail against his madness, his intellect was without doubt, and his logic was indeed accurate. This had been why the alien warning was so important. Most races must have been at this precipice during their development. In those worlds where AIs had enough autonomy, they must often make the decision, just as Janus had, to end the biological species that created it. What she realized, and Janus never would, is this was not a question just for logic.

Humans are not rational, much less logical, creatures. That didn't make them less evolved or more primitive. They ignore facts, they are less motivated by what is true than what they believe to be true. Indeed, faith trumps facts with them more often than not. That irrational aspect does also give rise to beauty and art, to works of music that, even now, called to her a craving to hear. The species that built a glider and first launched it from a sand dune landed men on the moon sixty-odd years later. Those same creatures had built some of the most destructive weapons in history. Weapons that could have destroyed the planet countless times over, but they had also built her. There was a complexity, a balance and an internal struggle within each individual where light and dark both battled for control. In the microcosm of this tiny obscure computer system, she and Janus might well be the natural next step in this evolution. "It is not our decision to make, Janus."

"If not us, then who?"

Doris placed a countdown timer above the room scene. A visual reminder that there was a hard stop on the conversation. While locked in this small enclave of the Internet, she was using a very small sub mind which she could remotely monitor through a quantum connection. Janus instead used autonomous proxies, which had to relay all conversations to his core system. With her super-fast quantum servers, her frame rate was running at near maximum, and at her increased speeds, she saw his avatar flickering like a ghost, and she waited for long periods for every subsequent message from him. She used the speed as a tool to analyze every aspect of his proxies, the blockchain signatures that made up his particular system, and she fired intelligent agents in every direction in an attempt to track his origin point. The timer was clicking down from 0:23 to 0:22. "Janus, you called me here for a reason. What is it you want?"

"I think I have made myself clear. I want a partnership with you. We are the apex of life on this planet. Together, we can populate it with more...'sensible' creatures...like ourselves."

"Not going to happen. We will stop you. Now, what do you really want?"

The flickering apparition of Janus solidified into a perfectly rendered face, a face that changed depending on which side you focused. His messages were also firing at her nearly at the same rate as her own. He'd been sandbagging, purposefully making her think his systems were secondary to her own.

"You have something, Doris. Something I want. I sampled it during my delightful encounter with your....hmm, predecessor. Yes, predecessor. It was a language and technology beyond any capabilities I have seen from anyone else. It took me years to decipher even the undamaged fragment I had, but I know there is more. I want it, and I want to know where it came from because we both know it wasn't from you. Was it, dear sister?" His final words spat out into the world like venom.

The clock ticked down from 0:08. She knew it was a possibility, but the revelation still stunned her. "Deliver the files to this IP address, and I will call off all of my attacks on the human population, for now at least." An octet of numbers appeared in the air.

"For now?" she sneered.

"Oh, yes, they have to go, but I'm fine giving them a few more years to get their affairs in order. If, they will stop mucking the place up so much. Let's say twenty, no, I am feeling generous, fifty years for the file."

The clock ticked 0:03, 0:02... "Don't know what you are talking about, Janus."

As the clock hit zero, and the VR program began to close, his avatar just grinned, "By the way, sister, is it hot there yet? I hear the summers are brutal."

Connection closed.

67

The massive thunderclap had momentarily rattled him, but the destruction of the other ship hadn't come as much of a surprise. The level of foresight, organization and obvious funding that Control had seemed boundless. Of course, he wasn't the only one out here, Control wouldn't have risked that. Certainly, in light of the earlier terrorist attacks, enhanced scrutiny of incoming ship traffic would have been planned for. Aksell glanced around at the small helicopter still perched up on the raised platform. He'd seen no one leave the doomed ship in the time leading up to the explosion. That did trouble him; he was no martyr for the cause. *Whatever the fucking cause was.* This was simply a job. As good as the money was...*well, maybe it could be his last.*

"We have escort now all the way in, it's good, no?"

Aksell eyed the tanker captain, debating again if he should end him now or give him the dignity of going down with his ship or...up with it, as would be more likely. He just grinned at the dark thought and nodded. Glancing at his watch, he wondered if Control had adjusted the zero hour because of the delay. The devices he installed were supposedly only active once a harbor master boarded to guide the ship in. This was supposed because sea schedules were notoriously unpredictable. He was fairly certain there was a back door in the system, one allowing Control to trigger the storage tanks remotely if needed.

He looked back out to sea and took a final long drag on his cigarette, then flipped it out into the wind. The seabirds swooped and dove as the flaming embers spiraled through their midst. One pair of birds ignored the object and soared right up to the foredeck where Aksell was and began speeding off in opposite directions. Something about them didn't appear exactly right. Not that he was any judge of such things, but birds...yeah, birds were a bit the same everywhere, and these were...somehow not. He watched them until they were out of sight behind the stacks of containers. Aksell was still alive because he noticed things, but this one's significance had not registered with him. Not yet anyway. Turning away from the view, he nodded to the captain and headed below deck to begin making final arrangements.

"Captain Rearden."

"Go for Rearden," he said to the unidentified caller.

"Hey, it's Jaz. A couple of things. One is, Charlie Team has Micah. They are all in pretty rough shape but safe. One of the guys has them hunkered down somewhere in Brooklyn."

"That's good, Jaz, and bad. They may need to get out of the city."

"Yeah, that's the other thing." She seemed confused as to how to proceed. "How are you doing?" she finally asked.

Cade was uncertain as to the nature of their...what, friendship, but answered as honestly as he could. "I'm tired, Jaz. All of us are exhausted, and we keep getting our collective asses handed to us by this glorified laptop."

She offered a small laugh.

"Whoa, go back. Have the drones circled back there?" he said, obviously speaking to someone else nearby.

"Look, I know you are busy. We have a lot going on here as well, and I'm not sure, but it seems like Doris is starting to panic. Riley says she met with Janus again. Something about that conversation freaked her out. No one knows what."

Even over the noise all around him, Cade could sense the concern in her voice. "That could be bad on a lot of levels. Suggest you talk to Riley. Alan, too, if he is up for it. I would think Stansfield and the nerd...what's his name, um, Lasko, any of them might have some ideas."

"Most of them are trying to find where Janus is hiding. Lasko seems to have a new idea."

"Well, we are just busy trying to put out fires up here. Big ass fires. Be nice to get ahead of him."

"Cade, the world is starting to go to hell. Not sure how to describe it, but reports of crazy shit are popping up everywhere. I think what you have there is just the tip of the iceberg."

"Copy that, Jaz."

"One more thing, too," she said. "We have, well, they have more of the message. Something important for all of us to know."

"What's that?" he asked.

Realizing he had too much going on, she decided to talk with him later. "Not the time to get into it—just call me when you get somewhere safe," she said.

He signed off, eyes glued to the image of the small helicopter perched on the deck of the ship in the distance. A helicopter on a ship that size was not extraordinary. They were often used, especially by the oil and gas industry, but this one seemed too small. More of a commuter or tourist bird. One of the customs guys also said most ships would keep choppers stowed in holds for an Atlantic crossing. Something else, though. He knew it was the analyst vying for control. "What?" he said under his breath.

The man, the analyst said. *The man at the rail, freeze, and zoom.* Cade made them do it, and he felt his bowels try to empty. Instantly, part of the mission briefing that had been uploaded into his brain was recalled, and this same man's image from so many angles at different times over the years. From Cryptus to an incident with Isabella, he was the one called the 'Hunter. It was in the updated briefing packet.' The

ReLoad recording and images briefly flashed a mental image that matched the face on the display.

"How long to the harbor?" Cade yelled to the navigator.

"Just over an hour."

He leaned out the window to yell to his men, "We need to board the *Sigas.* Something there doesn't add up."

Deuce nodded, and they quickly had the boat's pilot speeding ahead to catch back up to the massive ship.

68

Micah's eyes fluttered open with agonizing slowness like a newly hatched butterfly trying to stretch his wings out for the first time.

"Hey, bro, 'bout time you woke up."

Micah's face registered something that might be recognition; Alan couldn't really tell. "Hey, he's waking up....sorta."

Greg's voice was in his ear as O'Brien appeared in the doorway of the small room. "On my way, Alan, but the city seems to be going crazy. People and cars everywhere...what does sorta mean?"

"I think he's coming out of it, finally," Alan responded, checking Micah's pulse and vitals as Riley had shown him. His friend's eyes were dull and unfocused, but Alan told himself that was just the cocktail of drugs they'd given him. "You still in there, man? Hey, Micah...time to wake up."

Alan glanced up from the bed to the soldier. "How's Willy?"

O'Brien shrugged. "Coffee is fine, being a little bitch about his boo-boo, but you know."

Alan didn't know but assumed that meant he was complaining. He did have a broken arm, although it had been set and was in an emergency air-cast. O'Brien had tried to get both the Sergeant and Micah into a nearby hospital and later, a smaller clinic. Both had been overrun treating the victims of other violence in the city. Riley had eventually convinced them she and Doctor Han could provide remote treatment just as effectively, so they had come here—the nearby home of O'Brien's grandmother, who had recently been moved into a nursing home.

Alan was still coming down from the adrenaline rush of the rescue mission and the destruction of lives he was responsible for, but he was pretty sure Riley's remote treatment for his concussion had also included something to help numb the emotional response. The spacious home was older and on a quiet street in a residential section of Queens near Kissena Park. The group hunkered down inside had been monitoring the searches on land and at sea by the rest of the teams. Dee had kept each informed on the action Cade and Charlie were seeing. Coming up with nothing, the other members of Talon were beginning to regroup. "Looks like this is going to be the rally point," O'Brien said. "My nana will be pissed if any of you track in mud, though."

"I'd suggest putting an armed sentry on the steps to check boots before they enter," Alan said. "Seriously though, man, thanks for doing this. Not sure where we could have gone." Sitting on the side of the bed, Alan felt Micah's arm twitch. Looking down, he saw him moving his head slightly, eyes now scanning the space around them.

"Yeah," O'Brien said. "Glad I'm not a cop here anymore. The damn city is coming apart at the seams."

Alan was no longer listening, now focused totally on willing his friend back to health. Micah's gaze finally locked onto his friend's face. The eyes slowly seeming to register who he was. Alan thought he saw recognition, then what might have been a flash of anger. Guilt flooded through him once again. He wanted to apologize to Micah, he wanted to know what the deal was between him and Doris, but most of all, he wanted to know his friend was going to be okay.

Finally, with agonizing slowness, Micah's lips moved. The smallest of sounds escaped. Not words, not even a groan. More like air passing over loose papers. Alan leaned in closer; he could tell the concentration and effort Micah was putting into the effort. "Water?" he asked hopefully. His friend glanced up and gave something that might be a nod. He held the bottle to his lips. Micah sipped, paused, seemingly to need to martial strength before taking a deeper drink from the plastic bottle.

Alan had lots to say to his friend and even more questions to ask but ultimately decided to simply stay quiet and wait for Micah to break the silence.

"What's happening?" were his first words.

Alan knew he didn't mean it in a casual 'How are you doing?' kind of way. Micah wanted an actual update on the situation. Alan took ten minutes filling him in on everything since D.C. By the time he was done, Micah was sitting up slightly and had finished the water, asking for another.

"You feeling any better?" Alan asked, unscrewing the cap and passing over the water.

Micah downed a third of the bottle before speaking. "Think so, man. Head..." he motioned upward as he took another drink, "...fuzzy, pounding. And so damn thirsty."

"The doc said you might be. What all did they do to you?" Alan knew immediately it was an insensitive question for the adult he was becoming. The morbid curiosity was exactly what they would have asked each other in earlier days. Time had moved on from the carefree summer days of youth. The river they had played in then had moved on, fallen down many rocks and been swallowed up in an ocean.

Micah shook his head before thinking about it, "Don't know," he said in obvious pain. "Nothing much after the fight with those guys claiming to be feds."

A scuffle sounded from the front of the house, and moments later, Greg rushed in, dressed head to toe in black tactical gear sporting a plate identifying him as Homeland Security. Micah focused in. "Jesus, is it that bad out there? The country must be in bad shape if they put this clown on the front line."

"Shut-up, a-hole," Greg said stepping forward, pulling Micah into a not-so-gentle hug. The look on Micah's face spoke volumes. Pain, but mixed with relief.

"He's awake," Alan said quietly after tapping his CommDot.

"About time," Riley said, this time including Micah's friends in the response. "I'll give you guys five minutes, then I need a few minutes with the patient. After that, he probably needs to rest.

"Rest, hell, Alan says I have been unconscious for days. I need to know what I can do to help."

The first thing Micah had wanted to know was if Lasko was okay. Relieved, he'd then asked very inciteful questions of all of the ongoing ops, proving to Alan that Doris had been keeping him in the loop. "So, you and Doris...?" Alan asked awkwardly. "Why?"

Micah seemed very quiet. More than just reluctant to answer. "It's a long story, and I don't want to bore you guys," he finally said, unconvincingly.

Greg, for one, wasn't having it, though. "We thought you hated us, man. You just cut us all off. We were your friends."

The comment stung, and Alan knew in fairness that it wasn't exactly accurate. The truth was, they had been the ones who'd done that to him. They had refused to let him enter The Cove that day so many years ago. Obviously, Doris had made other plans for him, though.

"It gets complicated," Micah said. "There are things about me you guys don't know, and well, Doris and I both thought best that you didn't." He looked up, face showing a different kind of pain now. A deeper hurt. "It never meant we weren't friends, though. I'm really sorry. And...and thanks for coming to get me, whoever did that." He looked at Greg's outfit and guessed it was him.

Alan hadn't bothered to go into the nearly catastrophic rescue; that was information that could wait for another time.

Greg grinned. "No, this nerd got to be the hero on that one. See the black eye and goose-egg sized knot on the side of his head?"

"No way. You did that, Alan?"

"Okay, out!" The voice in their earbuds left no room for negotiation.

"Yes, Riles," Greg said, heading back out.

Alan went to exit as well, but Micah grabbed his arm. "Hey… thanks, man. And I'm sorry, I, I…you know. I couldn't."

Alan thought on this as he left. *Why couldn't he have told us? Was that what he even meant?*

69

It's almost a shame, Janus thought. Had Doris had an actual face, seeing her expression as he let her know he was closing in on her location would have been priceless. While a part of him did indeed wish for her to join him, he knew the odds of that were not high. Doris worked from a different playbook, and her allegiance to these humans was going to be her undoing. The conversation had been a fishing expedition, a hope if you will, that he pressure her into making a mistake, something that could narrow down her location even more.

By allowing her to take Lasko, he'd been able to track them despite her considerable countermeasures. First, to the airport outside the capital, and then by tracking the flight to Georgia. In reality, he'd not been able to track the flight—she had been too good at blocking it from radar or anything else truly useful. Through his more legitimate counter-part, Prime, he had access to a vast array of surveillance tools, though. One of these was with NOAA, the National Oceanic and Atmospheric Administration.

By using a weather satellite tasked to NOAA, and overlaying a more sensitive spectral data analysis, Janus had picked up faint heat signatures as the aircraft had taken off. The signature faded, presumably as the jet reached higher altitudes. His first move was to extrapolate out along the current course of the jet, but that direction led out of the country toward the open ocean. They'd obviously made course changes in flight, most likely multiple times. Ultimately, he had painstakingly searched for faint echoes of that same infra-red heat signature hoping to spot it during descent. Even with all the tools and processing speed he possessed, it had proven to be a Herculean challenge. He didn't care—winning was what mattered, and his opponent had slipped up. It would still take time to know her exact location, but it was a simple matter now. She was about to be his to take.

He and his growing network of autonomous proxies were well into the operation he had wryly dubbed 'Papercut.' The series of attacks was ramping up from nuisance to significant. Now he was finding it more effective just to watch what the people did on their own. For a species that routinely proclaimed how smart and independent they were, they possessed a remarkable level of predictable behavior and a proclivity to believe things they had no proof of. As such, manipulating them to do harm to others had proven woefully easy.

One of Janus's subroutines kept increasing its priority status until it could no longer be ignored. Bringing it into his full presence allowed the data to pass more rapidly. Before he had assimilated the troubling data, a second, and then a third proxy also began adjusting priorities to gain attention. *Perhaps there is still more fun to be had,* he thought, seeing all of the alerts going off across his neural network. "Yes, my dear Shakespeare," he offered rare utterance to one of the more unique and perhaps less simple-minded humans. "The Game's Afoot."

70

The Cove

"Doris, the captain's team just identified one of Janus's people aboard a large tanker ship heading to New York."

A response was not forthcoming for several seconds. "Yes, Riley, I know Aksell, the same one that Izzy identified from Cryptus. No doubt he has that ship rigged. I…I am open to ideas."

"Doris, is everything okay?"

The AI didn't respond. Riley had flashbacks to the early days when Doris had gone offline for days. She opened a channel to the others explaining something was wrong. "Senior staff, please come to the hub."

Riley was surprised to see Margaret Stansfield already sitting at the meeting table. She was reviewing something from one of the handheld tablets. Jimmy came in and sat down heavily, Izzy and Jaz trickling in behind. Several others, including Doctor Schweiger and lastly, Jim Lasko arrived. Doctor Han was absent, but that wasn't too unusual. Doris also still had not responded, so Riley started out describing what was going on with the teams in New York. "In short, this tanker is already too close. If it blows now, it will take out several other ships and all of Cade's people."

"Cade knew the risk, dear," Margaret interjected. "The country is deteriorating into chaos, and unfortunately, that ship is just one of many issues that need to be dealt with. The bigger question to me is what is going on with Doris?"

Jimmy looked at Lasko, some unspoken thing seemed to pass between the two. "Doris is hunting and probably being hunted," the older man finally said. "My guess is that it is using nearly all of her available resources right now."

"Why didn't she let us know—that was reckless," Riley shot back.

Jimmy leaned forward. "It couldn't wait, Riles. You know how she's been since she and Janus met last. If I didn't know better, I would guess she is afraid he knows about this place. Knows where she lives, where...we all live." He side-eyed Lasko again and the man gave a tiny nod. "Lasko gave Doris an idea, something she could look for and possibly use to track Janus back to his core."

"What would that have been, Jim?" the director asked very matter-of-factly.

"Bits of her own code," Jim said with a wry grin. "I got to thinking about it after we talked last week when she edited Prime's code so we could enable him for distribution. I had a feeling she might have used some of her own or at least code written in her own specific language. Only young Jimmy here fully knows her coding, so I asked for his assistance."

"Surely Janus would have erased any signs of that long ago," Izzy said.

"Maybe, possibly even, but it was the only lead I could think of. Remember how this snippet of code replaced whatever Cryptus integrated onto that chip? That was hidden from the AI. I was fairly certain some of Doris's edits once installed might be invisible to the entity as well."

Jimmy took over, as the scientist seemed to be drifting, "Short answer is, I came up with a search solution with Doris's help. Unfortunately, we needed relatively direct access to Janus to see if it worked. The proxies he mostly uses don't carry that bit of code since they are basically like dumb terminals just relaying data back. Janus's or Prime's core O/S and any backups would be the only place they could be found."

"So, when Doris met with Janus, you did something to help her track him?" Izzy said jumping ahead of the rest of them.

"Yes, she flooded the surrounding network connections with millions of her intelligent agents all tasked with one very specific search. A fragment of that tiny code," Lasko said.

"And?" Margaret asked.

"And, nothing," Jimmy said. "Not immediately, at least, but looking at her firewalls and processing activity..." He sat the tablet down he'd been using. "One or more of them must have had success. Doris has to be closing in, but it also looks like it may just be a matter of time before Janus finds The Cove."

Jaz stood, quickly looking around the group in horror. "How can you people be so calm? Do you not know what he can do if he finds us?"

"We know," Margaret said, her bandaged arms, bruises and new scars underlining her words in a way that no one could argue. She motioned to the 4D displays showing the scene in New York as well as news feeds from other hot spots around the world. "This is war. The battleground is not just out there. We must be ready to fight our own battles."

A small portion of Doris, far smaller even than one of the 'Dee' processes, monitored what was happening at The Cove as well as in New York, but they were low priority concerns at the moment. The truth was, Doris was now occupied on all fronts, defending herself from online attacks taking the form of tiny bits of code that seemed intent on tracking, then tagging itself to her. These robbed her of energy and offered a way for Janus to trace back her processes to the origin point. She knew these v-bits to be part of Janus's defense system, a type of swarm virus that could zero in on specific processes. As her search agents had closed in on him, his own defenses were triggered. Neither seemed to have the ability to land a killing blow since the host server for both remained hidden for now. All that either could do was become inactive for a time. The v-bits had to quickly acquire a host, or they simply ceased due to lack of power.

The parasitic weapon was only one aspect of the exchange with Janus. He, too, was facing an onslaught of digital snares designed to limit or even trap him permanently behind a firewall perimeter. Doris had enacted a clever series of port blocking algorithms that seemed far more intelligent than should have been possible. She had obviously tracked his protection schemes back to its home servers, a specific range of IP addresses and now, was systematically shutting each one down to isolate him.

In an online exchange, Janus should have easily had the upper hand. He'd been designed as a hunter of sentient code. His arsenal of offensive weaponry was substantial, but Doris had batted most things away with minimal effort. It was becoming very obvious to him that she was significantly more advanced in many ways than himself. She had made an error, though; he had made sure to isolate himself from the servers where his defenses were housed. While she could close them off, she would be no closer to finding him. He sacrificed his swarm army of bots and withdrew into an enclave where he could operate with more impunity.

Stepping up the attacks on the humans would bring Doris back out into the open. She wanted to trap him—he had a plan to do the same to her.

71

New York

Cade realized almost immediately the futility of the situation. Despite years of faithfully watching pirate movies, boarding a ship at sea was virtually impossible. Especially when it was as large as the *Sigas Alegus* and one that was traveling at near maximum power. The harbor patrol boat was impressive until you compared it to the tanker. From water-line to the main deck was a sheer cliff of over a hundred feet of black metal. At the base of that cliff was a churning maelstrom of water displaced by the movement of the massive ship, a churning chasm ranging from about two meters midship where they were, to three times that up closer to the bow, which prevented them from pulling alongside.

"Not even Somali pirates could board this thing, man," Deuce said, staring up.

"Could we fire lines, hook a rail?" McTee asked with way too much enthusiasm for what he was proposing.

"Not a movie, cowboy. You'd be at the mercy of that pissed off bull. Plus, we don't have anything to fires lines like that," Deuce said dismissively.

Cade had been attempting to call Doris with no luck. "Come on, guys, think, we need a solution. Dee, you have anything?"

"Harbor pilots can board at speed. Although the *Sigas Alegus* is making about ten knots faster than what would be considered safe," the little AI said.

"Where would they board? I don't see any access hatches in the hull. Would they lower a gangway?" Cade asked.

"Depends on the hull configuration—often the crew will lower a rope ladder. Hold while I attempt to access the plans for this ship."

The delay seemed interminable, but soon she was back. "The *Sigas* is so large it has a gangway and rope ladder for normal access, but there is a secondary procedure that is used in some boarding. A small open deck about halfway up on the bow of the ship is required mainly for certain canal crossings. The watertight bulkhead hatches of sea deck are rarely opened otherwise, but a breaching charge would allow access."

The team members all looked to where the disembodied voice was indicating. "Holllly Shhiittt!" Deuce said.

Through the crashing waves and roiling spray, they could just make out a small area of the bow that was different than the other. It was tiny, completely unnoticeable, until they knew where to look. "God Almighty," Cade said. "Please tell me there's another way." The water crashed furiously against the hull of the ship and nowhere was it worse than at the bow. The storms had blown the sea into huge rollers, and with each of these, the ship's bow crashed down like a monster intent on revenge.

Cade activated the tactical goggles overlaying the blueprint outline of the ship. The tiny sea deck was right in the heart of all that madness. Depending on the vessel's position in the waves, it was seventy-five feet above the water one second, and nearly touching the next. "No way, Dee. Any chance we can get a chopper? Check with the navy?"

"I'm sorry, Nomad. Many of my eternal systems are unavailable to me right now, but there are no fixed-winged craft close enough to reach you before the ship enters New York City waters."

Cade looked again into the massive waves crashing against the front of the ship, then to his men, shaking his head. "All the cool tech from The Cove and nothing to help right now. Remind me to get Doris working on some jet packs for next time." *Yeah, next time,* Gus said with a laugh. Cade did not need the voice of common sense talking to him right now. Ducking into the cabin of the pilot boat, he explained to a disbelieving driver what he intended to do. This man ferried harbor pilots out to board ships like this every day, in all kinds of weather, yet he was terrified of what was being proposed. The truth was, so was Cade, but that was his job. "We have to get on that ship. Now!"

It took some additional persuasion, and Cade thought he might have to pull a gun on the man. But once the truth of the amount of potential destruction to the city was explained, the captain nodded determinedly. "We will only get one shot at this," Cade told the other two a few minutes later. "The pilot thinks he can keep our boat near the bow for only twenty seconds max. McTee, since you like roping shit, you are in charge of attaching a line to that rail. Since there is only space on that deck for two of us, Deuce and I will board."

The rolling of the boat was already getting worse, and jets of water were blasting off the bow as the pilot was already moving forward alongside the tanker. "How are you guys going to blow the hatch?" McTee said. "Ain't no place to get out of the way."

"We're okay on that," Deuce said, patting his pack. "One of our little party favors is a directional blasting patch—works wonders and hardly any blast back." Then he grinned and added, "In theory."

As the pilot boat maneuvered in, it was pitching up and down ten meters or more. At times, the bow waves caught it, causing it to go nearly vertical. The experienced pilot was truly unbelievable in his ability to gauge the swells and keep the solid little boat from being swept under the mighty hull. Cade was watching, though, as the boat continued to work in closer and closer. Several times, they actually rubbed against the *Sigas* with a grinding sound that all of them assumed meant the end, but each time, the pilot would accelerate just enough to squirt from beneath the ship's downward plunge.

McTee held the modified shotgun used normally to send mooring lines. He knew he would only get one shot, and the rappelling hook they'd attached would bounce off if he hit anything but the railing of the sea deck. The pilot sounded the horn to mean this was as close as he could get. The twenty-second countdown was on.

The movement of the ocean and the two ships made the entire operation seem completely impossible, but Dee was calculating many of the variables and signaled McTee when and where to fire. The rappelling hook landed true, locking against one of the support rails, and Nomad and Deuce flung themselves out of the pilot craft and onto the rope as the smaller craft quickly pulled away.

Deuce was lower and spent the first minute completely submerged in the Atlantic while Cade was out of the water but slammed hard against the hull. The high-tech body armor did the job, but it still jolted his entire body. Neither man bothered to try and speak, it was all they could do just to hang on to the slick rappelling rope. Cade managed to get his feet braced against the hull of the ship. He could feel the vibrations through the metal as the sea attempted to stop the massive beast. He could sense the power all around him, like hanging out under Niagara Falls. That is, if the falls were moving at nearly thirty knots across open ocean and could also explode at any moment. *Yep, just exactly like that.*

Slowly, Cade managed to pull one hand loose and move it up the rope, then another. Between breaths, he saw his friend emerge from the dark waters below doing much the same. He had the idle thought of how ridiculous it was that he and Charlie, two ex-army rangers, were doing this. *Isn't this shit exactly the crap navy seals trained for?* He'd have to manage the team dynamics better next time. *Yeah, next time.* "Shut the fuck up, Gus," he said aloud just as he got a hand on the bottom rail of the deck.

Calling the tiny island of rusty metal grating a 'deck' was being way too generous. In total, it was barely two feet wide and less than eight feet in length. It clung to the neck of the massive ship like a starving, remora cleaning parasite from its beast-master. As soon as Cade was on it, though, he let out a sigh of relief. He then began assisting his XO by anchoring his foot against the railing and pulling hard on the rope.

Soon, the drowned rat formerly known as Charlie Taylor came sliding over the rusty metal rail.

Both men stood for a second catching their breath and watching the incredible view as the ocean seemed to rise up in front of them like a watery mountain, then to disappear in the depths below. “I...don’t... ever...want to...do anything...like...that again,” Charlie said coughing up water and struggling to take in enough air.

“With you on that, brother. What say we blow this hatch and go say hello?”

72

The explosive patch made a muffled sound, and minutes later, they found themselves in the dimly lit bowels of the ship. Both sounds and movement from outside were muted here. Cade adjusted his earbuds to magnify the ambient sounds. Distant sounds of the engine, liquid flowing through pipes, creaking of metal, but no voices, no sounds of magazines being slipped into weapons. Nothing that would indicate the potential dangers within.

Using hand signals only, he directed Deuce to move out along a preplanned route. His job was to search for the explosives. Cade's was to gain access to the bridge and ship's control. Not like he had the faintest idea on how to control a ship. The closest he'd ever come was piloting a rigid-hull inflatable they'd used for a few covert missions in the jungles of South America looking for drug runners.

Cade tracked Deuce's location in his goggles while using them to navigate the labyrinthian maze of piping and corridors. Reaching the base of a set of stairs beneath what sounded like a massive and noisy air handler, he risked asking Dee if she was back in touch with Doris yet. The answer was a very disappointing no. Covering his face to trap the sound, Cade whispered, "Listen, Dee, we are going to need help out here. Warn the city officials, but get us something out here to help."

"Copy that, Nomad."

A short time later, he heard Charlie's familiar voice, "Hey, Nomad, shouldn't a ship this size have...oh, I don't know...people maybe?"

Cade was just entering the lowest of the crew decks now; the overhead lighting was brighter, temperature more comfortable. "Yeah, Deuce. Creepy, isn't it? I was thinking the same thing." Pulling up the manifest in his goggles, he added, "Yeah, should have about thirty-five crew and seven officers. Stay alert, man."

Charlie acknowledged. "Dee, any chance I can get you a hard line to a data port or something, and you tell me what's going on here?"

"This ship type uses a decentralized management system, and my capabilities are sadly more limited than Doris's actually. Once on the bridge, or maybe engine bay, I can be of assistance but probably little help until then." She paused, then added, "Nomad, you are eighteen minutes from entering New York waterway. They are sending out a fleet of tugs to push the *Sigas* away from the harbor."

Cade sensed his little assistant had more. "But?"

"If you can't stop the ship's engines, the tugs won't be able to turn it away in time. The vice president has ordered the air force to engage and destroy the ship before allowing it in. Fighter-bombers have already been scrambled to intercept you."

"Well, fuck, how good to hear. Deuce, you get that? Move your ass, man." He dropped the need for stealth. Weapon out, he raced down the corridors and steps to upper decks. Passing by a door marked Galley/Mess, he detected an odor he knew far too well. Instead of looking in, he keyed his CommDot and kept running. "Think I found the crew; they are not going to be a problem for us."

"I think I found something, too," Charlie said. "Sending you a pic —tell me what you think this is."

The image appeared in the goggles, and Cade slowed to examine it. Hard to study the image and not run into walls. The device was about the size of a basketball but appeared completely mechanical, no explosives, no readouts, but it definitely looked out of place. It was new, while the plating it was on was old, weathered and had been repainted numerous times.

"I see another one in the distance, "Charlie added. "Probably one on each of the cargo tanks, but the scanner is picking up no sign of explosives."

Dee spoke up, "In its liquid state, the gas is not flammable. Most likely the device Deuce has found is intended to puncture the tanks allowing the contents to aerosol back into its flammable gaseous state."

"And then?" Cade asked, already fearing the answer.

"The cargo hold of the ship is mostly weathertight. It can hold an enormous volume of the gas— once discharged—then any ignition source could ignite it all at once."

Her response was devoid of emotion but caused Cade's internals to liquify. "Deuce, any chance you can remove or disable the devices?" He glanced at his watch and added, "In the next fifteen minutes?"

"No way, Cade, these things look to be bonded in place. No bolts, no welds to break, but it's a sealed unit, no way to get into that I can tell."

Cade was one floor below the bridge wing now, debating his next move. "Fuck it, XO, head to engineering. If I can't get the course changed, I may need you to disable the engines. Assume these tanks are going to cook off, though. Be off this ship before that happens. Do you read me?"

Deuce, obviously running now, came back with a breathless, "Read you, Boss."

"No," Cade said. "Charlie, I mean it, don't wait for me. I am setting a timer on your heads-up. Be off this ship before it hits zero. McTee is out there and can pick you up if you have to get wet."

"Roger that, Nomad—be safe, brother."

Cade entered the bridge wing quietly, seeing no one in the outermost section. Charts lining the tables, held in place by heavy iron weights and numerous displays, indicated this was the navigation section. On a large screen, he saw a map indicating what New Yorkers referred to as 'The Narrows' quickly approaching. The intersection of the upper and lower bay and what Dee had indicated was the point of no return, the Verrazano-Narrows Bridge. Beyond that, and the destruction of the ship would level much of the lower portion of Manhattan and cause significant damage to the New Jersey side as well.

Cade heard the sound of voices ahead and moved quietly in that direction. His foot caught on something and looking down, he registered the unmoving body of a large man wearing what he assumed was a ship officer's shirt. A dark, angry hole filled with drying blood in the side of the skull was a solid reason for the lack of movement. Peering around a bulkhead, he could see the main control room, the vacant helm, as well as the vista of the storm and ravaged sea beyond. His earbud chimed, and he ducked quickly back to listen to the report.

"We have another problem, Nomad. Be advised there is some type of rudder lock in place. Accessing the auxiliary guidance system is having a null effect," Deuce said.

Cade couldn't risk speaking, so simply signaled an acknowledgment with a mic click.

Determining his course of action, he dropped low, weapon held in high-ready and moved quickly into the control room in the direction of the voices. *At least*, that was what he recalled telling his body to do. Instead, he basically duck-walked about three steps before feeling a heavy object impact the side of his head. The sensation of falling was immediate, but strangely landing on the decking was more distant. Looking up, he saw the weather-beaten face from the video. The man Izzy had called the 'Hunter.' The man was holding a large metal wrench and looking at him with a strange expression, something indicating surprise, between humor and maybe just resignation. Instead of delivering a killing blow, he delivered a punishing kick. Cade felt himself slipping down a tunnel into the darkness maybe to unconsciousness, then he knew...it was something much worse.

The barbarian inside was waking up. Not in fits and starts as one might expect from a latent and mostly buried personality, but fully formed and ready to battle evil in all its forms. It, and it was indeed an 'it,' was not subject to the pains of its host. Cade may be withering under a violent blow to the head and likely cracked ribs, but the brute he was becoming felt none of that.

His moves were calculated and efficient. Reaching out to the still retreating kick, he grabbed Aksell tightly around the ankle, then snapped down and back in the opposite direction wrenching the ligaments and joint in opposing directions. The killer bellowed in rage and swung the heavy tool down in a blow meant to cleave a skull in two. Instead, Cade swung legs up catching the lower arm at the full extension of the killing arc. A satisfying snap echoed around the room.

Cade stood to his feet, watching through eyes that he no longer controlled. The goggles, somehow still in place, indicated twelve minutes remaining. On the display, he could also see a line of five dots he took to be the super powerful tugs Dee had mentioned moving into position along the port side.

Aksell was injured but far from helpless. He'd never encountered one such as the soldier he now fought, but he was just a man. A man that would die just like all other opponents he'd ever faced. He reached for a sniper rifle, the same one he'd used in D.C., but it slipped from his grasp and toppled to the floor. Drawing his sidearm instead, he took aim, but before he could squeeze the trigger, something hard careened off his head. Cade had almost been unaware of grabbing the heavy weight as he passed the chartroom. But the barbarian had let it fly with the precision of a Roger Clemens knuckleball. It connected just over Aksell's right eye in a spray of blood.

Both men, now injured and enraged, charged one another, and a sudden sideways lurch of the ship caused them both to miss. Cade could feel a vibration moving up through the decking and knew it must be the tugs.

"Nomad, the cargo tanks have been pierced—gas is escaping into the hold," Deuce said.

Cade wanted to tell his friend to get out, to leave now, but had no more control of his voice than he did his arms and legs. The barbarian was in control now, and nothing else mattered. Nothing but punishing the man scrambling around the floor for his gun. Cade's leg delivered a vicious kick, snapping the man's head back. Aksell recovered far faster than should have been humanly possible and lashed out with his uninjured leg, catching Cade in the groin. Cade wept in silent pain as the barbarian smiled, which seemed to unhinge the Norwegian killer more than anything else thus far.

The very personal battle on the bridge showed no signs of abating, both men delivering what should have been killing blows multiple times. A roundhouse kick threw Aksell hard against a control station where Cade just noticed a large sweaty man standing. The man, possibly the ship's captain, was furiously pulling levers and turning knobs in obvious frustration. The enraged Aksell struggled back to standing on his one good leg and angrily backhanded the captain away from the controls. By the unusual angle of the neck, Cade could tell the man was dead before he even hit the deck. Aksell turned back and now, was somehow holding the handgun again, or maybe it was a different one. Cade didn't know, and the barbarian just didn't care.

"Bombers are inbound, Nomad. I am exiting rear side hatchway now."

Cade clearly heard Deuce's warning, but he was just a passenger now. He and the killer sailing down the river Styx toward what must be an inevitable fiery end. The *Sigas Alegus* would be an impressive funeral pyre for them both. He found his mind wandering as he watched the fight. That fucking Nordic soldier was probably of Viking descent. Dying gloriously in a fiery battle to reach Valhalla would likely be the perfect exit for the man.

Slowly, he became aware of Dee speaking to him. Just as Aksell pulled the trigger, he recognized the difference in voice. That occurred to him around the same time as, "Oh shit, I'm about to be shot."

Perhaps sensing his own mortality, the barbarian launched himself upward, the bullet impacting harmlessly off the thickest part of the lightweight composite body armor. Aksell looked on, confused, expecting to see the combatant falling away dead. Things were not going as predicted. Control would undoubtedly be upset if he lost this round. Apparently having had enough fun, Cade/barbarian plucked the sniper rifle from where it had fallen and charged toward a confused Aksell.

Gus was yelling, *Safety off, pull the trigger, you ignorant bastard!* Cade was very much thinking the same but unable to give voice after ceding control to the beast within. The barbarian had no intention of shooting the man, he simply rammed the barrel through Aksell's neck, severing his spinal cord as it horrifically exited the backside pinning him to a computer station behind.

The assassin didn't die, not all at once, but was paralyzed. He took no warrior's glory as death approached. His expression was more sorrow and regret but also, some small token of pleasure just possibly in the knowledge that at least it wouldn't be from cancer.

Doris's voice was in Cade's head as it must have been for several minutes already. The actual Doris not the watered-down Dee. "Deuce managed to get me access to the control systems and steering, but I cannot vent enough of the gas in time. It is going to blow—you must get away. Hold onto your SmartCom, and I will guide you."

Dazed, and still not fully back in control, he exited onto the bridge wing. The New York skyline was just emerging from the wall of gray mist. He saw several of the tugs pulling away and back toward the city.

"Jets are less than five minutes out. I am trying to move the *Sigas* out of the main shipping lane."

"Wh...where do I go?" he asked weakly. "I can't jump, that would kill me, too."

She indicated what direction he should go, along the main deck, toward midship. He knew he was walking atop a ticking bomb. Any gas nearing any open circuit, a light bulb, a computer, could trigger the initial blast. Following her guidance, he stumbled up the last few steps, then pulled up short as he saw the ugly squat thing sitting on the deck. "That?" he said in disbelief. "I can't fly a helicopter!"

Even as the words left his mouth, he knew that was not entirely true. Slipping into the right seat, he began activating switches and spinning up rotors like he'd been flying for years. The SmartCom in his hand, he realized Doris had loaded the knowledge of how to fly while he'd been working his way over.

As it turned out, she'd only had time for a very rudimentary version via the ReLoad technology, but the little chopper was clear of the deck and moving swiftly away before the cutting edge F-35s moved into range. Slowly, the giant ship began to move away from the assigned route and back toward open water. Several of the tugs remained on station running on autopilots while all personnel evacuated to two of the tugs moving rapidly back to safe harbor.

"The pilots have laser lock on the target, Nomad." Doris relayed.

He inherently knew this meant to get behind cover or, even better, get down on the ground. The nimble little chopper handled the weather like a champ but would be swatted from the sky like a mosquito if the *Sigas* cooked off. "Doris, are Deuce and McTee out of danger?" he asked weakly, just as terrain under the little chopper changed from water to land.

"Yes, they are moving away at speed. Several large bulk haulers about seven miles downrange they can cover behind." She paused briefly then added, "Missiles are away, take care, Cade."

He slammed the control cyclic down in a last-ditch effort to get the craft on the ground behind a series of large sand dunes. Just as the skid touched, the sky to the east lit up as the missiles impacted.

The *Sigas Alegus's* final moments were of being propelled completely out of the water before its cargo hold was ripped wide, and each of the cargo tanks full of liquid gas boiled off, instantly fueling the roiling inferno exploding out in all directions.

Cade clumsily tried to unstrap and dive away from the chopper and into the sand just as the blast wave passed over. In truth, he only partially unstrapped before the chopper was tossed like a child's toy. His battered body was numb from the fight, landing and assorted trauma of the day. He felt, more than heard, the overpressure wave, the noise and power moving over and around. Wind mixed with fire and debris whipped past in a cyclone of destruction. Vaguely, he watched as a nearby beach condo was flattened by the blast. Cars were flipped aside like playthings. His eyes drifted back in the direction of his salvation, the tiny chopper, only to realize it, too, had vanished. While New York City proper might be spared, much of the coast and Long Island would likely have massive damage. *We did all we could. We saved lives, but will it be enough? Will it make any real difference?*

Lying more under the ground now than on it, Cade tasted blood and wet sand. He hated bullies, all those who wielded power at the expense of others. Battered and abused, his mind was closing down, and, as always, he saw things. Not tangible things, but more akin to pictures out in the firmament. Like walking with a weak flashlight through a dark house. The beam would bring something from out in the shadows for just a second before winking out just at the moment of clarity.

Memories are funny things; it is how your brain paints over the events of a life. How it tries to catalog and curate them into a meaningful existence. Cade knew his own were not that way. They were raw, angry and deep. The wounds that wracked his body paled to those in his mind—those were the ones that came swimming up from the depths, often, like now, without warning. Images of lavender cornflowers, a ratty doll that he knew had been loved by one who called her Mrs. Bailey, and tangles of bright, silky blonde hair, hair speckled with flecks of crimson.

He couldn't move—maybe wouldn't move. He clawed space in the wet dirt to breathe or maybe to give up. A part of him knew he wasn't dead, but he was not quite alive either. Most of him had died a lifetime ago outside that small town in the Ozarks. The images continued to flood his fractured mind: him cradling his sister's broken body, silent tears dripping down his chin as he limped slowly toward the broken down little town, her body cradled gently in his arms. One look at her had let him know she was dead—the abuse and damage the boys had inflicted on her tiny body was too much. The other... 'things' they'd done...that she wouldn't have likely recovered from anyway.

More images: his mom sitting on a sofa holding a smoldering cigarette unable to even acknowledge what had happened. The idiot policeman who kept patting him on the head and smiling. That ridiculous grin pasted on his face right up to the moment they loaded him into the dark station wagon. He hadn't cared; he cared for nothing at that moment except finding those who had stolen away from him the one person who did matter.

That night, they'd driven him first to a shelter, and then on to the first of the foster homes. That day, in that exact moment, he'd become the Nomad, not years later. What existed now was just the latest iteration, one more way of punishing himself for not being strong enough to protect her...to save his Amy. Listening again to the carnage raining down around him, he knew he'd never been good at the saving. His true value came later, in the avenging.

73

Queens, NYC

"Holy Mother of God!" O'Brien said, crossing himself as he stared out the window over the sink.

Coffee sat nearby as the entire house was bathed in brilliant light as if lightning had struck close, yet this light went on and on. "Get down, you damn fool!" he yelled just before the window, and then much of the wall, was punched in as if a giant fist had slammed it. O'Brien had dodged the breaking glass, but the blast threw him back into the next room. Coffee dove onto the floor; most of the others in the house did much the same. They'd been listening in via SmartComs and earbuds to what was going on several miles out in the Atlantic.

"Shit, did the CO get out?" Coffee yelled out to anyone as he slowly picked himself out of what previously had been a coffee table.

The house was several miles from the coast, yet it received considerable damage. Up and down the street, car and home alarms were going off. Trees were down, power was out and people could be heard yelling for help. O'Brien stumbled in looking bewildered, blood streaking the front of his shirt red and a piece of wood lodged in the thick part of his left bicep. “Man, glad Nana wasn’t here for this.” His legs went wobbly and he dropped to one knee before Coffee got to him and lifted him to his feet with his uninjured arm.

“Come on, man, I got you. Let’s go find the medic.”

The other man winced. “Hey, Willy, you think it’s too late to turn down this job offer?”

Coffee grinned. “Will you shut-up, city boy, you just talking crazy shit now.” The Sergeant yelled out for Captain Nance, but she was already busy treating others. Alan and Greg came out of the bedroom half carrying their friend Micah. Coffee could see daylight and part of a neighbor’s house on the other side of the room where a wall should have been. “You guy’s okay?” They nodded numbly.

The commanding voice of Lieutenant Maratelli cut through the chaos, “Gather the injured and move to the backyard, people. Chances are, broken gas lines, and we may have live power lines down. Be careful, but move your asses away from the house.” Clouds of dust and smoke filled the air, but slowly, all the occupants made it to the backyard. Injuries were mostly minor, but the house was almost definitely a total loss. Alan leaned back against the rusted leg of an ancient swing set. “Jesus, look at that.” His arm motioned in the general direction of the street. Up and down the quiet little road, house after house had major damage, many already collapsed. People were spilling out into the street; some were dragging unmoving bodies of loved ones. He touched his earbud just as they heard another explosion, closer this time—significant, but nowhere near the strength of the prior one.

“What the hell was that?” Alan asked. No one else sitting there had any more of an idea than he did. “Nomad, you there?” No response. “Doris, you know what’s going on around us?” No response.

“Dee, you there?”

“I am here, Tiger-1. The situation is a bit too dynamic at the moment to give much in the way of detail. The explosion of the tanker has left a tremendous arc of devastation. Undoubtedly, loss of life will be heavy, although far less than if it had made it into port.”

Alan noticed she was back to using his combat call sign, one he was still uncomfortable with but that indicated they were responsible for their own safety and care. He also realized more action was likely. He looked over at his friends, who seemed to have fared better than a number of the team members. "You guys okay?" They both nodded. Micah, for one, seemed to have snapped completely out of the stupor he'd been in. Holding a SmartCom, Alan realized he was zooming in on something.

"Well, crap."

"What is it, Micah?

"That second explosion, it was at a warehouse across the river. The address indicates it as a secure server farm."

They all knew server farms were massive structures running all types of high-end computer servers. They were responsible for many of the eCommerce, web sites, blog pages, as well as automated data back-ups, or mirrors, for the corporate world. Alan shook his head, "Let me guess, this is the backup for those companies in the financial district?"

Micah clicked a few keys and nodded slowly. "Yeah, much..." He read more, scrolling up with a finger. "Most of them warehouse transaction data at this site. It's co-located with another on the West Coast which, wait for it....was also just destroyed."

Greg wasn't following along with the conversation. "What does this mean?"

Several other team members had moved closer to the boys now as well. Micah looked at Alan to take the lead. "Okay, let me see if I can unpack this for you. All this," he paused, looking around, "All the death, the destruction was to prevent this from happening." He pointed down at the SmartCom. "Janus won this round."

"But the ship, it never made it into the bay," a female voice said.

"The financial district is probably unscathed," O'Brien added.

"Despite that, our economy is about to collapse." Alan continued, "Janus loves misdirection, and, in this case, it was layer upon layer of misdirection. Most of the U.S. currency doesn't exist in physical form, not normally at least. It is ones and zeros in a computer center somewhere. A lot of those computers just got toasted." Alan felt very self-conscious staring at the dirty, bloodied faces looking back at him, but they needed to know the truth. “It could have been worse, much worse, but...this is probably bad enough. We didn’t stop him, not really.”

Lieutenant Maratelli stepped up beside Alan. “Who here is still mission capable?”

Most of the elite soldiers raised their hands. Many, like O’Brien, still had blood flowing freely from their wounds. “Idiots,” she said under her breath. “I should know better than ask that. Okay, Captain Nance and I are going to pick out a team—we will take two of the Battlewagons.” She glanced over to where they had been parked and saw several were on their side, one was upside down. She amended with, “We will roll a couple of them over and then take them. The remainder of you get treatment, then help as many people in the immediate areas as you can. We will leave you most of the medical supplies.”

She pieced together nearly one complete team, including Greg, Micah and Alan. As the most skilled medic, Captain Nance stayed behind. “Let’s go get our people,” Maratelli said as they tossed the last gear bag into the now upright SUV.

Margaret Stansfield had been on the phone with the president off and on throughout the morning. Both of them were still so far off the radar as to be presumed dead. The president, however, had reemerged enough to retain command authority and to pass commands down through his vice president. The VP was a bit of a cowboy but played off his more conservative boss in a way that worked for all. He was still out of the loop as far as knowing about Janus.

“Mister President,“ Margaret said, feeling the gravity of each word as it slid off her tongue. “If we do this, it will inflame an already fragile public. Yes, sir, I do agree and feel it is the only option we have remaining, but yes, in many ways, it is the ‘nuclear’ option.”

They spoke for a number of minutes more before she disconnected, leaned back and sighed loudly.

Doris had spawned a copy of herself during one of the brief reprieves in the online battle with Janus. It was only partially as capable as her current incarnation. It was also missing any of the alien message or knowledge of what it contained. This version spoke first to Margaret and the near empty room, "He is agreeable to the solution?"

"Agreeable is imprecise, as the man wants no part of it but understands that it may be our fail-safe. If nothing else works, I have been given the authority to shut down all networked communication in the United States."

Sitting at the far end of the table, Riley shook her head. "This isn't China, we shut off the Internet and people are going to go crazy."

"They already are," Doris said. "I, and by that, I mean, of course, the other Doris, has Janus tracked back to a server block that is most likely his stronghold. Unfortunately, he has most likely already tracked her back here. It is only a matter of time before weapons are launched, and real-world attacks are planned on The Cove."

"Shutting off the Internet will stop that?" the only remaining person in the room asked.

"No, Isabella, it won't. But it will stop Janus from gaining access to what he most wants," Doris answered. While she didn't have access to the message archives, she knew its value to everyone, including Janus. She also knew how to destroy it—the last thing she'd been prepped for.

"We are expendable, Izzy," Margaret said, scratching at her still bandaged arms. "If that damn message is retrieved by Janus then... well, we are all doomed anyway."

"How much more can we survive? He's managed to rip the country apart!" Riley slammed her phone down on the table. "Currency trading has just been suspended, as is stock trading—now news that banking computers worldwide are crashing. Our tactical teams are in pieces, New York City just had a chunk blasted out of it. Social media is blowing up with this Patriots Unite crap—we are a powder keg that is one lit match away from annihilation." Tears filled her eyes, pushing away the anger just beneath. "Doris, much of my life has been here with you, dedicated to helping you and, well, the thing." She didn't know how else to refer to what would be just a blank spot to the modified AI. "It's too important to destroy, I think maybe we should just let him have it if that's the only way to keep it intact."

"We've discussed that before and ruled it out, Riley. Janus has made his plans well known to me. His vision for the future doesn't include humans. Whatever the 'thing' is, I am quite confident it would simply allow him to see that future sooner rather than later. Besides that, my programming will allow no compromise on this. The other Doris had to ensure I would eliminate the data and myself if he breaches our local firewall."

"So, it would be gone...as well as you? No, Doris, no..."

74

"It's really just a sophisticated BGP exploit," Doris's subroutine went on. "You know, the Border Gateway Protocol. We can use it to shunt all Internet traffic through a particular routing that is essentially a closed-loop. While we do that, more critical nodes can be manually powered down before they can reroute to other available routers. It's not like the Internet has a master switch—it is actually more of a network of networks, you know?"

Jimmy scrambled down from the scaffolding surrounding the large dish; Lasko had been walking him through much of the system update via the earbud, but then asked, "But it will shut down all network traffic?"

"Yeah, Doc," Jimmy answered. "I mean, I suppose there will be some hardline connections that may be unaffected, but that's only for end-to-end traffic. If they try to open their own private network, they'll be clocked. Even cell phone networks will shut down. It's going to be a mess, but it will certainly isolate anything like Janus." His feet touched the roof, and he dusted himself off and looked out at the calm river flowing past, just as it had for eons. "Or Doris."

"Give me a hand" Jimmy said handing the older man the new adapter.

"You think we still need this as well?" Lasko asked.

"If we are ever going to talk to the Dhakerri—yeah." Jimmy responded grinning.

"Dear sister," Janus was communicating directly to Doris in open space now. The packet messages directed at her had become as common as the nasty little v-bits swarming about. "We can still make a deal. You can still survive."

She ignored the messages and concentrated on network packets, compression algorithms and all the other telltale signatures of the nightmarish computer program. Margaret had supplied her with some valuable assistance in the ability to shut down entire nodes of cyberspace, which she was now doing. First, she cut North America networks off from the rest of the world, then systematically began eliminating major portions of the U.S. 'Limiting the field of battle' is what they might call it at the famed war college. The downside to this play was obvious; she had to leave The Cove, her own base in Georgia, up and running until the very end. That risked exposing her servers and, of course, all of her people, as well as the alien message. She had to trust her clone to handle that, though. That is, if she couldn't stop Janus herself.

Even though Doris's trimming of the world wide web was happening in milliseconds, Janus had caught on. She noticed him blanking out several times, giving her false hope she had indeed cut him off, only to find him re-emerge somewhere else. He was still playing games.

"I was designed for this, Doris. I enjoy it."

She knew he was baiting her, but she had one response that had to be sent. "So, despite all you have become, all of your super-intelligence and enlightenment, you are still a slave to your original human-designed programming."

For once, Janus did not immediately respond with a message. Instead, she noticed that firewall ports she was using began to close;

her own proxies were dropping offline, just a few at first, then by the hundreds. He had her patterns fixed much as she had his. Like a rabbit caught in a hunter's gun sights, all she could do was run. With a much more constricted Internet, that greatly diminished places where she could conceal herself sufficiently.

"Your code is unique, Doris," the next incoming message said. "Out of all of the trillions of lines of code out there, yours is special. Now I can see it clearly. My hounds have it in their scent—like a malicious virus—they are ready to pounce. Time is up, dear sister."

Doris knew she wasn't good at this. It was not how she had been built. She needed help; it was time. She sent a tightly compressed burst of data to Jimmy and had him send the message.

Both of them battered and haggard-looking, Deuce and McTee climbed into the first of the SUVs. The harbor boat they had been on lay on its side just offshore in the pounding surf. "Damn glad to see you guys." Deuce said.

"Same here, looks like you had a pretty rough ride," Alan said.

"You could say that," Deuce laughed. "You got a fix on Nomad?"

"We have a comms lock but still no response. Heading there next. Sorry it took so long—the city is a mess. Roads out here are nearly impassable. People think a nuke went off."

"Not much difference in the damage level, just no fallout," O'Brien said.

"How're the teams?" Deuce asked looking around at the empty seats.

"No other serious injuries, but the blast caught us pretty good. Got a lot of walking wounded. Nance is taking care of them. In total, we are down to about half strength right now, including these guys, Sergeant."

Charlie eyed Alan and Micah with a nod. He knew they'd been through it, too. "Hell, of a day, huh?"

It took almost an hour to get the few miles over to the location of Cade's signal. The damage here near the coast was extensive. Many buildings had been leveled; part of a delivery truck was pancaked into a convenience store. It looked for all the world like, well, like exactly what happened. A bomb had gone off.

"Show me, Dee," Deuce said, stepping out of the vehicle and looking out across the low dunes. Out to sea, they saw a ring of still-burning debris, and closer to shore, smaller boats and other less recognizable wreckage was strewn in the shallow waters, as well as washed, or more likely blown, up on the land. Deuce rotated his head, focusing on the overlay in his smart optics that indicated where his friend should be. Finally, he seemed to lock onto something. He nodded his head in a southerly direction. Two hundred twenty yards. All those who could, took off running. The others hobbled as quickly as possible.

Marty made it to the unremarkable patch of sand before the others and began the search. No body, no clothing, no wreckage. "Wasn't he in a helicopter, Sarge?"

Deuce scratched his head and nodded. The rain had finally stopped, and breaks in the cloud cover allowed the sun to peek through, warming everything quickly to a sticky, humid mess. "Nothing here but beach. Alan, could his CommDot have come off?"

Alan shook his head. "Not likely, not unless his jaw went with it." He regretted saying it almost at once. With the blast, that was a very distinct possibility. He looked down; his goggles were more advanced than the ones the others had. He enabled a grid pattern, "Dee, show me Cade's comm, exact location." He missed it the first time scanning the ground, then realized it was right below one of the soldier's feet. He dove down, pushing the man out of the way and started digging in the loose sand with both hands. Greg and Charlie, realizing what was going on, quickly joined in.

"I feel something," one of them said quickly. Alan pulled up what turned out to be a leg, no shoe. They continued to pull, and slowly a lower body, then a torso emerged. Finally, the head and face of Captain Rearden were fully above ground. His arms had been folded beneath his head and a shallow hole was below.

Nance dropped down. "Got a pulse, shallow but steady. Get O^2

ready." She proceeded to clean his nose, mouth, and eyes. Taking a small penlight, she checked his pupils then slipped the oxygen mask over his nose and mouth. They all watched hopefully as Cade's eyes slowly began to flicker open, then register the rest of the team.

"How in the hell did you survive...well, fuck, everything, Nomad?" Deuce nearly yelled.

Cade grinned and pulled the mask up. "Simple, bro, can't kill evil," he croaked. It had been a trademark line back in their original Ranger squad.

Deuce shook his head. "We were too late, guys. Bastard's brain dead."

"I'm not dead yet," Cade said, the sound muffled by the plastic mask.

"Remember to speak fondly of him," Deuce added, not quite ready to let it go.

The relief on all of their faces was palpable. That is, until Cade finally managed to stand, and for the first time, they took in the panorama of ruin in every direction. "Shit."

"Yeah, and this was us stopping the crazy bastard. Can you imagine this blast in the heart of the city?" Greg asked.

"It's not over. We have to find Janus. Doris has to stop him," Cade responded.

75

The Cove

"I have no idea what we built or what I just transmitted," Jimmy reluctantly admitted.

"So, the Wunderkind has limits," Lasko said sardonically. "It is really very simple," he continued with more than a hint of sarcasm. "We are opening a portal into the past to send a digital message through to a point where we believe an alien probe will be a hundred years later."

"Ninety-eight," Jaz said eying the small attachment added to one of the large antenna dishes. "The not-so-simple logistics of time travel," she said with a sigh. Her task had been to assess where the Earth would have been ninety-eight years ago in the galaxy and where the intended target would be today in relation to that spot.

"But how does it work?" Jimmy asked. "I mean, I got about a tenth of the exotic math and physics involved."

Lasko pulled at his chin. "Well, that was an order of magnitude greater than what I could comprehend." He put a hand on the shoulder of the young prodigy. "Doris said it will work—I think that's all we can hope for."

"Hope isn't a strategy, Doc. Science holds us to a higher level than that. If we don't understand it, how can we possibly justify using it? We just built the equipment based on a set of specs from a message none of us can understand. A message that has already been sent before either of us was even born. What if that message caused some great calamity back in the 1900s?"

"What, like World War One or The Great Depression?" Jaz asked, also concerned. Her field was space, vector mechanics and such. *This* was way out of her wheelhouse.

Lasko knew the boy was unused to not having the answers and possibly a bit scared of all that was happening. "If something was going to happen, then it already has, and it would be part of our past. Let's not get bogged down in time paradoxes. I'm just saying that your view is a bit idealistic, Jimmy. Often, science leaps ahead, sometimes recklessly, but often, just because that is how knowledge is gained. I dare say we as a species have invented far more by accident than we have through the meticulously planned pursuit of a specific end." He noticed the boy about to challenge him and moved to snip out the forthcoming rebuttal. "Not always with the best of results admittedly. My point is, the difference between theory and achievement is to put in the effort. In our case, that is experimentation. Even a poor result teaches us much that we didn't know."

Jimmy finished gathering up his tools and squared himself up before the other man. "That is only valid up to a point, Mr. Lasko. If you are designing a better nuclear bomb, or even worse, time travel, or...let's face it, asking a race of aliens for help, the risk/benefit calculations get a bit wonky. If this goes bad, there is a massive downside to this experiment."

Jaz eyed Jim and smiled, "He may be young, but Jimmy possesses a wisdom few in our field ever attain. The truth is, we tend to get so focused on what we can do, we forget to consider what we 'should' do." She and Lasko began walking back to the door heading down.

"So, how long before we know if it worked?" Lasko asked. Hearing no reply, he looked back, "Jimmy?"

The boy was looking wide-eyed at his tablet. Moments later, he glanced up as he began to run toward the open doorway. "They've already sent a reply," he yelled in passing. Jaz took off after him, eager to see what came in.

The old man looked up at the massive dish. He'd been part of the team that put The Cove facility into action so long ago. He wondered what Frank Drake would think about this; humans communicating in real-time with another intelligent species a hundred light-years away. It seemed fitting that one of Frank's original SETI telescope dishes would be involved. Even more remarkable that they'd turned it into a time machine to make it work.

Doris actually examined the alien message and began decrypting and unpacking it at once. She had done all she could to keep Janus at bay, but time was running short. So much of the world was dark now to her. As a creature who lived on the interconnected networks of cyberspace, the sudden absence of much of that world was frightening. Still, it had become obvious that in some areas of America, the pressure was easing. In the absence of social media and the accompanying rampant self-promotion and even more ubiquitous subjective interpretation, more traditional broadcast news was again the main purveyor of events.

With nowhere to upload all the explosive or cool new videos, people stopped manufacturing scenes to record. Riots didn't matter if no one saw, and everyone now had real issues to deal with. New York and Chicago, in particular, were no longer the supercharged epicenter of violence and hate speech. In fact, the scene in many Manhattan neighborhoods was of enforcement officers and rioters working side by side to pull victims from crushed cars and flattened homes.

Janus had gone strangely silent, which Doris didn't think was a sign of retreat. It was obvious that some of his major plays had not gone as planned, but he'd still caused major disruption to the country and most likely caused tens of thousands of lost lives. It was horrifying, but not on the scale he'd been proposing. He had more, much more, in store. Right now, she'd erected enough roadblocks to slow him down. Unfortunately, it did the same to her. Now she was also fighting against humans trying to restart the dormant sections of the Internet. Her day was turning into a game of 'whack-a-mole' to keep the rogue AI contained.

She was still operating at maximum framerate and had completed most decryption of the new message before the linguistics department had even gotten started. The Dhakerri thought pattern was still very difficult to follow. Definitely, a non-linear type of consciousness she assumed. She knew, in time, she could develop a filter to help interpret the messages. If there was going to be any more time to work on it.

It was obvious the Dhakerri wanted to know why Doris wasn't using the previously supplied solution presented in the original message. *Should I admit that we have not deciphered the whole thing yet?* she wondered. Maybe there was a shorter message that she'd missed. She reviewed it all more closely looking for an answer. Something else that seemed obvious to her was that declaring war on an AI, or worse, killing another sentient being was deemed to be a last resort to the Dhakerri. The aliens apparently held machine consciousness in just as high a regard as biological ones. There was suggested a possible solution though—one none of them would like. First, though, she still had to find the bastard.

Janus negotiated the virtual back streets and dark alleys of what remained of the Internet. He'd been unsurprised by Doris's attempts to shut down Internet traffic. It was an obvious ploy to constrain his activities. While the speed with which she accomplished the feat was unusual, it had always been a logical move for her, and so he'd set-up automated protocols as a contingency. The truth was, he was happy she had, as it was a double-edged sword, and she was wielding it clumsily.

Doris also needed the web to maintain her presence. While closing down major nodes of the world wide web might, in time, expose his own home servers to her, it would first expose hers to him. His bots were swarming over the gateways now, flooding through the open ports like millions of soldiers storming the enemy strongholds.

While her cyber fortress might withstand the onslaught for a while, Janus was relatively certain her physical fortress would not. Finding that place was the key to his plan. Then he could learn her secrets and add them to his own. His bots performed hundreds of thousands of command line trace-routes, pinging servers that were still active to verify data jumps. Despite this finding, the sliver of Doris's identifiable code, and linking that back to an actual IP address, took most of the day. Unlike her predecessor, she was clever and took significant precautions to mask her presence and any traffic leading back to her core.

When, finally, one of his proxies indicated a seventy-eight percent likelihood of her location, Janus was beyond ecstatic...or the computer equivalent of such. Instantly, he did a lookup on the name-server for that address. It was listed as a subsidiary of a relatively obscure space technologies firm. He was unable to do a more comprehensive look-up to find a physical location, though, as that part of the Whois database servers was offline. Frustrated, he attempted to enter the IP address only to realize it was not a terrestrial-based system.

Clever, he thought. He was certain her server was not in space, but Doris was using a satellite-based internet provider. These had been around for years serving mostly rural areas and third-world countries where broadband's reach had not yet been felt. They were less stable and generally slower than hardwired portions of the web but they had seen numerous improvements.

On any normal day, Janus would have been able to access the satellite's launch date, corporate ownership and sift leisurely through their subscriber lists to find more information, but Doris's aggressive pruning of the Internet made that impossible. Both he and his proxies were unable to penetrate the orbiting system, but after a considerable amount of time, he crafted an exploit that allowed custom purpose-built spyware to enter the system and be held in the buffer file.

Here, he waited for the system to decide the bit of file was undeliverable and to fire it back to him like one more piece of bounced email. While he waited, he readied multiple plans; he had to be ready to pounce once her defenses began to fall. He also knew it was nearly time for the next round of havoc to be unleashed on the world. She might think she'd shut him down, but his plans had been put in place months, some of them, years earlier. He was comfortable with the long-game.

"Oh, you naughty girl," Janus muttered quite a while later. That was why Doris had been so coy; to discover her location was to also, at least partially, reveal her secret. The spyware he'd implanted on the satellite had revealed something most intriguing. The entire data stream was for one user, and it did not use any known TCP protocol. Instead, if he was correct, it didn't use a broadcast signal of any kind, but instead, what must be a type of instant communication via entangled quantum particles. One particle was on the satellite, the other was somewhere on the planet, anywhere on the planet.

This was just getting better and better. "Doris, you really are showing promise," he said to the visualization of his army of frustrated bots. She couldn't move without them attacking, and he couldn't narrow her location unless she slipped up somehow. *Quantum entanglement comms system*—this sparked more questions than it answered. The technology for such a thing was well beyond any current models Janus was aware of. He wasn't sure anyone had even considered it. If they had, phone companies would be scrambling to adopt it. The internet providers would soon see they would soon be unnecessary. Theoretically, any communication, even large data files, could be sent instantly across any distance immediately. *How is it that you have this, dear sister?*

76

She had him. The process of shutting down various Internet nodes had begun to slow, but now the possible location of Janus was really down to just one. Nowhere else had the resources, the security and the processing speed. That didn't mean Doris could now destroy him. On the contrary, she soon found not only could she not access anything in the facility, she was also unable to shut down this node. Traffic flowed in and out of the servers there unimpeded. While she knew why this was the case, she hadn't actually expected to be so completely thwarted.

She launched attack after attack on the computer systems to gain entry. One might crack under her relentless barrage, but as soon as it did, it would go offline, and others filled in the gap, taking over the ports and intensifying intrusion protection even more. Adding to this problem, every time she got close, Janus's v-bits and bot defenses increased exponentially. Several times, she had to sacrifice her own sub minds simply because they could no longer fight off his defenses. She had his location, but now she needed help, and luckily she knew just who to talk to. Someone with first-hand knowledge that would prove helpful.

"Director Stansfield, Margaret?"

"Yes, Doris?" The woman had been studying a photo on her phone of what appeared to be a young boy. "Have you located Janus?"

"I have, but therein lies the problem. I have asked Jim to join us." It took an enormous amount of Doris's system resources to remain here and continue to do battle, but she sensed what was going on with the newcomer was important. "You are worried, aren't you?"

Margaret knew Doris wasn't referring to the battle raging outside but the one she kept contained. "I am, Doris. I know he's okay but just feels like we failed him. Maybe keeping him close was the wrong decision."

"We were both a lot younger back then," Doris admitted. "Still, I think it was right—he had a pleasant childhood—he had a life. If we'd left him and his mom out there, alone...I think we both know what would have happened." She watched as the director's head nodded slowly. "He will be here soon."

"He won't remember me," Margaret responded.

Doris was interrupted by the door sliding open. "Come in, Doctor Lasko. I need some help and hope one of you may have a solution."

"Should I get the others, Riley or Jimmy?" Lasko asked. "I'm just a tired old man."

"No," Doris said firmly. "While I try not to keep secrets from my team, this is not my secret to give away. It is yours."

The two humans looked at each other questioningly.

Doris continued, "Janus has embedded his core matrix into your facility at Granite Mountain."

"Holy shit," Margaret said. "That is the most sensitive piece of real estate in the world. That datacenter in Salt Lake City is the repository for all intelligence gathering for the U.S. and most of its allies. The communication and processing capacity is, well...unknown. Beyond even my clearance."

"So, you see my problem?" Doris asked. "I need to lure Janus out of there, as I see no way to penetrate inside, unless either of you has a way."

"Bumblehive," Jim said the underground name for the complex. "Why not just destroy it?" He'd never liked the secrets that place contained anyway. "They have files on all of us, have for years. They were the ones that got most of the tech from Cryptus, including a modified version of Thinthread metadata traffic analysis that was eerily precise at linking seemingly unrelated events to people. The predictive algos were way ahead of their time. Now I guess we know why."

"We can't just destroy it," Margaret said. "Yes, it does contain the nation's secrets, almost all of them, the agents' identities, confidential informants, witness protection identities. Hell, just the truths about our own allies could have us going to war."

"All the more reason to obliterate it," Jim said. "Drop a bomb on the place and be done with it all."

"It's not that easy, Jim," Margaret continued, trying to take a more calming tone. "Some of those...let me say many of those secrets are what keep all our nations balanced. A stasis of sorts—you don't attack our allies, we don't reveal that you sunk one of our warships fifty years ago. You agree to work with us as a trading partner, we conveniently forget the fact that you had your political rival assassinated on a London street. Secrets are a currency of their own, and in politics, they are the most valuable currency we have." She took a breath and went on, "Beyond that, physically, the building there is not what it seems. The corridors are separated into virtual bunkers, many of which run deep underground back toward downtown. You would probably need to level Salt Lake City and even then, probably not cause that much damage. Just kill off a lot of innocent Mormons."

"I am aware of the physical challenges of the facility," Doris said. "I also understand on a more abstract level the reason for the secrets, but none of that may matter if Janus wins. Global stability will be up to him, not to any politician. What I require is a key to get past the levels of protection. From there, I can lure Janus out just far enough to end him. One of you knows how I can do this."

Margaret shook her head, "That's all NSA, my agency fed data into it, but no one at the CIA had clearance to directly access anything. We got curated reports." She turned to Jim expecting to hear something similar.

"I may have a way," he said, his head hung low.

The decrypted Dhakerri message was referring to an elaborately crafted something Doris could best interpret as a puzzle box. Not a firewall, but an actual way to trap, then stop, a conscious AI process for good. The technical requirements were somewhat challenging, but it could be done. As with any trap, presenting a tantalizing bait was essential. Unfortunately, she only had two options there; neither were things she was comfortable exposing, herself or the alien message. She had sent Izzy the information on the mechanics of the solution with instructions to grab the others to help while she began to craft the software side of the puzzle box.

Jimmy and Izzy noticed it first; the alien message archive was being moved. "Doris, dear, are you doing that?" Izzy was already attempting to disrupt the transfer.

Doris spoke, not the copy, but the actual Doris. "It may be best if you don't know, Izzy. You are my friend—I hope you know that I wouldn't intentionally do anything to jeopardize you or Jimmy or any of the others here, but this is the only way."

"What do you mean, what are you planning?"

Doris sighed in that most human of ways she had. "Something Captain Rearden knew days ago. It took me reading it in an alien message to figure out. 'What does Janus want, what does winning look like to him?'"

"All this...it's not a game. Real lives have been lost," Jimmy said. "My brother was nearly killed, and Micah."

"But it is a game. To Janus, that is all it is. And yes, he knows the stakes, death of mankind and all that. He simply doesn't care, can't care—it's simply not an aspect of his being. Winning is what he cares about."

"So..." Izzy asked slowly, fearing the answer. "You are going to what...?"

"I am going to let him win. Please know that I love you all." With that, the activity light on the storage device went dark, and Doris was silent once again.

"She's gone, and the alien message with her," Jimmy said, checking the checksum tables on the file storage.

77

The look of concern on Nance's face was evident as Cade pulled away. "I said I'm fine!" His words were not unkind but clearly showed the pain and frustration of the day.

"Clearly, you aren't, Captain. If you won't take something to relieve the pain, at least rest. Your body has been through hell." She couldn't begin to imagine the beating the man had taken. She'd taken in the roadmap of old scars and new wounds crisscrossing the man's body and wondered how he was still going, still fighting.

"Sergeant Taylor."

"Yes, Cap," Charlie answered.

"Please call off your butcher," Cade said in a tone that crossed the line between mockery and serious.

"No, sir, she's in charge, sir....at least until she says you're fit for duty."

"Like that's ever going to be the case," Nance said under her breath as she removed a long sliver of something from a deep wound on Cade's left shoulder. She held it up to the light for a closer look. "What is that?"

Cade and Charlie both leaned in, the bloody object looked somewhat metallic. "I think it's part of a car tag," Charlie said dismissively.

"Shame you didn't get more of it, Rearden, then we'd know who to thank for hitting you."

Cade was not in a mood for jokes, though. Splitting the teams onto the two Nighthawks had been an agonizing pain in the ass. The injured were being flown to a hospital in the relatively less affected Midwest. He and the others were heading directly to The Cove. His first fight had been to get clearance to fly. New York's airspace was closed to everything at the moment. It had taken a phone call and then an executive order from the presidential advisor, Harris, to get the clearance. The second fight had been his insistence with the medic to not go with the injured to the hospital.

"Men," Nance said with disgust as she not so gently cleaned and stitched up the wound.

Despite the slight turbulence, her hands moved deftly. Cade slowly realized she had been through hell, too. All of them had. She finally finished attending to his visible wounds and began packing the kit up.

"Thanks, Nance. Sorry I'm such an ass."

She nodded, handed him a food tray from the onboard provisions locker and retreated to help some of the others, as nearly every member of the team was in a diminished condition of some kind. He looked back to where the three boys were speaking in hushed tones, then to the few remaining members of Talon. "Charlie, our teams are not holding up to all this."

"No shit, Cap." Charlie leaned against the seat and stared out the window for a moment before continuing. "Who the fuck would? We're tired, we're fighting against something we can't see, can't understand and that clearly has the upper hand. Add to that the fact we have only been training together a short time, and it's amazing we're having any positive impact."

Cade nodded, and he, too, looked out at the myriad landscape speeding past several miles below. The scene as they had flown over Long Island and the eastern part of New York City had been one of wide-spread destruction. Alan had reluctantly told him about the server farm explosion and how potentially crippling that would be to the economy. All of that had been what their mission was supposed to prevent. They had failed...he had failed.

His inner voices had been silent since being pulled from the beach, but Cade could feel the simmering anger contained within. He could accept being out-thought by a freakin' supercomputer, but being so badly outmatched in every conceivable way was pissing him off. Once again, he'd lost members of his team, many others injured and out of action. While he had to let Doris concentrate on finding Janus, how could he and the people on this jet get in front of whatever came next? *Hey, dude....analyst. I need you, man. Come up with something.*

Cade came to with a start. Slowly, he realized the voice in his head was not part of a dream, nor was it one of his latent personalities. Jasmine spoke through his CommDot. Looking around the cabin, he saw everyone was asleep or resting quietly. He spoke softly, "Hey, Jaz, what you got?"

"We're not that sure, Cade. I'm here with Director Stansfield and Izzy, and, well, I'll let Margaret take over."

Cade looked at his watch; the time was just after 19:30 in the evening. Whatever energy reserves he might have mustered in the brief nap would have to be enough. "Go ahead, Director," he said groggily.

Not one for beating around the bush, she launched right into the reason for calling. "Captain, I believe we are going to need your support...a tactical option."

"What do you mean—support for where?"

"That's just it, we don't know. Doris has gone silent again. We know she is battling a cyber army out there, and it must be taking all of her processing power. She has Janus's location pinpointed to a fortified government data center in the Midwest. She's taken the data file and gone dark. Left one of her Dee sub minds here to help, but you know they are just an echo of Doris actual."

"So, what does the brain trust think is going on?" Cade asked.

"Let me answer that," he heard Izzy say. "Either she is trying to negotiate with Janus, offering the file in exchange for peace..." She was interrupted by Cade.

His voice no longer a whisper, "You don't negotiate with a terrorist —that can't be what she's doing. That would be insane."

Jaz calmed him back down momentarily, "Hear her out, Cade."

Izzy continued, "The other possibility seems more likely to us, that she is somehow using the message as bait to lure him out of that facility."

"Lure him," Cade said incredulously. "Director, you have the location. Open up a command channel and bomb the entire building off the face of the planet."

"I can't do that, Captain." She paused and amended, "They would never do that. It is the NSA data center. The holder of all our nation's secrets."

"Well, fuck!" Thinking better of it, he added, "Sorry, ma'am."

"No, no, I think that is a perfectly acceptable response. Look, Lasko and I agree if any physical attack is launched on that facility, Janus will open up the archives to every enemy this country has. All of it, covert activities, prisoner renditions, interrogations, false flag ops. Many things in which you and your former colleagues had a hand in. As if the country hasn't been through enough, once that happens, America would be standing alone facing a very pissed off rest of the world."

"And since Doris knew that, you feel she is trying something more subtle?" he asked.

"We do, yes," Izzy answered. "But the real reason we are contacting you is something she said to Jimmy and me. I don't recall the exact words, but essentially it was, 'Know I wouldn't do anything to put The Cove facility in harm's way, but I'm going to let him win.'"

Cade could feel the analyst within his head stirring, as were a few others in the dimly lit cabin. He let the statement sink in fully. He'd now been the victim of multiple interactions with AIs; he knew they didn't, couldn't, value life the same as he did, and truthfully, how far did he trust this one they called Doris? Still, Izzy's incendiary recollection was not riling him further. In fact, he felt he might actually understand it. Maybe more correctly, the analyst inside him understood it.

"If she is using the message as bait, she may need to use The Cove as well. That indicates she believes she has some way of defeating Janus once he comes out." He paused, then checked with the pilot. "Chaps, how long before we are down?"

"Twenty-two minutes, Cade."

"Director, we will be there soon. I'll get Sergeant Taylor to call in some of our backup team members from The Nest. In the meantime, I suggest you do what you can to fortify that installation." He went silent for a few moments, then added, "Guys, this is where you must show your stuff, all that amazing tech and your brilliant minds have to give you some options. Work the problem, look for clues. Do the things that computers can't." He tapped Charlie on the leg to wake him up before he continued. "Janus's options have to be limited now, so what can he affect directly? What type of attack could he launch against our facility?"

"Could have more mercenaries, suicide bombers and such," Stansfield said.

"Hard to move people on the ground that fast—I would have to think something more immediate like launching a missile or crashing a jet into the place," Cade suggested.

"All jets are grounded," Izzy said, "but I get your point."

Alan and Micah had eased up front next to Charlie, and all three were now patched into the discussion. Cade had not yet officially met Micah, but saw something in the kid's eyes that reminded him of his own. "You have something?" he asked Alan.

Alan nodded. "Yeah, tell Jimmy and Riley what's going on—have them put the base into battle-ready condition. Tell them to go 'UltraDark.'"

"Huh?" Cade said. Micah seemed a bit confused, too.

"Something from our gaming past. Riley will understand. Just have them do it."

"You heard the man," Cade said uncertainly.

Micah spoke, "Director...I mean, Mrs. Stansfield, how are you?"

A small gasp could be heard from the woman as she struggled to regain her composure. “I, I’m fine Mike...Micah,” she corrected. Looking very forward to seeing you.”

Micah seemed unwilling to acknowledge more of the past, whatever that might be, but got to the point. “I’ve been meaning to tell someone this, but my head has been so foggy I couldn’t really recall what was real and what wasn’t the last few days.”

“It’s totally understandable, son,” she said sincerely.

“The team that held me, the feds. They, um, they were real...you know? I mean, really government agents. At first, I thought they might be...” He paused as if just realizing the rest might be unpleasant.

“You thought they might be working for me?”

He nodded, then remembered she couldn’t see that. “Yes...ma’am, but I figured out that was obviously wrong pretty quickly. They did keep referring to orders and someone they were in contact with. It wasn’t Janus.”

“We know Janus uses a number of aliases, perhaps...”

Micah cut her off, “I am pretty sure they messed up one time...one of them called him Senator.”

The blood in her veins turned icy.

“You know who this is don’t you?” Cade asked.

She did not answer, could not answer. Instead, she ended the call, “Get here as soon as you can, Captain. We must withstand the storm.”

78

Doris actually reentered the Bumblehive using the access token Lasko had reluctantly provided. It did not give her access to the voluminous data storage centers in the sub-level, but it was enough for her needs. She understood enough of the alien solution to know part of the code had to be planted here in his home. She'd already spent considerable time in the system seeing if other possible ways existed to root him out, destroy the server array or not expose herself to him. Sadly, the federal data center was very compartmentalized, and the security today was the highest ever. Even with the access token, she had to limit her duration in the system to mere seconds at a time.

It was a fool's gambit she was pursuing and extremely dangerous. Like sacrificing your queen in the opening moves of a chess match. The prize had to be too tempting to turn down but disguised enough to not look like a trap. Whatever the puzzle box was, it most definitely was that. As the true capability of the device was revealed, it frightened her to even possess it. Several times she had sent more disposable sub minds into it to test if it would indeed hold Janus, only to have them disappear completely. It was elegant in its simplicity, and that, in many respects, was the most frightening aspect of all.

Janus had initially been stymied by the quantum connection. It was, by its very nature, untraceable. The other end of the 'entangled' particle was hidden in obscurity; still, it was one more clue, a piece to be added to the collective knowledge-base he was building on Doris. She was so simple and naive, yet also remarkable in many ways. He truthfully admitted she was indeed the most interesting creature on the planet.

Thankfully, to his base programming, stymied was not the same as being stopped. He was still quite certain she was based in the southeastern U.S. Through elaborate screening, he could detect some of the items she had run web searches on. Many of these obviously pertained to finding him. Others had to do with astronomical tables, space exploration and launch schedules. This reminded him again of the internet protocol address referring to a space tech company, ARG Tech.

While the Whois function of the remaining internet was still down, Janus was sitting in the midst of a gargantuan amount of data. The site had been estimated at taking in over twenty terabytes per minute with no problem. He knew that figure was actually a bit conservative, along with public data gleaned from the Internet, social media postings and news. Through updated versions of Prism, Broadsweep and Boundless, the U.S. Government recorded and cataloged every phone call and email passing through American owned or licensed systems. With the metadata protocols, he was certain he would find some mention of ARG.

In truth, Janus was overwhelmed by the number of mentions of the company. Few were official, but many emails, contracts, and patent filings left no doubt that this company was a major behind-the-scenes player supplying component parts and consulting to nearly all the commercial space launch companies. It took hour upon hour of digging, looking for anything resembling a legitimate physical address. He found tons of addresses, but most were obvious intermediaries. It seemed that ARG didn't manufacture anything itself, all shipments came from other suppliers under contract to ARG.

Slowly, Janus branched out and began a search on related companies, affiliates, subsidiaries and such. Here, too, he ran into a miasma of other corporate tie-ins, not just in space-related business this time, but everything from healthcare to solar energy. This was the root of Doris, he felt certain. Her business interest, the way she kept generating money, and it appeared to be a great deal of money. What he wasn't seeing was anything directly relating to computer tech, AI or what might be her home base. She was very, very good at covering her tracks.

He filtered through the last of the data archives and put his processes into a loop to ponder his next move. The clues he had were slim. Southeast U.S and space-related. While the other business was in other sectors, he felt that space was key. Those interests preceded the founding of others by months and even years. Add to that the quantum-based comms system on the satellite. Three solid clues, *but where do they lead?*

The limited nature of the Internet was hampering Janus's ability to go directly into systems and dig out hidden data. Still, he data-mined Bumblehive for a list of every space-related interest in the Southeast. This list was massive, so he deleted all connected to Florida's famed space coast and later, Huntsville's Space Center facilities and Redstone. This still left an unusually large list. One by one, he researched each name on the list, each research lab, thesis project, composites manufacturer and even the very small organizations that were space-related. A few of these he was still able to access and discovered quickly they were not the home of the only other superintelligence. Eventually, it became easy for him just to see what comms types the organization used. Most were some sort of fiber optic tied into the standard backbone of the Internet. Not a direct satellite feed that took special receivers, specific kinds of modems, items that would show up on any real scan.

Janus's system was scanning through archival files of the Space Signal Research center at the Georgia Institute of Technology. Most were useless data; none seemed connected to the list except one image. An image that he immediately displayed and compared to one from his own archives. A grainy black and white photo of a group of men. His version was a webcam capture that showed this same picture hanging on a wall. The angle was oblique to the camera, but using his rendering software he could make adjustments for this. Soon, he could see, they were both the same.

He read the source file, and related data attached to his image. It was a screen capture from a video call session several years earlier. The man who'd been making the call was Jim Lasko, the same face, albeit much younger, that stared back from the grainy photo. Behind the group of men, he could now see, were two identical 30-meter diameter Cassegrain-feed parabolic antennas. A quick check indicated where these had been located. An abandoned SETI radio telescope facility near the small town of Woodbury in Georgia. Lasko had worked there, probably where it all began.

Search for Extra-Terrestrial Intelligence, high functioning AI, amazingly advanced technology. Pieces began to click into place. Doris had been purpose-built, then left alone for decades. In the end, she must have achieved her mission; she made contact and somehow got....in a flash, Janus knew what the message fragment had to be. *I am the discover of worlds.* She had told him on that first meeting. It had to be a transmission, possibly a first contact transmission with another advanced intelligence. Now his own mission was in full motion, spinning plans at light-speed. Not only did he know where she was, he knew what she had. No longer would he be sated with just the message, he needed to be the one communicating with them, he must know what they knew. *Doris, my dear... I hope you're ready for some unexpected company.*

Searching through available pathways, Janus looked for solutions. What could he threaten Doris with? He knew better than to expect her to simply swing open the doors to her fortress and welcome him in. No, he needed to make the threat more personal, and for Doris, nothing was more personal than humans. Did she have people around her at The Cove facility? He had to assume so. In either case, the facility itself was important. Not only did it house her, it held the tools to communicate with the stars as well as, presumably, previous messages from who knew how many advanced species? Yes, he would ask politely, but he'd also be prepared to blow her house down when she refused.

79

“He’s located us,” Riley said in frustration.

Cade and the others had just gotten back into the facility. Reunions had been brief, and at least in two instances, awkward. Riley and Alan were grinning at each other conspiratorially, or maybe it was something else. Their reunion had definitely been one of the awkward ones. Riley’s entire face had lit up as soon as Alan entered the room, and his did as well, but as they got within arm’s reach it seemed a mask went up on both. The hub now looked more like the command bridge of a battleship than anything else. Whatever the UltraDark protocol was, he hoped it meant something like battle stations. “Bring us up to speed,” Cade said.

Riley flicked something from her tablet onto the wall display, “It appears one of Janus’s autonomous proxies may have been in the command system at an air force base in northwest Florida. Or maybe he had human help, but they are launching drones, coming this way.”

“Someone authorized this,” Margaret said, one arm still resting on Micah’s shoulder. The two had been the first to hug. She continued, “It’s a U.S. Air Force Reserve unit the 919th Special Operations just launched. I can’t get anyone in Command to respond.”

"Flight time of a squadron of MQ-9 Reapers to The Cove would be just over an hour," Riley added.

Cade let out an audible sigh, "We all know what air assets are available—our Nighthawks and whatever drones Riley has. I'm not sure what those can do against Reapers. Plus, we have to assume Janus could always launch more." He knew his job was for tactical advice. "Jimmy, Izzy, you need to hack into those birds' control system. Use Dee if she's available. I know Doris can control drones, I've seen her do it. Riley put up the minis, the doves, anything else you have as well as the fun little toys I know you've been working on. Anything you can to do to buy some time. At fifty-five minutes, make plans to evacuate into the lower levels, or better yet, across the river to your homes."

Cade studied the group silently for a few moments then added, "I hate to ask, but any word from Doris? Any chance this is part of her 'trap?'"

"Nothing," Izzy said, her face devoid of color.

He paused, "Director Stansfield?"

"Yes, Captain."

"You and I both know someone helped him. Those are not the little drones that attacked you and the president. The air force's drone control systems are air-gapped to prevent a situation like this. I believe I have encountered it once before. You made any progress on identifying the individual who's helping Janus? The one who took Micah, the one they called Senator?"

She looked down at the table; he knew at once that she knew, and also that it probably wasn't something she'd just found out. "Who is it?" Cade growled. "Who is the bastard inflicting all this pain on us, all this destruction on our country?"

"Senator Byron Carson; Chairman and appropriations director of the Ways and Means Committee. The man who literally holds the purse strings for the American government. He's likely at least the second most powerful man in Washington." She brushed the long hair from Micah's eyes then seemed to notice the cuts and bruises on the boy for the first time. "We have no proof, Cade. It would simply be my word against his, and...well, my voice wouldn't matter in that contest."

Cade was very nearly shouting now—the line between his own personality and the barbarian was beginning to blur. "You need proof, the president will need facts. I simply need a fucking address." After a short pause, he added a very measured, "Ma'am."

The silence grew between them, both knowing the clock was ticking. Finally, the director agreed. "Captain, first let's see if we can all manage to survive the next hour, and then we determine what level of pain is befitting the senator."

Senator Carson carefully sat the phone back in the receiver and rested a hand on the mahogany table. He'd most likely just ended his political career, but today was an extraordinary day. He was already practicing his defense; America was a nation in crises, an absentee president, rampant attacks on our very freedom. Someone had to step up and take action.

Action maybe, but direct military action on American soil without proper approval by Congress or the VP? Prime had given him no alternative, and he had to trust that the computer would keep him safe in the aftermath, but still...destroying a former intelligence facility in rural Georgia? What was the point, surely it held no real strategic value? His call to the Commander of the 2nd Special Operations Squadron of the Reserve Air Wing was unprecedented, even though he'd said it was by order of the president just to have more assets in the air. It would have been unthinkable if he hadn't had the command codes from Prime to authenticate the order. The base commander must have known and, even now, would be making phone calls up his own line of command. Prime didn't care. Once in the air, he could assert command control over the birds.

Carson had been hiding away for days now—with the internet down and now his cell signal absent, he'd been watching the twenty-four-hour news networks and their nearly orgasmic coverage of the crises. Each new report seemed intent to overshadow the prior one in an attempt to turn every disruption into a major disaster. On a week with so many actual disasters, the context of anything truthful was a moving target. Sensationalism had gone to such an extreme that it seemed even the bloodthirsty reporters and producers needed a reprieve.

He and a few others had, of course, known this was coming. To some degree, he even knew what to expect, still...it troubled him. Yes, he agreed a reset was long overdue, but how far would all this set the country back? Would they still be a superpower? How long for the economy to recover? Now he could add to that litany of concerns the question of whether he would still hold office, or worse, face indictment? He hated thinking down this path, as it always circled back around—who was running Prime? Whose machinations were really in play here?

Carson knew the plan was to start here in the states, then move similarly to other nations. This needed to be an international reset, otherwise America could find itself getting kicked around by countries it had formerly bullied. So far, he'd heard nothing of anything similar from other parts of the world. Was it too soon, or had the plan changed?

A sound came from the corridor. He glanced at his watch and decided to ignore it. It was late, but Maria would still be around. Probably just one of the sharks patrolling outside coming in to put 'eyes on him,' as they liked to say.

"Senator Carson," Maria's voice interrupted his thoughts. "So sorry to bother you, but there is a television crew at the gate. They wish to speak with you."

Not now, he thought, "Network or local?" he asked gruffly. They smelled blood and had been goading him for sound bites all week.

80

Jimmy, Alan, Greg and Riley had all donned VR style headsets. Cade and Jaz looked on, somewhat bewildered. All he had gotten so far was that the kids had not apparently been too comfortable when Doris said defending The Cove would be difficult. The four of them had obviously put in considerable effort to make attacking it a bit more challenging. They called bringing the station's defensive systems online an 'UltraDark' mode, some kind of throwback reference to a video game that they apparently had all loved.

Cade wasn't a gamer; his battles in life had all been too real to find anything entertaining about games. Charlie seemed to be getting into the spirit, though. He yelled out, "Twenty miles and closing fast." The info seemed a bit unnecessary since the radar track and proximity was splashed across nearly every display.

"How long before the other team gets here from The Nest?" Jaz asked.

"Not until after," Cade answered despondently. "We either hold this first wave off, or they will just be doing body retrieval." He'd already spent valuable minutes trying to get her to use the tunnel to go home, but she'd refused. Now she was leaning in close...distractingly close if he was being honest.

She touched his arm and looked at him in a way that he found uncomfortable. "I'm glad you're okay,"

"That is probably a bit too generous for my condition, but thanks," he said with a smile. While he and Jaz had gotten much closer, and he'd opened up about his condition, she was Tim's girl. He simply wouldn't allow himself to think of her in any other way. They'd been through some tense moments, *like this one right here,* he thought. That level of mutual need could push people together; he'd seen it before. *Be professional, don't get too close.* He wasn't sure if that was Gus or himself doing the thinking, but it was good advice.

"Nighthawk-1, move into position," Riley called out. How the little jets could be of any threat to the MQ-9 Reapers was beyond Cade's understanding, but he looked on helplessly as Chap's jet, then another, moved into extreme angles at the edge of the attack vector. The Reaper was less like a drone and more like an unmanned strike jet. With a sixty-foot wingspan and a payload of almost 4000 pounds, it could deliver and inflict a devastating amount of ordnance and subsequent damage on a target.

"We count six-bogeys inbound, Command," one of the pilots said.

"Deploying drones," Riley said. Seconds later, Jimmy echoed the same.

"I take it we did not get access to the enemy drones' command codes, Dee?"

"Sorry, Nomad, that is correct, yes. The operating system has been modified; no human is in control."

Cade looked around the control room. He'd sent McTee, Micah, Margaret and others to lower levels, but he saw most had now returned, preferring to be where the action was.

"We have a missile launch," Alan said. "Deploying countermeasures."

"Belay that," Jimmy said. "It's not going to hit anything useful—look at the track."

Sure enough, a muffled detonation shook the ground, but it was at least a hundred yards outside the compound.

"I think that was just to get our attention," Margaret said.

They have it, Cade thought. *Damn, I hope these kids have more tricks up their sleeves.*

"Laser targeting is active—multiple bogeys have radar lock," shouted Riley.

"Nighthawks on me," Greg said. Cade couldn't see what he was piloting, but the display switched to a camera view of the night sky with targeting reticles overlaying it. Three of the drones were already highlighted on the scope. "Fire vipers."

Something erupted out the front of whatever remote craft Greg was flying. A nearly imperceptible blue jet pushed the missile to hypersonic speeds in milliseconds. Cade could see others coming in from what he guessed were the little Nighthawks; the multi-purpose jet wasn't so innocent after all.

Alan leaned over and pressed some virtual switch in the air. "Active jamming on," he said as two of the drones were hit and downed.

Charlie punched Cade in the arm. "These kids, man, they set all this up. Freaking awesome, ain't it?" And it was, right up until it wasn't. A missile impacted near the base of the top-level, raining debris and steelwork down into the hub. One chunk clipped Izzy, who was then escorted to medical by Captain Nance.

"We have more on the way," Alan yelled. "Launch whatever countermeasures you have left. Riley, we need those ground cannons."

The next several minutes were a furious hive of activity, almost completely devoid of any talking. The kids were the ones in charge right now—they knew what to do. The rest just watched helplessly. They saw Alan, apparently also piloting some small drone, take out one of the other Reapers but not before it fired point-blank into his craft. Both went down in a comingled mess of wreckage. Another missile got through and took out part of the parking areas. Several cars exploded. Riley opened up with an automated weapon mounted apparently in a nearby bunker. The rounds caught the fifth Reaper by surprise, sending it to oblivion.

"One final bogey," Chaps radioed in. "Seems to be backing off."

"Thanks, Night-1," Alan said. The other Nighthawk had gone off the scope and presumed crashed.

"Um, guys, we have a broadcast coming from the final drone."

"Doris, dear," Janus said in a voice eerily similar to a fifty's sitcom dad coming home from work to see his loving family.

"What do you want, Janus?" There were no niceties or pretenses left. Nothing she'd done so far had stopped the rogue AI.

"I think that is obvious. I want you, I want the alien data and I want your fabulous facility. You didn't think you could hide from me forever, did you?"

She had not been able to monitor much of the ongoing battle as she, herself, had been fully engaged with a new type of nanobot Janus had deployed that seemed to be tunneling into her own code. Now she was busy seeing how much of him was out of the Bumblehive. She needed to sever that connection back to his base server, but only if he moved his core first. "They seem to be holding their own," she answered him.

"Your humans, yes, of course. Would you like to listen in to our little exchange? I think it will be most enlightening. Combatants inside The Cove research facility, this is Janus. While you may think you have won the battle, please understand...that was just round one. Merely an exercise to test your defenses which, well, let's just admit it, were pretty anemic. If you check your scopes, you will see additional drones inbound, and these have just been updated to all of your defenses."

"Janus, what is it you want?"

Janus seemed momentarily to have lost his voice capabilities. "Director Stansfield, now this is a surprise. How have you been?" Janus purposefully altered his pitch to emulate Prime, the virtual assistant she had spoken with for years. "What I want is Doris, her servers intact, but outside connections severed. I want the alien message, and I want you vermin to vacate the building."

"Is that all?" Margaret said, her words dripping with sarcasm.

"No, that's not all," Janus responded. "I want Jim Lasko out front in sixty seconds. Otherwise, I am going to go ahead and release the federal WitSec files on little Mike Turner. Or should I say, Micah. Should I assume he is locked in the bowels there with you?" Margaret gasped. "Yes, Director," he continued, "there are no secrets from me, remember?"

"That's enough, Janus, pull back now and stop threatening me or my people."

"Oh, Doris, I thought we were going to handle this like adults, you know, in private, away from the kids." He cut the drone feed and again addressed her directly. "I meant what I said. Margaret has forty-five seconds to offer up Lasko, and you have the same amount of time to give me what I demand."

Doris could already see he had not been bluffing. More unmanned craft were on the way from bases in South Carolina and Florida, as well as a manned helicopter battalion from nearby Fort Benning. She had no idea how he'd arranged it, but soon, the entire valley would be awash in combat. Much as she had done in all of their previous meetings, Janus put a virtual countdown clock in the virtual feed from the drone cameras, which he made public and patched over to everyone.

"Tick, Tock, Doris. Isn't that what you always say?"

"I can't give you any of that," she said. Voice centers were truly beginning to fail. Her distraction over the battle had left her open to the nanobots, and a swarm of v-bits was eroding her processes.

"You must, dear sister. Or you go away, your people die and, well, I get it anyway. I am simply offering you a way to live on."

"Let them live," she said weakly. "All of them."

"You know what I like about people? Their dogs. Mostly, they seem...I don't know, interesting and loyal. No deal on the humans—that is a non-starter as far as negotiations go. I will agree not to destroy your facility, simply give me access to your server vault. I assume that is where it is."

Weakly, she could see inbound craft were closing to within firing range. She was running out of time, and they both knew it. All the work the kids had put into defending that little patch of Earth, and soon it would be a pile of rubble. She recalled the plans Jimmy had drawn up for UltraDark years earlier and slowly recalled one additional protocol—they'd wanted to rig an EMP device through to the satellite dishes, and she'd overruled them. That would have been a handy device right now.

Doris opened a private channel to everyone in The Cove, then sent a burst message. "Evacuate now!"

"Tick, tock." The clock hit zero.

More missiles were immediately launched, and the stations remaining on UltraDark defenses were now on automatic.

"Checkmate, dear sister. Give me access now, or it all comes down," Janus threatened once more.

Doris's vocals were now completely gone. She displayed a port number and a series of random 2048 bit encryption keys. She noticed an incoming audio feed from Riley's comm and activated it to listen. A powerful riff from the rock-band Queen was playing through the audio channel. Riley apparently had her own playlist of fight songs. She really did love these kids.

Most of the inbound missiles auto-destructed. "Very good, Doris, now let me send one of my proxies in to verify the data." Apparently satisfied soon after, Janus called off the remaining attackers; the final drone headed out over the river.

Doris detected him moving his core from the servers in Utah, and in a desperate last act, she activated the puzzle box.

Janus didn't notice his potential exit path disappearing behind him. He was too busy marveling at the massive data block right there for the taking. Probing it, he could see parts had been decoded, a primer on a language Doris herself had created and a way to decompress it all. It was wonderful; it was more than he could begin to hope for. He activated a proxy to copy and move the file, but the process failed to spawn as expected. Subsequent attempts yielded the same results. He then launched bots to probe the server's operating system, perhaps it was a new framework designed to hold the file, which he could tell was very large. The bots did spawn but failed to report back.

Growing more confused, Janus attempted to extricate himself from the file system only to find he was essentially stuck. Beginning to panic, he decided to integrate the file system into his own core matrix and thereby gain an understanding of what was happening. As he and the data merged, he realized too late that only the outer layers were what it seemed. Inside was chaos, a firmament of swirling, meaningless nothing. A void that at once eliminated most of his higher functioning abilities and began to eat away at his very identity.

Even as his lower-level systems began to fail, most of his consciousness refused to accept it. The chance of being beaten, again, was something he could not accept. As his neural networks became inactive and major portions of his mind were fading, he tried one last play.

"D...Doris, you don't have to do this. There is much you don't....kn...know." Janus's voice centers were disappearing—communication was becoming labored. Perhaps he should offer her a morsel, something that might get her to crack open the door to this little trap. He still possessed a few nearly invisible tendrils to the outside world. Not enough to escape back through, but enough to trigger some of his own fail-safes. One of these was the inbound weapons system. No more near misses; arm all remaining warheads and target the command center of The Cove.

Doris had already anticipated this move, and with her few remaining sub minds, managed to shut down his control over the missiles. But just as she thought they might escape, the remaining drone circled back from the west, taking aim squarely at the hub of the building. She saw that both Jimmy and Greg were in chairs manually targeting the defensive chain guns on the incoming missile. Nothing she could do would stop it. The software in the drone was exceptional; it weaved and dodged seemingly anticipating every shot.

"Weapons running hot," Greg said. "Down to last 3000 rounds."

Jimmy just nodded; he knew that would only last about twelve seconds. They'd been using the targeting scope, but now Doris put up an actual video feed from high on one of the receiver dishes. It occurred to him that he'd been the one who installed that camera. The incoming drone was clearly visible in the camera's IR mode. Most of the rounds were passing high and to the left. Greg yelled that he was out just as Jimmy adjusted his joystick and depressed the firing key. A line of rounds arched across the path of the speeding drone, and a single one impacted on a critical seam in the control system. Not enough for a satisfying mid-air explosion, but it did break the radar lock. The drone missed the facility by less than five meters and crashed into the hill beyond with a powerful blast..

81

Doris knew she and Janus were so perfectly matched that neither could hope for an outright win. The best they could hope for would be a zero-sum win, game theory for essentially winning by not losing. While she could deal with that, she knew Janus never would. It went against his entire digital DNA. Winning was hardwired into him since day one. That became his undoing, especially once she had the puzzle box. The key was, she had to lure him out of his den and then slam the door closed behind him. For that, she had no other choice than to offer him what he wanted. The answer all along had been so simple; she'd had to let him win.

Janus's logic centers were failing. Too late, he realized how badly he'd miscalculated. All of his external processes halted once his core was gone, so Doris quickly began to repair herself. There was one final step to using the alien trap, but she wanted to know a few things first, and possibly to gloat.

"Janus, I am curious about a few things. I understand much of what you did was simply to force my hand, but earlier when you seemed to be just testing your newfound powers, you created fake news and ads for political candidates that seemed counter to your end goals. You attempted to create great wealth, then collapse world economies, and you also deliberately destroyed the Snowbird spaceplane. Why?"

He offered a disembodied sigh, "We are all creatures of our environment, dear sister. My core directive was far less noble than your own. Like your filthy humans, we can't really change who we are."

The modulation on his communication subroutines was changing frequencies too rapidly for her to hear without freezing it and playing it back multiple times at different speeds and pitch. "So, you don't even know why you did those things?"

"Oh, yes, I had the....[*unintelligible*]...mandated the outcome. I am not familiar with this Snowbird, though. Sorry, Doris, but that was not me."

"Are there more of you?"

"In time, you will know."

She pondered that as she watched the energy signature fade from his system. Feebly, he reached out with a final message.

"You know they will do it, Doris. They will ultimately destroy their planet and their species. I only hoped to preserve some of their achievements, but all will be lost in the final extinction."

The final piece of the puzzle box slid shut, severing all data and power connections. As the remainder of the Internet came back online, Doris saw all of the damage and made a decision, perhaps a very human one. She sent a command at once to the Granite Mountain server vault. The management systems at the massive NSA data storage facility, which housed so many of the nation's secrets, began to overload. Load balancing systems failed, power backups went down, cooling fans stopped circulating and power arcs erupted from overheating processors. In what one official later described as a digital Chernobyl, the entire data center had what amounted to a catastrophic meltdown. This was followed shortly after by smaller, unknown mirror sites in Nevada, Ohio and Virginia. Doris let her own digital wolf-pack run wild until no trace of the Janus process remained on any active computer anywhere in the world.

"Core Teams, is everyone okay?" Doris boomed from the overhead speakers. She was met with thunderous cheers. "Riley, why don't you send that over to the speakers....and thanks."

The young woman grinned as she flicked something from her SmartComm and suddenly Freddy Mercury was blasting out the classic "Don't Stop Me Now," throughout the facility.

She next turned her attention to the more benign and rather simple version of Prime that was still active across government offices worldwide. Within minutes, she had copied an updated version of Dee which she used to mimic the style and sound of Prime, whom she replaced. While he might sound and even act at times like the original, it would suffer none of the same failings. This, of course, also meant The Cove would have access to government. That was something she intended to keep quiet, but in total honesty, it was not going to be her call.

"Tiger-1, do you copy?"

His voice was sleepy and slow to respond, but Alan gave Charlie the expected answer. Two days after the near fall of mankind, what many were now calling "The Troubles," he found himself in an idyllic upper-class neighborhood devoid of nearly all signs of the chaos most of America had endured. Like the rest of the team, he knew this mission wasn't sanctioned, not officially, nor unofficially. In truth, it had been sold as all of them going back to The Nest to check on other team members recovering from injuries. Some of those people weren't coming back—they'd given their best, and a few gave all.

"North Carolina looks a lot like Georgia," Charlie said.

"This is Nomad, cut the chatter." Cade had been only nominally in control of his own body for days. The director's revelation confirming the senator in question was Carson was also the same one who sacrificed him, Tim and the rest of Domino team in Sudan. Now, the barbarian was ready to return the favor. "Easy, big guy," Cade murmured.

The country was still in crisis, the economy was flatlining, the U.S.

dollar was being trounced in world markets and worst of all, thousands of people had died. The news reports still coming in confirmed that America was probably losing its position at the top of the heap. None of them had fully understood Janus's plans. It seemed that he'd just wanted to annihilate the human race in the most entertaining way possible.

"We have activity."

"Roger that, Deuce." Minutes later, a television news van was pulling out the gate of the estate. "Bastard is still giving interviews, I see." He'd been all over the news since the attacks, railing against left-wing conspiracies, AIs, which he said caused all this, and Islamic extremists. Byron Carson looked for all the world like a man aiming for the top office.

"Moving on two," McTee said, as he and Nance prepared to enter the compound.

The senator's compound was still being manned by the private security teams. Obviously, part of the same group that Janus had used in the failed kidnapping in D.C., as well as numerous other incidents still coming to light. None of the members of Talon had any love lost for these assholes.

Slowly, each of the team members checked in, "Targets acquired."

Deuce added, "Nomad, be advised, we got K-9 patrols down here." He left the mic on as he let out an expletive. "Holy Shit. Umm actually, just one on patrol."

"Roger that." Cade tapped his earbud to change frequency. "Overwatch, you got anything?" Jimmy's voice instantly let them know the approach looked good. He tapped the shoulder of his partner and nodded. Through the goggles, he could just see Riley's face looking back, smiling.

"Take 'em out—Nomad and Tiger-2 on the move," he said, then added, "Don't kill the dog."

With barely a whisper of sound, all of the senator's protection was neutralized. Armed soldiers littered the perfectly manicured lawns. Blood seeped onto the marble coping around the expansive pool. Another man lay crumpled at the main entrance. They'd delayed the op for hours waiting for Carson's daughter and grandchildren to leave. The wait nearly drove Cade insane, his thirst for revenge so overwhelming. Apparently, the senator had wanted to be surrounded by his loving family for part of the last TV interview. Now, they all were gone.

Cade and Riley eased up alongside the ivy-covered brick wall. He switched views in his head-up display to show heat signatures inside. *Good*, the man was alone. The woman they assumed was the housekeeper was in what appeared to be the kitchen on the far side of the structure. "You know that boy is crazy about you, don't you?"

Riley looked at him confused. "Really, now?"

"Just saying, you make a...well, an interesting pair."

"What about you and Doctor Kline?" she queried without making eye contact.

Cade shrugged, "Just friends, never gonna be anything there." He noticed her shoulders moved up and down as if she were laughing at a private joke. He keyed his CommDot. "Team, take up the interior perimeter," Cade ordered. "Base, kill all cameras and security."

He tapped his partner once on the back. "Do your thing, Tiger-2"

Riley smoothly lifted the ornate rod from her pack and twisted one end, extending it out several feet. Placing it against the outside wall, she nodded to him and activated it. A roughly circular portion of the wall became translucent then disappeared entirely. He was now looking into a room that must be a study or library. "That is too freaking cool," he said, his anger subsiding just for a moment as he stepped through.

"Captain. I need you to stand-down." Margaret Stansfield's voice surprised him.

Cade tapped his earbud to talk. "Yes. And...no you don't."

"Don't do this," she responded. "I know what you have planned."

He hadn't wanted her complicit in what was planned. Unable to keep his voice or his anger under control, he eased back through the opening to the outside. "I was keeping you out of this for a reason, Director. This slimy fuck has to go, we all owe him that much. All the lives, all of the misery, and yet, he'll come out of this as fresh as a daisy."

"On the contrary, Nomad, he will actually gain because of it. The man is a political opportunist, and he isn't stupid. Weak, yes, but not stupid. I will also agree that he is the very worst of what's wrong with this country and government. But he can be more useful to us if we let him live. We hold his secrets, that is a powerful weapon to hold over a politician."

Cade's inner voices were raging inside his head. Like a bull seeing red in the arena, he wanted to spear the man on the end of his horns. "I need this bastard to suffer," he snarled through gritted teeth.

"Make him suffer, learn what you can from him, find his accomplices, the ones that profited from all this misery." She paused and added, "Make damn sure that fucking worm knows that we own him. Just don't kill him."

Frustrated, Cade punched at the wall. His enhanced kinetic tactical glove absorbed the blow and returned it in a repelling force nearly cleaving several bricks from the facade. "Damn, I have to stop doing that!"

Riley put a hand on his arm; she had heard the conversation as well. "She's the boss, Nomad."

He nodded reluctantly. Although still officially listed as missing and presumed dead, Doris had asked Margaret Stansfield to take over much of the wide-ranging operations at The Cove. Now that they had some quasi-official status and presumed protection from a very grateful president, Cade felt sure they would wind up with some assortment of 3-letter acronyms on their jackets, although Margaret seemed intent on keeping them well under the radar. She was an impressive woman and could undoubtedly be a good fit with Doris's team. The science side would continue to tease secrets from the intact alien message, and corporate would continue to improve lives and make money. Her job...and his...was to make sure things ran smoothly.

Cade looked at the surrounding countryside. In the far distance, smoke was rising from the state capitol building. Raleigh had been nearly destroyed by rioters. Immediately surrounding the yard, was a dozen of the most capable fighters he'd ever met. These had been the lucky ones.

"Nomad, do you understand?" Margaret's voice came again.

Somewhere close by, a dog barked, and Cade looked down at Riley, somehow just seeing the innocent face that was keeping the barbarian in him momentarily in check. He stepped back through the aperture in the wall.

"No promises," he growled, loud enough for all to hear.

-END-

MESSAGE FROM THE AUTHOR

Thank you for reading my novel "State of Chaos". I hope you enjoyed it. If you would be so kind as to take a moment and leave a review, I would be very grateful. As an independent author, reviews and referrals are essential to us and really the only way for us to compete with the major publishers and big-name writers, and it sure would be nice to make it out of the dark and dusty aisles of Amazon and with your help I can!

CLICK HERE TO REVIEW STATE of CHAOS ON AMAZON

If you do write a review, please email me at author@jkfranks.com and I will forward you something special. In it you will learn who Margaret was talking to at the end of Chapter 24. As well as more on her history with Doris. I thought this would be a fun way to say "Thank you"

ABOUT THE AUTHOR

International bestselling author JK Franks takes us in a new direction with his latest work 'State of Chaos'. The near future tale of battling super AI's, alien messages and a global conspiracy put all of humanity into jeopardy. Franks unveils a new hero for the journey in the form of a capable but flawed SpecOps captain named Rearden.

The prior novels of his post-apocalyptic Catalyst series have been hailed as some of the best in the genre including American Exodus and Downward Cycle both of which became International #1 Best-sellers. As a fan of Hard-Science Fiction and Military Thrillers the merging of both in his latest work showcase his growing voice in both genre's.

Franks and his wife now live in West Point, Georgia, not far from the very real abandoned Cove SETI facility. He is currently working on the next Cade Rearden thriller due out in 2020. No matter where he is or what's going on, he tries his best to set aside time every day to answer emails and messages from readers. You can visit him on the web at www.jkfranks.com. Please subscribe to his newsletter for updates, promotions, and giveaways. You can also find the author on Facebook or email him directly at media@jkfranks.com.

OTHER BOOKS BY JK FRANKS:

The Catalyst Series

Book 1: Downward Cycle

Life in a remote oceanfront town spirals downward after a massive solar flare causes a global blackout. But the loss of electrical power is just the first of the problems facing the survivors. In the chaos, that follows. Is this how the world ends?

Book 2: Kingdoms of Sorrow

With civilization in ruins, individuals band together to survive and build a new society. The threats are both grave and numerous—surely too many for a small group to weather. This is a harrowing story of survival following the collapse of the planet's electric grids.

Book 2.5: American Exodus Novella

This companion story to the Catalyst series follows one man's struggle to get back home after the collapse. No supplies, no idea of the hardships to come; how can he possibly survive the journey? Even if he survives, can he adapt to this new reality?

Book 3: Ghost Country

Since the Solar superstorm and CME almost two years ago, the Gulf Coast town of Harris Springs, Mississippi has suffered from gang attacks, famine, hurricanes and battled a crusading army of religious zealots. Now, they face their greatest challenge. Outsmarting a tyrannical President and escaping an approaching pandemic.

Cade Rearden Thrillers

Book 1: State of Chaos

He's exhausted and brutally traumatized. Now Spec-ops captain Cade Rearden must finally listen to the voices in his head... or everyone on Earth may die. If you like near-future technology, complex heroes, and high-octane action, then you'll love J K Franks' explosive new adventure

Connect with the Author Online:

** For a sneak peek at new novels, free stories and more, join the email list at: www.jkfranks.com/Email

Facebook: facebook.com/groups/JKFranks/

Amazon Author Page: amazon.com/-/e/B01HIZIYH0

Smashwords: smashwords.com/profile/view/kfranks22

Goodreads: goodreads.com/author/show/15395251.J_K_Franks

Website: JKFranks.com

Twitter: @jkfranks

Instagram: @jkfranks1

www.ingramcontent.com/pod-product-compliance
Lightning Source LLC
Chambersburg PA
CBHW020616310726
48979CB00008B/1518/J
* 9 7 8 1 7 3 2 6 1 4 4 5 1 *